ISLE OF THE CHARRED MAIDEN

MAIDEN

GLIK'S FABLES
VOLUME ONE

H.D. SCOTT

First edition: November 2022
Printed in the USA

Cover & Map Art By: Cristina Tănase

Hardback ISBN: 979-8-9869636-0-0
Paperback ISBN: 979-8-9869636-1-7
Ebook ISBN: 979-8-9869636-2-4

Published by: H.D. Scott Creations LLC
www.hdscott.com

Dedication? Oh it took dedication all right! Thank you to everyone who made this book possible including my inspiring friends, brainstorm buds, beta readers, artists, editors, and my harshest critic (you know who you are). It's been a long roller coaster of a ride, and I'm hoping it's just the first of a long series of enjoyable reads to come.

CONTENTS

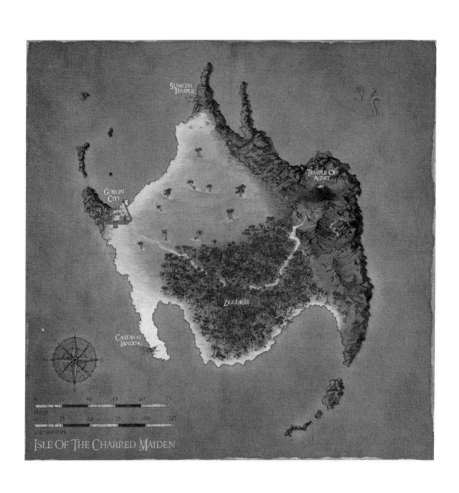

SUNKEN
TEMPLE

TEMPLE OF
AGNITH

GOBLIN
CITY

ZIGGURAT

CASTAWAY
LANDING

ISLE OF THE CHARRED MAIDEN

CHAPTER 1

BARNACLES & BIRD DROPPINGS

B utts, butts, butts, everywhere! Why do humans and elves have to be so tall!? When I was with my tribe, I could look everyone in the eye. Not here. In Partha, my nose is at crack level every time I step out the door! Don't get me wrong, these people are fascinating. The things they've built, what they do, how they function, even why they do what they do. It's all amazing. But even the most elegant elf begins to look a bit foppish if you see nothing except their butt all day. Oh, what I'd give for a gnome to walk by, or a halfling! Anyone I could glare at, right in the eye! Butt cheeks just don't respond to glares as well as I would like.

Partha is a large port city. I had only been here for a few weeks, but I was sad to be leaving so soon. The sights, sounds, smells, and flavors were all an experience. There were giant constructs at the ship-yard, tasty fish at the market, shady pickpockets in the grey quarter, and people over by the docks that never wore clothes and whistled as you walked by. All of it was fascinating. There was even a library where I acquired a couple of light tomes on history and magic! They would spice up my fables nicely without breaking my back when traveling.

I had finally gotten enough coin to broker passage to the mainland, a three-month journey by ship across the largest ocean in the world. The tavern owner at the edge of town was originally planning to only pay for room and board in exchange for my entertainment services. Fortunately for me, he realized quickly that I ate less than half of the normal fare, and I was fine with whatever food he was about to throw out. In my defense, that food was infinitely better than EVERYTHING we had at the goblin lair!

On the first night, after reciting my two favorite fables, which gathered a fair crowd, I shouted to them, "Don't bother tipping your storyteller, instead drink, drink, and drink some more! I want you up here where I am, telling the best stories you've ever heard!" It turned into one of the highest-selling nights the owner had ever seen. I, of course, got a few more tidbits of lore to add to my fables and learned a few dozen more things to avoid doing when telling stories. The owner was so impressed that he offered to give me a share of the profits if I could keep bringing in the crowds and the money. I didn't do the same stunt every night, but when there was a good crowd, we all got drunk and had a merry old time swapping stories on the main stage. Good times, but it was time to move on to new adventures.

According to the tavern patrons, goblins are mean little monsters that are usually attacked on sight. But Partha is a town built on trade and money. Anyone and everyone with coin who can keep their weapons sheathed is welcome to spend here. I didn't want to test that theory personally, and my gnomish clothing didn't disguise me very well when my hood was down.

There was also my past to think about. I escaped the disgusting caves I grew up in only a couple of months ago, and I'm certain my old tribe would love to see me dead. I gave the leaders no end of trouble. I would be disappointed if someone had not taken up my mantle of insanity and trickery, but either way, if they ever spotted me again, I was rat food. Best be on the other side of the world. Besides, if I successfully made myself famous, I could always come back with enough fame and fortune to hire bodyguards and keep people happy enough that they wouldn't want to kill me!

Thoughts of death in mind, I meandered my way toward the docks. I stopped by the market and grabbed my favorite fish (some kind of tuna or swordfish, I was told). I flipped Marco a tip as usual, then stopped by the mushroom vendor to get a nice little fungus that reminds me of home. It paired excellently with the raw fish. I had once tried to get the tavern to carry this recipe, but the tavern owner found it disgusting. He always burned his fish, the numpty. In retrospect, most of my memories of home involved some form of saving my own skin. Usually from the chief, his guards, the cook, or some form of monstrosity. Perhaps not remembering home too often was a good thing.

I was still chewing on the head of the fish when I reached the first prospective ship at the dock. It was a fine-looking, three-mast ship with golden sails and a mermaid at the prow. *The Elegant* was written on its side in wispy elven letters that were barely legible. Surely fine elven sailors would love to have a storyteller on board.

"Get off my ship, you miniature troll!"

"1000 marks. Do you have 1000 marks? Then stop wasting my time!"

"You look positively ill, little gnome. I don't want any disease on my vessel. Begone!"

"Only people on this ship are crew, and you look way too weak to be holdin' yer own on my ship. Off with ya!"

"Are you chewing on a raw fish head? Disgusting! Bugger off before you make the other passengers sick!"

"We don't haul nuthin' but cargo, n ya ain't no kinda cargo I'm willin' t' haul."

So much for the generosity of elves and humans. I had gone through every ship in the port that was bound for the mainland. Every one of them either jacked up the price, shot me down, or flat insulted me.

That's when she caught my eye. Hidden around the corner of the last pier in the harbor was one final option. Her sails were riddled with so much patchwork that little of the original sail remained. The boards of the hull had numerous repairs and obviously second-hand replacements. They were probably scavenged. It appeared to be held together by barnacles and bird droppings.

There was one little gem that stood out. Her name sparkled in mother-of-pearl lettering on her side with clearly legible and tasteful calligraphy. "*The Dolphin's Tear*". It looked like a good way to commit suicide, but also like it had seen a great many adventures.

I had a great feeling about this!

"You're eyeballing my vessel mighty hard there, little one."

His voice was bright, his smile brighter. He seemed to be a short human, but his ears had a slight point to them. He was stockier than most elves, so not one of them. Halfling blood, perhaps? Who knew? Nobody in this town really cared anyway.

"Hmm, a cloak, large pack, light books with heavy material. If I had to guess, I'd say you were a gnome quite far from home. But you don't move like any gnome I've ever seen. Most gnomes don't have that fine greyish-green skin like you do either."

The stranger straightened his collar and took a shallow bow. "No matter! I'm Raylin. Raylin Yfrit, first mate of the *Dolphin's Tear*."

"Oh, I'm eying your vessel all right! Are you headed to Shael? And do you have any cats on board?"

Raylin paused at the last question, blinked a few times, then smiled radiantly. "Nope. No cats. Our rat troubles have gone to nothing since Skia, the kobold, joined our crew. Suspicious since she's our cook, but the stew tastes damn good and we don't have any rats on board, so who am I to question the gods of luck?"

Ugh, kobolds. The only creatures I've ever seen that can be both hairy and scaly at the same time. Not the soft, fuzzy fur of a small animal either. More like the creepy, prickling hair of a spider. They all had a snout like an alligator, claws, and tiny holes where ears should be. They were usually short and gangly like a goblin too.

Raylin continued, "To your first question, yes. If you care to join us, fare is 300 local coins, 400 Shaelian marks, or 600 of that Imperial papyrus crap."

Dammit. I only had 200 of the local. Last week that was enough. We must be getting close to winter or something. Then again, maybe they just didn't want a goblin on their boat.

"How about 150 local, and I provide entertainment every night of the voyage? I might even be persuaded to find out about this cook's recipes. Have you heard of Glik's Fables?" It was a long shot, but if they had been in the city long, word may have spread from my tavern on the outskirts.

Raylin grinned. "No, but I'm sure I'll hear of them before long. No worries about the cook. I'm sure she'll try any recipes you give her. The crew might not, though." He glanced at the last bits of fish head still in my hand, his eyebrows cocked in suspicion. "Either way, we've got open spaces left and we leave at high tide one hour from now. You'd better hurry if you have anywhere to go first. The captain waits for no one."

"Deal! Name's Glik. Where do I put my stuff?"

Raylin smirked, entertained by my antics already. "Let me show you your bunk."

He led me up the gangplank to the deck. A crew of twenty was moving quickly, hauling the last provisions below, readying the sails for a quick release in an hour's time. The deck itself was immaculately clean, as was everything that was not currently in use. It was quite a contrast to the overall condition of the ship. The crew was also unexpectedly, quite efficient. They were rarely distracted and never needed instruction or reminder of their duties. Impressively, they were quite the diverse crew as well. Most showed primarily human and elven characteristics, but a handful of dwarves, halflings, and surprisingly, an orc appeared on board. The captain, however, was nowhere in sight.

Raylin took me below deck next. It was quite a shift from the bright daylight above. A few magical lanterns were placed in a few key spots between the stairs and the cargo hold. Other areas had dimly lit oil lamps. It was clean, like the deck above, but it was a cramped space to begin with, and box after box of cargo crowded it further. Far to the back of the ship, Raylin gestured toward a row of double-high hammocks. There were two trunks below each, securely fastened to the hull.

"Here's where the passengers sleep, unless of course, you paid a stupid amount of money for the two cabins in the back." He pointed his thumb over his shoulder to two wooden doors that could easily be mistaken for closets. "I'd love to give you the tour, but it will have to wait. In the meantime, I'd suggest staying either here, or up top near the front of the ship. Wherever you choose, stay out of the way."

It wasn't hard to see what he meant. Raylin almost got knocked on his butt trying to work his way back up deck. Too many people going to too many places, and all of them are in a hurry. Despite the challenge, I decided I'd be better off up top where I could see the sights. I only got knocked into a box twice on my way up!

It was there, on the bow of the ship, that I met a few of the other passengers. They were easily recognizable because they weren't running around carrying things or shouting at each other. Most of them were looking out to sea, deep in thought. One lady was busy looking inward at all the ship's commotion. She stood apart from the rest. Her clothes were a mottled green and black, like she wanted to blend into darkness. She actively sized up every person on board, judging how they would act around her.

"Best escape route is overboard once we leave." I smiled a toothy grin from under my wide-brimmed hat, craning my neck upward just enough for my eyes to connect with hers.

"I'll keep that in mind if you need 'help' escaping later." Her voice was a warm timbre, but had a sharp and irritating edge to it. Then again, most human speech was irritating to goblin ears, so maybe it was just me. "Is there a reason you are giving me your attention?"

"You seem to be the smartest person on the ship. I figure you have the best stories. Probably the best chance of survival when the bird droppings wash off and the ship sinks too."

Her eyes made a quick judgement. Then, with a slight hesitation, she forced a thin smile. "Of course. What makes you think that?"

"I thought that was obvious! Everyone else is gawking at the scenery. You're gawking at the crew and everyone else. Either you are quite the people person" *unlikely*, "or you're judging everyone's uses and any threats. Sadly, I've had to do both my entire life as a goblin. You seem potentially useful and practical. Care to form an alliance? I'd rather not worry about people rummaging through my things while I slept. Goblins aren't usually welcome anywhere you know."

Her eyebrows knitted together in a look of concern. "An alliance. With a goblin? I think not."

Her eyes darted away from me briefly, distracted by something or someone I couldn't hear. She started fidgeting with her amulet as her gaze returned to me. "Then again, you seem quite forthcoming and informed. Perhaps we'll speak more on the journey." Well, that was quite a quick shift. Maybe she's crazy and hearing voices? I've made worse friends.

I shrugged. "Okay." She was a strange one, but her initial lack of trust made me like her even more. I didn't trust her either, especially after that quick shift from a "piss off" attitude to, "you're useful. Let's talk later." But humans have a weird saying, something about "friends close, enemies closer, and lovers as far away as possible".

I suppose I should have expected it. She had been fidgeting with her amulet the whole time. It was the closed eye of the goddess of secrets.

I really liked my most recent literary acquisition. It was a book on religious history and was surprisingly useful. It was why I recognized that symbol and why I knew we would definitely talk later. Those who followed the goddess of secrets were directed to find new information wherever possible, especially if it was uncommon or secret information. A curious goblin storyteller in gnomish clothes mingling with "civilized" society was bound to have some uncommon secrets, right?

The book also mentioned that the truly devout followers wouldn't lie, but that sounded too good to be true. Then again, the best liars I had ever known technically just omitted key details and never actually lied. Half-truths I believe humans call it. In Goblin, we describe it using the same word we use for "lie".

Another passenger caught my attention. This one seemed exceptionally out of place with her elegant clothing trimmed in gold and silver. She also smelled of flowers and had long, thin ears that twitched as I approached. She was short enough that I could look up at her face without hurting my neck too! She turned toward me, a confused look appearing on her face.

She gave a slight nod before her gentle, mid-ranged voice articulated the words "Saleth, dwa'er" crisply and slowly.

"La duala!" I responded in High Elven with the most grating voice I could come up with.

She cringed at the obvious butchering of tone. "Quan, eomath?", which roughly translated into "you speak elven?"

"Ioa (yes)." I replied, and we continued our conversation in High Elven.

Her eyebrows knotted in confusion. "How is it you know my language? Few know it well. Far fewer that aren't elves. Sorry, I must apologize. Your appearance and unexplained knowledge have caught me off guard. My manners forget me. I am Orinne of the House Windwalker."

"No apologies necessary! I am Glik, soon-to-be famous author of the fabulous anthology known as Glik's Fables! As to your question, I once had a friend named Rakit. His disappearance saddled me with an almost endless stint of guard duty in the goblin holding pens where we kept the prisoners of... crap, I forget the elven word. Carnage? Fighting? Battle? Whatever, the important part is that prisoners will talk endlessly and tell you anything if they think you'll befriend them and set them loose. I couldn't do that without dying myself, but I learned a great many things from the endless hours of conversation. It truly is amazing how many languages some fighting people know!"

Her expression paled. "That's, um, quite a tale, little one. I suppose you withheld some gruesome details, thank you. Was there something I could help you with?"

"Not at all Orinne, or should I call you Miss Windwalker?"

She smirked at the breach of etiquette. "Orinne is fine, in your unique case."

"Orinne it is, then. I'm curious. What brings you here over all the other, more hospitable ships?"

"Hm, I shall not bore you with the details, but in short, the *Dolphin's Tear* once belonged to my family centuries ago."

She sighed and placed her hand on her temple. "Was there anything else? If not, I must apologize, but I am not in a fit state for conversation. My mind is elsewhere."

I took the hint, but made a note in my journal. Previous owner-ship, along with the ship's age, could be useful. "Until next time then, Lady Windwalker." I bowed and backed away.

I scanned the deck and decided against talking to the few remaining individuals I spotted. A pissed off human in silken robes was screaming at the crew, something about how valuable the merchandise was and how they were treating the crates. Something about "Manhandling them like a pig farmer". I may have to avoid him all together. But that was a lot of shiny stuff on just one outfit. Perhaps a visit to his quarters would be a good idea on the last few days of our voyage.

There was also a short, fat fellow with a long, red beard. He looked like he could split a person in half with a belch. The armor was quite intimidating as well. A look of irritation in his eyes let me know he would be better to approach later, if ever. That look, it clued me in. Well, that, and the oddly well-kept eyelashes. That wasn't a short guy at all. It was a dwarf woman!

With little left to focus on while everyone was busy, I risked a

little venture. I worked my way to a semi-private area at the front of
the ship, then settled my shoulder bag onto the rail and clicked my
tongue softly to signal the all clear.

Tck, Tck...Tck, Tck

Long whiskers emerged from my bag, followed cautiously by a
tiny black nose on a long snout. Round ears and beady eyes twitched
every which way to make sure the environment was safe.

"It's alright, Tinky. You probably won't get much air for the next
day or two while we settle in. Once we get close to the mainland
there's a lot of fun to be had, but until then I suggest you stay close
to me. There's a kobold cook on board who likes rat."

"Squeak."

"Help yourself to the bread. You did excellent today. Not a single
noise, and I didn't have to remind you to not take anything from the
market this time!"

Tinky squinted her grey eyes in the wind, enjoying a bit of fresh
air. The little monster was probably the only loyal friend I really had.
We had met in the holding pens of the goblin lair a few years ago. I
assume she had come in with some adventurer as a pet or something.
She was far too intelligent to be a regular wild animal. That's probably how she learned to steal so well too. It was sheer luck that let me
catch her with the keys while she was filching them off of me. Rather
than eat her, I let my curiosity guide me. After some time, we learned
to communicate. Still, I can't speak rat. We ended up escaping
together, finding mutual benefit in Tinky's keen senses and my knack
for confusing guards.

"ALL ABOARD! *If not, too bad for you, ya lazy overfed
bastards...*" Raylin was true to his word. With only that shout of
warning (and the not-so-subtle comment under his breath), the
gangplank was brought up, the anchor weighed, and the ship lurched
forward. The city of Partha shrank behind us, along with all my
worries of home. Only adventure on the endless blue horizon
remained.

CHAPTER 2

DOLPHIN TEARS & LIGHTNING-FINNED TUNA

URK! Another trip to the railing. Sea travel is for numpty humans. I had been nauseous every damn day for weeks! Most of the others were fine. Even Tinky didn't seem to have any issues. I would occasionally find solace by meandering to the kitchens, but the cook was a cantankerous old hag of a kobold named Skia. Should have called her Retchin, as the food was horrendous. Luckily, there were biscuits, dried meat, cheeses, and plenty of fungus growing around that required no cooking at all. We also caught some fish in nets.

"I wonder if I could snag one of those before they let ol' Skia burn it to ashes? Nice and fresh out of the water, that's when they are best."

"Squeak!"

I sighed. "Yes, yes, Tinky. I know you like the burned fish, but don't go in there. I'm sure she hunts down any rats herself. Probably eats them raw, but putting leftovers in the stew seems like something she'd find perfectly acceptable."

Despite the cuisine matching the nastiness of the old lair and the constant threat of it coming back up, I made sure to extract as much information as I could from the inhabitants of the ship.

The crew was mostly avoiding all contact with passengers. I presumed this was a standing order from Raylin. Nobody had seen the captain at all on this journey, but there was always a light in the captain's quarters. Luckily for me, the crew enjoyed my stories, more so than the aristocratic or secretive passengers at least.

One night after a few fables and some gambling by the crew, one of them named Erisal broke the silence. She was a nice, short, woman with strong arms, pointy ears, and a missing eye. She told me she was ready to be done with ship life. Raylin was too tight of a shipmaster, which meant he kept the crew busy, and any idle time was spent gambling or recovering from lost sleep. This was why the ship was so clean, despite looking like a patchwork disaster. Between the over-work and Erisal's hatred of kobold cooking, "life flinging arrows at hay bales for the crown" was preferable to seafaring on the *Dolphin's Tear*, according to her. She also let slip that she was the best archer on board, despite only having one eye.

Raylin had a few good stories to tell but always ended up jabbering about navigational junk. In spite of my natural curiosity about everything, I had little interest in the topic. Lines on paper, random points in the sky, more lines on paper. It seemed really stupid to keep directions at sea on a material that flies easily and gets destroyed when wet.

He did like to gamble, so maybe having paper maps that could fly away at any time made some sense to him. He always joined the nightly gambling sessions with the crew. Somehow, he lost more hands than he won but always walked away with more money than he put in. I suspect I was missing something important. I never gamble. It's too risky. I learned a lot watching the bigger goblins when they played dice with the hobs. The few that won the pot rarely left the table alive. It was too easy to slip something into a drink, poke a poisoned needle under the table, or just have someone walk up and slit a throat when a victim's attention was totally focused on the greed of the game.

The other passengers weren't all that talkative either. The well-articulated human who had been screaming about all of his precious cargo claimed to be our journey's sponsor. He ignored me and acted like I wasn't around when I tried talking to him. That fopdoodle almost stepped on me too! Tinky got revenge. She didn't wait to nip a few shiny baubles off of that guy's "private cabin" in the hold. The risk of him finding out early was worth it, just to know we had the upper hand on him.

The bearded redhead was scary. She had scars all over and was drinking constantly. I tried talking with her, but after hearing the fable of the fishing goblin, she wasn't keen on drinking with me. I guess she's known some dwarves that went missing during a goblin fight.

Then there was Orinne. She was quite proper but unfortunately spent most of her time on the bow of the ship. She always had a sad expression on her face and cut off any conversation politely, but quickly. Her mind was on something intense and elsewhere. I would have suspected she hated my kind, like most people did, except she didn't talk much to anyone else either. Considering how much wealthier she looked compared to the ship, perhaps she simply felt out of place and lonely.

There was also the halfling who spent most of his time in the hold. He dressed in rags, carried a single sack of meager possessions, and had a grand multitude of stories in his head. "I was once a miller... once a guard... once a royal vizier." Most of these tales were bollocks. Despite this, his eyes gave away some truth. He'd always look down in shame or start fidgeting with his rags when he wasn't lying.

After a few drinks, he got stuck on one topic. "It comes out only in a thunderstorm see!" Spittle and ale showered everything in front of him, his hands made a dramatic waving arc for emphasis. "Black as night it is, with three fins, blinding gold color. Don't touch 'em though! Those fins will shock you to kindling, sure as lightning itself! I came close to catching one once. Don't believe me? They have a few of them on the market up north, ya see. They'll tell ya straight and true, just like I'm a telling ya now. The Lightning-Finned Tuna! Or maybe it was a Thunder Fish. I can't remember. Name wasn't important..."

The strange part was, he thought he was telling the truth. Sounded embellished for sure, but I wondered. Could there be truth to it? Either way, his ramblings went on forever and rarely provided any real information. After the first hour, they failed to provide any entertainment value either.

Last, there was the secretive woman with the amulet that didn't seem to trust anyone. I approached her at the rail of the ship a few days into our journey, deciding that a direct approach would be best. "A closed eye isn't something you see hanging around everyone's neck."

Her muscles tensed for a moment. Not taking her eyes off the water, her fingers lightly grasped her amulet. She closed her eyes and mumbled something quietly. A short prayer perhaps? My sharp ears picked out just a little of it. "... ata, känna... iquin... dak li matea... " No language I had ever heard. Secret language for her secret goddess?

She relaxed a bit as she finished, her body going into a practiced stance of neutral stoicism. "What would you know of it, little storyteller?"

"No more than most secrets, but I'd love to know more."

She huffed in mild amusement, turning around to lean her back against the rail and look me in the eye. "I'm not in the habit of having my secrets cast to the world one tavern visit at a time. Why should I tell you anything?" Her tone said that this wasn't a rejection. It was a test, a probe. Her open body language invited me to try convincing her. Something about it was off. It was too obvious and somehow unnatural for her.

"Now, now, just because I tell great tales doesn't mean I don't keep secrets. Perhaps an agreement then? A few of my secrets for a few of yours, provided we keep them 'professionally' secret in the future? I'll even promise that I won't write them down."

It took her a few moments of concentration, eyes roaming over me repeatedly, coldly. Her look was much more intense than any person I had ever encountered. It was not aggressive but rational to the point where it could easily be considered a weapon. Her tongue quickly flicked over her lips, wetting her drying lips. My eyebrows shot up at what I saw, composure lost. Her tongue had a forked tip!

She continued without acknowledging my social guffaw. I wondered if she let her appearance slip on purpose. "Well, little story-teller. What would you ask of me?"

Curiosity smashed through the more intelligent parts of my brain, words pouring out of my mouth before she finished speaking. "Why is your tongue broken!?"

I had never seen anything like it, nor read anything about it. This was something that made great stories!

"What purpose does it have? Oooo, was it some kind of torture or punishment? Maybe it's one of those weird bed time things those elves at the tavern kept talking about?"

I was so excited that I almost missed the cold hesitation that preceded her energetic laugh. It was a bright, animated sound that could melt defenses and fool anyone. But her eyes didn't lie. They remained cold and focused. "You are quite observant, little story-teller. It is a defect from my birth. Nothing more."

She sounded like she was hiding something. Or maybe I just wanted a better story. Not everyone has a literal forked tongue! A birth defect fell far short of good storytelling. I couldn't use that. It reminded me of the peg legged pirate who convinced everyone that his leg was lost fighting some legendary sea creature. In reality, his ingrown toenail had got a nasty infection that spread up his leg. Much like him, I would have to embellish on this "birth defect" if I wanted to keep people listening to my tale.

"Too bad. That could have been interesting. Hmph, I suppose

you would like to know something in return for your boring explanation?" I emphasized the word boring, let my ears droop a bit.

Her eyes stayed cold, despite a faint smirk. "If you are offering.
How have you not been killed on sight? Most goblins don't mingle
so freely amongst humans and elves."

My shoulders slumped on reflex. I hated this question, and it
popped up frequently. Too many nights freezing in ditches, hiding
from torch-bearing jackanapes. Too many close calls just for a scrap
of food. "I'd rather not go into too many details. The clothes I wear
help me pass as a gnome. At least they should. I got them off of a
gnome right before I left my tribe. The hat helps cover the ears. I
think the biggest trick is to avoid running in naked, screaming 'I'll
kill you all and eat your children!' in a language that sounds like a cat
getting smacked with a lute. It is difficult to resist that urge. I'm sure
you can relate."

"HA! I suppose we must all make sacrifices and refrain from
our vices occasionally, little storyteller." Her laugh this time had a
sharp, cruel edge to it, but it was real. Dark humor worked,
interesting.

"Can we keep taking turns? This game is somewhat fun,
Miss...?"

"Serah. Serah Vihn. Normally Serah the Vagabond, but I'm sure
you've realized by now it's Serah the Faithful. Let's hope the Gatekeeper favors our conversation. And yes, this game is interesting. But
now you owe me your name as well."

"Glik! Soon-to-be Glik the Famous, author of the renowned
Glik's Fables!"

Serah's face tightened slightly, a mildly disgusted look crossing
her face. "Quite the introduction there, little storyteller. Best of luck
with fame and fortune. What do you wish to know?"

So many questions. Who is the Gatekeeper? Why is Serah going
to the mainland? What does Vihn mean? Why is the sky blue?

"What is a Lightning-Finned Tuna?" Crotchety mumpkins!
Damn curiosity took over my mouth again!

She scrunched up her eyebrows and blinked once, slowly. "What?"

"Lightning. Finned. Tuna. You keep secrets. I can only assume you know things that others don't. Maybe it was called a Thunder Fish instead."

She shook her head in disbelief, letting out a practiced giggle. It was almost perfect, except for her eyes. They didn't wrinkle right. They stayed hard and cold. Maybe she wasn't fully human and humor didn't reach her eyes like it did with everyone else? Many creatures look like humans but don't have the same expressions. Lizardmen for example. Except lizardmen are more pleasant to stare at.

"Aren't you just full of surprises, little storyteller? No, I do not know of any 'Thunder Fish', nor any 'Lightning-Finned Tuna'. If they exist, I suspect the crew would know more fish stories than I do. Whether the stories they tell are truth or exaggeration, that's up to you to decipher. Now for my question. Why did you choose this ship?"

"Oh, that's simple. No cats! My turn." I grinned from ear to ear, jagged teeth on full mischievous display. Easy questions like that were all too rare to pass up! Another question came to mind. Most likely she would lie about the answer, so I blinked a few times, making sure I wouldn't miss her reaction. "What sort of creature are you?"

Serah took a deep breath and looked up to the sky, contemplating what words to use. That alone confirmed she wasn't human. Any elf, human, dwarf, or even gnome would have been angry at me for insulting them; or they would have answered without a second thought. She glanced around for any bystanders who might hear her reply, then adopted a stance of controlled hostility. Her hand grabbed my shirt roughly, her face rushing forward. Our noses practically touched; eyes locked with one another. The smell of cucumbers and an odd aftertaste of rotting egg invaded my nostrils. Her breath maybe?

With a glare that promised pain and death, she spat a harsh

whisper in my face. "You will not write this, nor speak of it in any way that is related to me. I will kill you if you fail. Are we clear?"

My jaw dropped. Unholy crap! She was going to tell the truth! She had also just threatened to kill me, but that was a daily occurrence, so that didn't surprise me much anymore.

"Yup!" I squeaked.

She released her hold on my shirt. Her eyes scanned the area again, then she smiled maliciously, sticking out her tongue as she did. It was long, lithe, and flicked around on its own. Snakelike in every way. Two elongated fangs folded back nicely when she smiled like this, her mouth half-closed.

She watched my reaction, waiting for the perfect timing before stretching her jaw in a catlike yawn. Her needle-sharp fangs extended to their full length. They glistened in the daylight, venom forming a tiny drop on the tip of each fang. She quickly closed her mouth and took another cautious look around us.

"We are called naga, little storyteller. Should you run into another like me, I would recommend being much less inquisitive. Few of us take kindly to blown cover."

My heart raced as I stared, open-mouthed and wide-eyed. I found myself speechless, a rarity for sure. Now that was something to write about!

Her demeanor shifted back into a somewhat charming, yet distanced human. She sent a fake smile and a laugh my way. "Enough seriousness, Glik. Come talk to me some more tomorrow." With that, she turned and headed below deck.

That's how most of the trip turned out to be. Nights spent regaling the crew and a few passengers with strange tales, usually stories of goblins tweaked to fit the audience a little better. Days were spent reading my latest literary acquisitions (the two books I had brought, along with a nice little treatise on pirate activity, courtesy of our human "sponsor"). In the afternoons, Serah and I traded secrets for a few hours.

About six weeks into our journey, the weather shifted for the worse. The morning came, but the sun did not. I had woken up earlier than usual. The smell of the air had changed drastically. It was a nice clean salty mist before. But now, it went from a humid swelter to a damp cold in an instant. The fresh scent of rain wafted in from the horizon.

I went up on deck to investigate. Raylin would know something if I could find him. The crew was busy already, and it was plain to see why. Looming a few hours ahead was a wall of storm clouds shifting in a disturbing, greenish haze. "Make sure our stuff is strapped in tight, Tinky, including yourself and food for a couple days. I'm going to go grab a bucket to stick my head in."

Erisal noticed me staring at the storm, along with my horrified expression.

"Glik? You should get below deck and stay there until the storm lets up. We're going to get hit pretty hard and the waves can knock even the big boys off the deck. Raylin says this will be a tough one, especially since it's come out of nowhere. It's also against the current, which is odd for this time of year."

"Be careful, Erisal. Wouldn't want you to end up fish food. Thar's a too many hay bales that need a killin' back home!"

She smiled at the joke and nodded before hustling back to her duties. There was much to be done in preparation and little time to do it. Raylin's screaming at the crew wasn't helping things. He seemed tense, somewhat panicked in his movements, and the crew knew what they were doing already. This was going to be rough.

I headed back to my bunk and started packing my stuff a little tighter. I also wrapped my cloak around my books. It was water resistant, which would help protect them. Besides, if a good wind hit me, it was more likely to choke me to death than be useful for keeping me dry. I strapped everything tight in my pack, then threw the bag over my shoulders. The straps were just about right, but I tightened them a bit more anyway. If my books and food were going under, so was I, sod it!

"Tinky. You good in there? Better make sure you get snug. This may be a wet and wild ride!"

I settled in by the stairwell up to the deck. It had one of the magical lights, so less chance of accidental fire, even though I'd likely get wet from the water slopping down the stairs. If things went downhill, like the ship sinking, I wanted to be as close to the escape as possible. I also remembered a small boat lashed to the side of the ship, not that it would help much in the open ocean. But that's where I'd head if the ship started to sink. Best guess is that's where the crew would head too.

No sooner had I gotten settled and the waves grew choppy, shaking the ship in unpredictable patterns. Lightning flashed. I wondered where that halfling was. Maybe he could catch that Lightning-Finned Tuna he kept on about. URK! Where was my bucket?

ALL SARDING DAY, and all sarding night! The storm was still raging outside. Sheets of rain fell so hard that the crew couldn't see further than they could reach. Multiple runners were relaying messages as nobody could hear Raylin's shouts over the deluge. They could barely see his lantern signals. Waves half as high as the mainmast rocked the ship every which way. I recalled a layer of hell that matched this scenario. Endless nausea!

When the rocking finally stopped, I was too thankful to understand what was going on. The ship had jolted severely, slinging a few loose items flying and knocking all of us passengers on our butts.

"Ahhh, no more rocking!" The world was still spinning for me, but the promise of relief let me relax, just a bit.

"MAN OVERBOARD!" The unified screams of the crew carried over the noise of the storm. I barely noticed despite my large tufted ears. My nose, however, caught something. An odd smell permeated the air. It smelled a lot like some of the refuse pits near the hob caves. Not death so much as rot. Salty, with a hint of rotten kelp stench. It would make an interesting seasoning in Skia's cooking. Couldn't make it worse, that's for sure.

Serah stepped up the stairs beside me, barely slowing as she spoke. "You may want to follow me, little storyteller. Boats don't just stop in open water." She had her belongings strapped tight to her back; oilskin cloak thrown over it all.

I followed her slowly, still reeling from my empty stomach and the odd sensation of a stable floor after weeks at sea. We both stared at the scene on deck. The rain was still terrible, blocking most of our vision. We caught a few brief glimpses of crew members running past, struggling to hold their footing. I noticed the halfling had roped himself to the side rail. He was laughing wildly, holding a fishing pole. Guess he was going after that Thunder Fish after all!

BOOM!

A terrifyingly close bolt of lightning pierced the clouds, revealing everything in a brilliant light. The masts made for excellent contrast, appearing as dark silhouettes against the whitened sky. They contrasted almost as well as that giant tentacle.

GIANT TENTACLE!?

Soaring well above the masts, thicker than a dozen goblins could reach around, the gargantuan appendage loomed overhead. The light didn't last. In the blink of an eye, all was shrouded by the rain, yet again. I turned my head slowly toward Serah, eyes wide with fear. Maybe she knew a secret that would help with sea monsters?

Her eyes were riveted to the spot where the tentacle had been. A cold, emotionless expression dominated her face as she clenched her amulet in one hand. The roar of the rain drowned out her voice, but her mouth was moving quickly, praying.

A weird tingle flitted across my skin as her spell took shape. An odd, acrid smell invaded my nostrils, making them twitch. Serah closed her eyes as she spoke the last words, then thrust an open palm toward the sky. The rain surrounding us stopped abruptly, hitting an invisible wall all around the ship. We could see again. Shouts of the crew replaced the roar of the rain. The towering form of a tentacle was once again visible. So were the other seven of them. Four wrapped tightly around the front and rear of the ship. The other four loomed high, positioning themselves to crash down with as much force as possible. I guess that explained why the ship had stopped.

Every instinct told me exactly what to do. Run, hide, escape. I could swim as well as any goblin, mind you. That means I'd drown after about thirty seconds of flailing. Maybe a minute if the water was a calm lake. The only option left was to freeze in place. Not a bad idea considering how close I was to the only magic user on the ship.

We watched, too stunned to move, as the remaining four tentacles came crashing down to the deck, snapping through the sail rigging with no resistance whatsoever. The entire ship trembled and groaned under the impact when the tentacles hit. This was a lost cause.

The crew panicked. Raylin tried vainly to shout a few orders, then gave up and ordered an abandon ship as he sprinted toward the small boat on the side. I slapped Serah's leg as I bolted in the same direction. She snapped out of whatever stupor the spell had forced on her and followed quickly.

We arrived just in time. They cut the lines holding the boat to the ship right as we stumbled in. Raylin, Erisal, and the ratty-looking kobold with a cooking pot on her head, Skia, were the only three to make it in time. Our boat hit the water right as the *Dolphin's Tear* made one last groan of protest. The giant tentacles relaxed slightly before giving one final flex.

SNAP!

The entire deck exploded, blasting splinters everywhere at mind-numbing speeds. We gained a few cuts and bruises from it, but we had bigger concerns. The breaking of the ship created a fast wave that slammed the side of our boat, almost flipping us.

"ROW DAMMIT!" Raylin was screaming hard at Erisal. They both had the oars out and were pulling as hard as their lithe bodies would allow. The current from water rushing into the broken ship pulled us closer and closer, threatening to suck us under with the splintered hull. A few agonizing seconds of losing ground, then the current subsided, and we pulled further away from the ship. Luckily, Serah's spell followed her. The rain peeled away as we sped from the doomed vessel. The tentacles writhed and rolled, dragging the two broken halves of the *Dolphin's Tear* under the surface.

"AAAAH! SARD!" Serah screamed and grabbed her head as soon as the ship was gone. Magical backlash? Perhaps just realizing how screwed we were? We were totally screwed after all. The storm was still raging, despite Serah's magical reprieve from the rain. We no longer had a ship, just a tiny boat in the middle of the ocean, and a swell about the size of the *Dolphin's Tear* was just a few seconds away from flipping us and crushing the boat into splinters. What a great way to end a journey.

~

THE STORM CALMED QUICKLY over the next few hours, which likely spared our lives. The first massive waves would have killed us if they had broken, but luck was with us. Or maybe something else? Raylin's expertise had been critical those first hours, as he navigated us just well enough to keep us from capsizing.

Raylin glared at Serah, like she had caused the whole thing. "How in the nine green hells did we survive that?"

"Just because I can use a bit of magic doesn't mean I know everything, or really anything in this case. I should be asking YOU why some mythical sea creature just attacked YOUR ship! It probably only let us go because we're too small to care about. It really doesn't matter now does it? We're stranded without a ship in the middle of the ocean. Do you have any practical suggestions on what we do now, seafarer?"

His head drooped into his hands while he mumbled under his breath, "*We stick our heads between our legs and get prepared to kiss our...*" He stopped and looked up at us, noticing all our eyes fixed on him. "No. We'll likely die in a few days from dehydration and heat stroke once these clouds disappear and the sun roasts us all day."

I looked at him like he was the biggest idiot in the world. "Are you kidding!? We are literally surrounded by water. The only way we'd die of thirst is if we didn't touch the unlimited supply of water we are floating on! See!" I used my hand to spoon a handful of water into my mouth.

PFFFTT! "That's disgusting! Curses! Curses on every foul being that ever spawned under this forsaken sky! I should go back to my cave! What's in this crap anyway? Tastes like a salt miner's sweat wrapped in seaweed and served up from Skia's kitchen."

Everyone in the boat burst into laughter. Serah had her hand over her mouth, modestly blocking it, but Raylin and Erisal were howling so hard that they had trouble staying upright. Their cackling brought a smile to my face. I don't mind being the idiot every once in a while.

Skia, in her own special way, seemed to laugh along. It was quite a sight seeing her bouncing with laughter, the cooking pot almost falling off her head as she did so. Her laugh was a hissing noise of sorts, combined with what seemed like a light hacking. Her shoulders bounced like most creatures in mirth.

I never truly understood kobolds. Sure, there was plenty of common ground for me to relate to, but it just never clicked. They seemed almost like goblins to everyone else, but to goblins, kobolds had weird personalities. It was like a hairy goblin and a lizard had children, with the children getting the worst traits of both sides.

Erisal broke me out of my recollections, calming her laughter enough to bring us back to reality. "Well, now that we've determined Glik doesn't know crap about the ocean, what's next? Do we choose a heading and row blindly? I'm guessing we aren't likely to get picked up by a rescue. Unless, of course, you have some spell for that, Serah?"

Serah didn't bother with fake emotion. "No. I will pray for any instruction I can get, but don't count on it. I don't always get an answer. In the meantime, let's pick a direction and go. Perhaps we can stumble across some land."

Raylin shook his head. "Not likely. We were just about halfway through our journey when the storm hit. The charted course took us a fair bit further south than normal since we are traveling at an odd time of year. I had hoped that would let us get around the storms that hit the usual sea lanes. Unfortunately, that put us right smack in the middle of the largest body of water in the world. Nearest documented land is a tiny little island over two weeks travel out of our way. On the bright side, the current should pull us roughly east."

"Skrreeet, ihrrr rakjaw kaphuth." Skia looked at each of us in turn with what passed as a hopeful expression.

"Does anyone here speak kobold?" Raylin asked, eyeballing me, then glancing at Serah.

I blinked in response, realization smacking me in the face. "Wait a second, Raylin. You're telling me that nobody knew how to talk to the cook? No wonder the chow was always terrible! Who decided the menu?"

"Ha! There was one fellow who did the rigging that could speak kobold. He would talk with Skia. In hindsight, he did look a bit orcish. Probably explains the flavor. None of the crew complained, and I appreciated its uniqueness."

Erisal snarled and made a choking motion behind Raylin. Apparently, she did not approve of that "uniqueness" in her food. But she had never questioned it publicly for fear of retribution.

Serah ignored our banter, focused on our survival. "We head north then. Maybe another ship copied Raylin's thinking and is veering a few days south of the primary sea lanes."

"If you are suggesting we waste energy rowing, you are welcome to do whatever you want. I will be saving my strength as long as possible, hoping for a miracle." Raylin gestured grandly to the oars in the bottom of the boat.

Erisal let out an exasperated sigh. "Ugh, such drama. I for one would rather do something than nothing. I'll row with you, Serah. To the north we go."

Well then, I suppose I'd have to chip in. "If Skia takes a turn, so will I. Can't have us spinning in a circle because one rower is stronger than the other. Raylin, is there any way to tell if we veer off path?"

"Just the usual, but I don't have any navigation tools, so it'll be rough. We'll need the clouds to clear up too. Right now, I'll keep an eye on the swells, which direction they should be going. Once we can see the sun, we'll be able to tell if we're headed north just by watching it go overhead from east to west. At night, with any luck, the stars and moons will shine. So long as we point toward a few key stars, that should be enough."

Two days went by like this. Occasional jabber, a mild bit of story-telling, but mostly just lying around; hot and bored. We rowed more out of spite and boredom than any real hope of survival. All but one of us. She was subtle about it, but Serah made sure there was always someone at the oars. She learned from Raylin how to tell if we were going straight north. Luckily, the clouds did clear on day two, so his methods easily applied.

Once everyone fell asleep, I nudged Serah awake. She popped up instantly, alert and wary. Her body tensed, ready to fight. The rapid transition from sleep to functional would have impressed most elite soldiers. It definitely impressed me. Her eyes darted around rapidly, assessing the situation before she settled her gaze on me, irritated.

"What? Why wake me?"

I held my hands up defensively. "Nothing, Serah. Relax! I needed to ask you something. Privately. Do you speak Goblin?"

Her lips thinned, genuine anger seeping through her normally cool demeanor. "Why in the world would I speak Goblin?" She paused, taking a deep breath and closing her eyes. "Fine. If you want privacy, I know the language of the southern elves, high elves, peak dwarves, and deep dwarves. You?"

"Maybe high elven, but I suspect Erisal or Raylin may also know it. Better than nothing, I guess. I doubt you know Nomadic Orc or Grass Gnome."

Her lip curled with disgust. "Ugh, yes. I understand Nomadic Orc. I'd rather not recall how I came to need that." She grimaced with a little shiver at the memory. My curiosity began gnawing away at my mind. Not today, Glik, not today. Save that story for later.

"UnnGrakt Klibi Nombrakat" I replied, urging her to continue in the rough, guttural language.

"What is it, Glik?" she replied in butchered Orcish.

"North. It's important to you, and only you, that we head north."

She looked up and sighed before whispering to the sky, "Why pin me with the most observant goblin in all of creation? When did you get a sense of humor, Gatekeeper?" Her eyes lowered and settled back on me. "You observe too much, Glik. That curiosity is going to get you killed."

I wasn't sure if her words were a threat or not, so I assumed they were and noted death by backstabbing may be in my future.

"It hasn't yet. In fact, it's how I've lived to the ripe old age of eleven! Few of my kind can say the same, unless they are huge and mean."

"This secret stays between us, Glik. You may already know too much. Just after the *Dolphin's Tear* sank, I heard a voice. A powerful voice. It was not terribly unlike my own goddess in power, except it was different in intent and tone. I think it was the tentacled beast that ate our ship. It told me there was an island to the north. Considering our situation, any option is better than staying at sea. If this voice wanted us dead, it would have been easy to leave us stranded at sea."

"Huh." It was all the response I could pull together. First, sick for weeks. Then hit by a freak of nature storm. Follow it up with an attack by a monster and getting stranded at sea in a dingy. Now I find out that monster is some kind of sentient god, not just a big squid. This was becoming a bit too big for my first intentional adventure outside of the goblin caves. "Guess I should go back to sleep then." I stared off into space, trying to wrap my head around it all.

"You still owe me one little storyteller, two if I consider what you just asked me about north. How do you, a goblin, know so many languages at eleven years old? Most creatures take years to learn any language, even their first."

Grrr. Should I lie about this one? She had been honest about her secrets. I bet she could tell a lie better than I could. She had far more experience. If I wanted more secrets from her, I'd have to risk it.

"I'll hold you to secrecy on this one, Serah, much like you hold me to keep the secret of what you are. I don't think a death threat would mean much, but still. It's important.

"I remember almost everything. Whether I read it, hear it, see it, doesn't matter. Takes years for anything important to fade. I consider it a curse from the god that made goblins the dumbest laughingstock of all creation. Or maybe a gift from a different god with a twisted sense of humor. Some things are best forgotten."

Serah's muscles finally relaxed. "There is much truth to that last statement, little storyteller. Much truth indeed."

CHAPTER 3

SAND GETS EVERYWHERE, EVEN FOR HEROES

Two more days in that rowboat. It was messy, smelly, and nobody had any privacy at all. Privy use in the open air with a close audience brought back a lot of disgusting memories from the goblin lair.

Raylin wasn't kidding about the water. We had rationed out the two water skins that Serah and I always carried with us, but that wasn't nearly enough for five of us. I suspected I wasn't the only one hallucinating a bit. Luckily, I had us covered for a day or two on food. Travel rations, a staple of the travelers' packs, were quite filling and disgusting. I always kept some in my bag since they rarely went bad. Few creatures ever wanted to eat them, but they were still better than Skia's cooking. Her chow was usually better the second time around when my stomach heaved it over the ship's railings. Regardless, I knew keeping something in my bag for a rainy day was a must, so I chose the nasty stew over my reserve food supply on our journey.

At least the sun had been out, partially obscured by large, fluffy clouds overhead. We used our clothing and cloaks to rig some reliable shade. Raylin took some time to try fishing using an odd bone hook and some string he always kept in his pocket. He didn't expect to catch much without bait, but he managed to haul in a blue-streaked fish about the length of my forearm.

"Ha! I didn't think that would work without a pole or net. Oh well, can't cook it. Might as well throw it back."

"NOOO!!!"

"SKRAGIII!!!"

Skia and I both dove for the fish at the same time. Yanking it out of Raylin's hands, we both snarled and bit into either end like animals. I wrenched the head loose with a savage jerk of my teeth. Skia got the tail. We both smiled at each other, prize in hand, satisfied with the looks of horror on everyone else's face. They were too tame. That was fun! Besides, raw fish was quite tasty. I wondered briefly why Skia cooked hers on the ship if she also liked it raw. Maybe there was more to her terrible cooking than I gave her credit for.

The morning of day five, clear skies showed us what we needed to see. Slightly to the northeast, wreathed in a light fog, was land. Rocky cliffs dominated the southern coastline with large mountains looming in the east. Dense jungle overwhelmed the central island above the cliffs. To the west, a giant sandbar. What a perfect way to avoid a rough landing.

Raylin was the first to spot it. "Whoa! Land ho! That's unexpected, but I'm not complaining."

Erisal started giggling, obviously a little delirious. "You won't hear any complaints from me about it!"

Skia started doing some weird jumping dance that rocked the boat. "Klakjak! Whoopie!"

A smug little smirk appeared on Serah's lips, but it disappeared quickly, her thoughts weighing on her. The voice had led us here, but we didn't know why.

"Are you sure it's not a mirage?" I chimed merrily. The glares I got from everyone could have skewered a wild boar.

A few hours later, we made landfall. Raylin quickly took charge, dividing up the duties and tasks we needed for survival. Given our lack of experience, nobody complained about the hierarchy. Before long we had a fire, enough driftwood to keep it going, a small lean-to, a meager number of shellfish to cook, and enough freshwater to keep us going for the night. The water had come from a nearby stream. Raylin commandeered the pot Skia had been wearing on her head and used it to boil the freshwater before starting up on the shellfish. He shouldn't have messed with it in my opinion. Shellfish taste terrible whether you cook them or not.

I set up my own little sleeping area near the water. After that much close and personal time, I needed some space. I perked up my ears a bit as I built, listening in to the conversation at the fire. Skia was acting frustrated that Raylin had taken over the cooking duties and, more importantly, her helmet. He was ignoring her, trying his best to boil the meal without overcooking it. Serah and Erisal were in quiet conversation.

"Think we should say something?" Erisal whispered in Serah's ear, nodding her head in my general direction.

"About what?"

"Tides."

Serah looked down the hill at me briefly. I glanced up for a second and waved, then turned my eyes back to my task, ears perked the whole time.

"Nope." Serah whispered back as her lips curled into a smirk.

Huh, wonder what that meant. Oh well. I let Tinky have a break and cleaned out my shoulder bag. With Skia on board the rowboat, Tinky had to use it for ALL of her needs. It was disgusting enough that I was tempted to chuck the bag into the ocean. Alas, it was still nothing compared to the smell in the lair back home.

I regrouped with the others afterward. We knew nothing about this island. Raylin hadn't seen it on any map. It was too far from any other land masses to know what type of creatures inhabited it. Might be natural, or not. It may have an active volcano, but the lack of smoke during the day and lack of a glowing mountain at night suggested otherwise. I doubted any civilization was going to be here. We would decide what to do in the morning once our bodies had recuperated somewhat from dehydration. For now, we set up a rotating watch and slept in shifts.

I awoke to the chill of seawater spreading on the sand all around me, freezing my back and drenching my gear. "AAAH! What the ever-loving bakkarshnits!" I could hear Erisal laughing up at their camp, apparently taking her turn at watch. The water line had risen until my camp became submerged. What devilish magic changed the water level!?

Erisal yelled down at me from the camp, "High tide is in about an hour or two, Glik. You might want to join us up here. Come on up and I'll tell you all about it."

Oh, I'd go up to their camp all right. Where was my bucket? Someone else was getting drenched when I got up there! Or maybe I'd pour sand all over her. Yeah, that would be better. She'll have that crap stuck everywhere for a week!

She took the surprise bucket of sand over her head quite well actually. She laughed it off, surprised it wasn't seawater. She then told me all about the tides; how they rise and fall with the moons multiple times a day. She also taught me a bit about fishing and the best times of day to catch the squirmy rascals. Before long, it was time for her to go back to sleep, and me as well. The next few days were likely going to be painful.

RAYLIN WAS the first of us up, having volunteered for the last watch. Surprisingly, he had already gone to the trouble of cooking up a rather hearty breakfast of fish over the fire. "Food, water, sleep. Abundance makes people happy, but even light rationing gets everyone irritable. Not enough and people make bad decisions." He may have been a bit too engaged in his navigation and gambling, but he ran a tight, efficient ship. Too bad efficient ships can still sink.

"We should head up the coastline. Fill up as much water from the stream as we can. We'll boil it before we head out. There should be enough fish to keep us fed from a few hours of fishing a day."

"Why not just set up a camp here then explore out as we can?" I didn't see any reason to abandon the boat and the camp unless we had to.

"If there's civilization on this island, it's likely to be a port of some kind. We had a good view of the southern shore and got a fair look at the western too. I for one am not keen on traversing through a jungle and over mountains when I could enjoy a walk near the beach instead. You?"

"Fine fine. I suppose. At least we should take the boa—" Memories of our time in close proximity at sea came crashing back. Judging from the looks of distaste on everyone's face, the same idea hit them too. "Never mind, better to burn the boat."

Raylin snorted. "It wouldn't matter. The sea is choppy around the coast. We should be able to make better time on foot. On the off chance something hostile finds us, it would be easier to hide on foot as well. It's probably a good idea to pull it up from the shore and hide it. I like having a few stashes of stuff around for a rainy day."

We headed north that entire day, stopping just before sunset to set up camp. We saw next to nothing except the usual seagulls and sea life. Morale was good overall. Banter was frequent. I told many stories and extracted a few from Erisal. Her stories were interesting, but she was a terrible storyteller. She spent more time laughing at her jokes and jibes than she did telling the story.

I was starting to think Skia could understand Western Imperial even if she couldn't speak it. She laughed at the jokes in my stories often. At first, I thought it could be her way of fitting in when everyone laughed. But there were the few times she caught on to the more morbid goblin humor. She smiled even when nobody else caught on. Sneaky kobold.

Raylin seemed lost in his thoughts toward the end of the night. His normally bubbly personality from the ship was replaced with a shadow of sorts. Human grief I believe they call it. We goblins aren't plagued with such troubles. Everything changes. Usually quite quickly. Enjoy what we can, if we can, when we can, for it won't be that way for long. Life's usually more misery than fun for a goblin. Besides, fun usually meant pain for another in the goblin lair. I enjoyed this kind of fun a lot more.

The night went by uneventful until just before daybreak, when Raylin's voice woke me from a fitful sleep.

"What type of tracks, Erisal? What direction were they pointed?"

"Raylin, I'm not a tracker. They look webbed but about the size and shape of a large human. I don't know of anything with large, webbed feet other than birds. Large seagulls or pelicans wouldn't fit. They don't have that many toes and usually aren't that big.

"As for where they were going, I have no idea. They went every which way, like they were deciding which way to go. The tide had washed the tracks away before I got the chance to track where they headed."

"That's a lot less information than I'm comfortable with. But better too little than nothing at all. Let's get moving just in case. We'll talk it over with everyone as we walk."

Erisal packed up camp while Raylin woke everyone up and got us moving. We headed north again, this time at a quickened pace.

Raylin opened the discussion. "Erisal found some tracks this morning. Either of you know anything about walking sea creatures?"

I chuckled at a few odd memories before responding. "Nope. This is the most water I've ever seen. Best we had was an underground lake full of catfish with claws instead of whiskers."

Serah spoke next. "Erisal, could you draw one of those footprints from memory?"

"Of course."

Erisal headed toward the nearest sandy patch by the water. She dropped to the ground in a rush, then gave us all a panicked look while waving at us to do the same. We did. I lifted the flap on my shoulder bag and fanned in some of the air.

In as quiet a voice as possible, I whispered, "Tinky? Smell anything?"

"Squeak. Squeak squeak. Squeeeek!"

Her response was very quiet. She smelled danger. I crawled over to the tallest grass patch and hid as well as I could while keeping Erisal in sight. She wasn't stupid enough to get closer to what she had spotted. Good for her. Serah and Skia on the other hand, they had a death wish. They both crept closer, slowly and carefully.

A spear appeared in the air before I had any hope of shouting out a warning. It soared in a long, high arc then plunged right at the three of them. The hooked point ripped through Erisal's upper leg, burying itself into the sandy dirt below. This was an ambush; one I had failed to see until it was far too late.

"AAAAAHHHH!!!" Erisal screamed and started to get up, only to fail and fall back down as the pain in her leg flared.

"GLUUUGGGOOO!" A scaly, blue-green creature ran toward us from the south. It waved a second hooked spear threateningly as it sprinted towards us, wobbling awkwardly as it ran. Half again taller than Raylin, muscular, with tentacle-like hair hanging loose along the sharp spines of its back; it was not a creature I had ever seen or ever wanted to see again. Beady black eyes on either side of the head and sharp serrated teeth ensured it would live in my nightmares for months, if I lived at all.

Serah was up and running already, amulet in hand. "RUN! That's a myrrh! They don't take prisoners and never travel alone!" She glanced back once to see if she was being chased and sprinted as fast as she could.

I moved quickly, staying low in the grass and hoping to stay hidden. I had to be fast, but there was no reason to make myself a target. There wasn't any chance that I'd be able to outrun my group, so my only hope was to keep out of sight as I moved. Well, I'm sure I could outpace Erisal. Luck had chosen her as the first victim, so we might as well use her to escape.

Raylin took three steps toward Erisal before he stopped. She hadn't even had the time to get up before the other two myrrh emerged from their hiding places under the sand. They grabbed her flailing wrists, taking a few hits, but Erisal had no leverage or force to punch with in her position. With monstrous strength, they yanked her pinned leg free of the ground, spear still hanging from her upper leg. Her screams filled the air, a solemn, yet familiar sound to my ears. The myrrh were dragging her to the water when Raylin, tears in his eyes, turned back toward us. He quickly noticed that he was the farthest one back, and that the first myrrh was not satisfied with just catching a single person.

Raylin hesitated one last moment, his mind warring between saving his comrade or saving himself. It was just long enough for the myrrh to take advantage and throw his second spear. A little gust of wind made the extra distance too great for the spear throw. The deadly shaft flew so close that Raylin's hair shifted out of the way, causing him to flinch. It impaled the ground just past him, burying itself deep in the sandy soil. To his credit, Raylin jerked the spear free, slowing only briefly before he caught up with us. He was fast!

I chanced a quick glance back as Skia ran up beside me in the grass. The myrrh had given up the chase quickly; angry, but wanting to ensure its previous catch didn't fight back enough to overcome his fellow hunters. One sure kill is better than multiple uncertain kills, a good rule for survival.

Raylin and Serah outran us by a lot. Skia and I had to stop running to catch our breath long before we caught up. It took us a good two hours of jogging up the coast before we found them. They came out from their hiding spots in the grass to greet us as we walked by.

I puffed heavily, then clenched my jaw angrily. "Fancy meeting you two here, long legs! Next time would you mind carrying one of us, or should I just find a better hiding spot where nothing can find me for days!?" I eyed Raylin closely, watching for his response. He was staring, distantly, back the way we had come. My fury fell on deaf ears.

He kept staring as he spoke, eyes red and watery. "She was as good as dead the moment that spear hit her leg. There was nothing I could do. I had no weapons to fight something like that. I know a lost cause when I see it. Doesn't make it hurt any less."

Serah showed no emotion at all, ignoring Raylin completely. "You may have a point, Glik. While I'd like to say that the slowest in the pack makes a fine distraction so the rest of us can escape, that's not how the myrrh work most times. They will be back, and soon. Stay within five paces of me as we travel, Glik, and I'll carry you if we need to run. Raylin, can you do the same for Skia? They are both light enough to carry on our backs, gear included. It will make us slower, but we are still faster with a burden than they are on their own. The four of us together have a much better chance of survival than two. Or one." It dawned on me that if we were being shot at, I'd get hit first if I was being carried. Serah failed to mention that little detail.

Raylin huffed. "Fine. At least one of my crew is still alive. I might as well try to keep it that way."

We needed a morale boost. At least something minor. "Raylin, you have a spear now. I've got a pretty good knife I could lend to Skia. Do you think you two could take one of those things down?"

Raylin glared at me like I had taken a prized fish and stuffed it with Skia's burned cooking.

Serah interrupted us. "No, Glik. They would die trying. Myrrh are much stronger and better at battle than any normal sailor could ever hope to be. Scavenger parties like this take pride in dragging living creatures to the water and drowning them. They are heartless, efficient killers, in it mostly for the stuff they collect off the ship-wrecks and bodies they find. Unlike their cousins, the merfolk, they are hated by most creatures. They take pleasure in the suffering of others, often torturing instead of taking an easy kill. The only sure-fire way to kill a group of them is to keep them active and out of the water for hours. They can't breathe like we do, but it takes a while for them to die outside of water anyway."

Her knowledge was impressive. "I take it this is not your first time playing with a fish-faced menace?"

"Fortunately, it is. I've read books. Lots of books. These creatures are fairly common on the coastlines of both continents. They also favor areas with civilization more than wilderness. That means there may be some civilization here. It's not much, but it is a little bit of hope. We might survive."

My ears twitched, picking up Raylin's barely audible mumbling. "Tell that to Erisal. Drowning is one of the most horrible deaths a sailor can face." He sniffled a bit, gathered his composure, then spoke up so everyone could hear. "Every sailor has heard of the myrrh. Few of us have ever seen one. They prefer the shipwrecked and unfortunate. Guess that's us this time around. But everything else Serah said matches the tales as well. Those three myrrh may be satisfied for the night, but they will keep hunting tomorrow. We should go a few more hours north, catch as many fish as we can before sunset, then head inland until we can just barely see the coast. If all goes well, that'll be enough food for a couple days of hard marching. If the moons are out tonight, we should keep going as far as possible before we make camp. I'd rather not get ambushed in our sleep."

Serah furrowed her brow. "Raylin, there are much worse things than myrrh that live on islands. I don't have a better plan, but I doubt we've seen the worst this island has to offer. And don't forget, it was you who said 'food, water, sleep'. We need all three to keep going."

I tried to lighten the mood. Tense companions were a death sentence. "The weather is nice for a walk, and we won't have to worry about sand in every nook and cranny anymore!" I pulled off my boots one at a time, pouring out large piles of irritating granules. "Anyone ever take one of those 'bath' things I've heard about? Seems like that would get rid of this gritty crap!"

"Sssss, hrk, hrk, sssss!" At least Skia was laughing.

WE TRAVELED FAST the rest of the day and well into the night, stopping only to fish as Raylin had suggested. By this point we had made our way inland but could still see the shoreline. We set up camp hours after dark, not bothering with a fire as it would give away our location. The camp was along a hill and heavily obscured by tall grass. Anything looking for us would have quite a hard time.

The watch rotation began with Skia. I took second since both of us have exceptional "vision" at night. Raylin and Serah still had not figured out that the trick to seeing in the dark was to rely on the nose and the ears. Eyes play tricks.

My bag was laying close to Serah and Raylin while I gave my shoulders a break. They needed it after the fast pace of the day. Skia preferred to sleep on the other side of the camp with all her stuff. I suppose she still wasn't comfortable hiding near someone else or anyone as big as these two. I couldn't blame her. Being the smallest of the group usually meant being the first target.

The moons were out in full; illuminating everything with a soft, silvery shine. Grass swayed in the cool ocean breeze. It was a quiet, peaceful night. A welcome time of relaxation compared to recent events. I spent a few hours daydreaming, recalling various events from my past in the goblin lair. Our situation was bad but not hopeless. We had many advantages compared to being lost in the goblin caves. There was only one type of creature hunting us, that we knew of. We had food, water, and open area to move in. Great hiding places surrounded us thanks to the tall grass. We'd likely still die, but we could at least avoid the more lengthy, pain-filled deaths if we tried.

My shoulder bag jiggled slightly, drawing my attention. Probably just Tinky getting anxious. She had spent way too much time in that bag lately, but I didn't want her anywhere near Skia. The bag then slid its full length toward the edge of camp, further into the grass.

"HEY! That's mine!" I jumped up and ran to the bag, thinking Skia had woken up and finally caught Tinky's scent. A great shadow rose from the grass, lifting the bag in its giant maw. At full height, it was over three times my size, bulky, muscular, deadly. Two paws larger than my head spread to each side of the beast, claws extended. We were doomed. Again.

"AAAAAHH!!! RUN!!!!"

Serah woke and reacted first. "BEAR! GRAB YOUR GEAR AND RUN!"

Raylin scurried away in a panic, struggling to get up. "THROW THE FISH AT IT!"

I wasn't about to abandon Tinky. Thinking fast, I did the dumbest thing a goblin could do. I charged in heroically. The bear was standing on its hind legs, but its attention was focused on the taller members of our party. I pulled my dagger and slid into the grass near its legs.

"ROOOAAAR!!!"

Its bellow was terrible and loud. Anything within walking distance probably heard that! But it's hard to bellow with a bag in your mouth. My shoulder bag fell to the ground as the bear roared. I swooped between the bears legs, nipping the back of its ankle with my dagger as I went by. I hoped the pain would turn its attention behind it. Instead, the bear yelped and dropped to all fours. I dove to the ground, now directly beneath the bear. Giant paws smashed into the earth, narrowly missing me. I glanced to my left, stomach rising into my throat. The only part of my bag visible was the strap. A gargantuan paw crushed the rest of it. So much for the luck of heroes.

"Not again dammit!" Raylin screamed at the bear, seeing me trapped beneath it. He grabbed his spear and began poking at the bear's face with it, hoping to scare it back. The bear backed off a few paces, then rose to its full height again. It definitely wasn't afraid.

"ROOOAAAR!"

"Run, stupid! Leave the fish!" I grabbed my bag, knowing I had likely lost another friend, and ran toward Skia's sleeping spot. She wasn't there. I didn't waste time searching. My legs pumped hard, carrying me as fast as I could go. A few minutes later, I risked a look back and noticed that Serah and Raylin kept pace with me. Serah wasn't far behind, but Raylin, spear in hand, frequently looked back, losing ground every time. He was ready to engage any pursuers.

Winded, we stopped to assess the damage.

"Where's Skia?" I asked immediately. I had to check on Tinky, or at least her corpse. As rushed as I was, I still didn't want Tinky to become a snack for a scared kobold.

"Wait, she's not with you? Mother of sodding orc twins! SKIA! SKIA! Better show yourself, or we'll have to leave without you!" Raylin began searching, gradually tracing his way back toward camp, ignoring the threat of the bears.

I looked to Serah for guidance. She was much more level-headed. "I didn't see Skia in camp when we ran off. You called that monster a bear. Do bears eat kobolds or take hostages?"

Serah caught her breath quickly and shook her head at my question. "No. No hostages, but they could eat her. I think these scavengers were hungry and caught a whiff of our fish. I doubt they will chase us now that they've had a meal."

She put her hand to her forehead. "It doesn't matter, Glik. We should leave. At this rate, we'll all be dead before we find a way off the island."

So be it. Skia wasn't in my line of sight. I'd have to risk a look. I sat down with my shoulder bag and gently opened it. My ears flattened, expecting the worst. There was no blood, no stench of gore. "Tinky, you there?" No response. I carefully reached around inside. My fingers brushed fur, then a wet little nose. I grasped her gently, lifted her still form, and pulled her out of my bag. Her hind legs were grossly misshapen, shattered and held together loosely by skin. Her hips were distorted awkwardly, obviously damaged as well. She was done for.

Serah looked at me, eyebrow cocked with curiosity. She noticed my drooping ears and the woeful expression on my face. "My, my little storyteller. Secrets upon secrets with you, aren't there?"

Her expression grew soft, almost caring. My brain told me it had to be fake, but my gut said otherwise. "You'll owe me for this if it works, and I doubt my goddess will grant such a boon to a rat. Still, why not try?"

She began mumbling under her breath, eyes closed, hand clasped around her amulet. The surrounding air became calm, peaceful, fresh. Her palm emitted an eerie emerald haze that wafted lazily around her fingers.

Lines appeared on her forehead as her concentration deepened. Slowly, cautiously, she lowered her glowing hand to Tinky's soft fur. Green light laced lazily around her still body, enveloping it all in hazy, emerald smoke.

Serah lifted my chin with one finger and met my eyes with a comforting smile. "This is quite a story. Tinky's body accepted the spell. She may survive after all. But her legs are too far gone. There's nothing I can do about that."

My eyes bulged with excitement. "WHAT?"

I brought Tinky close to my face, studying her as the last tendrils of glowing haze drifted off. Her chest rose and fell. Warm air from her lungs gently escaped from her wet little nose.

"WHOOHOOO!!!" Okay, maybe goblins don't succumb to loss like humans do, but we can celebrate when a friend escapes imminent destruction. We're practical, not dead.

Raylin, to his credit, came back after a few minutes of shouting and searching. "She's gone. I'm not losing my last crew member without a fight, sod it! Sarding crap, this trip keeps getting worse! We'll head back to camp at dawn to see if we can find her. At least we all grabbed our bags, but her gear is probably still back there."

Raylin paused, then turned to me. "What are you so happy about?"

"I just had some good luck. That's all."

Raylin's eyes flared. "Good luck, huh? Skia's missing and you call it 'good luck'!"

"Whoa, whoa! That's not what I'm happy about. Skia's cooking was terrible, but she wasn't bad by any stretch! Let's go back and look for her!"

Serah turned to me. Her stern gaze told me everything I needed to know about how bad of an idea going back was. We were losing time, something we already didn't have enough of. But Raylin was human. That meant he was attached, grieving, and stubborn. If we didn't go back with him, he'd go by himself. Likely get killed too. But his skills were useful and necessary.

Raylin restrained his rage, but his fists were clenched around his spear. He'd soon look for any excuse to vent his anger on anyone. Maybe it was a good thing we got attacked at least once a day.

I tried to calm him slowly, taking a practical approach. "That bear won't be far off, and the wind isn't in our favor. It'll smell us before we can see it. Skia's a kobold. She knows how to hide, but if she's like most kobolds, can also track. If so, she'll likely find us before we find her. Especially if we wait until dawn." *But if she doesn't show up in the next two or three hours, she's probably dead.* The spear in his hands made sure I only said the last bit in my head.

Through all of this, Serah had maintained her composure. None of this disaster hit her emotionally. She even seemed happy healing Tinky. Maybe Serah expected all of this trouble or just didn't feel the same way humans do. Sort of like goblin practicality. Perhaps the naga had something similar.

I, however, stayed overly anxious while we waited for daylight. It was too open. I wanted my caves back where there were no hungry bears, scavenging myrrh, or even rat-hunting kobolds. The caves were terrible, yes, but a terrible I knew how to navigate and survive. Too much on this trip had just been luck. There was nothing to do about it now, except survive. To do that, I'd have to keep bigger targets than me around and stay hidden as much as possible. In goblin society the weaker, smaller people served as bait. I appreciated the reversal in my situation.

Raylin paced the whole night. He woke Serah the very second sunlight broke across the sky. Without complaints, we headed back to camp. It was ransacked. All the fish had been taken and Skia's bag had been torn apart and strewn everywhere. At least that's what it looked like. The collection of shells, rocks, shiny things, and string could have just been a trash heap. Kobolds.

I went over to the last place Skia had been. *Sniff, sniff.* Damn, we were still upwind from where the bears had come. I wouldn't be able to sniff out a trail with this breeze. I scanned the area visually. Bent grass. Perhaps we could follow it. But what if we did and just found the bears? I looked over at the patterns in the grass from where my bag had been attacked. They matched. Skia wouldn't have moved that much grass or been heavy enough to squish it so flat.

Not wanting another confrontation with Raylin, I quietly told Serah. "Skia is gone, most likely taken by the bears. You said they don't take hostages? So, she's probably bear chow? Do they maim first to prevent escape?"

Keeping her eyes on Raylin, Serah invited the confrontation head on. "Being dragged off in an animal's jaws isn't harmless. Look Raylin, we can either waste half a day tracking her down and facing off against the bears in their den or admit what we already know. Survival is my primary concern. Is there any way to put your mind at ease short of bringing her back from the dead and erasing this whole mess of a situation we're in?"

Raylin stared at the grass. His rage had cooled a bit, but he wanted to track down the bears and wear their skins as a cloak.

An idea sparked in my mind. "I've got it! Not just survival. We get off the island, then come back later with an entire armada. Settle the place and start our own tropical getaway experience halfway between both continents! Charge excessive amounts of money! Have strangers pay for the thrill of running away from bears and being dragged into the water by myrrh!"

Raylin's expression was death. "We come back with mages and level it all. Turn it into another flaming realm of hellish ash." Raylin took a deep breath, shoulders sagging. "Despite how I feel, you are right. We should go. I need time to think anyway."

We trudged away from the scene, traveling north yet again. Shoreline changed slowly from sandy beach and grassland into rocky foothills. Come dusk, we topped a small rise, which rewarded us with an excellent view of our surroundings. In front of us was a mountainous peninsula. The ocean stretched as far as I could see to its north, with a shoreline fading into the distance to the east.

Oh, one other tiny detail caught my attention. The towering dwarven walls of a city-fortress.

CHAPTER 4

GNOMISH PRESCIENCE? PRESENCE? PRESENTS? BAH!

Yet again, no fire at the camp. No fish to eat either. Water was running low again, and Skia had been wearing the only pot we had to boil water in. I wonder if bears could eat metal or maybe wood? Fine ability, that. If we had it, we wouldn't have been so damn hungry at camp that night!

"Raylin, any advice on how to approach this walled city? Personally, I'd scout it for days, making sure it's not inhabited by anything that eats or kills goblins. But given our current provisions and track record for survival out here, that's probably not going to work out so well."

Silence.

More silence.

I opened my mouth to ask again, thinking I might have slipped back into speaking Goblin, when Serah's voice gently broke the tension.

"They were a good crew. There was nothing you could have done to save them."

I'd heard of this type of thing happening with other races, but I was surprised it came from Serah. Her tone was empathetic, like she cared and knew the pangs of loss personally. She was trying to make him feel better, to snap him out of his guilt and grief.

She kept her face turned away from Raylin the whole time. But I could see. Her nose wrinkled and her lips curled in a slight snarl. The expression directly opposed everything she intended with her tone and her words. This conversation was a necessary chore for her, so she forced it, pushing through with the act despite her boredom and disgust. What an ability! She could put royal acting tropes out of business with skills like that!

Tears soaked Raylin's cheeks. He didn't bother looking at Serah when he answered. Instead, his head drooped heavily, voice speaking just loud enough that we could hear his weak, broken ramblings. "An admiral once told me, 'A captain isn't made from a handed over title. They are made by what they do, the respect they earn from their crew, and the love of their ship.'"

He turned his head up to the sky with a sniffle. "The end of the year. My contract with that lazy bastard captain that never lifted a finger and leeched off all the profits would have been done at the end of the sarding year! I would have had it all. I'd have been captain of the *Dolphin's Tear* and been able to put our profits toward the ship and the crew. No more scavenging up cheap parts and short-term fixes. No more sifting through the desperate populace to find the rare, reliable crew members willing to work for nothing. No more busting out every possible job as quickly as possible to maximize profits. It was all to get the sodding captain out of the way!"

Raylin's jaw clenched at the memory, his voice growing ragged. "For what!? All of them are dead now. Every. Single. One. Even that bloodsucking, whoreson of a captain. I should have gone down with her. I was the captain in all but name. Guess I'm getting what every captain that abandons his ship deserves. Why did I expect anything different?"

I timidly raised my hand. "Ummm, because they weren't all dead when you left the ship?"

I half expected Raylin to throw his spear before I finished the question. He was unstable. I'd seen this in dwarves mostly. They get so into their drink that emotions take over their mind. Then they do all sorts of stupid things, thinking that they are fun or important. They'd start fights, throw things, start sobbing randomly, and hug people. Some would even try to sing. Dwarves sing worse than goblins.

A few big goblins would drink like that and do stupid things too. But they usually forgot they could die and did whatever they wanted to do. Which usually got them killed!

Serah spoke again with a firm, yet caring tone; face turned away. "Raylin. You survived. You are the last part of the *Dolphin's Tear* that exists. Grieve if you must, but survive. It won't be the same, but the ship can be built again. A new crew can be assembled. You can start again, but this time your way, with no captain to stop you."

She took a deep, dramatic breath, pausing briefly to let Raylin absorb her words.

"But you have to live first. And we need off this island. Take some time to think about how to do that."

She shook her head slightly, then looked toward me. "Glik, you are correct. We need to scout and you see better in the dark than Raylin or me. Can you sleep now, under our guard, and go scout later tonight?"

Wait, what? Aw fraklestrüpt! She was right. I was the perfect scout for this group. Much better senses, especially at night. Small and stealthy. Damn it! At least I got to sleep, and these two were naively trustworthy.

"Grrr. Sard it! Fine. I'm faster without baggage. Protect it all with your life, especially Tinky!" I plopped to the ground, pouting angrily, and forced myself to try sleeping. It took an hour or so for me to calm down, but peaceful darkness won me over eventually.

IT TOOK a few long hours of trudging through dense grass and light forest to get to the wall. There weren't any torches or fires to signal anyone walking the walls, so I headed toward the gate under the cover of grass. The wall was at least ten times my height with a moat around it that was as far across as the wall was tall. Ramparts, arrow slits, what appeared to be murder holes; this was a fortress. But where was everyone? As I snuck my way to the gate, I found out. There was a drawbridge down but so was a wide set of two portcullises over the gatehouse. A cackling laughter filled the air.

"Yuz zo ztupid, Calak! Yuz dropped ze metal gatez on Guluk!"

Sure enough, there was a corpse underneath one portcullis. My shoulders slumped as I looked at it. Short, coppery green skin, big ears with little black fur tufts on the tips. Big bulbous nose and huge feet. If there had been any doubt, the language they used confirmed everything. This place was infested with goblins.

I didn't need to know anything else. I turned and snuck my way back toward camp. If there were guards, then there was something with a brain in there. That likely meant hobs. Where there are goblins, there are almost always hobs. One of our goblin magic users was possible, but unlikely. They didn't bother with guard duty assignments. Ugh, hopefully there weren't any orcs this time. But this was a large city, and large cities required a lot of muscle to enforce any semblance of order. What had I done to anger the gods of luck?

Apparently, not too much. When I returned, camp was right where I left it, and Serah was awake. In her hand was a shaky but conscious Tinky. She was tickling Tinky's whiskers, flicking them playfully with her forked tongue.

"Nagas don't play with their food, do they?" I asked suspiciously, realizing how snakelike Serah could be.

She let out a huff of amusement. "No, I don't eat rats unless I'm starving." She glanced up, taking a second to think. "Well, I won't eat Tinky, regardless. I've put too much effort into healing her fuzzy butt."

Interesting. Serah had feelings after all. No deceit, no hiding her face or shifting her tone. Her words were true and genuinely caring. Maybe she had a soft spot for small animals? Yet she cared little for other people. I wondered if that was normal for her kind or if there was some history.

"That's lucky for Tinky. Unfortunately, our own luck isn't as good. The whole frackin' place is crawling with goblins. They stationed guards, which means there are probably hobs. With a place that big, there are probably orcs too. You might want to start praying for something, because we're screwed."

Serah stared off into space, eyes shifting, as she thought about what to do next. The wind blew the grass softly, bringing the sea breeze to our noses. I played a bit with Tinky. She loved getting scratched behind the ears. She lifted her torso up with her front paws but didn't have the strength to drag her broken half very far before stopping. Raylin's soft breathing occasionally erupted into a loud snort or snore.

A few minutes later, Serah gave up. "We'll take another look tomorrow. We have to go that direction either way, so we might as well do it with the walls in sight. Unless you think they'll spot us."

"HA! A goblin guard won't notice anything that's not attacking it or bringing it food. Especially during the day. That's when most of us sleep, including the guards. Daylight is hard to see in unless you've spent months in it."

I paused, realization smacking me in the face as I spoke. "On second thought, our luck this trip has been terrible. Let's stay where we can barely see the wall. Just in case."

Since Serah had slept earlier, we passed the last few hours of her watch playing the trade secrets game. She taught me more about bears and a few things about the myrrh. In exchange, I regaled her with the intricacies of goblin social chains, focusing specifically on defense and law.

It's fairly straightforward, really. The goblin with the biggest stick makes the rules. Nobody follows those rules until that goblin is present and makes an example of someone. Usually by beating someone smaller with said stick until they stop being able to break the rules. Simple and practical, just how we like it.

Raylin woke right at dawn. We updated him on the situation, packed up camp, and headed out, not having any better idea of what we could do. Scout first, bypass the place all together if needed. We had just about given up on a better plan as the city came into view. An odd sound on the wind made my ears twitch. It was a bouncy, earworm of a tune, in some goofy language. Pixie maybe? Nah, too low-pitched. Must be Gnomish. I know Gnomish, but I'm far from fluent in it.

Only gnomes I had ever known were those that were in our goblin prisons or invading our caves. They left a bad taste in my mouth. Unlike most soldiers that attacked us, they were full of tricks, just like the hobs. It was hard to keep them in the prison too. Non-stop babbling and lots of them knew little magic tricks.

"There's a gnome up ahead. Well, someone singing in Gnomish anyway."

Sure enough. Over the rise, pulling a little hand cart, was a goblin singing in perfect Gnomish. The cart was brimming with boxes, bottles, and vials. Probably some kind of cook, as no self-respecting goblin would be an alchemist. The magic-using goblins might, but they wouldn't ever get their own ingredients. That's what weak goblins were for.

Raylin spoke first, "Let's ambush him. Can't have him running back to the city warning them that we're coming. Probably some useful stuff on that cart too."

I gave him a quick nod of approval. "Agreed, but I doubt there is much for us on the cart." I took a quick sniff to be certain of our bearings. "We're downwind. Don't make a sound and we should be able to surprise him with only a few paces between us."

We set up to ambush the goblin on both sides. Raylin dropped into the thick grass with spear in hand. I held my spare dagger out to Serah. She ignored it, pulling her own wicked-looking, wavy dagger from underneath her cloak. I believe some called this type of weapon a keris or kris. Sneaky.

Within a few minutes, the goblin pulled his cart into our trap. I was waiting for him to pass, hoping to kill him in a quick hit from behind, when Raylin pulled a completely idiotic move. He jumped out in front of the goblin, spear leveled at its face, and shouted "Hands where I can see them!"

Predictably, the goblin flung something hard at Raylin while falling backwards to dodge the anticipated spear thrust. Raylin didn't expect that at all. The bottle shattered on his chest as Raylin thrust out his spear, aiming low. Acid began burning through Raylin's shirt. Eyes wide with panic, he gave up on the goblin and started ripping off his clothes. The goblin hadn't been so lucky, however. Raylin's thrust had struck true. The hooked spear head was buried deep in the goblin's foot.

I rushed the gnome, putting my knife to his throat from behind, quiet and efficient. Wait... gnome?

"What in Skixfiggle's Fandactory are you!?" I held the blade tight to his neck, waiting for a response and hoping that whatever magical monstrosity turned this goblin into a gnome wasn't going to kill me.

"OOOWWWW! MY FOOOT! Don't kill me! You jumped out at me!"

A now naked Raylin stood in front of us, a few hairs still smoking from the fast-acting acid. There were a couple of red spots on his skin where the liquid had soaked through before he could wipe it off. "Hardy har har, ya little bastard! If you had hit my face with that crap I'd be a pile of poisonous goo on the side of the road. Give us one good reason not to take that spear out of yer foot and shove it somewhere less pleasant?"

"Because I'm not trying to kill you?" The gnome howled in his high-pitched, nasally voice.

"Everyone on this island hates gnomes, so I disguised myself as a goblin! Do you blame me?" He scanned us quickly, bushy eyebrows shifting left to right. "You don't hate gnomes, do you?"

Too easy. "Why, yes, I—"

"No, we don't!" Serah stopped me as I started to push the blade into his neck, hard enough to break skin. "I believe we all got off on the wrong foot here. No pun intended mister gnome. I am Serah."

I looked at her, staring with one eyebrow cocked and mouth open. What in kiggledig's boot stash was she doing? Acting all personable and charismatic to this idiot! Where was the survival-focused, cold-hearted snake of a woman I had grown to like?

"Gleeglum. Gleeglum the Tintapper. If you don't mind, can we take this conversation elsewhere? Preferably without blades at my neck and in my foot!" The gnome groaned and shifted a little, trying to back away from my dagger without putting weight on his foot.

Serah gave me a sly look that demanded I follow her lead. "Agreed, Gleeglum, but we're not putting our weapons down until we know we can trust you."

She paused, glanced at Raylin, then looked away with a smirk. "Raylin, you might want to put away both of your spears and get some clothes. It appears to be a bit chilly out here."

Gleeglum snickered, then moaned in pain as the laughter shook his foot. I removed the dagger from his throat and readied myself to thrust it hard into his back, right at heart level. Risky because I might hit ribs, but it would drop him fast if my aim was true. Raylin scowled at Serah, then carefully extracted the hooked spearhead from Gleeglum's foot.

"I don't suppose you have a spare set of clothes for someone my size, do you, Gleeglum? I doubt any of Serah's clothes would fit my build all that well."

Gleeglum grinned, enjoying friendly banter despite the pain in his foot. "Perhaps, but they would be back at my tower. For now, the best I can offer is a rather small mantle or cloak. For what it's worth, I apologize. I hope those rags of yours weren't nostalgic. Seriously, I am truly sorry, you three—" He stopped short, eyes settling on me, scrutinizing heavily "—are the first 'civilized' people I've been acquainted with outside the walls. There are only a handful of people inside the city that aren't orcs, goblins, or hobs, and most of them are more cruel than the monsters that run things. You three don't strike me as barbarous, just a bit overeager, which was technically my fault."

Serah gave a cautious look to Raylin, then moved to Gleeglum's foot, creating a familiar green glow around her free hand.

"Oh ho! A mage in your midst!" Gleeglum's eyes lidded over as Serah's magic enveloped his foot.

"Ahhhh, that feels glorious. You are no mage. You are some kind of priestess. Mage healing hurts, but that is sublime!"

Serah rolled her eyes as she got up and walked over to inspect Raylin's burns.

"Pft, those'll heal fine in a few days. Just wash them every night."

Raylin's scowl said more than words ever could. This was strange. Serah liked healing. What was she playing at?

Gleeglum tested his foot, flexing it a bit before standing. He was a relatively old gnome, grey-haired, long beard, bushy brows, and wide ears. He was exceptionally short, even for a gnome. Half of Serah's height at best. Heck, he was a full head shorter than me! He also smelled of raspberries and cinnamon, so Tinky approved.

"Now, now, Serah. It may not merit a miracle, but I do have something that will relieve any paresthesia or irritation around his burns."

He turned to his cart and produced a small container full of a clear, oily substance.

"It is a liniment I make specifically for epidermal burns and abrasions. Works wonders for erythema."

I stood there, blinking stupidly. What was he was talking about? Was he still speaking Imperial? Judging from the lost look on Raylin's face, I wasn't the only one stupefied. Gleeglum was oblivious to our reaction, too immersed in his own little world of technicality.

"Luckily, the bottles for that wonderful defensive concoction have to be coated in wax and they are fairly thick so that they don't shatter in my bandolier. That means"

Gleeglum's hands blurred through the air, his words blending together as he spoke. We could barely understand what he was saying.

"IHaveToAim ForTheBodyOrTheyWon't Break! VeryExpensive StuffThatYouCan't FindJustAnywhe."

He paused, finally noticing our lost expressions. His hands lowered slowly, and he took a deep breath, shoulders slumping with minor disappointment.

"Sorry. I get too excited when talking about my work. Will you be inquiring about my creations much longer? If so, I'll consume a mild sedative to slow myself down a bit."

Serah nodded in agreement. "That would probably be best. You should also grab that cloak for the spear master over there." She cocked her head toward Raylin with another smirk.

I missed something. Her tone was odd, and Raylin began having some sort of reaction. Poison maybe?

"Raylin! Are you ok? Your cheeks have turned red! That stuff didn't get on your face too, did it?"

I ran over, ready to help him wipe the stuff off.

He swatted at me before I could get too close. "Get off of me! No, I'm fine!" He turned roughly away, crossing his arms and huffing.

"Huh? I was just trying to help. Why are his cheeks red?"

Gleeglum had busied himself with the cart but was obviously snickering. Serah covered her mouth, shoulders shaking from her muffled laughter.

She waved me over and whispered in my ear. "He's embarrassed."

Yet another new human thing for me to learn. Or maybe it was elven.

Gleeglum returned, threw a large cloak to Raylin, then lit a long pipe. A few drags later, he looked at us expectantly. "Now that we've mended our disastrous first impressions, how may I assist you?"

"Mended" my sand-chafed butt! He still didn't say HOW he had looked like a goblin. I knew gnomes were trustworthy to their word, but they were almost always trouble. Exact wording was tricky.

Nothing too painful or permanent usually happened, but hijinks and mischief were the favored commodities of the little miscreants.

To be fair, the same could be said of goblins, but our hijinks were lethal. Well, and we lie a lot. Practicality before honor. He needed to prove himself a bit before I'd take my eyes off of him and put my dagger back in its sheath. The only thing going for him right now was Serah's strange approval.

She continued the conversation. "Gleeglum, we're shipwreck survivors. We need whatever we can get to survive. Is there anywhere else to barter passage off this island and get supplies other than the goblin city over there?"

"Aha! I knew you all were an exception!" Gleeglum hopped with excitement.

"You're trying to get off this sodding island too! How's this? You help me get out of here, and I'll give you anything you need. Except most of the useful stuff is at my shop in town. We'll need disguises. Luckily, your goblin friend here should fit in without one. I also have one concoction that gives an imbiber the appearance of a hob for a few hours. Regrettably, I have nothing for the last of you. Whoever is left will have to impersonate a servant or act absolutely, powerfully, evil." His eyes locked with Serah's, a maniacal grin spreading across his face as he slowly articulated the last three words.

Her civil persona ceased immediately. "What exactly do you mean by that, gnome?" The switch from happy customer to soul devouring demoness took everyone by surprise. Gleeglum almost fell over, stumbling backwards in a panic.

"MAGIC! You know some magic! Whew! On second thought, with a temper like that, you may not need any magic! I disguised myself earlier with a spell, but it only works on me. I was hoping you knew a similar incantation or at least some charm to make you appear intimidating."

She visibly relaxed, replacing her cold visage with a half-hearted smirk. "Sadly, I don't have magic that would make me look like a goblin or hob. I'm not inclined to go in as a meek servant either. I find displays of power work best to avoid being targeted. Don't you agree?"

"Um. Yes?" Gleeglum stammered.

I smiled and nodded appreciatively. She was a good student of goblin affairs. A display of aggression like that would have every goblin in town talking, and most of that talk would be about avoiding her.

Serah continued, still radiating power, but less aggressively than before. "First, please answer a few questions about the island, Gleeglum. That is, if you would like our help leaving it."

Gleeglum adjusted his tunic, regaining his composure. He kept a cautious eye on Serah.

"Sure thing! For the most part, I'll disclose anything you desire. Open book for a friendly face. Those have been in short supply the last few years."

Serah let out a light huff of amusement at being called a "friendly face". "Then I'll get straight to the point. There are snake people on this island, aren't there?"

My ears perked up in an instant. Had she known we would end up here from the very start of the voyage? How? Guess what topic was coming up in our next trade secrets game!

Gleeglum's expression matched mine. He subconsciously mouthed the words, *"How did you know that?"*

"Ahem. Hopefully, you weren't assaulted by them. They typically stay in the jungle to the southeast. I believe they occupy an old city and a ziggurat there. It's hard to tell who specifically, but I can see some action from my observatory. While we are on the topic of temples, there appear to be two others on the island. A small cult of goblins seems to have found the old shrine of Agnit at the top of that mountain over there," he pointed off toward a specific tall peak in the eastern mountains, "and there's a sunken temple in the northern sea caves."

He paused a moment, lost in thought. "I lost a colleague there. You see, I'm not technically here as a shipwreck victim. I've been here for over five years as part of a scientific expedition. We didn't realize this island was inhabited by a city of pirate goblins. As a result, the expedition was doomed. I survived through some cunning alchemy, as did my closest associate, Pikle. The others..."

Gleeglum grew pale and shifted a little, uncomfortable with the memory. "Well, they perished trying to survive in this city. I'm the last of us. Have been for three or more years now. Pikle left to study the sunken temple in the northern sea caves a few years ago but never returned. She was intrigued by the temple's origins and had to know what sort of creatures might still worship there. Unfortunately, I was in no position to accompany her at the time.

"To my surprise, her orc bodyguard returned last week with her notes and other belongings. Arrogant oaf wanted me to fulfill the remaining terms of her contract. I informed him that if she was deceased, then he had failed to uphold his end of the bargain and should not receive compensation. Enraged at my response, he insisted she went swimming and disappeared, which was no fault of his own. Quite improbable, considering he had her belongings, and we were talking about Pikle specifically. Not only was she an exceptional swimmer, but she knew how to brew her own concoctions of water breathing. That was a formula I never mastered myself. Regardless, I was loath to add an orc to my list of enemies, so I remunerated him half of the agreed upon sum as a compromise. It was only a few hundred coins anyway. A pittance compared to the value of Pikle's recovered notes."

Serah didn't hide her lack of compassion. "Do you have a map or any better information? Perhaps we could convince a crew to take a ship off the island?"

Gleeglum shrugged. "Nope. I never travel more than a few hours outside of the city. Too unpredictable. Alas, I have run into one of the aforementioned snake people. He fully intended to sacrifice me to the goddess Khabis. I knew little of her before that. I'd rather not investigate her further, either. Seems like begging for trouble." He shivered a little at the thought, apparently knowing too much already.

"As for the ship, nobody has embarked on a sea voyage in over a year. Everyone who made an attempt vanished, save the last ship a year ago. A handful of sailors returned on a rowboat. They claimed some tentacled monstrosity sank the ship roughly a day after they left port. It's impressive that they found their way back. Since then, no one leaves sight of the shoreline. The hobs even put out an order. They don't want any more ships disappearing. Makes sense to me. Hobs have terrible skills when it comes to naval construction methods. Orcs and goblins are not any better. That means, once the best vessels are gone, there's no way to get more."

Serah pondered that for a little while before asking, "Do the goblins fear the snake people much as you do?"

"More, much more. A few of them have come to the city for trade. The first time it happened, a guard mistook one of them for a human. That snake ripped the guard's throat out with his huge fangs, then bit a second guard on the arm and pinned him to the ground while the others watched. After a few seconds, the poor victim began seizing and drooling a frothy spittle from his mouth. The whole incident lasted less than thirty seconds. That poor guard's skin discolored to a purplish-blue, indicating some form of asphyxia. He expired while everyone watched." Gleeglum turned a sickly, pale color as he recalled the spectacle. I guess he had watched first hand.

"The snake person then demanded trade or else we would face the wrath of his people. One hob supervisor on duty saw an opportunity. He accepted, on condition that the snake people trade a modicum of venom to him and him alone. That's the legend of how our glorious leader, Kragga'k'tol, became the head hob in town."

Serah nodded, her plans falling into place. "Excellent. I can appear to have fangs given a bit of time to prepare. Would that get me in unscathed?"

Gleeglum's eyebrows rose. "Undoubtedly."

He began gathering his things and checking his cart. "I think our little scuffle has soured me on finding more reagents today. Would you care to escort me back to my shop now? I'm afraid I won't have enough lodging for the three of you, but I can at least get you started with supplies and a pittance of funding."

He sighed. "Admittedly, I'm at a loss for how to escape the island. Any assistance is appreciated. I'm really sick of goblin food, goblin smell, and goblin security."

I spoke up. Time for potential enemies to be closer. "Onward, Gleeglum! But give the disguise concoction to Raylin first."

I slowly meandered toward the rear of the group. I wanted to trust this gnome, but the setup was all too easy. First promise everything to desperate, shipwrecked people, then stab us in the back.

Gleeglum smiled at me. "Oh, so it does speak! Do you have a name, goblin?"

He pulled a vial from his bandolier and handed it to Raylin.

"Glik. How do we know you won't just hand us over to the guards when we get there?"

Serah rolled her eyes, then leaned over to whisper in my ear. "Trust me on this one. I think he'll be able to do something very specific for you once we get to his shop. Something very important to you personally. I know when people lie. This one never does. It will get him killed someday." I wondered why she trusted him so much. Another secret of hers.

Gleeglum snickered again. "You are welcome to linger here until tomorrow when your friends return and report that it was, in fact, safe."

Grrr. He had me there. Fine. My gut wasn't sending up any more warning signs. One last check and I'd go with it.

I sneaked a peek into my shoulder bag. "Tinky. Thoughts on this gnome?"

"Squeak."

Her response was tired and half-hearted, but the message was clear. He smelled of raspberries and cinnamon. How bad could he be?

CHAPTER 5
GOBLIN SECURITY AT ITS FINEST

I t took us a few short hours to get to the drawbridge. By now the sun was high in the sky, and the sentries were looking exhausted. They had retreated into the gate house but made certain the portcullis stayed up. They propped barrels underneath in case one of the goblins up top got any "funny" ideas.

Gleeglum, once again disguised as a goblin, led the group. Raylin had hidden himself behind the cart, wrapped in a spare cloak. He waited until the last possible moment before chugging the disguise concoction. He made a hideous hob. Well, hideous to other hobs at least. He was probably somewhat attractive to an elf. It didn't matter. The guards all focused on Serah. She made no attempt to hide her human appearance.

Gleeglum started the conversation promisingly, in perfect Goblin speech, albeit with an odd accent. "Yaklik! How did you get stuck with morning guard duty? Piss off the ol' Peg Leg again?" To their credit, the guards never took their eyes off of Serah.

Yaklik responded in a high-pitched, nasally voice with a similar, odd accent. "I tell you yesterday, I tell you day before, I tell you every day! I is Giant, the Tiny! Get. It. Right!"

Laughter erupted all around, including our party and every guard in earshot. Everyone except Serah. She looked like she was trying to bore a hole through Yaklik using nothing but her eyes.

"HAHAHAHA! Yaklik. Even if 'Giant the Tiny' was your real name, I still wouldn't use it because it's so sodding stupid!" Gleeglum was belly laughing so hard that he had doubled over and was slapping his knee.

Yaklik's face turned an angry red. "Bah! Who is these guys? You know rules." He turned and looked at the other guard, his bushy, black eyebrows cocked up in confusion. "Ogrip, what is rules agains?"

Ogrip partly opened his mouth and stared at Yaklik in disbelief. "You really are dumbest numpty in the whole city, aren't you? How you survive this long?"

He shook his head more and turned to our group. "Any newcomers must pay security tax. We use money to keep the pea—"

"AAAAAAAAAHHHHH!"

SPLAT!

The sickening packing sound of meat hammering into stone erupted next to us. It was accompanied by a large blast of fluids and body bits. A red-smeared corpse was all that remained of the goblin that had been flung off the top of the gatehouse. A large hob looked down at us with a toothy grin. Her deep voice carried through the air. "Slipped and fell. HA!" She tossed a small bag of belongings at the pile of remains, then left with a satisfied smile.

Ogrip put a hand on his face. "Never mind. Get in here. Keep an eye on your human pet. It looks fresh, so hobs will want it."

Ogrip's jibe didn't seem to affect Serah at all. We had all gotten in unscathed, with little effort.

The fragrance as we passed through the gates made my eyes water. It was familiar. Years, perhaps decades worth of unwashed goblin filth and refuse piling up everywhere. It was a fine mix of rot, feces, piss, and goblin cooking. Generally, it was hard to tell those four smells apart. GGRRPP. My stomach growled. Some habits are hard to break.

Gleeglum spared a quick glance back at us. "Straight ahead to that tower. Mind your belongings."

He moved swiftly down the narrow, crooked street, careful to dodge the many little hands that tried "bumping" into him or his cart. Far ahead, the cackling of an amused crowd filled the air. Some unfortunate fellow had been strung upside down from a tavern sign. The crowd was throwing all manner of objects at him. The sign read: "Stone'N". Huh, that was somewhat clever, both by the innkeeper and the crowd. I'd have to pay that place a visit later.

A scuffling noise near Serah caught my attention. She grabbed a small goblin child by the arm. "That is not yours, little one. Do I need to make an example for all of your friends to see?"

Her threat was cold, even by goblin standards. Stated clearly, with no emotion whatsoever on her face. The meaning went beyond the Imperial words she used, which was good. The goblin likely didn't understand any Imperial, but she obviously recognized the meaning.

The little goblin screamed and yanked about, struggling to free her hand. "Rikkish, Riikkissh!"

Within seconds, a hob of roughly Serah's height walked up to us. He puffed out his chest, trying to look intimidating. A deep, gravelly voice escaped his lips.

"Is there a problem here, human? We don't take kindly to others abusing our children."

So the thieving ring had a supervisor. His Imperial was spot on!

Serah's eyes switched instantly from emotionless to a sharp, predatory eagerness.

"Example it is."

Nobody saw her move. She was speaking one second, the next her fangs were buried fully inside the hobs neck. Her jaws convulsed weirdly as she pumped massive amounts of venom into the poor bastard's bleeding throat. All the while, her steel grip held the goblin urchin.

She pulled back after a second or two, the hob too shocked to react. She spit repeatedly on the ground, grabbing Gleeglum's water-skin and washing out what had to be an absolutely horrid taste. Even I wouldn't lick a hob!

The urchin screamed and clawed at Serah's arm. She yanked the child around, forcing her to watch her boss.

"Watch, child. See what happens to those who cross me. Spread the message well. Leave. Us. Alone."

The hob grabbed his neck and fell to the ground. He began spasming wildly, foaming from the mouth and clearing the crowded street around his flailing body. Everyone stopped to watch. They had seen death but not like this. His grunts and screams were painful to hear. His voice was strained, twisted, and partially muffled by a jaw that wouldn't do as he commanded. After less than a minute of nerve-wracking contortions, every muscle over tightened to the breaking point. His body froze. Dead. Tendons locked as though magic had turned him into a living statue.

Serah, satisfied that the urchin had seen it all, relaxed her grip and let the urchin slip free.

Raylin stared at her with a combination of awe and horror, like his mind was battling the need for survival with the potential for having a powerful ally. His fingers absentmindedly touched his teeth.

I gave Serah a genuine look of approval.

"Very nice, Serah! Better to be a respected enemy than potential prey, or likely property, judging from the looks of this town. Buuut, I probably should have told you this before we got here. Goblins are stupid. Imperial is known by about 90% of all creatures that can speak. Goblins are usually part of that lacking 10%."

Gleeglum snickered a little. "I really don't think the words mattered much just then, Glik. Besides, we're far enough east that Eastern Dominion is predominant."

Bugger. My Eastern Dominion was rough. I had hoped to sharpen up once I got to Shael, where both languages were used heavily. Time for some more books to get vocabulary! Wait, how the fizzlejig would I find a book in a city of goblins? Latrine maybe?

After that fine display of not so sensual violence, the crowd happily gave us space. Despite being able to see the tower from the gate, it still took us quite a while to get to Gleeglum's. I'm sure the original builders of the city had wide, well-constructed roads. But the goblins managed to build their ragtag shops and "houses" all over these ancient streets, creating a kind of unintentional maze of shacks and hovels. The resulting chaos allowed for easy pickpocketing and easy escape if you knew the area. It was smart. We did the same thing in the caves I grew up in. Well, as much as the caves themselves would allow.

We finally approached what appeared to be a four-story conglomeration of hastily thrown together gnomish tower building techniques. It had been built recently out of nearby stones from the ruins and leaned heavily to one side. Gleeglum scampered happily to the small wooden door and opened it without a thought.

The rest of us stood in open-mouthed shock. This fool likely had alchemical wealth beyond the comprehension of any goblin hidden in a giant building that could be spotted from anywhere in town. And he didn't lock the sodding door!

He met our expressions with a mischievous grin. "We all have our secrets. Come on in!" He waved us up, then hauled in the cart after.

We went up a set of narrow, spiral stairs lit dimly by magical lamps. Gleeglum left the cart in a special nook at the bottom. "Skip the red door, look for the green one."

The red door appeared to be on the second story, followed shortly by the green one. It was the same rickety looking wood that the front door was made from. It was also unlocked.

The place smelled like the library in Partha. Old paper and parchment mixed with the dust and burning wax smells from a dozen or more candles scattered around the place. The gnome was simply begging for this place to be torched! Shelves and clutter filled the otherwise spacious room from top to bottom. It was somewhat organized, if you considered organized to mean "like goods" were put into piles.

"I've got lots of stuff for you all. I think you are the best shot at getting me off of this rotten cesspool of an island. This stuff doesn't do me any real good here anyway. First thing, put on some clothes, Raylin! There, in the back, but keep away from the dark-grey cloak. It has teeth!"

We all took our time, browsing slowly. Serah went over to the pile of armor and weapons. I headed over to the books. Tinky decided that this was too good of an opportunity to miss, legs or no legs. She stuck her head and tiny front paws out the top of my shoulder bag and let her nose take the lead. I learned long ago to trust her instincts.

"What's got your attention?" I whispered.

"Squik, sqeeeak, squieak."

She pointed her nose toward the edge of the armor pile. It was filled with trinkets of all sorts, toys, contraptions, orbs.

"What's all this junk, Gleeglum?"

"Ah, those are the experiments that function properly. Mostly little distraction devices and, uh, toys." Gleeglum had been following closer than I realized. He was now quite fixated on my shoulder bag. "Mind if I meet your colleague? I don't care if you plan to liberate my belongings, as I would likely give them to you anyway. But I rather enjoy the company of diminutive animals. They are a rare sight in a town of goblins, as you can imagine."

I was still on the fence about trusting this gnome, but I had never met one that was cruel to animals. Most gnomes outright worshipped little critters.

"Up to you, Tinky." I said to the bag.

Her little nose popped out first, testing the air. Her fuzzy ears followed, twitching nervously. Finally, she raised her full head to see. Her head cocked to the side as her nose twitched. She then looked up at me.

"Squeak."

As relaxed an answer as I'd ever heard her give. Must be his smell.

If Tinky trusted him, I'd have to as well. I gently pulled her broken body out of the bag. Gleeglum had a fascinated look that quickly broke into horror once he saw her legs. His hands covered his mouth.

"That's terrible! What happened?"

"Crushed by a bear. Healing spell saved her life, but I doubt Tinky will ever walk again. It may be a trick for her to survive this adventure."

My ears drooped as I voiced the realization. Tinky was the closest person I had to a truly trustworthy friend. She had been there when I left the lair.

"May I?"

Tinky looked at me.

"Squeak."

I handed her over gently. Gleeglum was almost as careful as I had been. He swatted a bunch of trinkets off the desk haphazardly and tenderly set Tinky onto the cleared spot. His hands reached into a drawer and grabbed a set of goggles with various lenses and a few other odd instruments, including a notebook. Fully equipped, he began studying her in great detail, jotting down notes, listening to her breathing, and moving various body parts with exceptional care.

After what seemed like an eternity, he was satisfied. "It has been a long time since I engineered any prosthetics, but I'd be willing to bet Tinky's spine is fully intact and functional. I've been seeking a unique challenge, and I suspect Tinky is no normal rat."

He pulled off his goggles and looked me in the eye. "I beseech your permission to outfit her with newly designed, mechanical, and slightly magical posterior appendages. It would take a few days for me to fabricate them and a full day to perform the procedure. A few weeks of healing and calibration will be necessary afterwards. I use the term calibration loosely. She'll be learning how to use the prosthesis in recovery. She is fully matured, correct? No more growing?"

I was at a loss for words. Again. "Um, yes."

Gleeglum looked at Tinky. "Is that what you would like? I can make them special for you. Perhaps a bit faster, a bit quieter. Maybe include some gadgets like lock picks?"

Tinky began nodding enthusiastically.

"SQUEEEEEAAAK!"

It was settled then.

I scowled and put my nose right up in Gleeglum's face. "If she gets hurt or she dies... Well, I don't need to tell you what goblins do to their playthings for fun."

He rolled his eyes but nodded. That would have to do. I wouldn't go against Tinky's wishes.

"I'll begin immediately. I presume you'd like to observe during the process? Bring her here in three days. If the process is successful, she'll be a whole new rat! In the meantime, why don't you take her with you? Be sure there are no second thoughts. This is not reversible."

Gleeglum turned to put away his tools, then held up a finger, remembering something. "I have some books you may be interested in. Take a look. I also have a more robust travel bag, specifically designed to protect books, if you'd like. It's not waterproof, but it should resist the elements significantly better than that inferior thing you currently use."

Our group spent the better part of the day scouring through Gleeglum's wares. Raylin found a nice set of clothes that fit well enough despite being overly loose. He also procured a rapier, dagger, a stubby bow with a heavy draw, and some basic survival gear that would be useful in exploration. Serah grabbed some cloth armor with narrow, metal links sewn in, a bandolier full of various vials, and an odd flail with several blades embedded in its shaft.

I gave her a quizzical look.

She glanced at me and said, "It reminds me of home."

The possibilities of that comment made me cringe a little. Considering where I'm from, that says something.

I struggled to pick the right books, eventually settling on a book regarding "magic words" as well as a jungle survival manual. There were also extra writing supplies, a handy little crossbow, and a small set of leather armor that fit me acceptably well.

Gleeglum handed me a small bag. "A bit of pocket money to get you started. Don't die and don't give it away at the Blood Pits. In fact, it's better to avoid that cesspool all together. They have a nasty habit of recruiting bystanders unwillingly. Oh, I almost forgot. You'll need this, Raylin."

Gleeglum pulled an odd-looking glove from a drawer. All the fingers were open, and it appeared to be stitched together from at least four distinctly different hides.

"It will take some time to acclimate yourself to it. But concentrate hard enough and the magic will make your body a simulacrum of any creature that the gloves are made out of. So long as what you want is the same general dimensions in space as you are. It's just a trick of optics, so don't expect to be as strong as an orc if you look like one. The magic from the glove is a lot easier to penetrate than my concoctions, but it is stable and non-consumable. You can use it all the time. Just don't expect it to fool any overly religious or magically inclined creatures."

Serah was idly testing the sharpness of the blades on her new flail. She spoke without taking her eyes off of it. "Where should we start our search, Gleeglum?"

Gleeglum yelped and rushed over once he noticed what she was doing. "DON'T DO THAT! If it cuts you..." He sighed once she stopped. "It extracts blood directly from anything it lacerates! Nasty thing. I'm glad to be rid of it. Don't strike anything with it unless you want that thing dead. Permanently."

He shivered, then gathered his composure. "Ahem. As to your inquiry, you'll want lodgings first. That stone tavern we passed on the way here should suffice. Don't leave anything in your chambers there. Bring your own locks too."

He paused, placing his hand on his chin in thought. "Ugh, on second thought, don't bother with locks. I don't have any. There's no need with my security system. Any locks you get from the market are either easy to pick or there's a master key floating around for it. Just bar the door from inside the room."

I was still curious how Gleeglum kept his place secure without locks, but we took his advice and headed back toward the "Stone'N". As soon as we left the tower a loud "POP" drew our attention, followed by "GAGAJGIGRRRRMMMMPH!"

A spasming goblin was trying to steal Gleeglum's sign from above the door. Blue lines of lightning crackled repeatedly over the goblin's body, forcing his muscles to twitch and his teeth to chatter uncontrollably. It was over in a few seconds. The still convulsing body fell to the ground in a smoking heap. I guess that answered the lock question.

It was a short walk, but now that we were out of earshot, my curiosity demanded answers. "Serah. What's with the buddy-buddy routine on Gleeglum?"

Serah sighed and dropped her shoulders a little, not taking her eyes off the road. "Trying for another free answer, Glik?"

"Yes!" I interjected as quickly as possible. "Now we're even. An answer for an answer!"

Serah glanced down at me. "Hm. I suppose so, little storyteller. But don't expect quality answers if you play dirty. Gleeglum is useful. The friendly approach bypassed his mental defenses and left him as a willing ally. It is a risk, but I judged a gnome alchemist to be relatively safe compared to the threats he may help us avoid."

We turned the corner and got our first full view of the tavern that we were intending to call home. It was an impressive, albeit crumbling, stone temple. Graceful spires and buttresses betrayed its elven influence, yet the heavy stone foundation and reinforced stone doors were of dwarven make. Odd to say the least. Part of the roof had collapsed, and much of the intricate stonework had crumbled to dust. It was a testament to ages, how time would return everything to dust.

The crowd from before had dispersed, but the corpse of the stoned goblin still hung from the tavern sign. It was a grim reminder of this morning's "entertainment". Nowhere was safe in this city. It didn't matter where we settled.

Raylin stopped us. "Before we go in, I suggest we stick together and set a watch. Any disagreements?" His eyes shifted around rapidly, obviously nervous.

I expected him to last less than a week here.

Serah answered. "Agreed. Once this business with Gleeglum is done, I'm headed to the jungle. I suspect if anyone knows this island, it'll be the snake people there."

She wasn't nervous at all. Emotionless as ever.

I nodded and pushed through the stone door. Inside, I was greeted by a familiar sight. A pleasant ruckus of goblins celebrating for the sake of celebrating. Drink was flowing, food was flying, and despite the malicious forms of mischief, it was a generally happy atmosphere. An orc sat on a tall stool next to the doorway. He was the usual sculpted slab of muscle, but he was also surprisingly symmetrical and unscarred.

"Don't start trouble, you three."

It was not said as a threat, just a bored statement. He hated his job.

Looking further into the tavern, past a dozen tables of drinking goblins, there was a large, stone column that had fallen across a raised dais. The goblin behind it had converted the fallen column into a makeshift bar. There was a small cooking fire behind it as well.

All of this did little to distract from the centerpiece behind the bar. An ornately carved, vertical slab, roughly the height of the orc at the door, dominated the room. The stele was made from a shiny, black glass, likely onyx or obsidian. Its center had a perfectly cut, spherical relief, almost the entire size of the slab. Intricate, silver-gilded engravings portrayed arcing paths that swarmed around the sphere. Thirteen archaic symbols lined the outer edges in an almost haphazard, floating pattern. Various colored enamels had been used to accent the symbols, but centuries of wear had taken their toll. Most of the color had chipped away, little by little. The bartender had placed a crude mockup of a goblin right in the center of the stele. Judging from the knives and darts embedded in the wood, they used it for some sort of game.

As we made our way toward the bar, the tavern keeper looked at us with suspicion, sizing us up. He probably thought we had money but might be more trouble than we were worth. His left ear was missing several pieces. His nose was halfway lobbed off, showing a grotesque hole in the right side of his face where his nostril entered his skull. He had no shortage of scarring all over his mostly bald scalp. He knew how much trouble was too much.

"Whaddaya want?" His voice was abnormally nasally with a sort of "pebbles under a wheel" grinding noise in it. "Only drink we got is rotgut. Only food is blackened fish with turnips. Place to stay is—" he paused for a few seconds, guessing how much we had to spend. "Ten coins a night. None of that Imperial parchment crap."

"Ten it is and we'll split the largest room you have." I tossed ten tin coins on the table, the old western continent currency that held little value anymore. The old goblin grimaced, suddenly realizing his mistake.

"Oh no, that won't do. Ten gold coins."

"Ten silver and you have a deal. I'd be willing to up to fifteen if it covered a few drinks and some fish for the three of us each day we are here."

"Bah, and they call me crooked. Fine. Room is that one in back. Get yer own lock if you want one. It bars from the inside and there's a trunk to leave yer crap." He turned and began fishing three cups worth of rotgut out of an open barrel. He then tossed a fish directly in the fire and chucked a few sickly-looking turnips onto plates. They still had fertilizer and dirt clinging to them. By the time he had our stuff ready, the fish was black on the outside. He dragged it out of the flames by its still raw tail, then hacked it into three pieces with a cleaver, right there on the floor.

Flop. Flop. Flop.

"There! Now leave me to better paying customers!"

Raylin had the raw tail. It still had a pinkish, clear liquid oozing out of it, scales and bone fully intact. Serah had gotten the middle, with its cracked, charred exterior failing to hide the still cold center. It was complete with all the guts and innards of a freshly caught fish. I had scored the head. While I lamented the loss of the outermost layers, the eyes were still delicious, as was the rest of the pickings around the gills. Burned outside or not, the inside of a fish head was still great compared to most goblin cooking. If only he had some mushrooms.

Serah, obviously not interested in the food, sniffed her cup. She slid it over to me, then grabbed her water skin from her pack. One swig later and she wandered over to the room. I guess standard goblin cuisine was not her thing.

Raylin at least made an attempt at the rotgut. He took a deep breath, slammed a mouthful in, and promptly sprayed it all over the bar. "Pfft! I've tasted piss that was better than this." He sniffed the cup. "Actually, this IS piss, isn't it!?"

The bartender smirked. I knew piss was not part of the typical recipe. But nobody ever stuck to a recipe in goblin cooking, if they even had a recipe. Every chef had their own "unique spices" to add, particularly when alcohol was involved. I gracefully sipped my rotgut. Huh. Maybe Raylin was right. This didn't have the burn of most rotgut. It really did taste like piss. Waterskin it is.

Raylin headed over to the room next. It was late evening by this point, and we had been through quite a few rough nights. I, on the other hand, was way too curious about the stele in the back. "Barkeep! Mind if I take a closer look at that stone slab your dartboard is hanging from?"

"So long as you don't rig the game, do what you want!"

I approached the stele with a mix of fascination and awe. The stone had no seams or connection points. It was standing on a base made of speckled grey and black stone, granite perhaps? I can't imagine how long it must have taken to get it right, particularly the spherical relief in the center. Maybe the craftsmanship had been magical. It didn't have any elements of typical elven, dwarven, gnomish, or human construction. The haphazard symbols didn't appear to be any specific language, either. They seemed to represent particular shapes:

- A shining sun, traces of a white enamel still visible
- Another sun, this one blackened
- Fish, hopefully tuna
- Keris dagger, with a drop of something falling off the tip
- Island
- Feather
- Tower, eastern style construction
- Octopus or squid of some sort
- Flaming bird
- Three interlinked rings
- Three interlinked triangles
- Three more interlinked triangles, upside down
- Compass

Outside of each symbol, scratched roughly into the stone itself, were notes in a language I had never seen. Perhaps Gleeglum would know something, or maybe Serah. I tried to memorize as much of it as possible. It wasn't too hard with the images themselves, but the language, that was tricky. I broke out some of my writing materials and made some notes, along with some rubbings.

After a few hours of study, I headed to the room. Raylin was already passed out on a stone bench that was supposed to be a bed. Serah was organizing her equipment on the floor, assessing if anything was missing, and deciding if anything could be abandoned.

"Does this script mean anything to you?" I tossed a page of rubbings over to her.

She looked up, annoyed, lamenting the interruption to her thoughts. Her hand snatched up the page as her eyes quickly scanned it. A spark of recognition crossed her face.

"This is a language used in high religious groups. Said to be the language of the old gods. I am not fluent by any means, but I may be able to piece together a general meaning. AFTER I'm done here."

"Whenever you like, Serah. The original is on the stele just outside our room."

"Fine." She huffed and threw her things back into her bag. "I'll let you know what secrets I find in the morning. For now, I need to sleep. Take watch."

I shrugged, then went to inspect the door, checking the pre-installed fasteners for the crossbar. Ugh, goblin construction. At least the owner could have had an orc do it. The fasteners would pop off with a single hefty tug. I took a look at the handle and the hinges as well. Wow, these goblins really were dumb. The hinges themselves were on the outside of the door, which opened outward. The door didn't quite fit either, just a "reinforced wood" door that had been taken from somewhere else.

I loosened the fasteners on the door handle. If anyone pulled hard enough to dislodge the bar, they'd pull off the handle instead. Hopefully, that would buy us enough time to be ready if the intruders dismantled the hinges. There wasn't an easy escape route either. A slit window for ventilation was in the wall, but it was too small to pass through. We'd have to smash through the wooden ceiling of the room, then climb ten times my height of stonework to the roof if we wanted out. At least that made it unlikely we'd get ambushed.

Once the room was "secured" I popped open the new-to-me book on "magic words". It started off as a primer on halfling diplomacy, migrating into generic diplomacy for different levels of society. It was strange, often using archaic forms of the Imperial language that simply did not match context or timeframe. After getting a bit frustrated at this, I skimmed through and found a few abnormal chapters and blurbs hidden throughout the book. They were in no particular order, not included in the table of contents, and made almost no sense at all. They spoke of actual magic contained within words and how to empower words with magic. I was no wizard, but the last I checked, spells were much harder than just screaming "boogety woogety" and waving your fingers around. It added more questions to ask Gleeglum.

When Raylin awoke, I filled him in on the situation with the door and the stele outside our room. He was in a depressed mood again. Poor humans. How did they ever manage to survive when every time a friend died they had to spend weeks getting over it?

Oh well, time to sleep on a nice, hard rock. Just like being back in the lair, minus the pile of other goblins and the stench they gave off. I handed Tinky a piece of cheese I had nipped from Gleeglum's and tried to fall asleep, belongings within easy reach.

CHAPTER 6

WHO SEWS AROUND HAY STACKS?

"It might be a means off the island. It might be a surefire way to die. I can't be sure." Serah chucked my notes to the ground, frustrated.

That was an emotion I had never seen her show. I couldn't tell if it was fake or not.

I wondered. "Do you think Gleeglum could figure something out?" I wasn't keen on giving the gnome too much information, but any way off the island was worth pursuing.

Serah huffed. "Possibly. He'll need time, but testing the stele won't go unnoticed. We may meet resistance if we take too long. In the meantime, we should find out what we can about this sea monster and the history of the island."

She picked up my notes and handed them back to me, gingerly. "You're well on your way to being my only reliable option for help. There are many secrets on this island. I want to find as many of them as possible. If we must wait while Tinky recovers, we should learn what we can here. After that, we head to the jungle."

I nodded. "What do you have in mind? I'm thinking we'll need to swing by Gleeglum's for some more questions. Then we'll probably need to go to the market to get something more edible for you and something more alcoholic than the literal piss water here for me."

Raylin interjected, having woken up while we talked. "Well, you two, I don't really like the idea of poking around uninvited in a bloodthirsty monster den. But, if you find some way around this sea monster, I might be able to procure a ship. These goblins look like they love a good gamble, and who am I to turn down easy coin? I'll need a bodyguard to pull this hustle off without getting robbed, but get me some starter money and I'll 'invest' it into the local gaming scene until we have enough to buy anything you want in this city."

He took a swig of rotgut from his wineskin, grimacing as he forced it down. "Besides, it'll focus my mind on something. I'd rather not be alone with my thoughts. Idle boredom will kill me."

Huh. I never expected him to know a way to snap out of an emotional haze. I'd have to note that for future use. I wonder if other human types could do the same thing? Then again, maybe he had some halfling or elven blood in him that gave him some practical reasoning beyond the normal human. Both were likely considering his slightly pointed ears and short stature.

Serah watched him closely, judging whether he was foolish or talented. "We start with Gleeglum, now that we know what to look for. I doubt there are any other books in this city."

We gathered our gear and headed out the door. It was early morning, and only a few patrons remained. A different goblin had taken up the role of barkeep. By goblin standards, she was much less attractive. That meant she wasn't missing any pieces and had no visible scars! Likely a smart goblin, or at least a sneaky one.

She sat there with a skewer, rotating it slowly over a much more concentrated fire. Fish again but with some sort of bacon wrapped around it. On each end, a plump mushroom. This goblin knew how to cook real food!

I couldn't contain my excitement. "I'll have some of that!" The

Imperial words left my mouth before I had control, spittle flying with them.

The cook glared at me, furious. She then did a double take and realized I was staring at the food, not at her. In a roughly accented Imperial, she responded, "Ah, fish. It's been a long night of gnash-gabbing puttock's in here. They act like they own the place. And me too! Good thing Ruk works late for me. See the six bodies in the corner?"

She pointed over to a pile of bodies and grinned wickedly. "All his handiwork. They might wake up. They might not. Guess which way I like better? He didn't use any weapons. Just his bare hands. Means some of them might survive. But I wouldn't count on it."

She tested the sharpness of her cleaver and licked her lips. I couldn't tell if she was happily threatening to kill the rest of the goblins in the corner or just making sure I didn't say anything stupid.

Ruk was nodding off on his stool by the door, trying to keep his head upright. But, every so often, one eye would open and check the pile of idiots that had crossed him the night before.

The savory smell of a fine meal took priority for me.

"Yes, the food. Mushrooms, fish. Not burned. Genius wrapping it in bacon to protect the flavor. You gutted it too! I'm Glik. What might I call you?" I was choosing my words more awkwardly than normal. Quite a rare occurrence. My excitement for the fish had spilled over a bit too much.

She narrowed her eyes and clenched her lips. "Chunx. Shut up before you ask!"

She stuck her finger in my face and glared, articulating every word until it was sharp enough to cut.

"I grew out of it. Sarding puttocks kept calling me Chunx anyway. Bloody lubberworts!"

Apparently, my tribe wasn't the only one that was ruthless with names.

I held up my hands defensively but licked my lips at the delicious scent wafting through the air.

"When it's done, the three of us would like some of that fine meal you are cooking. Is there anything other than rotgut to drink?"

Chunx glanced at us with a bit more scrutiny than before. Her eyes glinted with unmistakable greed. "You came out of the room, so I guess you got a tab. If not, Flugspur can sit on a stick. I'm not paid enough to care."

She looked around the room suspiciously, then leaned in a whispered. "My partner's been trying to brew 'ale'. Don't tell any goblins. They try to cheat me. They don't pay. But any humans like her can buy some. One silver coin per pitcher."

I tossed three silvers to her, hoping to buy some leniency in conversation. "Sure thing! I'll give it a shot! One mug for each of us to start."

I gestured toward the pile of bodies. "You said Ruk over there had six different fights last night? Is that normal?"

She gathered the coins and pocketed them instead of putting them into the till.

"No. Pay attention."

She pulled a large jug out of a hidden stash in the column's side and began pouring for us.

"One fight. The idiots started it. Guess they didn't think about Ruk. One orc couldn't handle his rotgut. He beat on two hob supervisors. They deserved it. In here slacking. Not on patrol where they should be. They had nine goblins with them. Numptys thought they could beat the drunk orc. Numbers don't matter in a fight like that."

She paused, sliding each of us a cup of her "ale".

"Ruk took down six in one charge. Never knew what hit them! They're in the corner still."

She chuckled as she recalled the fight. Her laugh was lighter than most goblins but still had a gritty quality to it.

"The other morons fought back. They got smashed up bad! Definitely dead. All but two. We chucked the bodies into the rotgut fermenter. Flugspur's orders. Imbecile doesn't waste anything.

Someday that drink will kill someone. He won't want that heat. Not if it's a hob."

Color drained from Raylin's face as he realized what was in the rotgut. He turned and vomited violently, then poured out his half full skin of rotgut on the floor. Pfft, like he'd never tasted a corpse before. Teetotaler.

"Ruk smashed the dead faces into the floor. Nobody recognized any faces after that. Didn't matter much, but in case someone checks the fermenter. He also set an example. The survivors watched Ruk killing, then Ruk let them go. I told Ruk that's the wrong kind of attention. He's still pretty new. He'll learn. Until then he says 'Gotta set an example. Nobody plays hero in here!'"

I cracked up. Chunx deep vocal imitation of Ruk was spot on and absolutely hilarious!

Raylin was still recovering, but a curious expression grew on his face. His gaze had turned to Ruk. He was plotting something.

Chunx told a good story, but one orc against a room full of angry goblins, hobs, and another orc. What crap! There was no way one orc could go through that many assailants and walk away unscathed, much less do it bare-handed.

I called her out on it. "That was a marvelous story, Chunx! You tell it like it was true!"

Chunx clenched her jaw, then finished dishing up all of our food, slamming it down on the plates as she went. Once she was done, she leaned in close to my ear, her whispered words dripping with malice.

"Go ask Ruk. After he beats you, come back. Call me liar again. I'll put more nasty things than piss in your rotgut."

Raylin attempted to rescue me from my mouth.

"I don't know, Glik. Ruk over there may just be what I'm looking for. HEY, RUK! CARE FOR A MEAL?" Raylin waved the half-asleep orc to the bar.

The orc's voice was deep, yet abnormally smooth, especially when speaking Imperial. "Hm? Why not? I'm done with this shift."

He stretched and yawned as he got up. Every muscle he had rippled and flexed. Nasty sharp fangs jutted out from his lower jaw. The man was a beast, even for an orc. Watching him stretch was terrifying.

Raylin and Ruk began discussing the terms of bodyguard work. More accurately, they discussed how many limbs Raylin could be missing before Ruk no longer got paid. Serah, who had been sniffing her drink and waiting for the food, tore into her fish. She seemed to genuinely enjoy it, along with the drink.

I was failing to be Chunx's best friend, so I wisely focused my attention on the meal. It wasn't tuna, but it was excellent. Cooked to perfection, just enough time to be juicy.

I took a sip of the "ale" next. It was hard but pleasant. The flavor was similar to a drink that I had helped brew back in Partha. The recipe was just about perfect but missing something sweet that would give it just a bit more kick. Plums I believe they were called. Grew on trees. In fact, there were a few of those trees just outside the city. My curiosity took over again, ending my silence.

"Chunx, I'm sorry I doubted you. This drink is amazing. Add some of the purple fruit the imperials call plums. There are a few trees not too far from the city, but they weren't ripe yet. Your friend timed the rice harvest perfectly for this brew, not too ripe, yet not too raw. When you sell it, call it 'sake' instead of ale. It's common in the Eastern Dominion and a fair bit more expensive than ale, so it should fetch a better price. I'd love to buy more of it."

Chunx expression softened a bit, but she was still furious.

"Fine. We'll try that. If you pay, you can keep buying. I only work during the day. You won't get any from Flugspur. Don't ask him either. He will try to take over. I won't give you any more if you do that."

I bit back a thousand compliments, some refined, some vulgar, and none of them likely to do anything but infuriate her more.

"Thanks." I sat silently and savored the rest of the meal.

ARMED with a few extra bottles of sake and some leftover fish, we headed over to Gleeglum's. Serah led the group as a test for yesterday's intimidation tactics. Raylin walked beside me disguised as a legitimate hob, albeit a scrawny one. He started asking me about orcs.

"I think Ruk may be an able bodyguard. Are most orcs trustworthy when paid well? What should I look out for to prevent backstabbing? Any particular weaknesses that I should know about?"

There's an idea. Hire a big orc to keep other big orcs from beating the crap out of you when they lose. It will probably piss off Chunx too, since she'll need a new bouncer.

"Well, make sure he knows you pay better than anyone else. Tell him to come to you first if someone offers more. It's a good idea to keep him well fed and well liquored too. Make sure to get him at least some physical action every few days to keep him from getting bored."

I felt like I was giving instructions for taking care of a pet.

"I wouldn't take on an orc myself. Most of them are stupid and greedy. Makes them easy to manipulate. They are terrible at picking out assassins and thieves. It's not that they don't sense them, but everything seems weak and harmless to them. Then again, depending on what you are trying to protect against, the imposing presence would cut down on emotional outbursts and poorly picked fights. Best of luck!"

Raylin stroked his chin in thought. "Okay. Once we're done with Gleeglum, I think I'll go talk to Ruk. Maybe he'll come with me to the docks. Sailors love gambling. Hopefully, I won't lose the fifty silver Gleeglum gave us, but it's best to start a reputation as an easy score."

I shrugged. "Meh. Gnome looks like he has all the coin anyone could ask for. He won't lament the loss of a few hundred. You should ask him if he has anything he'd like you to sell."

Raylin's eyebrows rose. "Good point. It is easy to hawk stuff through a good gamble. I'm not sure he wants to give good quality stuff to goblins though."

"Pfft. Let him decide. He wouldn't sell anything in this city if he were afraid of it going to goblins."

"Point taken."

Serah remained quiet and alert the whole way. Probably wasn't convinced that she wouldn't get attacked. Once we arrived, she simply walked up to the door and knocked before any of us could stop her. I remembered the crispy critter from his sign the night before.

A few seconds later, the door opened on its own. No lightning or shocking defenses for Serah. We headed up, noticing the cart in the alcove was now empty. The red door was open.

Gleeglum's nasally voice carried into the hallway. "Enter, my friendly adventurers. But don't touch anything!"

The red room was everything that the green room was not. Meticulously clean, everything in a specific, identified place. A large workbench and various machines lined the outside of the room. In the center there was a large washbasin next to a massive alchemist setup with various forms of glassware, mortars, stills, and any other combining device imaginable. Gleeglum had an odd device on his head that directed magical light wherever he looked. He also wore a similar set of goggles to the day before, one with multiple lenses he could switch. His hands were working slowly, carefully, on some intricate mechanical device.

"Give me a few more minutes of uninterrupted focus, then I'll join you upstairs. Peruse my collection if you like. Green door only, no further if you please."

We headed upstairs, not wanting to distract him. He was likely working on Tinky's new legs. I immediately scanned the books for anything related to the history of the island or of this stele. Serah began searching through the rings and amulets, and Raylin migrated to a pile of clothing.

Gleeglum entered a few minutes later, pipe in hand, and closed the door.

"Thank you for the silence. I hope whatever items you've pilfered serve you well. Provide egress from this island, and I'll consider it a fair transaction."

"Squeak."

I looked down at Tinky. She held a small, somewhat tarnished, silver chain, likely a bracelet. A white sun symbol hung from it, identical to a symbol on the stele.

"Nice find, Tinky. Someone is getting extra snacks later!"

"Squeeeak!"

She held her chin high and squinted her eyes in satisfaction. The pride of a job well-done.

I held the bracelet out to Gleeglum.

"What do you know about this?"

He took it and inspected it, a puzzled look taking over his features.

"Ancient history. Archaeology that escapes my investigations. Supposedly, that old goblin running the Stone'N' discovered it when he first took ownership of the tavern. They excavated it from under some ruins in one of the side alcoves. It was probably a holy symbol of whichever god or goddess the temple builders worshipped. Then again, it could be some frivolous good luck trinket."

Gleeglum sighed in resignation.

"Sadly, in all my years here, I've yet to find any useful history of the place. It has some elven and dwarven architecture, but time has obfuscated most of the elven records. Anything hidden has been discovered and eradicated long ago. That only leaves the dwarven chronicles, which are often engraved and sculpted deep into the stone. It's a dubious possibility, but they may have recorded some sort of instructions or manuals over in the keep. But that is hob territory and I abstain from dealing with them. It's difficult to do business when the other party has a reputation of deceit."

Ugh, hobs. They look like overgrown goblins but bulkier with sharper, longer teeth. Yellow, cat-slit eyes are the easiest way to tell them apart from the larger goblins in a group. That, and they liked braiding their hair. Every damn one of them was smart too. The dumbest hob was easily a match for the smartest goblins. They used that to make traps. Traps for the body, traps for the mind, traps in business, and traps just to embarrass each other regularly. Tricking each other was a social pastime and a game of status. Leaders emerged only so long as none could trick them into failure. Thus, the hierarchy was upset regularly. Rules were meant to be bent and bypassed. Breaking them was for the orcs.

My mind was made up. "Serah, I don't think we should worry about the keep. The hobs will probably be too much of a pain. There may not be anything there anyway."

She watched my body language more than she listened to my words.

"I'll heed your warning. Gleeglum, is anything in this shop magical other than the potions?"

"HAHAHAHA! Nope! I keep the exemplary creations in my personal quarters, notwithstanding a few necessary items in the observatory. Why do you think I let you dig around in here? That bladed flail is as much a curse as a blessing, and it was probably the most powerful item in here."

He noticed our eager expressions.

"And before you ask, the answer is no. I won't surrender any of those inventions. They are too hazardous and I don't want them falling into use by a gang of hobs. I doubt any of them would be particularly helpful for investigating history anyway."

His rapid-fire speech shifted toward me.

"Speaking of books, how do you fancy the book on 'magic words', Glik?"

What? When did he say anything about books? GAH!

Gleeglum started talking again before I could utter a single word. "Utter nonsense from what I could make of it. Only spells I know of that need vocal elements require incredibly precise articulation. You can't just wish energy into your lips and spit fire! However, the publication is passably accurate on the intricacies of diplomacy, assuming the populace you are dealing with is over a century old and archaic in habit."

I guess that's one topic crossed off the list. I rushed to get my next question in before he resumed his verbal onslaught.

"Have you looked at the giant stele in the tavern?"

He smiled condescendingly, like he knew what I was going to ask before I opened my mouth.

"Nope! I've heard of it, but I'm not about to set foot in a goblin tavern. It's one thing to convince a twosome of idiot guards to squabble with each other for five minutes about the intricacies of onomastics. It's a whole different trick to convince a room full of inebriated monsters that I'm the same species as them. Especially if drinking rotgut is involved. From what I hear, that stuff is more toxic than sewer water."

I thrust my handful of notes at him, hoping to pique his interest.

"Here. You may find these interesting. This stele isn't just an everyday dart board."

He took a few moments to flip through them, mostly looking at the rubbings. He stopped when he got to the scratched notes on the stele's edge.

"Wow. That's a script I haven't seen in ages. I can't translate it. Linguistics were never my focus, but I know someone who might assist us. I'll message him once everyone leaves. Can you duplicate your notes for me? I'll replenish your supplies, of course."

I clapped my hands together. Finally, something that might not be a dead end! "Absolutely. Do you think this stele may be a way off the island or some way to control that sea monster?"

Gleeglum shook his head from side to side.

"Nope. It definitely appears arcane or at least ritualistic, but my gut says it's inutile. If it was a means of egression, someone would have used it by now. They would probably protect and hide it too."

Pigglefluff! So much for that lead. The book on magic is supposedly a flop too. I went back to the bookshelf to continue my search. My only hope now was this "contact" Gleeglum had mentioned. Well, that or some miracle in the jungle. I thought the real miracle on that trek would simply be getting out of the place alive! I want adventure, but I'm not a huge fan of pain, suffering, disease, and death.

Raylin was eager to get going. "Gleeglum, I'm going to get out and make some contacts, perhaps get a ship on the off chance that one of you three find us a way past that smelly set of tentacles out there. Do you have anything you'd like me to sell for you?"

"Of course. Send them to my shop for whatever they want. Just make sure they knock first, hehehe."

Raylin grinned and looked down with his hand on his chin. "Perhaps I'm not being clear enough. I'm good at getting a lot out of practically nothing. But the more I have to start with, the faster I can make something happen."

Gleeglum stopped messing around with a trinket on the desk and focused on Raylin with a sly smirk.

"You'll fit right in here. Understand that the hobs are not stupid, so don't expect to get far with them. Orcs and goblins will cooperate nicely, just don't let them think they've been cheated. Orcs will bludgeon you in the face, goblins will knife you in the back."

Gleeglum paused for emphasis and focused on Raylin, eye to eye. "I resolutely suggest that you resist going to the Blood Pits. Every fight is rigged, and very few know what cheat is involved until it's too late. The prevailing penalty for any perceived dishonesty is throwing the perpetrator into the pit for the next brawl. I stress, perceived dishonesty. As for your 'items of value', let's begin with some basic trinkets and 'shiny things'. Return with your earnings when you want more items, and we'll keep 'upping the ante' as it were."

Raylin worked out the details in a few minutes, then headed on his way. Serah waited for me to finish my review of the books, but it was no use. After an hour I had determined that, while there was plenty of valuable information on Gleeglum's shelves, none of it would help us get off the island. Disappointed, we left Gleeglum to his work on Tinky's new legs.

I walked side by side with Serah, picking her brain for more insights. "Why do you think the jungle will have answers?"

"I suppose I can give you a history lesson, Glik. Let's head to the market as we talk."

We turned toward the bazaar. Her pace was livelier than I expected, forcing me to jaunt every so often to keep up. Perhaps this was a story she liked, or maybe she just wanted to outpace any eavesdroppers.

"Naga were once the dominant species of this world, born to lead it to greatness. Benevolent leaders, top-notch mages, a benefit to all of creation. Over time we grew into the largest population of the world, yet we ruled fairly and efficiently.

"The creator god was impressed with our accomplishments and sought to reward our success. He created a utopia for all naga. It was an entirely new world crafted specifically with us in mind. It was free from the trials of leadership and survival. An easy life. Millions left until only a few hundred naga remained. They were tasked to usher in the next species and continue the ways of civilization. We believe this was but one of many cycles where a species gained dominant power; then intentionally handed it all over. This world is a trial designed by the creator god."

She paused for a moment to collect her thoughts and choose her wording.

"However, there is another version of this story. Some say the creator god grew leery of the naga, worried that we were too powerful. He thought that once we ruled every corner of the map, ambition would corrupt us, and we would challenge the gods themselves. To prevent our ascension, he sent us to another world. Some say he sent us to our doom instead of a paradise.

"In this version, the few hundred naga that remained knew the truth. A rebellious faction grew and vowed to reclaim the world for the naga, despite the treacherous creator god."

"That is quite a story, Serah. While I love a good tale, how does this relate to getting off the island?"

"The largest group of naga I know of only numbered around fifteen, including myself, but the naga on this island have a full temple. Regardless of whether they want to conquer the world or collect the faithful, they would need a means of transport."

She could tell I was getting impatient. "Hear me out, Glik. If they relied on ships, they would have made the temple on the coast, not in a jungle. This leads me to believe their method of transport is magical.

"Naga also value knowledge. Once the temple was completed, they would record as much history as possible and ensure it was preserved somewhere. They would assign a historian and task them with upkeep and maintenance of records. If that historian is cooperative, they could speed up our search for information significantly.

"Here's where the story comes in. Trekking through the jungle is deadly, even for those who know it well. To go in blindly is suicidal, and the naga are unlikely to welcome visitors. If we are lucky, they are the benevolent sect of naga and will welcome me. You would have to stay outside the temple grounds."

Her features darkened. "If the naga are rebels, both of us will be welcomed generously and turned into dream slaves for their goddess. I'm uncertain, but I think they worship the old naga goddess of sleep and inspiration, Khabis. Since our fall, she developed a preference for nightmares. Her worshippers torture the dream slaves, exposing them to their worst fears repeatedly while they are awake, then drugging them into a forced sleep full of nightmares. That is the myth anyway. Until Gleeglum said otherwise, I had never heard of anyone actively worshipping her."

Well, that's terrifying. "You make the hob's keep sound like a pleasant option. They try to kill you with traps, or at least get bored after a few days of torture and finish you off."

"Maybe it is. But what are the chances any records are left there? I am no expert, but I don't recall dwarven history being of much use in the way of secrets. Family names, paragons, military victories and campaigns. At best we find out what this city was for. I highly doubt we find any way off the island, if one still exists."

I shrugged. "You don't have to tell me twice to not dance with the hobs on their own turf! What's the plan? Why are we headed to the bazaar?"

"Scouting run. I want to see if we can put together enough provisions and people to get us safely to the naga temple. I suspect Raylin can help with hirelings later if he's as good with money as he says. My guess is it will take us a week or two to gather everything we need. We should probably hit the docks after the market, and despite Gleeglum's warning, the Blood Pits would be a good place for fighters and desperate mercenaries that blew too much coin.

"Unfortunately, that still leaves a guide to the jungle. That may prove our downfall. I've had no luck finding one of those. Might get lucky at the pits, or Raylin may find someone, but probably not. Any guide that knows the jungle well would likely still be in the jungle. Few intelligent creatures spend time in a goblin city unless they fit in explicitly and have few other options."

She stopped walking and turned to face me, feigning empathy. "Understand, Glik, I say 'we' in all of this because I need your help. Goblin cities are not my specialty. I understand if you don't want to risk the trip, but it will be one hell of a story, even if I end up dead."

She didn't need to give me the expectant look, but she did. It was almost as perfect as the unnecessary bait.

"I'm curious, Serah. Of all the angles you could have chosen, why emphasize how good this adventure would be as a story? You know you are the only person on this island that I somewhat trust. I obviously care about survival too, and you are most likely my best chance at getting off this island. You also know that the goblins here are not the same as the goblins I grew up with, so my 'help' may be limited. All that and you chose the story angle."

She gave me the most genuine smile I have ever seen. There were even wrinkles under her eyes, betraying her authentic emotions.

"Because you are not with your tribe, hiding in goblin caves. You are trekking across an undocumented island with a gambling sailor, a creature of myth, and a rat."

She paused, then gave an amused huff. "And most of the space in your pack is taken up by books."

CHAPTER 7

THOSE BEST FORGOTTEN

A few days had passed since our last visit with Gleeglum. Serah and Raylin had been exceptionally busy. Raylin was already pulling in a small fortune. He had talent, that was for sure. The items he took, he would lose intentionally as part of his plan to gather information and set the stage for larger hauls. Then, once bigger fish had made themselves known, he would up the bets carefully, slowly, strategically. By the end of the night, the goods were still in the hands of the goblins, keeping them happy. Raylin, however, would have triple the item's value in his purse.

Serah was not happy with the information she had gained. She knew that the expedition could be properly supplied with materials and muscle, but at much greater time and cost than she wanted. Luckily, she had Raylin's financial skills to work with.

He needed a few weeks to acquire enough funds. It would take another week after that to round up supplies. This gave us all time to try scrounging up a guide to the jungle, but every day here was spent with a looming threat of danger. Serah had made it clear that we would go without one if that was all that remained, but she was prepared to secure a lot of extra supplies if that was the case.

Her other major concern was the lack of quality in hirelings. Loyalty was iffy and survival skills were poor at best. There were several orcs willing to join up that would be great in a fight. However, none of us trusted them to follow through if things got bad. At least they wouldn't run away in terror like a goblin. They weren't likely to slit your throat in your sleep like a hob either (they would wake you up first so you could know who killed you face to face). The only option left was to search the Blood Pits.

As for me, Gleeglum's contact had agreed to meet on the same day that the preparations for Tinky would be ready. Serah agreed to come with me in case this contact had more information that she could use. Once Tinky was in stable condition and recuperating, she wanted my help at the Blood Pits. But that would be a day or two according to Gleeglum's estimates.

Knock, knock.

Gleeglum's voice carried to the door. "YES, YES, impertinent, impatient, inconvenient interruptions, GIVE ME A MINUTE... Ok, you are safe to enter. Blue door this time. Please be civil with our guest."

Serah and I climbed up three floors this time, to the blue door that was decorated significantly better than the others. Silver plants ran the entire length of the door in graceful arches. Small gemstones accented several spots, depicting flowers and fruits on the silver vine. It was elaborate, particularly for Gleeglum. I wondered what traps he had rigged on it.

We opened the door slowly and heard a quiet conversation in a language I had never heard. The room had a hearth like coziness to it. Soft furniture was placed strategically for entertaining visitors. A small fire with cooking equipment separated the entrance half of the room from what could be considered "private quarters". A small curtain obscured a quaint little bedroom toward the back. Gleeglum and his guest were seated comfortably on two large floor cushions, a drink in hand and a large elaborate smoking contraption in between them.

"Welcome, Glik. Welcome, Serah. Have a seat. You are welcome to partake in our refreshments. This fine gentleman—"

I interrupted, "Is no fine gentleman at all! Valas! I didn't think I'd ever see you again! How on an earth jabbers wart did you end up on this island?"

The man looked up at me with surprise, his large-brimmed hat masking his face until his neck was craned completely upward.

"Wow. You're still alive? I did not expect that." His smooth and exceptionally well-articulated voice pronounced each goblin word like a work of art. It sounded terrible and wrong.

"It does warm my heart just a little to know that Glik's Fables may end up as more than just a dream after all."

Valas rose to give me a hearty handshake and a hug. His stature was at least double my own, all wiry and lean. He was no weakling, but his body was made to move itself not those around him. His skin and long hair were both a pale white, devoid of any kind of coloration. He had shiny trinkets in his braids and his usual wide-brimmed black hat sat on top of his head. His ears were exceptionally long, folding under his hat and accenting his razor-sharp facial features.

"What happened to the blindfold, Valas? That shade of blazing red in your eyes is nice and all, but the blindfold added a lot to your mystique."

"Well, unlike some places I travel, the residents here tend to take advantage of disabilities like blindness. I'd prefer to not be a target. Besides, moving by smell is terrible in a place that has this kind of stench! I could probably fashion an illusion, but that takes too much energy to keep up all day every day. It's much easier to kick up a protective spell or two and make an example every once in a while. Someone as unique looking as me can make quite the urban myth. I wish I had more time to discuss the details, among other things, but time is short. I'm sure we'll get to do some catching up later. For now, tell me about this stele."

Gleeglum, eyebrow cocked in amused suspicion, handed me the

hose from the hookah. "Agreed. Let's begin. We have a grueling day ahead of us once we get started on Tinky's procedure. It's best that we don't perpetuate this discussion any longer than necessary."

Valas's eyebrows arched at the mention of Tinky. "I'm impressed, Glik. Not only have you survived, but you didn't get my favorite animal eaten along the way. Let her out to see her old friend!"

I hesitated. Valas was an instrumental part of my survival when I first escaped the lair. He had taken quite a liking to Tinky and would not be pleased with her condition. But he deserved the truth. I sat down my shoulder bag and opened the flap. "Before you ask, she was stomped on by a bear."

His look of concern appeared in a flash, then melted away with a heartfelt smile as Tinky scooted her way out of the bag. He quickly reached for her, stopping himself a fingers length away. "May I?"

"Of cour—"

"Squeak!"

Tinky interrupted me excitedly, scooting quickly to close the remaining distance.

"Ha! Thatta girl, Tinky!" He fished out some odd, little snack from his pocket and handed it to her. She gobbled it up without as much as a precautionary sniff.

Serah had stealthily settled down on the remaining cushion. Her hand was on her amulet, and her emotionless expression had taken over. Had I not known her, I would have called her tense or nervous, but no. She was interested. She was also mumbling under her breath, much like she did when using magic.

"Ah-hem!" Gleeglum cleared his throat. He was happy, but less interested in reunions and more interested in getting started with his latest project, Tinky's legs. The promise of information that may lead off the island paled in comparison to his mechanizations. "I've educated Valas regarding how and where you came upon the stele, but that is all."

I nodded, pulling out my set of notes and the rubbings for Valas to peruse. He sifted through them with little interest in the stele itself, then paused with a look of concern at the carved notations. "That is a language that I wish I could forget. Sadly, to do that I would have to forget my own native tongue as they share the same root language. I can't imagine who would have used this to take notes, much less scratch them into solid stone. Give me a moment, I'll jot down a translation for you. Perhaps you can tell me what you are planning to do to poor Tinky while I work?"

Gleeglum bolted up with excitement. "BALDIO MMENAON FAO GIBBIRON RILOPS!" Gnomish words and slang competed for space on his tongue as he tried to blurt out everything his brain was thinking at once. After a second he stopped, took a deep breath of air, then a deeper drag off the hose. "Okay, one word at a time, Gleeglum." He then rambled off an obscenely long and technical explanation of Tinky's new mechanical hindquarters and how they worked. He might as well have been speaking the language of pixies for all I could understand of it.

My attention meandered toward Serah. Her eyes flicked up at me, relaxed and attentive, then settled on Valas, studying him closely. I leaned over and whispered in her ear. "Like what you see there, Serah?"

"Do not distract me, Glik. This is important."

So be it. I would pry more out of her later.

"—and that is how she will pick locks with the utilization of her replaced central claw. I thought about adminis—"

Valas interrupted Gleeglum with a warm smile. "Thank you, Gleeglum. The translation is complete. It is an instruction manual on using an arcane machine. It is an old transporter of some sort. I'll wrap up my prior business and start studying this contraption by the end of the week. I highly doubt it still works, but this is a much better lead than trying to kill or divert the legendary kraken."

"Wait, the what!?" I had seen it on maps, but I never thought it was a real thing. I just assumed whatever monster attacked our ship was some overgrown squid. This and possibly a way off the island.

And meeting up with an old friend. My bounty of luck for the day almost matched my bad luck last week.

"The legendary kraken. Only one in the world if stories are to be believed. I'm not sure why it would hang around the warm waters near this island. I'd think it would like the colder waters of the depths. It sank my ship and stranded me here a few months ago. Any case, this stele is my best lead yet on a way out of here."

He stood, adjusted his clothes, and gathered his gear. "I must get a move on. Lots to do before I can shift my focus properly. Please stop by the Stone'N during the day, Glik. I'm sure we can spare a few minutes every so often to reminisce and catch up a bit."

He paused at my side and cocked his eyebrows with curiosity, then leaned down to my shoulder bag and slid a book out so he could see the cover. "A very old acquaintance of mine wrote this. I presume someone as clever as you figured out that it is more than what it appears. Bring it the next time we meet and I'll show you."

Gleeglum gasped, spraying some of his drink out of his nose. Valas laughed, a rich, pleasant, and earthy sound. "I'll make sure you are informed as well, Gleeglum. It would be a pity to leave such curious minds shrouded in darkness."

With that, Valas headed to the door, looking back to Serah at the last moment. "I trust my words have been true enough for you, Miss Serah. Goodbye!" He winked at her, waved to us, then closed the door gently.

"Is it time for Tinky?" I asked eagerly.

Gleeglum nodded. "Yes, give me a few moments to compound the most unstable concoctions. You may relax here if you like." He headed out the door.

"Care to play one round of trade secret, Glik?" Serah wasn't hiding her excitement one bit. She had a bright smile and had leaned forward, eager as a child at story time. How could I say no?

"Of course. You start this time."

"What is Valas?"

She was practically shaking with anticipation. Stringing her along would be cruel in ways that most goblins wouldn't understand. This was too good. When was Serah EVER excited about anything?

"Well, I could go on about his merits and charming lack of skin color, but I suspect you want something more specific. Remember, this must remain a secret, more so than your own origins. He assures me that the reason his people are called what they are is because it must remain true. Terrible things may happen should his people become more than just a myth."

She opened her mouth in excitement, so much that her fangs began to unfurl. "Forgotten!"

I nodded in confirmation.

She grabbed her amulet with both hands and mumbled some sort of thanks to her goddess. It took a full ten seconds for her to calm back down and regain her composure. The sight was almost as rare as the Forgotten themselves.

"Set Tinky on the operating table over there. The restraints are just a precaution in case of fasciculations or premature awakening at an inopportune time during the procedure. It'll take a few minutes for the anesthetics to render her unconscious."

I nervously placed Tinky as instructed. This seemed like a bad idea now that I had to go through with it. Probably just nerves, but my gut told me that this was riskier than I knew. "What's the chance that this goes bad?"

"Define bad."

Gleeglum let the words linger in the air for a few seconds before giving a chuckle.

"Unlikely. There's always a slim chance of death, but the most likely result of failure for this procedure is that she would lose full functionality of her hindquarters. Shockingly similar to the pre-surgical condition, isn't it? That said, I'd advise not observing the process too closely. It's never pleasant seeing the insides of a friend. If you don't mind, I would actually prefer you leave the tower all together or at least loiter in the blue room. I find it easier to concentrate alone, and interruptions would increase the risk of failure significantly. While the task is not complicated, the precision required is immense."

I took the hint, but couldn't bring myself to leave her alone. That was, for the first six hours. I finally caved and went upstairs for a nap at that point.

"KLEE KROTCHET'S INFERNAL GEARSTRAPS! IMBECILIC. INCONSISTENT. BAH!!!" Gleeglum's shouts carried up the hall, waking me from my slumber. I vaulted down the stairs to the lab, nearly tripping. Gleeglum was rushing back and forth, trying to grab things off of the center alchemy bench while holding down Tinky. Her forelegs were spasming hard, coming loose from the straps. Her lower half, save the spine and the tail, had been mostly removed, organs slid to the side. A variety of white threads spread out like a spider web from her backbone.

Gleeglum noticed me immediately. "You! Hold her for precisely three seconds, then move away quickly! Don't stare, just do it!"

He moved before I had a chance to react, but I took my place and put a hand on Tinky. She was jerking around, eyes wide with fear and panic. Gleeglum grabbed a bandage of some sort and a vial off the center table, then bolted over to us.

"Three! Move! MOVE!" He pinned her with one hand, sliding the vial to her mouth, letting it spill around her. He then threw the bandage onto the open mess of her lower half. Within a few seconds, the spasming stopped.

I was shaking. What happened? Was it too late?

"Whew, that was close. Thank you for the assistance. Now please, go upstairs. Speak the word 'Hiphorlac' BEFORE you pull the curtain aside. Under the bed there are various drawers. Far right, bottom compartment is the correct one. You are searching for a crescent moon pendant made of silver metal. Bring it here. Be quick, but do not hurry and do not forget, 'Hiphorlac'."

I moved as fast as I could without falling. I crashed through the door, almost forgetting to open the latch, and raced to the back screaming "HIPHORLAC" as I ran. I threw back the curtain and paused. What I saw was no simple bed like before (yes, I had snuck a peek before taking a nap on the floor cushions). It was a massive bedroom, complete with a gargantuan, four-post bed. Sneaky gnome.

True to his word, there was a set of drawers at the bottom of the bed and a whole rat's nest of necklaces in the bottom right compartment. I grabbed a handful and sifted as quick as my green fingertips would move. Luckily, the crescent moon stabbed me, giving away its position! I snatched the amulet, dragging along the other necklaces tangled up with it, and headed back to the lab.

Gleeglum spoke as soon as I passed the doorway, eyes focused on Tinky. "Good, give it here."

He waved an outstretched hand. "What's the hold up?"

I was hurrying to pop the necklace free of the others. Gleeglum looked up for just a second.

"Oh, that is a bit of a mess. Been meaning to organize that. Let me know when it is recombobulated. The biggest emergency is past, but I need to get her vitals under control, and magic is the most expeditious method I'm aware of."

"What happened, Gleeglum? Is she going to make it?"

"Herbal medications aren't consistent in dosage because of natural variations in the plant structures. As such, Tinky woke up while I was separating the contact points from her spine. I had to render her unconscious quickly, so I used a concentrated anesthetic. There's a risk that she may not wake up at all. There is also a risk that if she wakes up, she may not have complete neuromuscular control and may have permanently damaged tactile senses. But her life is no longer in direct danger, and the procedure may resume."

I finally freed the amulet and handed it to Gleeglum. He pressed it gingerly against Tinky. "Libram, incantantus, lyctropa, infusimo."

The amulet glowed softly with a silver light, flared briefly, then winked out.

Gleeglum wiped his forehead. "That should suffice. Hand me that pipe. I could use a breather before I get started connecting everything. This phase of the operation will only take four or five hours. You should sleep. When it is complete, Tinky will need your assistance acclimating to her new equipment. If she wakes up. Either way, it's been an arduous endeavor. I'll need rest once it's done!"

"Hmph." I walked away nervously. Not a chance I was going back to sleep. I'd be down here checking on her every half hour. In the meantime, maybe I'd see just how much interesting stuff was in that bedroom. I didn't like the idea of setting off a trap in another compartment, so I'd settle for the drawer.

There were a lot of necklaces in there, and Tinky would need something pretty and shiny when she woke up. She had better wake up. Otherwise Gleeglum might not.

CHAPTER 8
A RAT'S HINDQUARTERS

Tinky was still unconscious, days after the surgery. Gleeglum assured me it could take some time for her to recover and offered to let me stay at his tower while giving her natural healing and sleep. I accepted without hesitation.

"I don't get it, Gleeglum, what went wrong? You were so certain that she would be fine, yet there she is. Dead to the world."

"Not dead, Glik. I share your frustration. Unforeseen variation changes outcomes, regardless of how much preparation is achieved. The initial dosage of anesthetic that I administered was insufficient. I utilized an herbal source, as most creatures have fewer reactions and faster recovery, but vegetation is inconsistent in potency."

Gleeglum sighed and looked up, putting his hands on his hips. "There might have been too much sedative in the second round. The extract I crafted is a consistent concoction, but I had to grab and measure it quickly. If I made a mistake, the substance could act as a poison. Like most medications, the difference between harmful and helpful is often a matter of dosage."

He started to put a reassuring hand on my shoulder but thought better of it and stopped. "There is also a possibility that her unconsciousness is perfectly normal. Her body is adapting, connecting to new appendages, and adjusting to the loss of others. I found a lot of scarring and fibrous tissue when I cut into her, likely from prior magical healing. I made every attempt to repair what I could, but natural healing is almost always best for long term recovery. Regardless, if she's still asleep tomorrow we'll employ some magic and get her conscious."

I was not comforted in the slightest. If Tinky was still unconscious at the end of the week, I'd see if Serah knew anything more about healing. And possibly what she knew about poisoning gnomes.

A few hours later, I was mentally recalling the many things I already knew about poisons when Serah walked through the door. She wore her neutral expression, but I was learning the little tells that betrayed her irritation. Today's tell was her shoulders. They were held up higher and further back than normal.

"No luck finding a guide, Glik. I've tapped everything but the Blood Pits. Nobody I've found knows anything useful about the jungle. How long are you going to stay here?"

I sighed. Serah was just being realistic. "I'll stay one more day at least. I should be here when Tinky wakes up."

This was worse than death. I couldn't leave if Tinky was going to survive. If she was dead, I could get furious, kick the crap out of something, and move on.

Serah gave a tense nod. "Then I'll return tomorrow, ready with what little healing magic I know. I'll go to the Blood Pits with Raylin if you aren't able." She paused, making sure I made eye contact with her before finishing. "Glik. It may be time to say goodbye."

Her words were mechanical, but there was a hint of sadness as she said the word goodbye. Perhaps she didn't feel much, but it was more likely she had already accepted the loss.

I nodded as she left, more to myself than to her.

The day after that, Valas knocked on the tower door. He was stoic about Tinky's condition, likely hiding his own sadness as he was quite fond of the little rat. He said he would provide extra research on healing magic should her condition not improve soon. Thinking back on it all, I am amazed what everyone was willing to do for the sake of Tinky. It was more than most people would do for someone of their own species.

Valas's best gift was effectively distracting me and passing the time. Instead of reminiscing about the past, he tutored Gleeglum and me regarding the book of "magic words".

By the end of the day, I understood what he was saying but couldn't do anything with it. I lacked the ability to push and pull magic in the way he instructed. Gleeglum, however, managed a few simple effects, such as making a dim ball of light or lighting a candle with a single word.

It confused him greatly. He had a fair bit of magical ability without the book, but he was used to long, complex formulae that bent energy to his will. This method was something new to him entirely. It was less of a manipulation of physics and more of a force of emotional will. Or so he said. I had no idea what he was talking about.

Valas handed me a small iron ring as he left. "It may do nothing for you, but wear it on one of your toes just in case. It will magnify any magic ability you have. Practice what we talked about in the book. If it ever works, you'll probably get really tired. Keep practicing and it'll get easier."

Valas was a smart one. Keeping jewelry in your boots made it much harder to lose and less likely to be stolen.

I spent most of the night reading and practicing. It was a welcome distraction from the furry little body that slept on my lap. A few hours before dawn, I cuddled up on the floor cushions and turned myself into a nice, warm little nest for Tinky to sleep in.

"You had better wake up, girl. Tomorrow I have to keep moving. I don't want to do it without you, but we need off this island. Every new day is a risk."

I patted her head, then fell asleep.

SERAH SHOOK ME AWAKE. I had overslept, by a lot. Those cushions bore the curse of drowsiness and stupor!

"I see she's not awake yet. Gleeglum agreed that I should try what I can. There is nothing that will wake the unconscious that I know of, but I might be able to speed her natural healing."

I shrugged. "Go ahead. If it doesn't wake her, I'll go with you. We have to get off the island, and there's a much better chance together."

She whispered her prayer under her breath as one hand went to her amulet and the other rested on Tinky's fuzzy hips, where her flesh met metal. A familiar emerald glow swirled around her hand and wreathed its way around Tinky's body. After a few seconds, the light dissipated and Serah opened her eyes.

She remained expressionless. "That's all I can do for her. I'm going to search for a few more things in the green room before I leave. Come find me in an hour."

Tinky laid there on the cushions, breathing shallowly. My frustration grew into a rage. Tinky was my friend. Without her hind legs she would have died on our journey. But this? She had endured horrendous pain during the process, and now she was as good as dead. Grrr!

I put my face right next to Tinky's ear, letting the rage boil over into my voice. "Get up! Get up, Tinky! We don't have any more time! We have to get off the island! Grrr, SKRAGGAFRAKT! GET! UP!"

The final words erupted with rage. My toe suddenly burned, the smell of singed hair wafted to my nostrils, and my eyes drooped with a wave of fatigue.

Tinky spasmed once. Twice. Then her chest rose with a long, deep breath. She let it out slowly, then stopped moving. Seconds went by.

"Tinky? TINKY!?" Nothing.

Seconds turned into minutes. I clenched my fists in desperation, then took a deep breath and let them relax. I had to let go of yet another attachment that couldn't last.

"Goodbye, friend. I'll make sure your body doesn't get eaten by kobolds."

One beady little eye shined at me through a half-closed eyelid. Her chest rose, barely enough to notice, as she drew in a single breath.

"Squeak?"

"TINKY!" I jumped up screaming, "ALIVE! SHE'S ALIVE! Muahahahaha!" I did a little jig of celebration, too excited to contain myself.

Her breathing slowly picked up as I rejoiced, and she cracked opened both eyes.

"Don't bother getting up, Tinky. I've got some things for you. First and foremost, some food and water. Maybe later I'll get you some more of that sake from Chunx. Oh, and don't tell Gleeglum, but I've got a pocket full of shiny stuff to paw through once we leave his shop!"

We relaxed in the room with Tinky nibbling on some food and both of us checking out her new prosthesis. She seemed quite impressed, but they seemed heavy and painful when she moved around.

Serah interrupted us a little over an hour later. She smiled and gave Tinky a light pat on the head. "Hi, Tinky. Glad to see you're alive."

"Squeak."

"Are you ready to go, Glik? Tinky should rest here."

I grudgingly agreed. "Tinky, I'll get Gleeglum to take good care of you. Stay here and rest. I'm going with Serah to help find a way out of here."

I glanced at Serah and headed to the door. "I'm going to tell Gleeglum how to keep her happy before we go. Hopefully, he has more of that cheese. Did you find what you were looking for?"

Sera's eyes lingered on Tinky as her lips curled into a satisfied smile. "Yes."

I grabbed my gear, then went to find Gleeglum. He may fear the Blood Pits, but they sounded entertaining to me. Now that Tinky was no longer my mind's primary concern, it was time to have some fun!

WE HEADED to the Stone'N to find Raylin. Chunx was trying to stay awake behind the bar. There were no customers. Valas had constructed a scaffold around the stele and removed the wooden "dart goblin". He was busy studying every inch of the structure in great detail. Several books littered the floor, along with a handful of magical lanterns.

"Hey, Valas. That ring you gave me left a blister on my foot! Is it supposed to burn like that?"

Valas cocked an eyebrow in thought. "Never heard of that before. What were you doing when it happened?"

I explained what happened, including the events since we last talked.

"Huh, that might explain it. The ring is supposed to magnify your will. In this case it might have magnified the rage. That's a good thing. It means you might have a shot at using magic after all! Then again, what you said about Tinky is strange. I wonder what happened there. It is too coincidental to be nothing. Most likely she woke up from Serah's healing spell, but you may want to be careful what you say when you really feel the meaning behind it. If you threw angry magic at Tinky, you might have killed her. Then again, that rage may have fueled a command, like 'Get Up!'"

"Are you saying what I think you're saying, Valas?"

"Not exactly, but it's possible you're figuring out what my friend wrote about in that book. With the ring's help to put enough power into your words, they might take shape and effect the world around you directly. Keep practicing. In the meantime, good luck at the Blood Pits. Try not to get on anyone's bad side." He turned quickly with a soft smile, resuming his extensive study of the stele.

I chuckled, shaking my head as I headed to the room. Valas had always been a bit scatterbrained with his time management. He seemed to have a dozen things that needed his attention at any given time. But he was always helpful, even to a goblin with a pet rat.

I opened the door to find Raylin, sewing dozens of gems and coins into various new "pockets" he had fashioned on his clothing. He answered before I could say a word. "I don't want to get robbed while we're there. The gems are also lighter than coins, and I suspect there will be some big betting. Goblins seem to love shiny things, so gems are worth a lot more than normal here. How's Tinky? You seem to care quite a bit about that rat."

"She woke up but is still resting. I don't know if her legs work or not yet. She was too tired to try them out before I left." It was odd that he seemed to care. He must have recovered a bit from that human depression thing and decided that he needed me. Or maybe Serah had been working to accomplish something in our group and talked him into acting less distanced. I still wasn't sure what odd relationship was going on between those two.

"That's good news. I wish we had her nose with us for this little venture. It should be profitable, but I'm nervous about it. My disguise has gotten better now that I found a mirror to check it with, but I still don't understand the body language or customs. It makes for some awkward conversations and a fair bit of lost coin. It is interesting that the goblins will play with me as a big goblin or a small orc, but not if I try the appearance of a hob."

He had done quite the job with his appearance. That glove worked wonders. For now, he appeared to be an extremely small orc. He complimented it with youthful features, but even the youngest orcs are highly muscular. This would get him bullied in all kinds of ways by any orcs, but the goblins and hobs would still leave him alone for the most part. The smallest orc could still crush a goblin's skull with its bare hands.

Serah gave Raylin a quick once over with her eyes. "That's quite a disguise. With all that crap sewn into your clothes, you almost look muscular, in a totally asymmetric and ugly fashion. Was there anything else you needed before we go? Remember, our priority is to find a guide."

Raylin rolled his eyes. "No. I'm all done here and we know your priorities. Let's go."

We walked the few hours toward the Blood Pits with little interruption, weaving through the rat maze of shacks and hovels as we went. Raylin's disguise was working well, but the real defense was Serah's reputation. Word had spread all over that a snake person was in town. Anger her at your own risk. The usual enforcers had been advised to simply avoid her unless she started trouble somewhere important.

WHACK!

"OW! You have a death wish, little monster!?" Raylin yelled at a little hooded creature that had just hit him with its cane.

It looked up and spoke to a nearby hob, scaly nostrils poking out from under its hood. The voice was high-pitched like a gnome, but less nasally. Its pronunciation slurred around s's and t's. "That one crap fodder. You lisssten Kraz?"

A deep, grating voice escaped the hobs fanged maw. "No. Why test the smallest orc in the city? Might as well smack that human female and tell me she's no use. We should be back at the pits scouring the crowd for black-listers if we want fodder."

The little monster responded by whacking the hob in the shin. This gave Raylin pause and caused the monster's hood to slide back further. A kobold! She had much longer tufts of fur than most, golden in color. It clashed terribly with the rusty red color of her skin. Worse yet, she managed to braid all sorts of cheap, gaudy jewelry into her fur. She also wore a dozen necklaces and multiple rings on every finger. She carried her own little dragon hoard of junk!

"For hob, you densse, Kraz! Why catch black-lisster? They be numpty and place bet. If win, we catch, throw in pit. If losse, we take money!"

"Ah... good point." The hob grudgingly replied.

The kobold squinted at Serah with catlike, silvery eyes. "Hmm, human look like ssnake woman from goblin rumor. Lady! You want money? You bite goblin in pit, I pay you big money!"

Serah gave the kobold a predatory grin. "No. I do not fight for money. However, I may be willing to buy a fighter. You interested? I'm looking for any that were caught in the jungle."

"What sshame. No, no buy people, no buy animal. Esscape too often. Ssell people too hard. Angry relativess. You want fighter, you hire. Today normal fightss. Tournament in ten day. Good warriors fighting today. Maybe you hire. Lizzzardman maybe from jungle. Hairy old dwarf alsso fight. He alwayss win."

Serah betrayed a hint of frustration, then went back to her emotionless neutral. "I'll keep that in mind. I presume you run the pits then? What should I call you?"

"Hck, hck, hck, hssss." The kobold's laugh sounded quite similar to Skia's. "Kraz. He runs all. I not exisst!"

She stabbed her cane hard into the ground and vanished. My nostrils twitched. She was still standing there. I looked at Serah, unamused, and pointed to my nose. It was still impressive magic, to be sure, but useless for those who don't rely on sight.

Serah rolled her eyes. "Very well. Let me know if you think of more exceptional fighters. I could always use a few good mercenaries, or prisoners for that matter." We turned our backs and began walking again.

The kobold voice followed us. "Yesss yesss. You enjoy pitsss!"

Great, another incompetent idiot in control.

～

THE BLOOD PITS were everything I had hoped for. They were in truth, a single, two-person tall pit, not multiple pits (goblin naming logic for you). There was a full amphitheater of crowded benches surrounding it. Food was everywhere, along with ample amounts of rotgut. Some of the audience was chewing on random leg meat, presumably turkey or chicken. Others had some sort of roasted sausages on a stick. There was one orc that had scrounged up a live cockroach the size of my hand. He swallowed it whole, relishing in its squirming and wriggling as it struggled down his throat.

The crowd consisted mostly of goblins, but a fair number of orcs and hobs were also in attendance. The stench of sweat, blood, and dirt saturated the air. A dull roar from the crowd forced everyone to yell if they wanted anyone to hear them. A few vendors were roaming the crowd, barking out to sell their wares or take side bets.

We arrived just in time for the latest fight to begin. Three fully armed and armored goblins had just walked through the door on one side of the pit. Two held crossbows while the third had a club and shield. On the other end, a large, mud-scaled creature emerged that looked like a crocodile had figured out how to stand on two legs and use weapons. He wore a sparse leather war harness, held a spear in one hand, and a bone shield in the other.

As soon as the goblins realized what they were fighting, panic took over. The two with crossbows shot wildly, one bolt going wide, the other whizzing off into the stands, impaling one poor goblin's mug of rotgut. The club wielder spun her weapon wildly before throwing it as hard as she could. The club smacked one of the crossbow wielders in the knee, dropping him to the ground. Wild howls erupted from the crowd.

The lizardman shook his head in disgust. This was no challenge. He walked slowly over to the goblin with the broken knee as it tried to crawl away. One quick thrust and it was no more. The remaining crossbow wielder had regained enough sense to keep the shield bearer between himself and the lizardman. He also reloaded, taking time to aim with shaky hands.

Pffew!

The bolt whizzed through the air, nearly clipping the shield bearer as it flew over her shoulder. Despite the shakiness, his aim had been true. The bolt was right on target. The crowd hushed.

Thunk!

Metal splintered bone as the bolt slammed into the lizardman's shield, spraying fragments everywhere. He had waited until the last possible second before defending himself.

Raylin appreciated the showmanship, fully absorbed by the spectacle. "That creature knows how to work a crowd. He could have dodged that shot in his sleep."

I glanced over at Serah. She had no interest in the fight at all. Her eyes surveyed the crowd. She knew exactly what kind of person she was looking for. A guide, not a showman or a brute like the lizardman in the pit. Her loss!

My attention returned to the action. The shield bearer had retrieved her club and was attempting to keep the crossbow wielder free of pursuit. She failed miserably. The lizardman didn't bother dodging the club at all as she swung it. He took one full force blow after another, not flinching one bit. Instead, he knocked her to the ground with his shield, then dropped it. He locked eyes with the crossbow wielder as he grabbed the shield bearer by the scruff of the neck. She struggled in a stupor, waving her limbs lazily. The lizardman ended her struggles with a vicious snap of his jaws. His maw locked over her small goblin skull. He then worried her back and forth, his savage teeth slicing through tendon and bone.

The lizardman, eyes still locked onto the crossbow wielder, spit the shield bearer's head to the ground. Blood running through his teeth, nostrils flaring, the lizardman decided to end this spectacle. The crossbow wielder ran in terror as the shield bearers body thudded to the dirt. He abandoned the crossbow and tried vainly to climb the walls. The lizardman, not wanting to chance it, reared back and put his whole weight behind his spear, launching it across the pit. It flew straight and true, seemingly faster than the bolts had flown from the crossbows.

BAM!

The spear shook the wall as it slammed into place. The crossbow wielder shrieked, clutching the spear where it had impaled his back and nailed him to the wall. His screams were drowned out completely by the celebration of the crowd. The lizardman walked by slowly as he left, spitting on the twitching, soon-to-be corpse as he passed. This was the Blood Pits. This was why they were all here.

"Huh, I guess goblin doesn't taste good. No surprise there." I turned to Serah. "Have you found what you are looking for? I have certainly been entertained by this visit!" Hey, I am a goblin after all. Don't begrudge me some bloodshed.

"I'm not here for entertainment, Glik, and no. No one in the crowd moves like a hunter or a survivor. Unless we wait and see more fighters, we're wasting our time. Even then, I suspect the gladiators are more likely to be brutes than guides. I have enough untrust-worthy muscle lined up already."

Raylin was grinning ear to ear. "Let's stay for one more fight. Supposedly they are every half hour. I'll put in a good bet for this one. Just to get some flavor. This place is where the real money flows." His smile was far too big. So this is why he was working on a ship instead of rolling in money when we found him.

Serah beat me to a proper reaction. "We need off this island, Raylin. You can't do that dead. You just watched how one-sided these fights can be."

He lowered his head and sighed heavily. "Just one bout then. But no promises that I won't come back if we need money fast."

I smirked. Guess you can't keep a gambler out of debt after all. "One fight, Raylin. Unless you think you can best that lizardman we just watched on your own."

He glanced at me, head still hung low. "Good point. I guess I should learn the game before I count my winnings."

We wandered over to the main bookie.

The creature behind the cage was something I had never seen before. Its razor-sharp features, long, pointed nose, and thin, blade-like ears reminded me of some odd artwork depicting denizens of the various hells. It was only about half my size, wearing fine clothing custom cut to size. Two bony wings with translucent, blue-tinted membranes sprouted from its back. Solid silver eyes rose to meet us.

"You know the rules?" Its voice was deceptively low, with a sooty feel.

Raylin raised a hand in greeting and answered. "What rules?"

The creature's wings drooped in disappointment. "I don't have all day for games. Fights are to submission, but nobody is going to stop a kill. Winner keeps the gear, entry fees, and a percentage of the bets. No magic allowed. Single combat and group fights are available. You can also go for a raw match. That means unarmed and unarmored for all combatants."

The silver eyes sized each of us up slowly. "Judging from your looks, you don't want to fight. Bets are weighted. Next fight is five to one odds in favor of the orc. He's got a death wish and is fighting a few goblins that tried to cheat. Should be a landslide for the orc anyway, hence the low payout if you bet on him, but quite a win if you back the goblins instead. The orc has chosen to triple his pay by fighting bare-handed and unarmored."

Raylin was not impressed. "Even odds for the orc, and I'll put this in as my bet. You can keep it and give me the coin if I win." He pulled out a red jewel, perfectly cut and polished to a mirror shine.

The creature glanced at it with a bored expression. "Still one to five odds, but I'll count the ruby as ten thousand gold coin. I'm sure 'Kraz' will love it. I'll be sure she knows where it came from."

Raylin shook his head in the affirmative, smirking as he caught the slip of Kraz's pronouns. "So be it. How do I collect?"

"Here's your ticket. Don't lose it or your bet is forfeit."

Raylin finished the transaction, and we headed back down to the pit. We had been lucky. Serah's reputation preceded us in exceptional fashion. There were dozens of small fights and countless incidents of theft, but few goblins would get within reach of her. Some hobs eyed us suspiciously, then thought better of starting a fight with her at the pits. It was a good way to get thrown in.

I couldn't hide my curiosity. "How much is that rock actually worth, Raylin?"

"Pfft, like I know. Ask Gleeglum." That was reassuring.

I turned my attention to Serah. "Any idea what that bookie was?"

"I wondered if you would ask. They aren't common, but a few magic users figured out how to make use of their unique skills. They are called demon pixies, devil pixies, or hellspawn faeries. Nobody seems to know if they actually are from pixie bloodlines, but everyone agrees that somehow, they ended up corrupted by greed. This led to some demonic appearance and personality traits. They are highly magical beings, much like pixies, so after a few generations of similar, heavy emotions, physical traits emerged that reflect those emotions.

"My turn. Does every goblin society love bloodshed enough to have one of these arenas?"

"Love it enough, yes. Do most of them actually have one? No. They are superb entertainment but take out a sizeable chunk of the population. I'm not really sure how they manage it here."

The next fight began with no formal warning. The cheer of the crowd was all the announcement and ceremony needed. One door creaked open slowly. Goblins squeezed out of it, one by one. Two, five, twelve, they just kept coming. By the time the door closed, eighteen goblins were in the pit. Each was fully armed and armored, half with clubs, spears, and shields, the other half with crossbows and small axes.

Raylin's eyebrows raised. "No sarding way! What kind of super orc gets one to five betting odds against a damn hoard!?"

"BRAAAAAAHHHHH!"

The orc's bellowing war cry could be heard clearly over the crowd and through the door of the pit.

BAM!

Wood splinters rained across the arena as pieces of the door flew outward. A massive orc, twice the size of any I had ever seen, made his way through the opening. He wore a light war harness over oiled skin. Flawless skin. His name was Ruk.

Raylin's face turned solid red. "Why that sarding idiot! If he wanted money, he should have asked me. Now he's going to die!"

Serah chuckled lightly. "I doubt that. Ruk didn't have trouble fitting through a doorway when we last met. I'd bet his skin is harder than most armor right now if he went to the trouble of doubling his size and strength. A little magical preparation can go a long way in a battle like this, and I doubt any goblins will cry foul of cheating since it's not terribly obvious like throwing fire."

A few of the goblins were cowering from Ruk's impressive display of power. But this group was not untrained. It had two leaders that aggressively smacked the fearful few back to attention. They approached slowly, the lead goblins holding up their shields to block for the crossbows behind them. This was no band of debtors. This was a military group. They had been trained, and not by goblins or orcs, but judging from the tactics, dwarves or humans. That fact raised a whole slew of questions.

Ruk didn't wait for the first volley to fly. He flung a large chunk of the door into the midst of the goblins, following it with such speed that before the goblins knew what had hit them, he was already within reach.

"SHOOT IT!" One leader screamed in vain as Ruk grabbed her by the shield and swung her like a club.

The crossbow wielders obliged, loosing bolts in a random spray of chaos.

"GGGRRAAAAAA!!!"

Another battle cry from Ruk shook the goblins' morale, albeit not as much as the leader's demise. She was screaming in pain and terror as her arm was wrangled around at terrible angles, anchored tightly to the shield. A disgusting wet smack followed as Ruk slammed her body into his nearest enemy, then another, and another.

The other leader decided now was his time to shine. He lunged forward, low and accurate with a spear. It would have skewered Ruk's lower leg had the leader not been crushed by a flying goblin as he lunged. Ruk had thrown his "weapon" of choice, choosing to free both hands before furthering his rampage.

With both leaders laying silent in a puddle of gore and dirt, the other goblins broke formation. Ruk took the opportunity and pressed his advantage. He grabbed the nearest goblin by the head and squeezed. A loud "POP" silenced most of the crowd. They had seen quite a bit of violence in this arena, but the goblins in the stands were beginning to understand just how pitiful they were compared to the few orcs that sat among them.

For orcs, once the violence started, a wild surge of hormones often sent their minds spiraling into a euphoria. If they let themselves go too far, those hormones allowed them to ignore self-preservation as they sought greater levels of destruction. Many orcs in the stands, seeing such a wanton display of reckless carnage, had begun to fall into such a bloodlust. The tension in the arena was suddenly noticeable.

Ruk was oblivious to it, lost in his own little circle of brutality. Six corpses lay at his feet, and he had barely warmed up. The remaining goblins refused to be anywhere near Ruk. Most of them were struggling up the pit walls instead. Ruk grabbed anything he could find from the ground to use as a projectile. He chucked a shield like a discus, shattering it on the back of one goblin climbing the wall. Next came a spear, impaling another goblin's leg before it could reach the wall. Then he picked up a loaded crossbow and flung it sidearm, shattering it next to one goblin's head. The goblin reacted, causing it to fall as it was sprayed with splinters. This was a one-sided massacre.

Raylin stood open-mouthed at the display, oblivious to the still building tension in the air. Serah and I, we were not so naïve. She crouched over and crept toward an exit, trying to avoid obstructing the view or drawing undue attention. I nodded as she went by, then tugged on Raylin's shirt. "We need to get out of here. Now. This bloodbath is about to overflow."

Snapped out of his trancelike state, Raylin looked around. The crowd remained eerily quiet, except for a low, rumbling growl coming from the orcs. They were breathing heavily, flexing their muscles and stretching subconsciously. The nearest goblins caught the smell of murder and responded with a fearful sweat.

"Agreed."

We evacuated the pits hastily, and none too soon. Within minutes we could hear an all-out war erupt as orc war cries filled the air, followed by goblin screams. I guess Gleeglum was right about the pits being trouble!

CHAPTER 9

FOR INFORMATION ON ESCAPING UNCHARTED ISLANDS, SEE PAGE 42

I didn't bother hiding my grin as we left the Blood Pits. That had been a healthy dose of excitement. Unfortunately, Raylin was brooding again, letting the loss of Ruk send him back into a depressed state.

I nudged him as we walked, hoping to improve his mood a bit. "I hope Ruk makes it out of there alive, Raylin. You chose an excellent bodyguard. I wonder where he rounded up those magical enhancements? That nameless kobold doesn't strike me as helpful to anyone, even if being helpful would make her money. Any ideas, Serah? You know more about magic than most."

Her tone was neutral, unlike her words. "Why do both of you insist I know about magic? I pray for a few miracles. That's it. You want magic? Go ask your friend Valas or Gleeglum."

Hmmm, Gleeglum. That gnome owes me for Tinky. He's lucky she woke up.

Raylin slumped his shoulders. "Ruk is probably dead after that mob. What a waste. Did you at least find a guide, Serah? If not, you better get started prepping for your excursion. I think I've got enough money to cover your expenses. Well, I will have enough after

I go back to the pits and quietly collect my winnings. Nasty little demon pixie better pay up. Ruk obviously won the match, even if he is dead."

Serah growled out her answer. "No. There isn't anyone in this city that I would trust as a guide."

She clenched her fist and her jaw. "Who am I kidding? There isn't anyone that has any worthwhile jungle survival skills in the whole godsforsaken city, let alone someone I would trust. Let's just get this done. Every day we spend here, we risk death. My display of power may have worked for a while but inevitably there will be challengers who want to make their name off of me. You've got five days, Raylin. We leave in five days unless something goes terribly wrong."

I nodded, planning out my next week in my head. Five days. That should work fine. I could split my time between Tinky and Valas, hopefully learning more about the black stele, and more about this "magic word" spell casting, while helping Tinky get healthy enough for the trip. "Okay. Let's all meet at the tavern in five days, morning preferably."

Raylin's eyes shifted back and forth between us in a panic. "Uh-uh! You two have a merry old time in the jungle. I know when my skills would be better used elsewhere. I'll stay here and get us a ship, even if I have to build the sodding thing myself!"

Serah sighed as though she expected Raylin's response. "He's right, Glik. He can't fight worth a damn, and a silver tongue doesn't work well on snakes and bog water. Can you ask Gleeglum for help when you visit Tinky? We'll need as many ways to fight off disease and jungle sicknesses as he can muster. Poison too."

"Sure, Serah. See you both later. Don't get dead." I let my gaze linger on Raylin as they walked off. It was not a good idea for him to be anywhere near the pits again, but good luck pushing the issue.

I made my way to Gleeglum's tower. Our soiree to the Blood Pits had taken most of the day, and I was already getting tired. It had been a rough week. I wondered what we would find in this jungle.

Certainly, a lot of things we didn't want to find, and probably a few things that didn't want to be found.

Suppose we made it to the naga there. What were the chances they would give us any useful information? If they were anything like Serah, they wouldn't tell us a thing. She's as secretive as they come. During our games of trade secret, she wouldn't lie, but rarely told the full story of anything, sticking to specifically what was asked. The few instances she let more slip seemed to be an effort to lower my defenses or gain reciprocation on unwritten topics like goblin subcultures.

A nasally goblin voice snapped my thoughts back to reality. "Well, well, well, what do we have here? A nicely dressed little gob just beggin' to be robbed. Whaddaya say, Irma? Fresh meat?" Crap, I had let down my guard too much. Serah was the reason we hadn't been harassed in town, and she was not with me.

The slow, deep voice of an orc answered. "Heh. Heh. Heh. Yup!"

Skraggafrakt! I slowly reached into my secondary money pouch, grabbed a handful of tin coins, then chucked them with a fluid motion into the big orc's face. I bolted down the street while the two were distracted.

The goblin shouted at me as I ran. "Hahahaha! Nice doing business with ya! Come back anytime!"

I didn't stop running until I got to Gleeglum's tower. The encounter had cost me practically nothing. Tin looks a lot like silver when flung through the air. I kept the secondary pouch out in the open for just that reason. That and pickpockets. The whole situation was way too close. Things like this would get worse and more frequent the longer I stayed here. I needed to be back around creatures with crappier senses, or at least fewer creatures in general. I needed Tinky's keen nose back.

When I arrived at Gleeglum's, I knocked using a fickle pattern of rapid knocks and short pauses just for fun. He already had some means to know it was me or he'd never open the door. Too many heavy-handed thugs in this city.

The door opened on its own again, creepy as usual. I headed up toward the living quarters but was stopped by Gleeglum as I passed the door to the lab.

"Glik, come here! You need to learn how to perform the preventative maintenance for Tinky's prosthesis."

"I hope it's not too hard. We get into some nasty situations for long periods of time. How is she doing?"

"You'll see. Bring that bag there. The best method for learning is to teach, but hands-on learning can be sufficient in a time crunch."

We headed up to the living area. Tinky was in rat heaven, all four paws clenched around a wheel of cheese that was twice her size. She had already devoured a chunk the size of her head. A few bits of meat were left over on a nearby plate, as well as the rind of some fruit.

"SQUEEEEAAAAK!!!"

Tinky launched herself toward me as soon as I walked through the door. Her new legs were quite strong, propelling her clear across the room in a single bound. But her aim was off. I had to lunge to the side to catch her. She flinched as she landed in my arms. Her skin was still red and sensitive where flesh met metal.

"I missed you too, Tinky. I see you've eaten well. How do you pack that much food in such a tiny stomach?"

"Squeak."

She looked away, trying her best to appear innocent.

I smiled and turned to Gleeglum. "Thanks for keeping her well fed and comfy while I was gone. I thought we might have lost her."

"Yes, yes. She almost perished. But that's in the past. Now it's time for maintenance training. Her new hindquarters are mostly self-sustaining. However, they will need additional lubrication at specific intervals throughout the year. Cooking grease should suffice in a pinch, but common lantern oil is the preferred substance. Mechanical oils are ideal, but good luck acquiring any of that in the field. Apply a single drop at the marked points here, here, and here. Then repeat on the opposing side."

Gleeglum pointed to each spot but had me do the actual work.

"It is fueled by Tinky's metabolic system, so she's going to eat a lot more, especially for the next few weeks while her body adjusts to the increased energy demands. She can also expend her energy in rapid bursts. This provides additional strength to her legs for things like jumping across the room, but it means she will starve to death if she strains excessively and ignores her limits. Her body can't replenish energy as fast as her new legs can consume it. With practice, she'll learn to balance the energy levels, but start slowly!" He glared at Tinky with his last exclamation.

"I also invented this device to help with the energy balance." He pointed to a small gem where Tinky's belly button used to be. It was barely visible under a protective web of metal plating.

"The prosthesis can be fueled magically if you have the means. It wouldn't take much magic to overload her systems, but she can be exceptionally strong and fast for an extended duration if she drains the gem. Just make sure she's not caught in any sort of raw magical storm or any high energy spells. Her metabolism will slowly refill the gem within a few days if it is completely drained and she is allowed to rest.

"The gem also doubles as a safeguard. It should absorb incoming energy and burn out instead of killing Tinky, but the prosthesis will have no power once the gem is destroyed. However, if you have a way to leech magic into the gem at a slow, controlled pace, Tinky can also be nourished via magic instead of food. Don't rely on that method for long, only in short emergency bursts. Her digestive tract needs to function at least once a week or it may start shutting down, and magic energy isn't likely to provide the necessary nutritional elements for her body to survive. Only the energy."

Gleeglum handed me a small bag of tools and the bottle of oil. "The tools are unnecessary for upkeep, but in case of combat or emergency, it's best to be prepared."

"Squeak."

Tinky squinted at me suspiciously.

I glared back at her. "No, I won't! Why would you think I'd lose something that important?"

She kept squinting at me.

"We'll see. I'll make a special pouch just for it. Something I never take off. Just for you."

Gleeglum's eyes lit up. "Why didn't I think of that? Give me another week and I'll have 'Tinky Butt 2.0' ready for testing. They'll install seamlessly to the existing mounting plates. No need for additional surgery. I can integrate the tools into the legs so you can remove them whenever you need. I might even be able to add self-lubrication so that you just need to fill a reservoir when it's low! In the meantime, document the current version's shortcomings. Identify anything else that should be added!"

Gleeglum's rapid-fire speech was something else. If he didn't smoke that sedative every time we talked, I'd never understand a word of what he said.

I nodded. "We'll keep any improvements in mind. For now, Tinky likely still needs some rest. Mind if we both sleep here one more night?"

"Be my guest." Gleeglum turned to leave us in peace.

"Before you go, have you sold any potions lately that would make a person physically larger and stronger, or something that hardens their skin?"

He looked over his shoulder and answered hastily as he edged out the door. He was eager to get started on the upgraded prosthesis. "Nope! I can craft a concoction with similar effects, but the ingredients are expensive and the effects would wear off quickly, or it would overload the imbiber's nervous system and paralyze them permanently. I wouldn't sell anything like that in this city. There would be too many repeat customers and eventually some cunning hob would try to enslave me so that they had control of the supply lines. I have to maintain a low profile."

HA! Low profile, says the gnome with a giant tower in the middle of a goblin city!

"I see. Well, Serah was asking for any concoctions that will help us in the jungle. Care to spare any? We plan to leave in a few days."

He sighed and drooped his shoulders, annoyed at the delay. "Yes, yes, of course. I suppose disease suppressants, antidotes, and antivenom would be the most useful. You'll likely need to sterilize water as well. I'll gather everything I can spare. Stop by on your way out of the city and I'll have a crate ready."

I nodded, and Gleeglum vanished before I could say another word. Tinky waddled around the room, still trying to get used to her new legs.

I sat and watched her. "Off to the jungle then, huh Tinky? It could be worse. At least I have a nice, new bag that should keep you dry while we wander aimlessly. How do you like snake meat?"

Tinky wrinkled up her nose.

"Yeah, I'm not looking forward to this either. It's hard to get famous with nobody watching. But we need off the island. There will be lots of stories to tell too. If we make it back alive." I picked Tinky up, then settled onto a cushion for a long night's sleep.

THE REST of the week went by as well as I could hope for. Tinky practiced constantly, usually by traveling from one form of food to another. She got basic control of her mechanical legs quickly. Jumping was awkward, but she could walk and run without falling over. We also practiced her lock-picking skills on a padlock Gleeglum picked up from the bazaar. She was a natural, despite the awkwardness of using her hind legs instead of her front paws. Unfortunately, she was also eating four times more food than normal! I was glad we had a caravan of provisions, not just what I could carry.

I also managed to pry my mind off of the book on magic words long enough to skim through the survival book. It was insightful, but more of a reference manual.

I thumbed through a few entries. "In case of snake bite, see page

56. For lacerations, see 'medical emergencies'. Magical ailments and curses, find a different book." It had a bit on jungles specifically, but without knowing what issues we'd face, I'd have to memorize the whole thing to know what to do. Oh well, I'd take it with us and hopefully have time to consult it when something bad happened.

Before I knew it, the days had passed, and it was time to go. I caught up with Serah in the morning, assembling her caravan. She had her hands on her hips, looking up at a large, heavily scarred orc woman.

The orc's deep, grating voice carried through the air, the voice of a commander. "All here, snake woman. Twenty orcs. Five of them work armor, weapons, tools, and the like. Five of them hunters. The rest kill. All twenty have let blood in battle." She held her chin high, proud and confident of her crew. "We want double pay for the jungle hazards."

Serah's lips narrowed and her nostrils flared as she faked irritation. Her stance and body language didn't flinch or change, which told me she was acting. She expected this. "Ungra. I didn't expect an honorable leader like yourself to be fickle on the terms of a deal. Are you saying you lied to me when we first negotiated?"

Ungra the orc raised a hand to her chin in thought. "I underestimated the danger. No one has come back from this jungle in years. Well, those three goblins and other snake people like you, but nobody else. Better pay is warranted."

Serah bared her teeth slightly, growling out her words. "And you bring this up as we are packing, with no time left for me to find alternate options without incurring additional costs. Shrewd indeed."

She paused, presumably for effect. "You will not get double. I will agree to a thirty percent bonus upon our return, to be paid to each person individually. I have already paid you the agreed upon thirty percent up front. Do not push this further."

Ouch, minus one point for Serah on the leadership front. Terrible idea to let an orc muscle you in a negotiation. On the other hand, plus ten points for her acting. She could fool a royal inquisitor if they didn't have time to get a baseline! I'm glad I had learned what to look for, but it made me wonder what I was still missing.

Ungra grinned eagerly at Serah's response. "Agreed."

Serah raised one finger as Ungra made to leave. "Don't forget, Ungra. If I don't make it back alive and well, nobody gets paid, and the money is not on my body." She gestured towards me. "That same protection covers my friend, Glik here as well. Understood?"

Ungra's grin disappeared, replaced by a scowl as she realized the "Glik" she agreed to protect as part of the original contract was a goblin and not another snake person. "Grrr. Agreed."

Serah put her hand on my shoulder as Ungra left. "Did you bring enough parchment to chronicle the journey? The three goblins I hired might be able to get us a few days into the jungle without getting us killed, but I doubt it. They specifically said they could get us 'to' the jungle without issue but failed to mention anything about going 'inside' the jungle. Any brain-dead idiot with eyes could get to the edge of the forest from here, but these are the best guides in the city. So we'll have to make do."

I side-eyed her and showed a bit of anxiety. "Tinky and I will bring up the rear so none of the orcs stab me in the back. Hopefully, there will be a cross wind most of the time so we don't have to smell them either. It would be best if our presence stayed hidden from the jungle's native predators as long as possible. Then again, I can't imagine too many animals that would think the smell of orc is tasty. Buzzards maybe?"

Serah rolled her eyes at the joke. "I'll alternate watches with you when we camp so both of us can sleep. No reason to trust these hirelings any more than necessary."

She filled the role of leader out of necessity, but not easily. It wasn't her nature to lead, but she had to try. We hadn't left the city yet, and her posture was already tensing up a little, showing the weight of the position. It truly is amazing what people will do with the right motivation.

I wondered why she was so certain the jungle held her answers. A trek through the jungle without a guide sounded much more deadly than waiting things out in a goblin city, regardless of the possibility of escaping the island.

For my part, this would make for quite the story, and I had no intention of dying for anyone. Between Tinky and my usual pack of goodies, I was confident I could survive a week out there if I had to. More if Serah stuck with me. Besides, our way back out of the jungle should be obvious. Twenty lumbering orcs hacking through undergrowth would leave a huge trail. I couldn't say the same back in the city, unless Gleeglum let me hide away in his tower indefinitely.

We finished packing and verifying all the equipment together. Six hand-pulled carts loaded with a few tents, plenty of camping gear, hunting gear, spare weapons, tools, torches, Gleeglum's crate of goodies, and enough provisions to last the entire group a couple of weeks. Unfortunately, the food was mostly this disgusting orc ration paste that nobody else would eat, not even the goblins. But there were enough basics like rice, hard biscuits, and water to get us by, as long as nobody got greedy. Each orc ate triple or more than what a goblin ate, so it made sense that our provisions were minimal in comparison. Time to head out.

All packed up, the carts looked like a small war caravan from back in my goblin lair days. Minus the decorative bones and skins of fallen enemies, of course. We rolled past the gates and got some suspicious looks from the guards as we did, but none of them dared stop us. Between the carts and the heavily armed orc mercenaries, we could, in fact, be mistaken for a war party. I hope the naga didn't think we were the first wave of an invasion!

An hour later we crested a small hill overlooking the entire city. I stopped to take one last look at it as we marched away. The mountain mines with their orcish forges. The keep that we treated like a haunted graveyard thanks to the hobs. The docks with ragtag ships that never left. Gleeglum's tower. The sandy beaches to the east. Pipfiglets, I even took a moment to reflect on the little islands just off the shore.

Something nagged at my thoughts as I looked at them.

"Tinky. Wasn't that circular island further out to sea when we first got here? It looks like it's a lot closer, and now it's on the west side of the bay instead of the east."

She popped her head out of my shoulder bag and looked at me with her head cocked to the side. "Squeak?"

"Yeah, I probably just mistook it for a different island. What's more likely, my memory getting fuzzy or an island floating off? Either way, kiss it goodbye, Tinky. This might be the last time we ever see a city, much less a beach." One twitch of a whisker later and we rejoined the group, leaving civilization once again.

CHAPTER 10

WHAT PATH OF NO RETURN? THERE WAS NO PATH TO BEGIN WITH!

Ungra's rumbling voice bludgeoned its way through the sticky air. "How. Much. Longer. Kiggles?"

The goblin named Kiggles responded like a cowering dog, hanging his head and wringing his hands together. "N-N-Next rise." He pointed a trembling finger at the next hill.

"You said that last time!"

"B-b-but they looks the same! I'm sure. This one. H-h-has to be t-t-this one!" Kiggles edged away from Ungra.

Serah marched between them, her cold visage stopping the conflict without so much as a glance. "It is almost sundown. We'll camp as soon as the jungle is within sight and rest just long enough to regain our strength. Ungra, ready scouts to look for paths and passages on the edge of the jungle. Nobody scouts alone. Always have a partner in sight."

"Aye." Ungra feinted a lunge toward Kiggles, making him flinch. The orc grinned, chuckling to herself as she headed toward the main host of orcs.

Our group had divided itself naturally into subgroups, forming a sort of hierarchy. The hunters and crafters kept to themselves respectively, but the remaining mercenaries broke into two squads, each with a formidable leader. The two squads coordinated well, setting up defensive lines surrounding the carts. They kept a fairly sharp lookout as we marched and didn't waste much energy on friendly banter.

For better or worse, the wind was at our backs. This was good for Tinky and I who were bringing up the rear. We didn't have to smell the sweaty orc stench. Unfortunately, the slow breeze carried the scent directly to the jungle instead. If anything in there liked the taste of orc, its mouth would be watering long before we made our first step into the predator's territory.

Within the hour, Kiggles was proven right. The goblins leading our caravan topped a hill, then started jumping around excitedly when they spotted the jungle. I followed the caravan up the rise and lost my breath at the sight. Trees, trees, an occasional clearing full of overgrown vines and bushes, then more plopaflotzin trees! We were about to enter some kind of endless, sticky, tree infested hell.

Ungra immediately barked orders and started setting up camp. We were right on the hill where we would be spotted but could easily spot any intruders as well. I guess she thought twenty orcs were a formidable enough force to deter any attackers.

Clouds formed rapidly out of nowhere, dumping a light mist on us and obscuring our vision. Before long, the mist shifted into a downpour. Glad we brought tents!

I found Serah. She was checking over the camp setup, ignoring the pouring rain falling on her hooded cloak.

"Serah, do you mind taking watch while I rest?"

She sighed. "That would be best. It will give me time to dry off and think."

We settled into a central tent, and I let Tinky out for some exercise and food. The rain had peeled off the worst of the humidity, but it was still hot and uncomfortable. I curled up on a dry blanket and caught a few hours of sleep.

~

SERAH WOKE me with a gentle kick and handed me a waterskin. Tinky was already awake, tearing into some dried fish nearby.

Dark circles lined Serah's tired eyes. "The dried provisions aren't going to last well. One more thing to worry about. Now get out of my sleeping spot."

She nudged me off the blanket. I didn't resist. She had earned some sleep. I peeled back the tent flap and looked outside. It was still pouring rain. The ground had gotten soft and muddy, and any attempt to make a fire had been abandoned by the orcs. Everyone had clustered into the tents except the handful of orcs on watch rotation.

A few hours passed in pleasant silence, though the heat was still uncomfortable. I pulled out a tinderbox and a candle from my bag, courtesy of Gleeglum. They provided enough light for me to read and experiment with magic while Serah slept.

I tried to light a second candle with magic, like Gleeglum had done in our training session with Valas.

I focused hard on what I wanted to happen. Light the candle.

"Ignius!" Nothing.

"Ignité!" More nothing.

"Catch fire!" Still nothing.

I grabbed the candle with both hands and shook it. "Flammare! Burnicus! Incindio! Light you Kikkleflaken candle!" A searing heat burned my toe as the last few words tore from my lips, fueled by my frustration.

"Ow! You little son-of-a..." I trailed off, distracted by a tiny tendril of smoke rising from the candle wick. Huh. I didn't expect that to work. I wouldn't be calling lightning from the skies and thwarting armies with fireballs anytime soon, but any magic at all was a welcome sign.

Tinky had watched the whole scene while chewing on a bit of cheese. She shook her head at me; her bored expression saying more than any squeak could convey. I had been judged by a rat. Marvelous.

I gave up and went back to reading for a few hours. The sounds of rain subsided, and I poked my head out of the tent to take a look. The rain had stopped quickly, the clouds had already dissipated, and the bright dual moons peeked through overhead. It was almost bright enough to read under their light.

A handful of orcs were reloading the carts and packing up. Either Ungra was one relentless taskmaster, or everyone wanted to get this jungle job done with and go home as quick as possible. Probably both.

I ducked back into the tent and woke Serah with a quick tap to her foot. Her eyes snapped open, immediately awake, alert, and assessing her surroundings, as usual.

She grabbed a waterskin and spoke. "The rain stopped. Good. Help pack where you can, Glik. Let's get moving as quickly as possible."

She pulled on her cloak, grabbed her gear, and headed outside. I packed what little remained and listened closely to Serah's conversation just outside the tent.

"Ungra, what did your scouts report?"

Ungra's guttural voice replied with a subtle hint of challenge. "What scouts?"

I risked poking my head out to see what Serah's reaction was to that. Her visage did not disappoint. There was no faking it this time. Her nostrils flared, eyes narrowed, and her jaw clenched tight. One hand formed a fist at her side, and the other was creeping up to her amulet. She was pissed!

She spoke quietly through her clenched teeth. "The scouts that were finding a path into the jungle, Ungra."

Ungra smiled, feigning ignorance. "Aye. Those scouts. I didn't send 'em. Rain made it too hard to see. No point in exhausting the troops for nothing."

Serah dropped her gaze to her amulet. "Ungra, I have heard that orcs are highly resistant to poison. Is this true?"

Ungra's smile disappeared. "Aye. Care to find out?"

My eyes shot wide at the exchange. The tension had grown thicker than the humidity!

Serah pulled a small vial from her pocket and unsheathed her dagger. She swirled the contents of the vial absentmindedly as she spoke, which made the thick amber liquid stick to the sides of the mostly empty vial.

"I think it would be best to test the orc resistance, yes. We will find all sorts of toxic plants, venomous bites, and poison coated animals once we enter the jungle. It would be best to know how fast we need to treat our troops, if we need to treat them at all. Please, cut your hand, and apply a single drop of this to the wound."

She held out the blade and opened vial.

Ungra hesitated.

"No? I thought you were the toughest orc in the crew? Should I ask Ligs or Grung for their assistance?"

Ungra's face tightened as she scowled. She snatched the items from Serah's hand, sliced open her palm, and emptied the vial onto her hand. That was at least ten times the amount of liquid Serah had told her to use! Ungra shoved the items back into Serah's hands, glaring down at her as she did.

Serah smiled, politely putting away the vial and dagger. "Thank you, Ungra. You made a wise call with the scouts, but next time consult with me before canceling my orders."

Serah turned back to the tent and bumped into me as she passed, stealthily depositing a different vial into my hand. She whispered, "For when Ungra collapses."

Then, loud enough for everyone nearby to hear, she said, "Oh, sorry, Glik. I didn't see you there. Help Ungra pack up camp."

I took a quick glance at the vial, making sure that Ungra didn't see it as I did. This one was completely full of a lighter yellow substance. I pocketed it and turned to Ungra.

"You heard the lady. What do you need help with?"

Ungra snorted. "A goblin. Help. Stay out of our way, runt."

She shoved me to the side as she walked by, wiping her cut hand on her trousers. I followed her quietly, waiting for the inevitable. The orc made it a full fifty paces before a squishy, wet thumping noise announced that her body had lost the battle. It had been less than five minutes after Serah's poison entered Ungra's wound, and the big, tough orc was already face down in the mud.

I rushed over and tried rolling Ungra on to her side. Ogliferinkets was she HEAVY!

"Over here! Someone help me roll Ungra over!"

"Heh heh, after some tail, goblin?" Great. It was Ligs. The most obscene and worthless of the orcs I had met so far.

"Shut your yap, and get over here." I didn't mention she was dying. The lug would probably think that was an opportunity for promotion.

He lumbered over slowly, put a foot under her shoulder, and rolled her over with a grunt. "Have fun!"

What an idiot. I pried open her mouth and poured in the contents of the vial. She didn't seem to react at all. I suppose that was a good thing, since she was still breathing. At least she hadn't started foaming at the mouth and contorting into odd positions like the last victim of Serah's poison.

I shook my head in admiration. Serah may not like to lead, but that was a major win for her. Ungra was experienced and powerful, which was required to lead a group of vicious mercenary orcs. But her game was intimidation and displays of brute strength. Serah had just slapped Ungra's bravado down with a few tiny drops of liquid. The orc would have to watch over her shoulder from now on. That meant she had less time to plot a hostile takeover.

We took our time packing up with Serah directing the effort since Ungra was unconscious. She pointed to Raga, the head huntress.

"Form scouting groups. Same orders as last night, but move quickly. You'll meet the group at the tree line in four hours. Do not enter the jungle, and do not split up from your partners."

She shook her head at the unconscious Ungra and waved Grung over to help. "Grung, toss her in the cart with the tents. Then get your squad ready to move. We head down the hill as soon as you are ready."

"Ar" was his reply. Quite the linguist, that one.

Once the carts were packed up, we headed down the hill. The rain had softened the dirt tremendously. The wheels of each cart cut into the muddy terrain, getting stuck frequently. Eventually, Ligs got angry and heaved a cart onto his back. This worked for a little while, but his feet sank deep into the ground, wearing him out faster than he expected. We were less than fifty paces into this leg of the journey, and we were already losing time.

Grung's deep, grating voice reverberated in the air. "Ligs, ya overgrown turnip, put that cart down. We'll carry 'em in pairs." Following orders, the orcs split up in groups of two and simply lifted the carts off the ground. They made it look easy, but this could not go well in the long run.

We took a short breather when we reached the tree line, or more accurately, the impenetrable wall of vines, bushes, and other various thorny foliage. Ungra woke up while we waited for the scouts.

"Ugh. My head!" She rose groggily from her cart and looked around, trying to recall what happened, where she was, and why she was in a cart. Her memories all came back when she saw Serah. Rage turned her olive-skinned cheeks a fine red hue as she stood on shaky legs in the cart. They didn't hold, and she fell face first into the mud.

Serah didn't bother saying a word to Ungra as she made her way to the scouting teams who had just returned.

"Raga, report."

Raga replied meekly, her voice smoother and higher than most of the other mercenaries in our group. "Nothing. No paths in. Only wild jungle." She pulled away from Serah slowly, watching her reactions nervously.

Made sense to me. Orc commanders rarely accepted bad news without punishing the messenger. Orcs didn't have much control when they were angry, and it seemed like an orc's temper was directly proportional to their size.

Serah was no orc commander. She simply nodded and walked to the nearest wall of undergrowth, assessing the best way to proceed. Raga glanced around suspiciously, then cautiously pressed her luck by speaking to Serah again.

"We could hack or burn through."

Serah smirked. "I doubt we can burn anything this wet, but twenty strong orcs hacking away could do some damage. Thank you, Raga."

The orc visibly flinched at the appreciation. It was then I noticed her scars. Hundreds of faint lines overlapped each other where her skin was showing, particularly on the back of her neck and all over her arms. Life had not been kind to her, which was a common story amongst orcs. She was smaller than the others, which meant she had probably been picked on. But it worked to her advantage as a hunter, and amongst the hunters, her skill was more important than her size.

Serah paid no heed to Raga's reaction, instead focusing on giving more orders. Daylight was fast approaching. It was time to make some real progress.

"Grung. Grab your squad. We hack our way through. Make a path just wide enough to carry the carts."

"Ar." He turned and shouted commands to his squad in Nomadic Orcish.

Serah narrowed her eyes at the undergrowth. "Raga. Can your hunters make their way through this vegetation?"

Raga's eyes darted across various parts of the overgrowth, assessing. "Yes. Slowly."

Serah nodded, her expression neutral as always. "Travel in pairs. Cover at least fifty paces out on all sides. Take whatever help you need from Ungra's squad. Watch closely for animal nests and signs we are being followed."

Raga grabbed one of her fellow hunters and began rounding up the scouting pairs she needed. The remaining orcs paired up and lifted the carts, ready to head out.

Our travel was painfully slow and messy. The jungle itself had much softer earth than the hill. That meant more mud, deeper holes, and more stumbling. Our vanguard of weed-whacking orcs was efficient and practiced but still slower than the carts. After the first few hours, we got into the habit of stopping for about fifteen minutes at a time, then catching back up to the vanguard. Serah and Ungra didn't like this as it split the group, but they didn't stop it as the rest was necessary for the cart carriers.

By noon Serah had enough of it. "Ungra. Are you well enough to lead again?"

Humbled by her ordeal with the venom, Ungra appeared somewhat surprised by Serah's request. "Aye, snake woman." She got out of the cart she had been resting in and stood up without a problem.

"Then have your crew find us a suitable camp spot. We rest for the remainder of the day and head out again at dusk."

Ungra nodded, then began barking orders to the others in Nomadic Orcish. Before long we changed direction, heading to a small circle of taller trees. It was still overgrown and wet, but it was slightly elevated, lacked standing water, and was easier to clear than the rest of the jungle underbrush had been.

As everyone set up camp, I looked through the survival book for anything useful. "How to start a fire, pg 166. Use tinderbox on dried twigs, leaves, and wood." I looked around the camp. My clothes were soaked. Sweat dripped off the tip of my nose. The top two inches of the dirt were mud. Every tree and bush was waterlogged from last night's rain and the oppressive humidity. Where in Farkkagiggle's Snout was I going to find "dry wood"? Mighty lot of good this survival guide was.

I glanced over at Grung who was trying to help a younger orc light a pile of wet wood with a tinderbox. My Orcish isn't the best, but judging from the creativity of their swearing, they were having about as much luck as I expected. Grung finally lost his temper and chucked a branch into the jungle before stomping off. I suppose a fire wasn't really necessary since we had plenty of rations and water, but drying off would have been nice.

Once the tents were up and guards posted, I tracked down Serah. She was toward the edge of camp, speaking with Raga.

"Nothing follows us, snake woman."

Serah nodded, but Raga looked around nervously and continued.

"We leave a big path, easy to find, easy to track."

Serah stared at the wide swath of butchered vegetation we had carved into the jungle behind us. "Nothing we can do about that."

Raga nodded and left, more confident now than she had been on her last encounter with Serah.

I got Serah's attention. "Ready to take a break?"

"Glik. Do you know anything about jungles?"

"Nothing I haven't already said. Why?"

She let out an exasperated sigh. "Let's hope this undergrowth doesn't span the whole jungle, or we'll never make it without getting hopelessly lost. Kiggles isn't much of a guide."

On that note, we headed to the tent and took our usual turns resting.

Ungra's pounding voice jarred me awake. "Snake woman. Ligs is missing."

Serah stood at the open flap of the tent with an annoyed scowl on her face. Ungra was there, appearing eager with her shoulders back, chest out, and eyebrows up. Odd considering she was missing one of her warriors. It meant that she cared about Ligs as much as I did, which was not at all, and that this was another opportunity to test Serah. Was Serah hardened, willing to do what was necessary? Or was she soft like most humans, willing to sacrifice everything for sentiment and attachment? In orc terms, was she a worthy leader or another weak target for elimination in the endless struggle for power and position?

I would have thought getting poisoned for a day would have been enough of an answer, but Ungra was apparently stubborn. Or stupid. Probably both.

Serah's tone was cold. "When was he last seen?"

"Two hours ago. Taking a piss."

Serah sighed and shot me a quick glance before setting her jaw defiantly. "So be it, Ungra. Have one patrol look around where he was last seen, but we leave as soon as we finish packing camp. I won't waste resources on one person who's likely lost or in the belly of some animal."

Ungra bowed her head in acceptance.

"And Ungra, that applies to everyone. Let them all know, if they aren't around when we pack up camp every day, we wait for no one."

Ungra's lips curled into a ruthless, terrifying grin of approval. "Aye."

Serah closed the tent flap and began packing her things. I couldn't help but comment on her performance. "That was a fine leadership decision, but I hope there aren't any grudges in camp. If there are, we'll be missing a few more people tomorrow due to 'moments of opportunity' amongst the orc ranks."

Serah nodded in acknowledgement but said nothing. She had passed Ungra's test, but she didn't seem to like it.

We set out again at dark, the dense canopy above blotting out the light of the dual moons. The orcs hacked with extra vigor, eager to be out of the underbrush. It rained gently, and despite still being oppressively nasty weather, this was much better than trudging through the underbrush in the heat of the day with maximum humidity.

Many hours later, the glow of dawn brightened the sky and the underbrush waned. Serah put her hand on Kiggles' shoulder and squeezed firmly.

"Where do we go from here, guide?" She spit out the word "guide" with such ferocity that I thought she might bite the poor goblin if he answered wrong.

Kiggles' whole body began shaking as he looked around, eyes darting all over the place. He didn't have a clue.

He lifted a trembling arm, pointing straight ahead. "Th-th-that way."

Serah glared at him and huffed, unconvinced but lacking a better alternative. She barked a few orders to Ungra, and we adjusted our path.

A few more hours of travel into the rainforest and, while we still couldn't roll the carts, we made much better time. The canopy in this part of the jungle was thicker, which provided much-needed shade during the day and reduced the thickness of the underbrush.

As we set camp that day, I watched Grung attempt to start a fire again. This time the mercenary had given up on the flint and tinder method. Instead, he had a pointed stick pressed onto a cutaway chunk of a log with bits of tinder scattered around where the two pieces of wood met. He rubbed the pointed stick between his hands, spinning it rapidly, over and over again.

I had to comment. "Grung, you look like an idiot. What are you doing?"

He growled at me, not taking his eyes off of the stick. His muscles rippled as he pressed the pointed stick even harder into the wood, spinning it faster and faster. My mild taunting seemed to have motivated him. To my surprise, a tiny plume of white smoke wafted up from where the stick met the log.

"Ha! Eat that, stupid goblin."

I smirked and crossed my arms, enjoying the spectacle. Smoke does not mean fire. A few minutes passed as he continued spinning the stick and making white wisps of smoke. No fire. Eventually, he gave up. He was completely drenched with sweat and panting from the effort.

"Eat that, huh? Oh, I'm eating it up, Grung. What genius idea are you going to try next, spitting on the wood to light the fire?"

His hands clenched, snapping the pointed stick. That was all the warning I needed. I bolted back to the tent before Grung had finished getting up!

I quickly closed the tent flap, knowing Grung wouldn't risk interrupting Serah. She was already inside, checking her belongings.

"Squeak."

I glanced down at my shoulder bag. Tinky had stuck her entire head out of it and was staring me down with narrowed eyes.

"I know, Tinky, but I can't help it. Something inside me just screams out to make fun of the orcs. I've been doing it since I was little. It works wonders when I can use that instinct to frame an enemy!"

She was not amused. A little twitch of her nose and a small huff was her only response before tucking back into the shoulder bag.

Serah pulled a piece of parchment from her bag and unrolled it on top of the bedroll. "Glik. Don't antagonize the orcs. I'm having enough trouble keeping them under control. Come here and look at this instead. Bring one of your candles."

I obliged and pulled out a candle. This was a great time to test that magic again! I focused hard, concentrating on what I wanted. Fire. Burning. A lit candle to read by.

"Inflamare! Inflickitus! Torcharanicus! Poof! Burn you Skrag-gafrakting piece of OW!"

I jumped, grabbing my foot and dropping the candle. My toe was on fire! I could smell seared flesh and burning leather coming from inside my boot. I yanked it off and looked at the ring on my toe. The iron band glowed with bright, burning runes. Luckily, no flame was coming off of them or my foot, just a tiny bit of smoke.

A warm light drew my eyes away from my foot as Serah lifted the candle off the ground. She raised her eyebrows at it.

"That's no fireball, Glik, but I'm still impressed. I've never seen a goblin use any kind of magic before." She smiled and suppressed a laugh. "Especially with such fine, arcane linguistics."

It worked! I looked back at my foot. The runes on the ring were already fading and my toe still hurt, but the magic had worked! I pulled the ring off my toe to inspect the damage. The skin was pink and raw but nothing permanent.

"Um, thanks? At least the candle is lit. What are we looking at?"

I put the ring and my boot back in place and glanced at the illuminated parchment. It appeared to be some sort of map.

"I got this from Gleeglum. It's a crude map of the island based on what he could see from his tower observatory. We should be here." She pointed to a spot on the map just to the left of a badly sketched temple.

"If that's correct and we keep heading east, we should run into the center of the jungle. That's where the ziggurat is. If it takes more than a day or two we either missed it, or we got turned around."

I looked at the map closely, not entirely sure what I was looking at. "What's this squiggly line that stops at the trees?"

"That's the river. It goes through the goblin city."

"Why don't we follow it?"

"I asked Gleeglum the same question during our preparations. The jungle is thick enough that he can't see where the river goes once it gets inside the jungle. He also mentioned that paddling upstream could be difficult, and we'd need shallow boats for the river. That meant more time spent in the city making preparations. If we had a guide, it wouldn't matter."

Seemed logical. "What about Kiggles?"

Serah rubbed her face, obviously stressed by the topic. "That goblin has never been this far in the jungle. Sadly, nobody else in this group really knows any better."

I thought for a few seconds. Most of the orcs were having the usual power struggle. But Raga had been fairly helpful so far and had managed to lead most of the deeper scouting treks.

"What about Raga?"

"She hasn't died or gotten lost yet. Doesn't mean she knows where we're going. Let's get some rest."

∽

I AWOKE to Ungra's familiar, grating vocalizations, again. Serah was at the flap of the tent with Ungra, just like the day before. And just like the day before, Serah was already irritated.

"Snake woman. Vols and Ekegr did not return from patrol. Two goblins are dead too."

Vols and Ekegr were two of the better hunters. It wasn't like them to get lost. This was bad.

Serah narrowed her eyes at Ungra. "What exactly happened to the goblins?"

Ungra raised her hands innocently. "Nothing violent. Dead when we found them. No wounds."

Serah huffed. "Point me to the bodies, then pack camp."

She gestured for me to come with her, so I grabbed my shoulder bag and followed. Tinky's nose might be helpful. Ungra brought us to the center of the camp, where two goblin corpses had been tossed in a haphazard pile. Kiggles was there, frantically jumping around, pointing at anyone who passed by and accusing them all with his rough Goblin dialect.

"You all kill! Yous fault Miks and Maks dead! Yous be sorry!"

A single, cold look from Serah ended his tirade. She might not speak goblin, but she understood what he was doing. Kiggles quickly sat down and put his hands over his mouth in a forced act of self-preservation. It was odd to see a goblin caring this much for fellow goblins. Maybe they had been partners for a really long time, but more likely, they owed him money.

Serah crouched down and examined the bodies, methodically comparing them to each other. She moved their limbs around, sniffed their mouths, and bleck tasted their fingertips. She then pulled open their eyelids and inspected their bloodshot, lifeless eyeballs.

She rose and directed her gaze toward Kiggles. "Miks and Maks. Where did you find their bodies?"

Kiggles was still upset, but he collected himself enough to point toward a tent at the edge of camp and mutter, "Behind the tent."

Serah strode toward the tent with her neutral expression on her face. I followed, curious what would entice her to lick a goblin's fingers! She stopped as soon as the forest behind the tent was in view and gave a shallow nod of affirmation.

There was a small patch of blue mushrooms that had been picked over, along with a handful of half-eaten ones and a small pile that was ready to eat.

I cocked an eyebrow at Serah. "Mushrooms are a common staple of goblin cooking, but I've never seen these before."

Serah smiled maliciously. "I'm not a chef, but I know a lot of poisons. Mushrooms are a key ingredient for many of them. I don't know what this specific species is, but it's obvious that Miks and Maks ate some of them, and now Miks and Maks are dead."

I tapped my bag twice to get a certain rat's attention. "This is why we don't eat everything we find, Tinky."

A soft scratching inside my bag was her response.

I returned my attention to Serah. "At least it wasn't the orcs."

She gave me a sidelong glance and turned to walk back toward the corpses. "Unless the orcs told them the mushrooms were food."

I shivered. Ruthless and cunning. That was more of a hob move, but I wouldn't put it past an orc if they knew they could get away with it. Ungra's group of warriors probably shunned using poison and likely wouldn't realize the mushrooms were poisonous even if they ate them (gnashgabbing, poison-resistant orcs). It would have had to be Raga's crew, and they didn't seem to notice the goblins, much less care enough to kill them. Luckily, that meant it was most likely just a case of goblin stupidity.

Serah found Kiggles by the bodies and put the situation to rest. "Miks and Maks ate some poisonous mushrooms. Make sure you don't repeat their mistake."

Kiggles nodded and sniffled a little. He began inspecting the corpses again as we left, paying particular attention to the fingers and looking back toward the mushroom patch. I couldn't help but think about grabbing a few of those for future use, but I didn't want Tinky to mistake them for food. Poison wasn't in my general arsenal of tricks anyway. Too risky.

Not long after, camp was packed and we were traveling again. Our pace was much faster than before without the need to hack through underbrush. A few snakebites and some scratches from a very surprised cat were the only issues of the night. We camped at daybreak, following the same routine as the day before. And yes, Grung failed to make a fire, again.

AT TWILIGHT I was awakened by the tickling sensation of whiskers on my neck. Tinky's beady little eyes were waiting for me, letting me know it was time for breakfast. I gave her some cheese from my pack, got my gear all situated, and headed out to find Serah. She was in the center of the camp, looking up at the canopy.

I stood beside her and craned my neck as high as possible, trying to see what she was staring at. "Whatcha looking at?"

"Nothing."

She dropped her gaze back to the camp, expression neutral. "Nobody went missing today. The naga have probably noticed our presence by now. They might send a welcoming team but, considering our orc companions, they might send an armed patrol instead. We need to be alert. If these naga are not the benevolent beings we hope for, they might set an ambush."

Our travel that night was as uneventful as the last, which was becoming worrisome. We camped, following the same routine we were growing accustomed to. Serah kept silent except for the handful of commands she gave out. I watched over her as she slept a fitful sleep, tossing and turning frequently.

My turn to sleep ended at dusk, with Ungra's guttural report, yet again. "Graggatok and Milok are missing."

Serah didn't look irritated or particularly stressed at the news. She must have expected it. She gave the now common series of orders for missing persons, then silently packed for another night of travel.

I watched Ungra leave and tried to gauge Serah's mood. I wanted to ask her more, to confirm what she was thinking. She should be on edge, but her body language said everything was normal. That was more suspicious than anything.

I took the cautious approach and left her alone. She had said we would arrive at the temple yesterday. If we had veered off target, we might have passed it all together. If that was the case, in another day or two, we should reach the opposite side of the jungle. Maybe that's what she was thinking.

We headed out again, falling into our routine. The night went by, but no temple. We camped, rested, and traveled again the next night, and the next, and the next. Serah remained quiet most of the time, and I started losing track of how many days we had been traveling.

Occasionally, another person would go missing, but the travel had become an uneventful slog. Exhaustion was setting in for all of us. Heat and humidity never ceased, even when it rained. We were never dry, and some of our provisions rotted or grew enough mold that even the orcs wouldn't eat it.

Close to dawn on what might have been the ninth or tenth day of our venture, we stumbled across a clearing.

Serah held her hand up, signaling a halt to the procession. "Ungra, does this place look familiar?"

"No. Why?"

Serah narrowed her eyes. "Find Raga. We've camped at this site before. Raga might remember when."

She stormed over to Kiggles, not waiting for Raga or an answer from Ungra. When she found him, she spoke with an eerie pacing, like a predator waiting for an opening to pounce. "Kiggles, my dear guide. What direction are we traveling?"

Kiggles stood perfectly still and squeaked out a wild guess. "East."

Serah licked her lips, displaying her forked tongue prominently.

"In a few hours, when the sun rises, we will see if you have outlived your usefulness."

Serah began setting up camp, despite it being earlier than usual. Raga found her right as the dawn broke above the canopy.

"Raga. Have we been here before?"

The orc looked down but had learned that Serah preferred truth and did not punish messengers like orc commanders. "Yes."

"Do you remember when we camped here last?"

"No. The camp is old. Four or five days?"

Serah sighed and looked up at the slowly brightening canopy. "Which direction is east?"

Raga's eyebrows knit in confusion. She glanced upward, then pointed back in the direction we had come from.

I heard Serah's knuckles pop as she clenched her fists. "Glik. Find Kiggles. He may follow the group until we are out of the jungle. Make sure he stays as far away from me as possible."

I gulped, then scurried away. Serah was scary when she was angry!

After warning Kiggles about his impending doom, I headed to the tent. Serah was standing by the entrance, map in hand.

"Glik, good. Let's look at this together, inside."

I obliged, lighting a short stub of a candle and looking over the parchment.

Serah's eyes roamed. "We're lost. Do you have any idea where we are?"

I looked closely at the map. I remembered where Serah said we were back when we expected to find the temple in a day. But there were no landmarks, just an endless rainforest.

"No, Serah. There's nothing to go by. If Kiggles didn't know which direction we were going, we could be anywhere."

Serah rubbed her eyes. "Then we pick a direction and stick with it. Raga will lead as our new guide. At least she can tell what direction we are traveling."

I nodded. We had already lost almost a third of our original group. Food might also be an issue soon, thanks to the humidity. We were all tired. Rest was better than walking, but it was too hot to truly recover. If we lost much more time in the jungle, morale would break.

Serah didn't sleep at all during her turn to rest. She spent her time staring at maps and my survival book, searching for a solution that wasn't there. I slept fitfully, dreaming of wet, rainy days that never ended. It was bad enough that I almost welcomed Ungra's horrible voice when I awoke to it.

"Snake woman, more missing orcs today. This time, supplies are missing too."

Serah blinked slowly before answering. "How many?"

"Raga, her hunters, and three of the crafters."

She kept her expression cold and neutral. "How many supplies?"

"The gnome's crate, a tent, and one cart of food."

Serah took a deep breath. "Inventory what we have left. We'll pack up later than usual. From here out, we travel during the day."

Ungra snarled reflexively at the idea but obeyed anyway.

That was unfortunate. Raga had probably gathered anyone who cared more about survival than pay and deserted. I couldn't blame her. If she played her cards right, she might be able to take credit for Serah's death and gain some power in the hierarchy back at the goblin city.

What a fine way to start the day!

CHAPTER II

ALWAYS THE LITTLE THINGS

We traveled an extra half day and set camp a few hours before dusk. Serah finally got some sleep, and I read some more of my book on magic words. Near the end of my watch, a soft rustling outside the tent caught my attention. Hopefully, it was just some animal looking for food.

I nudged Serah. She awoke slower than normal, but got up and grabbed her flail when I motioned toward the sound. We snuck slowly out of the tent and searched. Nothing. I shrugged and turned back toward the tent while Serah looked into the jungle a little longer.

A strange rolling voice whispered from somewhere out of sight, directed at Serah. "Icreassia, fissali, miass."

Serah's eyes lit up at the sound, a genuine smile breaking her icy demeanor. "Finally! Show yourself so we can speak."

There was no response. She furrowed her eyebrows and shifted out of the Imperial language. "Icreassia, fissali, miass. Tut ri firasi memanos tre?"

The voice replied. "Fet ricast."

Serah signaled me to stay put, then crept back behind the tent. I listened carefully but couldn't pick out anything useful over the noise of the jungle.

After a few minutes, Serah returned, more animated than she had been in days but obviously agitated. "The noise was a hunter named Ixchel that speaks the naga language. She stayed hidden the whole time we spoke and insisted on hurrying the conversation. I wasn't able to confirm if she was from the temple or not, but I talked her into leading us there. She says our camp will be attacked soon, so she won't join us right now, but if we survive, we are to meet her by the river to the north."

I gave her a skeptical look. This sounded far too convenient.

"I don't like it either, Glik, but we have little choice and desperately need a guide. If we don't trust her, we'll probably die, lost in this humid green hell."

At least we got a warning this time. "Why don't you and I follow her?"

She shook her head. "I'm not that trusting. I'd like our muscle to be with us when we get to the temple."

She stepped to the center of camp and began issuing commands in a loud, yet controlled voice. "To arms. Prepare defenses. Something is coming."

The orcs understood and began hacking nearby saplings into crude wooden spike barriers. The tents were dropped and packed, placed with everything else inside a defensive circle. Spears and shields were handed out to each defender. Kiggles, the only non-orc left other than Serah and me, grabbed a janky-looking bow with a few somewhat straight arrows.

"Tinky, I'm not sure we're safe in this circle, but I don't see any good place to hide outside of it either. Ideas?"

Tinky cocked an eyebrow sarcastically as she shook her head no. The expression seemed to convey "You're asking a rat about defense tactics? Did you hit your head recently?"

"Fine, Tinky, it's your butt too."

Rain poured on us in the darkness as we took up our defensive positions. A few hours later, the rain calmed to a fine mist, and little yellow lights began glowing in the underbrush. They floated lazily in pairs, like lightning bugs. A slight breeze crept into our camp, smelling of flowers and wet earth. My mind drifted, thinking of how exhausting the trip had been, how nice a cool mug of ale and a soft bed sounded. A nap sounded like a great idea.

Thump!

Kiggles fell face first to the ground, fast asleep.

Serah rattled off a hasty prayer in less than a second. "Aghti dak li matea ai!"

Blinding light erupted from her upraised hand, illuminating the entire area for a fraction of a second. Her light showed the true nature of the yellow dots in the darkness. We were surrounded. Various wild animals had been waiting for us, their eyes camouflaged by the glowing lights of the lighting bugs. They were waiting until we fell asleep so they could finish us off at their leisure.

The orcs went into a practiced set of motions. Each had a unique style, but all were veterans of countless battles, resistant to panic, and ready for bloodshed. They chucked a flight of spears into the forest, then grabbed their shields and more spears. The barrage skewered some of the dazed animals, killing a few and injuring others. Serah began praying again, enacting who knows what sort of protective magic.

A handful of crocodiles charged shortly after. They distracted the orcs as several giant snakes slithered under the barriers, tangling up some of the orcs' feet, causing them to stumble. Smaller snakes joined in, quickly choosing targets to bite with venomous fangs before retreating. The orcs barely noticed, easily resisting the normally deadly toxins.

A rustling of leaves from high above alerted me to a new danger. Lithe, shadowy cats had climbed the trees and were readying to pounce.

"Above! Attack from above!"

The orcs heeded my warning just in time. Three of the night cats sprang at once. Two landed on orcish spears, impaling themselves. The other tackled its target with claws and teeth bared. The orc went down in a flurry of black fur and bloody mist as the cat tore in, rear claws raking the poor orc's torso savagely. Another orc noticed and ended the distracted cat's fight with a well-placed thrust of his spear.

We were losing. Each fallen orc took down their fair share of animals with them, but numbers were not on our side.

I couldn't take my eyes off the carnage in front of me. "Serah, this is not working. How do we get out of here?"

She didn't respond. I spared a quick glance at her. Her eyes were closed, both hands grasped her amulet, and her lips moved rapidly under her breath. I hoped she was casting something good for both of us.

Two hawks swooped down from above, adding to the fray. They weren't able to carry off a full-grown orc, but their talon slashes were precise and lightning quick. One orc lost an eye. Another was distracted just enough to trip and fall over the barricade. A waiting crocodile wasted no time clamping its jaws onto the orc's face. It rolled hard, snapping the orc's neck and dragging it across the jungle floor.

After the first thirty seconds of fighting, only three orc warriors remained. What sort of thing could cause such an organized attack from animals?

Something grabbed my arm, yanking away my attention. "Quickly. We leave now, Glik."

I couldn't see her, but Serah's scent gave away her position beside me. I looked around for her and noticed that I couldn't see my own body! Serah had turned us invisible.

I scanned the area in a rush. "We'll need to mask our scent, Serah. Cat guts. Neck, arms, legs."

I grabbed a handful of night cat entrails as we ran by, rubbing them all over myself. It wasn't perfect, but it would have to do. I hoped Serah had done the same but couldn't tell. The guts had turned invisible as soon as I touched them. Regrettably, masking our scent like this worked both ways. I wouldn't be able to smell out our enemies, or Serah, for that matter.

We crept quickly out of the defensive circle, hand in hand, so we wouldn't lose each other. We snuck by the barricade near the crocodile enjoying its orc snack and made our way into the jungle. A sharp tug halted me. Serah whispered in my ear, almost imperceptibly quiet.

"Up".

I looked above us. Staring at the camp was a softly glowing little body, no bigger than Tinky. Two translucent dragonfly wings twitched nervously on its back as it twirled a carved stick and paced back and forth along a branch. A Pixie! Magical little troublemakers!

It was mumbling in the language of sprites, a language I was vaguely familiar with but far from fluent in. I perked my ears and listened, picking out a handful of words that made sense.

"... invaders... chopping and burning... not edible... not in my forest... be dead in minutes... where's the human?"

Another sharp tug from Serah kept us moving. We headed north for hours, eventually stumbling across a calm stream. It was larger than I liked, but we could swim across it if needed.

Serah whispered to me, still cautious. "We cross, then wait until dawn. Our guide said she would meet us here. Can you recognize her smell?"

I shook my head (for what little good it did when invisible). "Not a chance. Orc stench overwhelmed the camp. I'd be lucky to recognize her voice, much less her smell. Besides, we're going to smell like cat guts for a few days, no matter how much we wash."

Serah let out an exasperated huff. "I wanted to stay invisible in case she set up an ambush, but that won't work if you can't identify her. Let's hole up near that overcropping of rocks. I'll try to keep us invisible until just before dawn, then I'll let myself be seen."

We crossed the creek. It was an oddly pleasant swim. The water was cool compared to the stagnant, humid air, but it wasn't cold.

Serah let her invisibility spell drop after we rested a few hours, but she kept mine going. She looked terrible. Dark circles lined her eyes, her shoulders drooped, and she flopped to the ground with less grace than an orc. Maintaining the spell was pushing her already stretched limits.

"Don't get caught, Glik. I've already told you what happens to prisoners of a Khabis cult. It's possible our new guide captures dream slaves for them."

I shivered a little, remembering the hellish treatment Serah had described for dream slaves. I did not want to spend my next few years being tortured during the day and forced to dream endless nightmares at night.

"What do you think, Tinky? Will you recognize the smell of our mysterious guide?"

She shook her head no, then went back to stuffing her face full of cheese. It was an understandable reaction. We had spent far too much time around orcs. That stink overpowers everything and is hard to get rid of.

DAWN CAME EARLIER than I expected. The jungle near the river was thicker with underbrush, but the canopy did not completely cover the river. It was strangely pleasant seeing open blue sky.

Serah made her way closer to the bank as the sun rose. I stepped a few paces away, mindful of the breeze and far enough from the bank that my footprints wouldn't show in the mud. It took less than an hour before Ixchel appeared, paddling upstream in a small boat that looked like a hollowed-out log.

She was a darkly tanned, raven-haired, humanish creature with light points on her ears. Seashells and plants were tied like jewelry around her neck and wrists, providing colorful accents to her hide clothing. A broadhead spear and a club, studded with volcanic glass blades, sat in her boat with her, along with a quiver of long darts and an oddly shaped stick.

She spotted Serah, gave a half-hearted wave of acknowledgment, then pulled her boat to the shore. She was as tall as a small orc with an athletic build of lean, sinewy muscle. Her movements were precise, well-honed, and purposeful. A look into her golden eyes confirmed what I suspected. Whatever else she was, first and foremost, she was a predator.

They greeted each other in the naga tongue and had a fairly animated conversation. Serah was uncharacteristically charismatic, much like she had been with Gleeglum. I suppose she was trying to disarm the guide and extract any extra information she could.

Once she was done with the initial scrutiny, Serah called to me. "Come out, Glik. If Ixchel wanted to spring a trap, she would have done it by now." Serah let her spell dissipate and waved me over.

I emerged from hiding and walked over to our guide. Tinky took the opportunity to sneak in a quick, covert sniff while I introduced myself. No warning squeak. Good sign.

"Glik." I said, introducing myself with a half bow, hand to my chest. I did not take my eyes off of her for a second.

Despite our lack of shared language, she understood well enough, awkwardly returning the gesture. "Ixchel".

A soft shift of weight in my bag alerted me to Tinky's conclusions. I turned and snuck a glance at her, out of Ixchel's sight. She was hiding under everything in the bottom of my bag, shivering. Well, she wasn't warning me of danger, but she was obviously scared of our new companion.

Serah pulled my attention back to the conversation. "Ixchel has agreed to take us to the temple. Apparently, it's on the river, next to a village. I never imagined the temple would house more than a handful of naga, much less a village."

"Ikchen wa uligeg, Serah." Ixchel's voice was rich and deep, forceful enough to command, but with a soft edge to it. She had trouble with Serah's name, pronouncing it slowly and awkwardly, much like we pronounced hers.

"Fet." Serah acknowledged her, then spoke to me.

"The naga here are definitely worshippers of Khabis. That doesn't guarantee they are malicious, but it's not good. Also, Ixchel's partner was captured some time ago. She wants our help freeing her partner in exchange for her assistance as our guide."

"Inyanga." Ixchel held up her hands as though they were bound, then quickly spread them wide apart. "Inyanga, fr-ee." She stumbled on the new word but was trying hard to fit in with us already.

Serah turned to her, a quizzical expression on her face. "Inyanga tut platoksis?"

Ixchel nodded.

"Inyanga is the name of her partner. When we arrive at the village, I need you and Ixchel to stay well hidden. I will speak with the temple leaders and hopefully find the whereabouts of Inyanga. Once I'm certain they will not harm us, I will come and get you. If two days pass before I return, run."

We loaded the boat and set off. Ixchel paddled upstream with surprising ease, sticking close to the sides of the creek where the current was slower. We made excellent time compared to our days of slogging through the underbrush and the rainforest. She somehow kept the boat stable as well. No seasickness for Glik on this trip!

Serah spent some time teaching me the bare-bones basics of the naga tongue. Formally, it was known as Patalic. It was a somewhat fluid language, filled with exceptions and extensive rules, particularly around the pronunciation of certain "s" and "t" sounds. It seemed somewhat basic to understand but a total nightmare to master. She did mention that the particular dialect that Ixchel used was odd. It felt old, almost like a completely different language with the same core.

We took turns napping as we went, glad to have the opportunity. Dusk came, and we waited for our guide to pull back onto shore for camp. Hours went by until the sunlight was long gone, yet Ixchel didn't slow in the slightest.

The glow of the dual moons shined bright above us, reflecting on the streams surface. It was amazing. I shifted my shoulder bag and opened it just enough to give Tinky a view.

"Wow, when the moons are full together, it almost turns night into day!"

Tinky refused to come out but climbed over enough stuff to take a look. She was still scared of our guide. It bothered me, but Tinky had never failed to tell me of immediate danger, and she hadn't alerted me directly yet.

"Serah, how often do the moons get full at the same time?"

"I don't know, but I do know that they aren't full yet. It will probably be another few days before they reach their peak. It is rare that they both synchronize."

Serah spoke to Ixchel for a few minutes. Our guide got a stern look as they spoke. Her jaw clenched several times and she glanced skyward frequently.

Serah turned her attention back to me. "Once every five hundred and sixty-three years. The dual moons hold significant power and meaning for Ixchel's people. She says that the moons will be full three nights from now and insists we free Inyanga before then, or her gods will be enraged."

I nodded. Great, another condition added.

I pulled out my book and read some more on the "magic of words" by moonlight, then went to sleep in the boat. Ixchel apparently wasn't going to camp tonight.

I AWOKE to Serah nudging me with her foot.

"Glik, we're almost there."

I nodded, wiping the sleep from my eyes and adjusting to the morning daylight. Small columns of smoke, like those from cooking fires, wafted up behind the trees in the distance. Ixchel paddled on, rounding a bend in the river.

The village before us was massive, almost the size of a true city.

The buildings were all made of ancient stone and while many were in disrepair or overgrown by the nearby jungle, they were still impressive.

We tied the boat to a stone-lined dock and left it where we could quickly re-embark. Serah handed me her hooded cloak, hoping it would let me blend in and keep a low profile as we made our way to a central street. The villagers gave us a few sidelong glances, probably noting how oversized the cloak was, despite my attempts to fold and tie it. But most people kept their distance, shying away as we went by.

We turned a corner onto the main street of the village, and my jaw dropped at the sight of the massive boulevard. It was paved in intricately placed stone mosaics depicting various tales using only the stone's color rather than paint or enamel. Elaborate buildings ran as far as the eye could see on both sides. But none of that held my attention.

At the very end of the road was a massive, five-tiered ziggurat. It was the largest structure I had ever seen! The lowest tiers sucked in the light, built from some smokey, darkened-grey stone. The middle tiers were a polished white and black marbled pattern. But the top tier, along with the small altar on top of it, was made of a shiny black glass. The whole structure towered over the village and the jungle. I wondered how we hadn't spotted it until just now.

We walked for a good hour or two toward the ziggurat, staying close to the edge of the road so we could duck behind a building if needed. Considering the size of the road, the city felt abandoned. Only a handful of people meandered around.

As we neared the ziggurat, it became apparent why. Hundreds of villagers were crowded around the base of the structure, vying for the best spots to watch the ceremony taking place at the ziggurat's pinnacle. Someone dressed in bright, elaborately colored feathers stood there, shouting something down at the crowd. We were too far away to see or hear what was happening, but it was obviously important.

Serah looked concerned. She squinted intensely at the ziggurat and spoke without turning her gaze. "Go hide, Glik. Keep close to the boat in case you need a way out. I will meet you at the dock tomorrow night."

Serah said a few more things to Ixchel in Naga, then popped her neck, took a deep breath, and strolled down the road as if she ruled the place. I had to give her credit for confidence.

Ixchel and I ducked between a few buildings and headed back down to the river using a side street. I was wondering whether it would be best to hide by staying on the river or in one of the abandoned stone buildings, or even in the jungle, but I didn't fully trust Ixchel yet. A potentially civilized area seemed less likely to be lethal, particularly while I slept.

Ixchel noticed me looking at the boat when we reached the docks. She pointed to it and shook her head from side to side, then nodded at a small mud-brick building that was slightly larger than the others. It had smoke coming from a short chimney. Ixchel put her hand to her mouth, then rubbed her belly.

She began walking over to it before I could protest. Perhaps the locals could give us some information, hopefully without us raising suspicion. We opened the door and walked into what appeared to be an ordinary tavern. A human stood behind the bar, the only person in the room. A few tables were scattered around, arranged for patrons to sit at them on floor cushions, and a bank of seven doors surrounded the place, presumably guest rooms.

The bartender was an older, light-skinned man with whitening hair. He was wearing some heavily worn clothes of a style that I had never seen. It was not different in cut per se, but it was something I would expect from an Imperial history book. Outdated, not entirely practical, and somewhat basic, so that one set of clothes could easily fit a person of almost any size.

I opened with my customary tavern greeting. "Start us off with some food and drink!"

The man gave me an odd look but started getting the requested order ready as I sat at a table near the back of the room.

He served up some excellent, well-cooked, and moderately

seasoned fish with some sort of cheese and colorful fruit. He poured an amber beer from a clay urn and left us both two tankards instead of one. I let Tinky have a sniff and a bite before we both chowed down.

Ixchel hadn't touched her food. She was busy watching me, trying to figure something out. After a few minutes, she nodded to herself, then walked over to the barkeep. They began speaking yet another language I did not know. Many of the words were similar to Western Imperial, but it simply didn't track. The language seemed to be some offshoot that shared a common ancestor. They nodded to each other in agreement, then joined me at my table.

We sat together eating, Ixchel finally digging into her plate of fish now that the bartender had joined us. I caught a few tidbits of their conversation.

"... ziggurat... sacrifice... dreamers... two moons... power..."

I was getting frustrated. I hated not understanding anyone. There had to be some way to fix this without learning every language in the world.

Not knowing what else to do and not wanting to lose our guide in case we needed her later, I kept close to Ixchel after the meal. She left the tavern and kept to side streets until we got to another tavern. She ordered another drink and questioned the barkeep, another light-skinned human in ancient Imperial clothing. Once again, similar words popped up. "... ziggurat... sacrifice... dreamers..."

Less than an hour later, we were on the streets again, zigzagging to avoid any crowded areas as we headed to yet another tavern. Same process as before, same keywords popping up during questioning.

All day we wandered from tavern, to inn, to boarding house, to gambling den, talking to anyone who might know something. It was always the same. They gave her a few odd looks, but they seemed to accept her as one of their own. They would speak of ziggurats and sacrifice, occasionally bringing up something about dreamers. This was making me nervous. No matter how undescriptive and discreet we were being, this would leave a trail to pick up.

After a few stops, it occurred to me that most people in this town dressed quite sparingly, if not outright poorly. It was drastically different from Ixchel's well-cut hide clothes. They looked different than Ixchel too, despite being human. Ixchel had higher cheekbones, narrower eyes, and a smaller nose. They had larger, squared jaws, thinner lips, and curlier hair. Neither of them had features that matched any of the humans I had encountered before. Admittedly, I hadn't met many humans in my life, other than those in Partha.

As dusk came, Ixchel led us back to the first tavern. Speaking to the bartender, she gestured to one of the rooms and pulled a few shells off of her necklace. She handed them to the barkeep, who took them without a thought and handed Ixchel a key. That was a first. I never thought about shells being used as money. Seemed like everyone should be on the beach trying to collect more!

We shared the room, Ixchel gesturing me to sleep. I gave my bag a double tap, signaling Tinky to stay alert, then risked a short nap. Tinky would catch up as we traveled.

Ixchel didn't sleep again. She always seemed alert in her own way and did not seem to tire. She sniffed the air a lot and often squinted while looking out the small window of our room. Her movements reminded me of some type of animal that my mind just couldn't pin down.

The next morning we started off with a fine breakfast. More fish and beer, of course, but there were also eggs and some sort of yellowish grain that had been ground up and fried. It was great! I wish I had a way to get the recipe and ingredients, but the language barrier proved too great. Perhaps I should include a cookbook as a companion to my fables!

As soon as I finished, Ixchel got up and headed to the door.

"Ixchel, wait! We should stay here!"

She glanced over her shoulder once, waved for me to hurry up, then left. Grrr. Sarding, long-legged, numpty human!

We avoided the main road, but meandered closer to the temple through the side streets as Ixchel resumed her questioning from the day before. Her pace was getting faster, the conversations shorter, and each interaction was less friendly than the one before. She wasn't finding what she was looking for, and it was making her anxious.

We stumbled across a small market area. It was a tiny slice of the heavens after our trek through the jungle. Barking vendors were everywhere, but I couldn't understand most of what they said. What I did understand was the aroma of food! It was everywhere! Tinky's nose was sticking out of my shoulder bag, apparently valuing the smell of food more than her fear of Ixchel.

There were a few stalls with a variety of weaponry and other equipment almost exclusively made from a shiny black glass instead of metal. Another merchant sold varieties of green stone armor. That crap had to be heavy! More vendors peddled colorful stone amulets, shell bracelets, and golden chains! Shiny stuff was always nice and seemed to sell well in every culture.

My bag jerked slightly, catching my attention. "No, Tinky. We don't want any attention here." I didn't have to look to know what she was thinking. With her new legs, the extra mobility might have gone to her head and made her think she could get away with stealing some of that shiny stuff. We couldn't risk the heat if she failed.

Instead, I ended up buying us a skewer loaded with a variety of spiced meats while I waited for Ixchel. She finished just in time to head back and meet with Serah before nightfall. We chose a different set of side streets to return by, trying to ensure that our tracks were mostly covered. Dusk approached quickly, and Ixchel walked fast enough that I occasionally had to jog to keep up.

There were fewer people on our route back. At first I assumed this was a less popular part of town, but after a few quick encounters, I noticed that everyone vanished hastily when they spotted us. Something was wrong. Ixchel slowed and began sniffing the air cautiously, noticing something was amiss as well. Her eyes scanned the area around us as we walked.

"SQUEAK!!!"

I dropped to the ground instantly and rolled to the side, then pulled my legs back underneath me and sprinted toward the docks. I didn't know what I was running from or which direction to go, but Tinky's warning squeak had been clear and absolute. There was no time to search or question, just escape.

Opening my senses as I bolted, I heard Ixchel grunt as something soft smacked into her. An overpowering, peppery scent blasted into the air right behind me. Ixchel gagged and choked, causing me to glance back on reflex. A white-yellow cloud rolled over us, obscuring my view. My eyes burned and blurred as the dust cloud wafted around me. I turned to run further and tried to hold my breath. I failed, inhaling a lungful after just a few steps. My throat tingled and contracted as soon as the cloud crossed my nostrils. I dropped to the ground and pawed at my face, trying in vain to get the evil, burning sensation out of my eyes and nostrils.

Strong hands pulled my fingers from my face, placing a hood over my head. It helped filter out the cloud but made it harder to breathe. I started to stand but a foot kicked my legs out from under me and dropped me onto my stomach. My hands were yanked roughly behind my back. I jerked around and thrashed, blindly trying to escape. It was no use. My feet and hands were bound, and a gag was pulled into place over the hood.

I was lifted from the ground and carried. I struggled hard, but it made no difference. After a half hour of being carried, my mind cleared enough to realize I had been caught, not killed. Serah's warnings rang in my mind. The attackers had been silent, all but invisible, and quick. Despite Tinky's alert, there had been no time to escape once the trap was sprung. I wondered if it had been an ambush or if they had simply followed us faster than we had walked. It didn't matter, really. I was caught either way.

THEY CARRIED me for over an hour. I heard lots of footsteps, the sounds of people shuffling out of the way, and hushed voices talking as I was carried by. At some point, I was handed off to another person and taken into a darker, cooler place. Stone grinding against stone indicated a door of some sort, followed by the creaking of metal hinges. They dropped me onto a cold, hard floor, and cut the bonds on my hands. I quickly ripped off the gag and hood as they slammed the metal door, locking it quickly before I could do anything drastic.

I surveyed my surroundings as I worked my legs free, focusing on potential escape routes. There was a large hole in the center of the room running completely through the ceiling and the floor. Judging from the dim light coming through it from outside, the hole went all the way out the top of the building. I didn't want to think about how far down it could go.

The room itself was a large square with two doors. One was made of stone that blended in well with the wall. It was set in the room's corner, presumably where I had entered. I took a second to think about the way the light was coming in from the central hole and guessed that the door was in the northeast corner of the room. The other door was a reinforced wooden door in the middle of the eastern wall, directly across the room from me.

Eight prison cells, including my own, surrounded the central hole in a big circle. From above, it probably looked like a pinwheel with the hole as the center hub and the walls of the cells making the spokes and outer wheel. In this configuration prisoners could see the light coming in from above, as well as the darkness below. They could touch the sunlight at midday by simply reaching through the bars in the back of their cell. This place was unnecessarily cruel. It gave prisoners hope, letting them see and touch the freedom they could not have.

The cell walls were built with metal bars and large, well-maintained locks. Each one had a cot with restraints on it and manacles bolted to the bars near the central hole. A small bucket in the corner appeared to be for refuse. Compared to goblin prisons, this was relatively comfortable looking, but far more difficult to escape.

The walls of the room caught my eye. The colors were hard to see in the dim light, but there were pictures and hieroglyphs all over the walls depicting stories of some sort. Some of the pictures involved what appeared to be naga, but most of them seemed to tell the story of a pixie queen. After noticing a few depicting torture, my curiosity shifted back to my current predicament.

I was not alone in this room. Three strong humans were conversing by my cell, presumably the guards or jailors. They spoke in the naga tongue, and despite looking like the villagers outside, each had some trait that betrayed their true nature. They weren't human at all, they were naga. One of them had a forked tongue like Serah's, and another's eyes narrowed to vertical, catlike slits when he looked at the light. The last had patches of scales on her neck and arms. I did not want to find out if they all had fangs.

There were five prisoners, including myself. My cell was presumably facing east, closest to the wooden door in the eastern wall. In the northeast cell, Serah lay on her cot, unbound and visibly unharmed, sound asleep. Her cell shared a wall with mine and was the closest cell to the stone door in the northeast corner of the room.

In the northmost cell, sharing a wall with Serah's, there was an older lady, also fast asleep. She had a curved spine, a hooked nose, and grey hair coming out of her ears. Her wrinkled skin didn't hide her high cheekbones and sharp features. She was also somewhat fat, which made me think she hadn't been here for very long.

The northwest and west cells were empty. But directly across from Serah, in the southwest cell, there was a strange-looking woman in threadbare rags. She resembled Ixchel in many ways, but she looked sick and starved. She was almost skeletal, no muscle tone at all. I could also smell her from my cell. If I had to guess, she hadn't woken up in days, perhaps weeks; sleeping in her own filth.

The southernmost cell was empty too. But the southeast cell, which shared a wall with me, held a woman that appeared much like the naga in the room. Human, but with scaled patches of skin that gave away her heritage. She wore robes like some sort of religious figure and wore a gold necklace adorned with the symbol of a blackened sun set in a flame-colored jewel. A blackened sun! That same symbol had been on the obsidian stele back at the Stone'N!

"Squeak." Tinky's soft voice drew my attention.

She was probably still in my shoulder bag. Where did they put my stuff? I glanced around the room. My travel bag and shoulder bag sat in plain view against the outer wall, right across from my cell. Serah's gear was along the wall across from her cell too. Across from every occupied cell, sitting against the outer walls, were haphazard piles of gear. Why would the naga make it so easy for a prisoner to grab their gear if they escaped? I glanced back at the hole in the ceiling. They want their prisoners to see their things, their old life. Once again, the lingering torture of hope.

I gave Tinky the "it's okay but stay hidden" signal.

Tck, tck, tck.

Best if she remained in the bag until I figured out how to get out of here.

The sound of grinding stone snapped my attention to the corner of the room, where the stone door slowly slid open. Screams and grunts from a rough struggle poured through the opening. Ixchel was dragged through the door, bound like I had been, but she had much more strength and was not afraid to use it. Four people, presumably more naga, slowly wrangled her over to the west cell directly across from me.

They slammed her face first into the bars at the back of the cell and clamped a manacle around her throat, securing her in. Two more cuffs were placed around her ankles, just above the rope bindings, ensuring she couldn't kick. With two naga on each arm, and help from the three jailors that were already there, they untied her arms and secured them with manacles to the bars as well. They cut off the gag and removed her hood last. Ixchel cursed, spit, and snapped her teeth at anything she could, but with the collar pinning her to the bars, it made little difference. She was facing away from them and securely bound.

They locked the door and flung her belongings into a pile across from her cell, just like they had done with everyone else's. Ixchel's assailants made their way back to the door, each one limping, favoring an appendage, or rubbing some part of their body in pain. Ixchel had made quite an impression. The stone door ground shut behind them, blending in almost perfectly with the wall as it shuddered to a stop.

The three jailors said something to each other, then separated. Two of them sat down at a gaming table in the northeast corner and began playing a game with a large board and two piles of colored stones. The other casually went through the wooden door across from my cell. I caught a quick glimpse of the hall behind the door. It appeared to be living quarters or a preparation area, as there was a table with food on it.

I sat down and tried to gather my thoughts. It had been a rough day. My face was still a mess, my eyes were watery, and drying snot coated my mouth, chin, and really everything below my nostrils. At least my breathing was returning to normal. Looking across the hole, I could see that Ixchel's face was much worse off than my own. Her eyes were just as watery, but she also had blood all over her mouth, and an angry red and black bruise had formed over one eye, close to the bridge of her nose. She appeared to be breathing fine, albeit much faster than normal. A bubble of blood and snot expanded and contracted in her nostril. She looked terrible, but she was still terrifying.

Her eyes rarely left the two guards playing at the table. A low, growling rumble escaped her throat. It was a constant reminder to the guards that she was still a threat, despite being bound. She sounded and acted like a caged animal.

That would be a great distraction. I flopped down on the cot and propped my head up to look at my shoulder bag. My position gave a semi-occupied appearance to the guards without letting them see my face. I hoped between that, Ixchel's growling, and their own game of stones, they wouldn't notice what happened next.

It was time to check on Tinky.

Tck, tck.

I clicked my tongue twice and watched my bag. The flap jiggled ever so slightly once, then again.

Tck

I clicked once more, acknowledging Tinky's signal. She was fine. We may have to try out those leg lock picks soon.

I got back up and faced Ixchel. She looked me over as I stood there, trying to think of something to say. There wasn't much we could do for communication. She didn't understand my words, and in her current bound state we couldn't use signals either. Bah! Frustrating communication barriers!

The wooden door slammed behind me, announcing the return of the third jailor. She walked up to my cell casually, opened one of several small bags she was carrying, and reached in. I turned and looked at her, my curiosity getting the better of me. Quicker than I could react, the jailor chucked a handful of sandy dust in my face.

"Pfft! You snarfliggin jobby! What was that for?"

She laughed and made her way around the cells toward Ixchel.

I tried to wipe the grittiness from my already tortured eyes. Bad enough that I had been gassed by some kind of fire powder earlier, but hitting me in the face with sand right as I recovered was low! As I cleared the largest chunks of grit, my eyelids grew heavy. A wave of drowsiness crashed into me. Every bit of exhaustion from today's earlier struggles crept up on me and pounced all at once. I flopped down hard on my cot, my arms growing lethargically slow with their attempts at wiping my eyes. They soon failed me as I toppled backwards onto the cot, still blinking back tears. I closed my eyes and gave up. Let my eyes take care of themselves. Just for a minute. Or two. Maybe a quick nap would help. Zzzzzz...

CHAPTER 12

GOBLIN DREAMS & PIXIE QUEENS

Shining magic lights illuminated every inch of the royal ballroom in fantastic golds, whites, and occasional hues of blue or green. Massive tapestries and banners hung from towering columns. Gargantuan tables formed a U-shape banquet, with the royal family positioned at the head table. Her highness sat tall, elaborate jeweled crown high upon her head. Her face was familiar, sharp, almost pixie-like, but I couldn't place it with a name. Active couples moved gracefully across the ballroom floor, keeping time with a well-trained symphony orchestra. This was the very definition of a party for the high-born humans of the Western Empire.

A small girl approached me wearing a fine silken dress with silvery lace. "Come here, Glik! Come dance with me!"

"I don't know this dance, miss."

"Oh, that's fine. I'll teach you." She said with a devilish little smirk.

Her hand grabbed mine and jerked me onto the dance floor. She showed me the steps once, then flung me into the midst of it all. I got one step right, two wrong, then stumbled into her and another couple. She giggled at me and covered her mouth with a gloved hand.

"It's ok, Glik. Everyone starts off bad."

She grabbed my hands again, went through the steps again quickly, then threw me back to the wolves. Unfortunately, the steps had changed slightly as the dance progressed. I misstepped again, tripped over another couple, and went sprawling onto the floor.

Dozens of aristocrats snickered and pointed at me with half-covered mouths. Public humiliation from the most powerful opinion makers of the land, how grand.

The girl was relentless. "It's ok, Glik, let's do it again. I'm sure you'll get it right this time." Her smile bored into me, compelling me to obey despite the impish glint in her eyes.

She guided me back to my feet, and we took our starting positions yet again. We repeated this effort once, twice, and again, over and over. For hours upon hours I stumbled, failed, and was mocked, unable to pull myself away.

At last, one final crash to the floor brought me close to the food.

"Sorry, miss, but I am famished. Let me rest a bit."

Her smile shifted into a pout. "Very well, Glik, I suppose I'll have to find someone ELSE to dance with. *Someone I can humiliate worse.*" Her last few words had been mumbled quietly. She must not have known how well goblins can hear.

The feast tables were massive. Dozens of full food trays and multiple fountains of various refreshing liquids were everywhere. All of it had been prepared by the top gourmet talents of the empire and promised a rare glimpse at the elegant tastes of high society. I daintily grabbed a plate and mimicked the ridiculous etiquette I had seen from the surrounding nobility.

The first tray held a variety of leafy greens. I didn't like any of them. In goblin cooking, green coloring on food was often a sign that it had spoiled. The next tray had some carrots, celery, tomatoes, sprouts, and other vegetables. A third held large turnips, onions, and eggplants. The next, sour melons, dried grapes, and hard, stale bread heels. They were ALL like this. No meats, no fish, no mushrooms of any kind. The soups and stews were just as bad. This banquet was exclusively disgusting to a goblin! Skrag-gafrakt!

Fine, I'd get drunk then. Should be easy to do on an empty stomach. I vengefully discarded my empty plate next to the table of green nastiness and headed toward the fountain with red liquid and silver goblets. Wine should do the trick. I grabbed a goblet, ignored etiquette, and dunked it right in. The liquid smelled heavily of grapes, but some odd sweetness tainted the scent. I took a deep draw, looking forward to the satisfying bouquet of flavors.

PFFFT!!

Grape juice!? With other fruits mingled in and maybe extra sweeteners? Is this that junk the humans call punch!? It was so sweet that it made me gag. I put the goblet back down and shuffled over to the next fountain. It was another type of punch! This one based on some disgustingly sour apple flavor.

I spotted a third potential flavor and braced myself for disappointment. This fountain was different, heavier, with clear liquid bursting out of its top in a delicate dance that sprawled across several ornate levels before reaching the pool at its base.

"Let it be rum, vodka, grain alcohol, anything worth drinking!" I grabbed a goblet and took a cautious swig. Of all the idiotic things to serve at a banquet! It was water!

The fourth and final fountain sprayed four jets of a fine amber liquid over the head of a small, but exceptionally well-carved, angel statue. It had drinking horns instead of goblets or cups. This had to be it. This had to be some kind of beer, ale, mead, piss liquor, anything! Everyone in the room was merry and tipsy acting. Surely they weren't sober. I filled a horn and chugged, swallowing hard. My teeth clenched as my tongue registered the flavors. Apple cider. Regular, non-alcoholic, apple cider. BAH!

I dropped the horn where I stood, not caring about the mess. Let the servants clean and the nobility snark. Maybe it would give someone a hint about their food selection.

A finely uniformed man approached me as I fumed about the

dining situation. He spared a sidelong glance at the puddle of cider on the floor, closed his eyes with a shiver to ignore it, then spoke to me. "You are Glik, I presume? The famous author of Glik's Fables?"

I puffed up my chest. "Of course!" Perhaps this night would not be a total waste after all!

"Then please accompany me to my table. My fellows and I would love to have someone of your talents and stature in our presence. There is so much to discuss."

I nodded and followed. This was a good chance to observe their habits, to learn how to mingle with the rich and famous. I would need these skills to fit in as my fame continued to grow.

We arrived at a small side table with four other people, all dressed in similarly decorated uniforms or finely tailored robes with expensive trim and accessories.

The largest man at the table held a long pipe and blew four perfect smoke rings as he watched us approach. He bellowed at us just before we took our seats. "Bartholomew! Who is your esteemed guest?"

My host replied. "Chauncey, how many times must I remind you? My title is General Flakisbur."

The large man rolled his eyes and cleared his throat. "Ahem. My apologies to you, my esteemed, Holy, Lord Highness Flakisbur!"

The general sneered, then gestured to me. "May I introduce the famous Glik! This little creature authored the text for this month's 'Intrigue and Analysis' book group. I hope the four of you have finished reading it before our discussion next week. 'Glik's Fables', as it were."

A hawk-faced, weaselly fellow gave me a condescending grin. "A goblin! Now that's something I did not expect to see. I had understood this to be an original text, not a transcription of oral tales."

One of the robed figures spoke next. "Count Lilithorne, I refuse to believe someone with such pure heritage as yourself would fall prey to pretentious stereotypes such as goblin illiteracy."

PFFFT! The other robed figure sprayed his drink all over the table.

"Bwahaha! Proctinus has gotcha there, Lili! Ya got the finest bloodline in the kingdom, and of course ya never, ever wield it over anyone's head. Unless, of course, they ain't a Lilithorne! How's that bastard son of yers anyway? Half dwarf is he? Or was that half orc? I never could keep track of yer taste in women."

The hawk-faced count turned red and stabbed a finger at the commenter. "Origus, you crude mutt of a noble, I will not have my name tarnished at such a "

The general interrupted them with a deep, commanding voice. "GENTLEMEN! We have a guest. Let us conduct ourselves accordingly. Personal disputes shall be dealt with at a more appropriate time. Agreed?"

The men settled down, grabbing more drinks and lighting more pipes. I sat down in the human-sized chair. My eyes were barely over the edge of the table.

The large man, Chauncey, took it upon himself to notice. "Servant! Servant! A children's adjusting chair for our esteemed guest!"

I suppressed my glare. It was bad enough to be stuck staring at butts all day, but to be treated as a child on top of it. Grrr.

The robed elven figure, Proctinus, spoke again in his lighter, more graceful speech. "Count Illariate, I have heard that your wife has taken issue with your latest contracts. As an elf, I must agree with her assessment. This latest batch of merchandise is far from a defensive preparation."

Chauncey, having been addressed by his formal title, rolled his eyes at the accusation. "And that is precisely why the woman is not allowed to have any interaction with my business holdings. If I was concerned about where my merchandise was used, I'd never turn a profit, and we wouldn't have these fine conversations, Kilwe. Now, I am curious what makes you think elves have anything to do with it."

The general interjected, raising his hand and glancing between the two. "Illariate, you know as well as I do that your wife has a soft spot for beauty and loathes war. If she so much as suspected you were making shoes out of fluffy animals or supplying hats to conscripted soldiers, she'd make a fuss. Duke Proctinus, you should know better than to assume this is anything but baseless rumor."

Origus leaned over to Lilithorne and whispered something in his ear. The hawk-faced noble curled his face up in disgust, causing Origus to belt out an excessively loud, obnoxious laugh.

Duke Proctinus, the elf, took the chance to shift topics again. "What is it, Lilithorne? Did the baron remind you of your last quarterly earnings? Quite the disappointment, if I recall?"

The hawk-faced count did not hesitate to deflect the accusation. "Speaking of disappointments, Proctinus, what is this I hear of your daughter's betrothal? Marrying her off to a mercenary, and a commoner at that?"

The general, ever controlling, thwarted this new wave of attacks as well. "A mercenary is nothing to shun at gentlemen, nor is a commoner. Must I remind you of my own humble beginnings?"

PFFT! Origus blasted another mouthful of cider all over the table.

"HUMBLE! Flakisbur, the only thing humble about yer beginnings is that they involved bumping uglies just like the rest of us!"

The table erupted in laughter. Illariate joined Origus with full-throated, bellowing guffaws. Lilithorne and Proctinus both covered their mouths, bouncing their shoulders as they snickered. Even the general smirked at the lewd commentary.

A servant arrived and switched out my chair. Despite my instinct to protest, it did its job, elevating me so my face was above the table.

Lilithorne filled the silence that followed the group's collective merriment with more snarkiness. "Perhaps, general, you can tell us another of your war stories. They all seem to involve your superior supervision from the rear of the army."

The five of them continued in this pattern incessantly. I couldn't have gotten a word in if I had tried. Pointless discussions about the relationships of some other nobles, how the family intrigue was going, different slights and public blunders that each of them had committed, etc. They then dove into a discussion regarding the intricacies of placing a ceremonial sword on the right hip compared to the left hip. Hour after hour went by, and I learned nothing.

I buried my face in my hands. I couldn't leave. I wanted to. I mentally tried to. Something kept me there, rooted to the spot, bored beyond all imagination, yet compelling me to stay and listen.

Finally, the queen stood and announced an end to the festivities. Whatever spell held me in this nauseating discussion broke when the men stood and left the table. I chugged a goblet of water and hurried out of the room. This was all too strange for my liking.

THE NEXT ROOM was a large throne room where they were holding court. I looked at the judge and did a double take. It was Serah! She was dressed in some odd, ceremonial robe and sitting in a tall-backed chair on a raised platform next to the main throne.

She waved cheerily as I entered, lacking her usual reserved manner. Odd. "Over here, Glik. I need you to take notes for me. We have to record what these people have done and what sentence they have merited. You'll be the royal writer for the day!" Something in my mind nudged me to obey, despite the suspicious mannerisms of my companion.

I stepped over to a little desk next to her chair that had parchment, ink, and quill already prepared. A small man in rags and chains was dragged to the bottom of Serah's platform.

Serah cleared her throat, then put on a comically overdone serious expression. "Failure to obey article 16 of Her Majesty's Treatise on the Amiability of Animals Housed Outside of Commercial Structures. Five months of hard labor. Next!"

I wrote quickly and mechanically. What in Rikarak's jugular was the "treatise on the amiability of... blah blah blah"? I didn't have time to figure it out as the next subject was already being led up for Serah's judgement.

This one was a well-decorated officer of the military. He spoke before he had permission. "I demand an appeal!"

Serah didn't hesitate for an instant. "Appeal granted and scheduled for five days from now. Charges for contempt of court, interruption of proceedings, and flagrant disregard of decorum, as per article 574-6137 of Her Majesty's Acts of Court Proceedings, seven months of imprisonment. To be carried out immediately. Please see that you aren't late for your appeal, or the sentence will be subject to a mandatory minimum of five years hard labor for repeated offense. Next!"

The man's eyes bulged out of his head in surprise. But he kept his mouth shut as he was led away. I scribbled down everything that was said, my wrist already aching from the speed of the writing.

A third person was led in for Serah's judgement. This one was a stout-looking gnome, skin stained in all variety of colors. He wore a soot-stained leather apron and goggles.

Serah pointed at the gnome and snarled. "You, Mr. Icktingles. I don't want to hear a word from you. You know EXACTLY what you've done. Guards! Wait until low tide, then take him to the water's edge and bury him up to his neck in the sand."

The gnome dropped his head and started sobbing. My hands worked meticulously, recording everything without my brain realizing what they were doing.

Next up was a woman with a silk dress and her small child.

"Countess Delamrit. Your little demon in children's clothing has caused us all quite a bit of trouble, hasn't it? But it is still a child, is it not? Thereby, you shall be personally responsible for the destruction of seventeen buildings and the death of six cattle. Per affluent precedence regarding merchant disputes, article 17-934 of the Queen's Legislation regarding Outsider Commerce, you are hereby to pay double the market value of such destroyed estates. Should you not have such compensation readily available, the court will direct the sale of your own estates until such funds have been levied. Best of luck."

She broke her stern expression to smirk and give a little wave to the child. It grinned back with a devious little expression.

The woman left with a huff, jerking the childlike figure by the arm behind her. I couldn't help but stare as they left. The "child" had a long, devil-like tail.

I hurriedly scratched the court's verdict onto the parchment as another person was led into the court, a large, armored dwarf. The prisoner was bound with chains and covered in mud. He jerked his arms free of the three guards that escorted him and spat towards the throne.

Serah's expression grew sharp, her brows knotting with anger. "BAILIFF! How dare a prisoner be presented to this court in such a state! I can smell his filth from here! Have the orderly responsible for this farce whipped publicly. Fifty lashes for gross insubordination per ordinance 976 of Her Majesty's 'Articles on Prisoner Etiquette'. Return with the prisoner tomorrow once he is presentable."

The dwarf grinned and gave a sly wink to the soldier on his left before they dragged him out of the room.

We continued in this manner, case after case, for what seemed like days. Each defendant was brought before the stand and judged without a single word allowed in their defense. The pain in my hands got worse and worse. My hands were stiff and bleeding before Serah took notice.

She let out a disappointed sigh. "I expected better of you, Glik. I thought you would enjoy being the royal writer. Very well, let's take a break. Guards, bring Glik today's specialty."

A silver platter was brought out and set before me. Fine cutlery was placed on either side and finally, an actual glass of wine! I gulped down the glorious vintage before lifting the domed cloche from the platter. The visual before me kicked my mind hard. There were more hideous vegetables lining the edges of the single serving of meat. A well-roasted rat, still on the spit, with hind legs that had been replaced with a set of scalded metal appendages.

The scene melted away into darkness as my mind realized that this was not real. I was dreaming. It was time to wake up.

A small, glowing speck of silver appeared in the darkness, growing as it came closer. A pulsing sound carried to my ears like the flapping of wings. The smell of fresh rain blew gently by my nose. After a moment, the silvery glow settled, then dimmed enough for me to see what caused it.

She was half my size, maybe less, and had gorgeous silver-lined dragonfly wings with violet-tinged webbing sprouting from her back. Long, leaf-green hair flowed to her knees, with just a few lines of silver betraying her age. Dark, emerald eyes pierced through me as she looked me over and awaited my reaction. Her long, silver dress flowed around her legs, swaying in the breeze as she hovered in front of me. There was an odd harshness to her beauty, something I couldn't pin down that made her visage painful more than pleasant.

After a slight hesitation, she took a deep draw from a silver chalice in her right hand. A hint of scarlet on her dainty little fangs was enough to know that she was drinking blood. Even so, she licked her lips, coloring them a deep crimson, just to be sure I knew.

I couldn't help myself. "A bit dramatic, don't you think?"

She leveled her harshly sharp features at me and huffed like a child before she spoke. "You have shown me so much, 'little story-teller', yet still you resist. My people will have to prepare you some more before our next little play date."

She reached in to a small bag at her side and brought a handful of sparkling dust to her mouth. With a mischievous grin, she gently blew the dust in my face. At first it smelled of exotic spices and flowers, but the feeling was quickly replaced by the same burning sensation as the crap I'd been drugged with in the streets. I frantically pawed at my nose and started wheezing.

She laughed with a high-pitched, bell-like giggle. "See you tomorrow, Glik."

CHAPTER 13
SMELLS LIKE WET DOG

I forced an eye open, straining against the yellow-green mucus that glued it closed, and got a magnificent view of the floor for my trouble. My body laid halfway off the cot, one leg on top of it, the other dangling in the air. Most of my weight pressed on my right shoulder and my face, pinning my arm at an odd angle. There was a small puddle of blood, snot, and drool on the floor where it had leaked from all the orifices in my head.

I slowly rolled over onto my back, dragging my leg off the cot. Good grief, was I sore! I stretched a bit, popped a few joints, then got onto all fours and wiped off my face. Clumps of sand had pooled into the gunk around my irritated eyes. It felt like my whole eye socket was filled with abrasive grit. I needed water, but there was nothing around.

I gave up and got into a sitting position on the cot. The old lady was missing, but the rest of the prisoners were fast asleep. Ixchel was still chained to the side of her cell with the manacle-like collar around her neck. She was going to have a serious neck cramp when she woke up! Two of the guards were playing a game of stones in the corner again. The third jailor was nowhere in sight.

I took a few minutes to let the grogginess of sleep slip away and studied the hieroglyphs on the walls as I regained my senses. The stories made more sense now. I didn't know much of pixies or of naga history, but what I did know matched up with the pictures on the wall. There was a pixie queen of sorts, a goddess of inspiration and dreams. The stories showed darkness and destruction, the fall of some civilization. Seems that this goddess of dreams fell into despair and her nature changed with it, creating a goddess of nightmares.

How was I going to get out of this? I needed a decent distraction. A plan would be even better. Admittedly, this wasn't my first time in a cell. But it was the first time I had been in a well-constructed cell with competent guards. I could have Tinky pick the lock, but it would do little good if I was spotted or if they noticed Tinky hanging off the door, jiggling her mechanical foot in the keyhole. Maybe if Serah woke up she could use some magic to help us out. Perhaps invisibility, timed with Tinky's lock picking? I wasn't so sure about that. Tinky was small but still noticeable. She also smelled like a rat and made little tapping noises when her metal feet hit hard surfaces.

I perked my ears up and glanced at the soft glow of twilight coming through the hole in the ceiling. There was a noise coming from outside. It sounded like a large crowd. My suspicion was confirmed a few seconds later when a booming voice, speaking in the village's language, made a declaration that I couldn't decipher. The crowd roared and cheered.

A wet "smack" accompanied a wet sensation on my hand as a glob of spit splattered all over it. I looked around for the source and found her glaring at me. Serah had rolled over on her cot so that she could face me, back to the guards and face out of their view. She seemed impatient, like she had been trying to get my attention for a while.

I got up, went over to her side of my cell, then sat down; putting my legs between the bars so that my feet dangled over the hole in the floor. I leaned my head against the bars between our cells, putting my head so close to Serah's mouth that I could feel her breath tickling the tuft of hair on my ear.

Serah whispered to me. "Any ideas how to get out of here?"

I made my best imitation of Tinky in a whisper. "Squeak."

She understood, quickly developing the start of a plan. "Tinky can pick our locks?"

I nodded discreetly.

"Wait until darkness falls. The guards will probably be distracted by the double moon celebration. They might even leave. If they do, we'll break the other prisoners free as well. They might keep the guards distracted. I think the one by Ixchel is Inyanga. She hasn't been awake at all yet. She might not be able to wake if she's been here too long."

She gave me a knowing look that said what I was thinking. If she can't wake up, we leave her. Ixchel too if she won't leave Inyanga behind. Survival first. Maybe they'd make a decent distraction?

Serah rolled over and pretended to sleep again. I kicked my legs playfully over the edge of the hole and started tossing pebbles down it absentmindedly.

That irked one of the guards. "Hey! Knock that off! You're lucky the ceremony is tonight, otherwise the high priest would be working you over already!"

Interesting. That particular guard was no fun at all but easy to irritate. It wouldn't do to taunt her right now, though. Taunting worked as a distraction, but it usually came at the cost of a sound beating and increased attention later. I'd wait. If they didn't leave like Serah said, I'd annoy them enough to keep their focus on me while Tinky opened Serah's cell. It seemed like a risky maneuver that had a slim chance of success. I'd have to perform magnificently to keep them from noticing Serah leaving the cell right next to mine. They might use me as a meat shield when Serah picked up her flail. This was a crappy plan. Those numpty guards better go get drunk and celebrate!

A few minutes later, the priestess in the cell next to me woke from her slumber and sat up.

"Ooow, my head!"

She groaned and looked around groggily, wiping the sandy gunk out of her eyes as she tried to regain her senses. A look of recognition washed over her face.

"Oh for the love of flaming serpents, I'm still here!" She put her hands over her face and flopped back down on the cot with a huff of exasperation.

The guards snickered at her.

Night came and the crowd outside began chanting, "Kha-bis, Kha-bis, Kha-bis".

A commanding voice carried over the crowd, silencing them. The man, presumably the high priest, chanted something I could not understand. His final words roared into the air, and a thunderous cheer erupted from the crowd.

The guards opened the cell next to Serah and stood in it, staring upward to see and hear as much as they could. They began laughing as soon as they heard the crowd cheering.

A few drops of something fell from above, passing through the hole in the ceiling and the hole in the floor. Then more drops, faster and faster, until the liquid rained down. It reeked of copper and rust. I held out my hand, catching a few drops as the torrent slowed, mere seconds after it started. The dull red color confirmed what my nose already knew. Blood.

I looked at Serah quizzically. She was still laying on her cot, but her eyes were open, watching me. She gave the barest hint of a nod, trying to avoid detection with the guards so close to her, but still confirming my suspicion. They were making sacrifices as part of the dual moon festival.

A low growl drew my attention. Ixchel was giving a not-so-subtle threat to the guards again, but there was something different about it this time. Her nostrils opened and closed rapidly, drinking in the coppery flavor of the blood in the air. Her bloodshot eyes were locked onto the guards, alert and wild. The normal look of humanity behind them was gone.

The guards barely noticed. They were chanting along with the crowd. One of them held a reflective brass mirror out so they could see directly up the shaft through the hole in the ceiling.

This was it. With Ixchel's growls, their chanting, and the mirror distracting their vision, I doubted I'd get a better chance. Time for Tinky.

Tck. Tck.

A light shuffle inside my shoulder bag opened it just enough for a beady little eye to shine through the opening. I walked over to my cell door and blocked the guards' sight lines to the lock. I pointed to the lock, then gestured to Serah's, followed by the priestess's next to us. The bag jiggled slightly in acknowledgement. Freeing the priestess was an added risk, but my curiosity overrode my objections. Her amulet matched one of the symbols on the stele, which meant she might know more about it and what it was for.

I turned my back to the lock, giving me a good view of the guards who were still watching the mirror from the old lady's open cell. Another chant came from outside, followed by screams and a cheer. More red rain poured down, drenching the guard's mirror and drawing a renewed vigor from Ixchel's growling.

Sccrrrccch, sccrreeeach,

The faint sounds of metal scratching metal sent a shiver down my spine. Tinky was at it, but this was her first time using her new legs as lock picks when it mattered. We had practiced at Gleeglum's, but this was different. Rear legs were not optimal for control, and she was hanging on to the bars with her front paws. Luckily, no one else heard enough to draw their attention, and the rusty scent of blood was too great for Tinky's scent to make any difference.

Ten minutes later, a heavy click sounded Tinky's success. One guard cocked his head slightly, but the cheering of the crowd drew his attention back to the hole in the ceiling. A soft *click-click, click-click* tapping sounded as Tinky moved on to Serah's cell. She was quiet enough for now, but we would need to do something about that noise later.

I glanced at Serah. She was still watching me. I smiled, winked, and gave a subtle nod toward the lock on my door. She took the hint, got up, and leaned against the door of her cell, blocking the guards' view of the lock.

Five minutes went by before Serah's cell clicked free. Another torrent of blood streamed down from above, drawing more celebration from the crowd outside, drowning out the heavy "thunk" of the lock mechanism releasing. Tinky's timing was impeccable. I wondered if she was intentionally waiting for the noise.

I shifted position in my cell, trying hard to discreetly block the guards' view as Tinky snuck her way toward the priestess. Serah narrowed her eyes at me when she noticed what Tinky was doing. I ignored her. She'd thank me for the information if we survived this.

Unfortunately, I couldn't block the guards' view of the priestess's lock terribly well. I was too short, and it was too far away. The priestess herself was lying on the cot with her face still buried in her hands. I'd have no luck getting her attention to help without alerting the guards too.

The high priest overhead had relaxed the pace of sacrifices and was giving a long sermon. I suppose the pinnacle of the celebration was approaching. Guess that meant the moons were reaching their peak fullness soon. Too bad that also meant there was less distraction. The guards were getting bored.

The guard holding the mirror pulled it back into the cell and began wiping some of the blood off of it with her shirt. The man popped his neck and stretched, looking around as he did so.

"Thunk!"

The sound of the priestess's lock popping in place was deafening in my ears. My heart leapt up my throat as one guard's eyes snapped to the source of the sound.

"What the!?"

The guard raced out of the cell. His footsteps were enough

warning that Tinky scurried fast through the cell bars over to me, scuttling up my leg and hiding under my shirt near the small of my back. The other guard followed him, shuffling to get her keys off of her belt.

"What's that rat doing, goblin? Pet of yours?"

I backed up reflexively. This was going to hurt. I hope Serah made her move soon.

The guard was stumbling to pick the correct key for my lock when the other guard's demeanor took a drastic shift. He cocked his eyebrows in confusion first, but they quickly shot wide at whatever he was looking at. He shakily tapped the other guard on her shoulder, causing her to look up and stop messing with the keys.

At first I thought they were staring at me, but no. Their eyes were looking above my head, across the cells to Ixchel's face. I realized Ixchel had stopped growling. Metal groaned and strained as I turned around.

Ixchel's face was red with exertion, muscles tight and clenching. Her hands shook as she gripped the bars, pulling them hard enough that they bent ever so slightly.

Light from the full dual moons above crept slowly toward her. And touched.

POP!

"RRRRAAAAAAAAAAHHHH!!!"

The blood drained from my face at her feral scream. She contorted in rage and pain, golden eyes fixating on the guards with an untamed hatred as she fought her restraints. Her veins pulsed visibly under her skin, shifting and contorting like worms.

CRACK! POP!

Her joints contorted wildly, causing her to grunt and scream in terrifying agony. Coarse black hair began sprouting from her skin as bone and muscle grew, tearing apart the seams of her clothing. The manacles which had fit a few seconds before were now biting into her flesh, far too tight.

"GGGRRRAAAAAA!"

With a vicious jerk, Ixchel bent the bars inward. She then yanked back brutally, popping the chain link between the bar and her wrist restraints. Her muscles at this point were triple their original size.

The guards panicked, rushing away from my cell as fast as their feet could carry them. They dashed to the stone exit door, sliding it open and stumbling over each other in the process.

PING!

"RRRRROOOOAAAAARR!"

Ixchel had popped the neck restraint off. She began tearing at the iron manacles on her wrists and ankles using claws that were not there a few minutes ago. She ripped into her own flesh as she did, her frenzy overwhelming rational thought. The manacles gave out long before her rage. As soon as they did, her joints deformed sickeningly. The flesh on her wrists knitted itself back together in seconds as her body continued to grow into some tortured monstrosity.

SNAP!

Her jaw unhinged, sticking out at a grotesque angle as it elongated chaotically into a snout. Razor-sharp, predatory fangs emerged, turning her human snarl into a bloodthirsty maw. She dropped to the floor as the transition finished. Her giant, black-furred body paused, breathing deeply, slowly recovering.

"HAAAAROOOOOOOO!!!"

A hand grabbed my shoulder as Ixchel's howl raised every hair on my body in alarm. Serah's hushed yet hurried voice whispered harshly in my ear.

"Now!"

I ran out of the cell, grabbed my gear, and strapped up as quickly as I could with Tinky scurrying back into my shoulder bag. Serah made her way to the stone door and started opening it, trying in vain to stay quiet.

I opened the priestess's cell and tugged on her pant leg, beckoning her to follow. Her hands trembled, but she followed me anyway, eager to be anywhere that wasn't close to Ixchel.

She mumbled under her breath in a panic as we headed to the

door. "Oh crap, oh crap, oh holy maiden, get us the sarding crap out of here!" Her high, melodious voice didn't fit the panic in her movements at all.

Heavy breathing drew my attention back to the cells. Inyanga was shifting fitfully in her sleep. A deep growl rumbled in her throat as her body began to jerk and spasm. The moonlight had reached her exposed foot.

The three of us pushed the door hard, trying to be quiet but failing miserably.

"HAAAAROOOOOOO!"

Ixchel's second howl pierced through us, drowning out all rational thought with a primal fear that screamed RUN! The bustling noise of the crowd outside ceased immediately, replaced by a deafening silence. Ixchel, now a fully transformed lupine creature, turned to us, golden eyes burning with ferocity. Her nostrils flared as she sniffed the air. Her eyes narrowed as she sniffed again, turning her nose up toward the hole in the ceiling.

"NAAAAAAAAGGGAAAAAAAA!!!"

The priestess gave a high-pitched squeak of terror. "Go! Go! Go! Sard it all, GO! I don't want to die here!"

We squeezed through the door while it was still half open, stumbling over each other in a rush.

Clang! Clang! Clang!

"AAAAGGGGGGH!!!"

Metallic banging sounds followed us through the door, along with a new, tortured voice roaring in agony. Inyanga was shifting too!

A spiral stairwell led us upward to a wooden door. Serah yanked hard on it, to no avail. Locked.

The priestess threw up her head in exasperation, struggling to keep quiet. "So dead, so very dead. Wolf meat, dog chow. I really don't want to be turned into poop!"

"Tinky, you had better make this quick!"

She popped out of my shoulder bag with blinding speed, bouncing off of Serah's shoulder and to the door handle. She hung off of it with her forelegs and began working her lock picks furiously, but she was off balance and didn't have a way to hold her weight up and still get a good angle on the lock. I quickly grabbed her around the waist, giving her the extra support she needed.

Click. Click click. Click, ting!

"Wow, Tinky. Less than ten seconds!"

She bounded back into my bag as Serah poked her head out, quickly scanning for any guards.

"Empty hall, doors on both ends. Let's hope this isn't a maze."

We sprinted to the closest door; stealth be damned.

EERRRNNNGG

"HAROOO!"

"HAAAARRROOOOOO!!!"

Metal screeched and two horrifying howls echoed from the stairwell behind us as we reached the door at the end of the hall. It opened easily, revealing a small guardroom with a large, wide-open stone door to the outside. A single guard stood in the doorway, staring upward toward the top of the ziggurat.

She jumped as we entered. "Oneka! Tota ri tut rasi!"

Serah bared her fangs with a hiss, yanked her bladed flail free, and charged, taking advantage of the surprise. The guard leveled her spear across her body defensively. Serah adjusted her aim and threw her full weight behind her flail, attacking with an overhead chop. The flail's handle struck the shaft of the spear hard. But the flail's head pivoted on its chain, whipping over the spear shaft with all the momentum Serah had generated, right into the guard's face. Sharp metal blades bit into flesh as the force of the flail crushed through the guard's skull. Bone splintered, blood splattered, and the guard's body collapsed, twitching as it crumpled to the floor.

Serah glanced back to make sure we were still following. Her eyes were wild, drinking in the exhilaration of the fight. I knew the feeling. I was terrified but excited, and truly ALIVE! We were too close to dying, but this was an adventure!

BAM!

Serah's smile vanished, eyes bulging in fear as her gaze looked past me. "RUN!"

"RRRRAAAAAAAAAAAGGGGHHH!"

Ixchel had broken free and come up the stairwell. The lupine beast had obliterated the door, blasting splinters all over the hallway. She gave the air one quick sniff and fixed her gaze on us. Without hesitation, she launched herself down the hall, rushing toward us on all fours.

We stumbled out of the doorway in a panic, tangling up with each other as we fled. The first step came out of nowhere, and all three of us fell, rolling down the stairs in a jumbled mass of body parts. We gained various cuts, bruises, and a few cracked bones as we bounced and slid down to the ground level. It hurt a lot, but it got us away from the raging beast in the hall much faster than running!

I pulled myself free from Serah and the priestess. We were all dazed from the fall down the stairs, but my survival instincts kicked in fast. I looked back up the side of the ziggurat, hoping that we had gained enough ground to escape the raging beast in the hall. My vision was still spinning, but I saw a great furry mass standing at the door, sniffing the air. It was Ixchel, and she was distracted by some scent.

"NNNNNNNAAAAAAAGGGGGAAAAAA!!!"

Serah was up and running instantly, legs pumping faster than I had ever seen. She headed straight toward the river, swaying slightly as the dizziness wore off. Ixchel didn't seem to care. Her massive head turned to look further up the ziggurat. A second beast emerged from the door. This one had brown fur instead of black. It appeared weaker and atrophied, yet still strong enough to crush my skull if it wanted. Inyanga was awake too.

Both of the lupine creatures shot up the stairs toward the top of the ziggurat, abandoning us for more favorable targets. I scrambled to my feet and looked back toward the docks. The priestess had joined Serah, both of them running as fast as they were able.

I screamed at them. "Son of a kecklefrapp! Gnashgabbing long legs, wait for me! Dammit, Tinky! They better not leave us here!" I sprinted as fast as I could, shouting more as I ran. "We're not being chased, you numptys! Don't leave me behind! Nobody will write your story if I die!"

Huff, huff, huff.

"Tinky saved your life!"

CHAPTER 14

BITE ME

Ixchel's boat was in the water by the time I caught up to Serah and the priestess. At least they had waited for us before pushing off shore. Savage howls and blood-curdling screams echoed in the distance, centered on the ziggurat. The massive crowd that had gathered at its base was now scattered throughout the village. Ixchel and Inyanga were hunting down people selectively and methodically. I had no intention of finding out why. We pushed off.

The priestess began talking in a nonstop torrent of words and wide gestures. Her light voice somehow articulated each word like a small pinprick. At least I could understand her Imperial.

"Upstream. Let's go upstream. My temple is that way, far up in the mountains. She'll want to thank you. My name is Eldi. I am not one of the snake people, even though I look like it. Who are you? Why are you here? Why does the goblin carry a half-mechanical rat?"

Serah narrowed her eyes and pressed her lips into a tight line, keeping her gaze out on the water and intentionally avoiding eye contact with Eldi. But she did turn the boat upstream and start paddling. "You talk to her, Glik. I need to think."

"Glik? Your name is Glik? That's a weird name. Where did it

come from? How many other Gliks are out there? Oh crap, I'm sorry. I get this way when I see new people. Just remind me to stop when I interru—"

"STOP!" I held up both hands, then inhaled slowly. Silence, glorious silence... except for the massacre going on in the village behind us, of course.

I exhaled; trying to relax. "First, grab an oar and paddle with Serah. Stay close to the shore. The water is slower there, according to the survival book."

Eldi opened her mouth to reply, then stopped herself. She nodded, chewing on her lip as she did, then picked up the oar.

This could be a long journey. I wanted to head downstream, back to the goblin city to resupply and tell Gleeglum and Valas what Serah had discovered. But Serah had turned upstream. That didn't bode well.

Our supply situation was terrible, and we both knew it. I only had a few days' worth of cheese and rations left in my pack. I presumed Serah had similar or less. Eldi had nothing but the clothes on her back and that amulet of the blackened sun. She didn't seem like the survival type, and we would have to share resources. We could use the river, but between Raga's theft and that fopdoodle pixie's ambush, we had lost all of Gleeglum's methods to purify water and had no way to boil it. At least I could snag some fish if I was lucky.

I sighed. The silence was amazing, but we needed information more than I needed to collect my thoughts. "Eldi."

She perked up with a big grin at the mention of her name. I spoke slowly, trying to avoid releasing the tsunami of verbiage waiting behind her lips. "Pick a single question. One. Then I will answer. After that, I will ask one question that you answer, briefly. We take turns, back and forth, so everything gets covered. Go ahead. One. Single. Question."

She stopped rowing, opened her mouth repeatedly, then stopped herself; over and over again. She looked off into the distance, put her hand on her chin, and tapped her finger on her lips.

Serah's irritation grew thick enough I could taste it in the air. After a minute or so of Eldi's delay, her anger boiled over.

"Keep rowing!"

Eldi's concentration broke at the scolding, and she started rowing again while avoiding eye contact with Serah.

That was enough for me. "Ok, I'll go first, Eldi. How long will it take to get to your temple?"

Eldi perked up with another bright smile but continued rowing at a disjointed, uneven pace. "Oh, that's an easy one!"

I rolled my eyes; This wasn't supposed to be a challenge.

"It takes a couple of hours to fly to it. I guess that's about four days of walking? Probably add another day going upstream?"

I cocked an eyebrow. Fly? That's a weird first reaction. Hopefully, there would be a pass through the mountains. If not, that four-day walk could easily double or worse.

I let Tinky out of my shoulder bag for some air as I thought about the implications. She came out calmly, barely giving Eldi a second glance. She stretched wholeheartedly and perched herself on the side of the boat so she could see better.

Eldi continued. "My turn! What happened to your rat?"

"Squeak."

Tinky realized that we were talking about her. She hopped casually over to Eldi's leg, then climbed up onto her thigh and stared her in the eye. At least that meant Eldi wasn't a threat.

I gave Tinky a look of bewilderment, then answered. "Her name is Tinky. A bear attacked her. Now, do you know exactly how to get to this temple? On foot?"

"A bear! Wow! I bet that's an interesting story. But how di—"

"Focus! One question, one answer." Fizpiggle's codpiece! This was worse than training an orc to dance!

"Oh right. Sorry. Yes. Well, no. Not exactly. I've seen the path, but I've never used it to walk the entire way." She rowed silently for a minute after that statement, actively avoiding eye contact.

"Ahem. Your turn."

"Oh, right! Sorry, I was thinking of my temple and," her eyes glanced up, scanning all of us, including Tinky, "other things. I suppose the next question should be important. Do you have any food or water? They didn't give me much while I was stuck in that cell."

Serah huffed.

I handed over my waterskin. "This has to last until we can get more. Hopefully, you have food and drink at this temple of yours."

She gripped it carefully with both hands, took a small sip, and respectfully returned it. My jaw fell open in surprise. I had expected her to chug the whole thing without thinking!

She started rowing again. "How much is too much? I don't really know how much we need for the trip."

Serah grumbled, side-eying Eldi. "Probably about triple what we have."

I suddenly remembered something from the survival manual. "Once we get to the mountains, the water may be fresh enough to drink without getting sick. Drinking straight from the river is risky without boiling it, and we don't have a pot."

Eldi nodded solemnly. I took her brief pause to interject my next question before she could open her mouth again.

"Who is this temple for, and is it the same goddess you worship?"

She gave me a cheeky smile and winked. "That's two questions, Glik, but I'll give you a pass since I just asked two myself."

How could someone be so naively chipper after spending days in a prison cell? Especially after being forced to have nightmares every night!

"I worship the Charred Maiden! This entire island is her domain. Except for a few small blights such as that ziggurat, we welcome everything here within her warm embrace. Honestly, the original builders made her temple for someone else. Agnit, I think it was? Doesn't matter, he's long gone now, and she loves her temple.

"Next question, Glik. Why were you in that naga prison?"

"Because we didn't pay enough attention, and I got caught." I smiled sarcastically. Eldi returned the look mockingly, unimpressed. "Fine, we are trying to get off this island. We thought the naga might know a way."

"Huh. Why would anyone want to leave here? It is paradise!" She spread her arms in a grand gesture to the hot, sticky jungle around us, almost dropping her oar into the water.

I studied her expression. There was no sign of deceit, sarcasm, or any form of maliciousness. She was serious.

Nope, nope, nope. I was not taking that bait and going down an endless spiral of discussion regarding how miserable this chunk of rock really is!

"I have important business elsewhere. Now I get two questions, right, Eldi?"

She smirked with her chin up in satisfaction. "You got me! Tricky little goblin, aren't you?"

I rolled my eyes. "Do you know a way off this island?"

"Sure, you can fly-er take a ship! I bet you could find one in that gigantic city to the northwest."

I facepalmed reflexively.

"What? What did I say? Why is a ship not a good idea?"

"Sorry, Eldi, goblins, hobs, and orcs run that city. Getting a ship may be problematic. Even if we could get a ship, the waters outside the island are hunting grounds for the legendary Kraken. Nothing has gotten off this island by ship in years. We're only here because the Kraken sank us as we passed by."

Eldi's eyebrows knotted up, confused. "But why would she do that?" The comment was quiet, spoken to herself.

"Wait, the Kraken is a she? Do you know her?"

"Hahaha, no silly. George is a male kraken. Well, don't call him George. He hates that. By 'she', I meant the Maiden. George is only here because she asked him to come. I didn't think she would bring him to sink ships. That seems so destructive and mean. Not like the Maiden at all." She paused for a second, then shrugged it off.

"My turn. Next question! Who do you worship?"

If Serah was listening to us, she gave no indication. One quiet stroke after another to keep us moving. There was much more to this situation than we could see, and Eldi was giving me far more questions than answers. Focus Glik, one thing at a time. Survival first.

"No one."

"That's a disappointing answer."

I shrugged in response. I had spent too much time already following leaders that didn't care about their followers. It led me to believe that no being in power was worth the trouble. Since all ends lead to death, I might as well choose my own path.

"My turn then. How do you fly, and could you carry us?"

Serah's shoulders shifted slightly, giving away that her curiosity was getting the better of her, and that she was listening in.

"I, um, no. I can't right now. I don't. Well, crap! You aren't supposed to know that! It doesn't matter. I'm too weak to fly right now, especially if I have to carry people. How did you — never mind."

She pulled her arms in defensively and crunched her legs up close. At least she continued rowing; badly.

"Your turn, Eldi."

She responded meekly, "Maybe later, I'm tired of this game."

Huh. Guess I hit a sore spot.

Everyone on the boat stayed silent as she stared off into space, appearing lonely and lost. The sound of the oars sliding gently into the water kept us company, along with the cacophony of wildlife in the surrounding jungle. Raindrops started trickling down on us as another small cloudburst prepared to "liven" our spirits.

∾

WE TOOK turns rowing and sleeping throughout the night. It rained in short, frequent bursts, keeping it less humid but also keeping us wet and filling the bottom of the boat with a small pool. Eventually, the sun rose and invited us to another hot, humid, and miserable day.

Serah broke the silence while she rowed. "I've reflected on what was at the naga temple. The guards enjoyed the prospect of a new recruit and the possibility of a satellite temple, so they let me in and allowed me access to their library. It contained nothing but a mass of blind worship texts for the goddess Khabis. Anything useful was probably in a restricted area on a different tier of the ziggurat.

"I assume the high priest had different priorities than the guards did. I never saw him, but I was roughly arrested in the library. No warning, no explanation. They just walked up behind me, yanked my arms back, and dragged me to a cell.

"By sheer luck, the prisoners had more information than the library, especially the old lady. Through some clumsy hand signaling, she told me she could read minds. With a spell, I can too.

"Keep in mind, conversing with thoughts is a strange thing, even for those experienced at it. Ideas and emotions are tough to control and often relay a cluttered, confused message. Something clear in one speaker's mind gets twisted through the lens of the beholder, making imagery unreliable. But we managed.

"First, let me tell you what she wanted me to believe. They had captured her for worshipping a god other than Khabis. Instead of torturing her into endless nightmares, they noted her magical talents and intended to sacrifice her under the dual moons. She wanted my help to escape. I agreed in exchange for a few pieces of information.

"One. She told me that the naga have no way on or off the island, except ships. She gave no explanation but inferred that she knew this through the process of elimination.

"Two. She discovered that their power is limited. Khabis is still feeding off dreams, but the power she grants to the naga is weak and fickle. They retain their authority through brute force and cunning, not magic.

"Now for what she didn't want me to know. The old lady expected to take more information than she gave me during our mental conversation, but she couldn't hide everything. Her undercurrent emotions were eager, cruel, corrupt, and easy for me to detect. She twisted magic and relied on grotesque methods of gaining power. In truth, the naga were sacrificing her because they lacked the ability to overcome her considerable mental defenses. Better to use her as a sacrifice than to keep her as a prisoner they could not use. I suspect she could have blocked me from reading her if her focus was not split on reading me as well.

"Her mind also let slip that she had twelve other 'sisters' that she came to the island with. Life on the island is free of interference from 'holy headhunters', so they came here to corrupt and consume without interruption. But now she was alone. Her sisters had cast her out of the coven. I could not determine why.

"Thanks to her, we know the naga are a dead end for us. They might have information in a guarded library, but conducting research during a break-in would be impossible. The old witch might have been another lead, but the naga probably sacrificed her the night we escaped. That leaves our only remaining lead."

Serah stared at Eldi, a cold anger resting just behind her eyes. "Ms. Eldi and her friends, 'George' and the Charred Maiden."

I nodded at Serah's explanation. So that's why we were heading to Eldi's temple.

Eldi blushed a little and mumbled, "He really doesn't like to be called George, but the name fits him so well that I can't help it."

I shook my head, bewildered. What kind of creature has the guts to give a legendary monster a pet name?

We spent the next day and night taking turns rowing and resting. I read a bit more of the survival manual and made sure Tinky got her fair share of the rations.

Eldi spent most of her time wrapped up in any extra clothing we could spare, yet she was still shivering.

"How are you two not cold?"

This island was a disgusting, sweltering, sticky green hell! Even more so in the jungle where the wet air didn't flow easily. I couldn't figure this woman out.

"It's hot enough to make an imp sweat, Eldi! More humid than an orc's armpit! How the Jirktaflog are you cold! Were you born in a bonfire or something?"

"Yes, I mean, no, um. It's just, I get cold easily. Thanks for the spare cloak." She tried to avoid eye contact again as she nested herself into a ball underneath the cloak.

The current got stronger as we approached the mountains. We had to make sure that two of us were on the oars at all times to maintain speed, but eventually, we were paddling twice as hard and going half as fast.

By noon I was done with it. "This is more work than it's worth!" I said, panting as I tried to paddle faster than the water was pulling us. "We should ditch the boat and walk."

Serah responded, the voice of reason. "Glik. We are still in the jungle..." she trailed off as we rounded a bend.

The roaring of crashing water drowned out the usual noises of the jungle. The river led us up to a small pond under a towering cliff where a narrow but powerful waterfall had carved a groove into the rock.

I smiled and pointed at the base of the waterfall where little flopping creatures were splashing about. "There's fish!"

Eldi perked up, and her childish voice heralded my impending doom. "Then go get them!"

A hard shove knocked me off the boat and into the water. It was surprisingly cold compared to the sticky jungle air, but after the initial shock, it was exceptionally refreshing. A swim wasn't a bad idea, but doing it with all of my gear was.

My head popped back up to the surface, letting me get a good deep breath so I could scream at Eldi. "Skraggafrakt you sarding numpty! Where's Tinky!?"

Eldi's playful grin dissolved into a look of horror as she realized what she'd done. She dove into the water with surprising grace and disappeared under the surface.

Tinky's head popped out of the water beside me less than a second after Eldi dove in. Her mechanical legs were heavy, but they were also powerful. She struggled to swim, but it seemed to be more of an issue with balance and form than an issue with buoyancy and swimming strength. I helped her into the boat, then hoisted myself up as well.

I smirked at Serah mischievously. "Let's leave her."

Serah rolled her eyes at our semi-playful banter and handed me the oar. "Leave me out of this."

Eldi surfaced as I was paddling away. She gasped for breath and looked around frantically. "I can't find her, Glik!"

"Squeak!"

Tinky stared daggers at Eldi from the edge of the boat.

Eldi gave a great sigh of relief, then leaned back to float on the water. I started paddling harder.

The splashing of the oars got her attention. "Hey! Wait for me!"

I bolted, paddling as hard as I could. We raced to the shore and the boat proved that despite my terrible strength and form, it was still faster than swimming. We were both winded by the time we finished.

The playful mirth and the promise of decent food brought smiles all around. For me, it was bittersweet. I grudgingly pulled my books out of my bag. Soaked, as expected. Eldi owed me for this.

To her credit, she noticed me gently placing my books in the sun to dry. Her eyes welled up a bit when she noticed the one entitled "Glik's Fables."

"Glik. I'm so sorry. When we get to the temple, I'll give you something, anything, to help. I didn't realize your books would get damaged!"

I shrugged, knowing there was nothing she could do. "We'll see how the drying goes. They might not be beyond repair." *But I doubt it*, I thought to myself.

I tried to focus on other things and enjoy the rare opportunity to relax a bit. With the cool water nearby and the spray of the waterfall, the place was a welcome reprieve from the usual harshness of the jungle.

Serah struggled but eventually managed to start a small fire with her tinderbox and a variety of scraggly branches growing out of the rock face. She took a bunch more of the knotty wood and set it close to the fire to dry out more, so we'd have a fire throughout the night as well, assuming it didn't rain any more. I set my books out beside the fire to dry, propping them up with sticks to maximize their exposure without getting too close to the flames.

Serah fashioned a spear with her wavy dagger and a nearby sapling. Within the hour, she had caught the first three fish of the day and had one propped over the fire. I grabbed one and tore into it raw. Fish tasted fine both ways, but if there wasn't any seasoning, cooking them seemed like a waste of effort. Eldi surprised me. She grabbed the last fish and mimicked me, tearing into the raw meat savagely, without a second thought.

We had no container to boil water, but I recalled the survival guide mentioning that running water over stone can clean out contaminants, so we took our chances collecting water from the falls. It made little sense to me, but the manual wasn't the type of book that misled people on purpose. Either way, the water was refreshing, and having full water skins for the trip up the mountains was a necessity.

We spent the rest of the day stuffing ourselves stupid, taking short swimming breaks to cool off, and resting. That night we took turns sleeping with full bellies and the satisfying knowledge that the jungle was behind us.

∼

I woke up as soon as the sky was bright enough to read by and immediately noticed that my drying rack had collapsed at some point while I slept. One book had fallen into the fire and was laying in the ashes. Horrified, I ran over and lifted it out by one corner of the spine, dreading what I would find. The binding held firm, but the charred and cracked cover was beyond repair. I gently opened it, carefully flipping to the front. My journal! My irreplaceable journal! NO!

I gingerly thumbed through it, hoping the damage was not too severe inside. Maybe the combination of the leather cover and water-soaked pages had saved enough of it? Maybe I could copy it to a new tome later? I scanned page after page of notes written in my harsh, rapid sketch handwriting. Some of the pages were still wet, but the ink had held, and the burns had only destroyed the edges. The writing was fuzzy in a few spots and there was some bleed-through, but enough of it was legible that I could make a new copy.

Whew! I set it out in the sun, hoping to dry the center pages a bit more. The minimal interior damage meant that it hadn't been in the fire for long. Serah would have rescued it if she had noticed, but she was fishing for breakfast and couldn't see the collapsed drying rack from the edge of the lake.

I sighed and took a look at the book on magic words. It had dried out nicely, leaving the pages with a crisp, almost brittle quality. They did not stick together much, and the leather took the ordeal without complaint. The ink on the pages had remained detailed and clear. That was a lucky surprise. A bit too lucky. I wondered if there was some mild enchantment on the book. It hadn't fallen directly in the fire like my journal, but I still expected more damage. Especially once I looked at the last book.

The survival guide hadn't fared well at all. The binding had come loose, and the book had fallen into a weird position on the ground. As a result, the back cover was browning with burn spots while the pages farthest from the fire were still soggy. It didn't matter. The ink had run and smeared enough that little of the book was legible anymore. Total loss. Hmph. I hurled the remains into the bushes, frustrated.

Serah had already started packing up our gear, and Eldi was busy getting warm by the fire, mindlessly watching it as I took care of my books. She was sitting so close that her clothes smoldered, sending small tendrils of smoke curling into the air.

I yelled to get her attention. "Eldi! Scoot back before you catch on fire!"

"Hmm?" She glanced at me, oblivious and still daydreaming. "Oh, the fire. Yes, it's still chilly, but the fire does help."

Serah walked over, packing complete, and kicked dirt into the flames, smothering them. "Your clothes are smoking, Eldi."

Eldi ignored that comment too. She was busy watching the campfire sputter and die. Her eyes focused on it mournfully, as though the flames were an old friend that she was saying goodbye to. As soon as the last orange flicker was gone, her demeanor shifted back to her bubbly self. She adjusted the spare cloak for maximum warmth and smiled at us.

"Mountains! We're getting close now! Come on, let's go!"

The three of us made our way to the base of the cliff. Serah tilted her head back and looked straight up, emotionless.

"How exactly do we climb this thing?"

Eldi answered her. "We don't. We stick to the valleys. There's a tiny little path that leads up about halfway through the mountains."

I cocked my eyebrow at her, surprised at her burst of unexpected wisdom. She pointed north along the cliff face.

Serah nodded. "Lead the way, Eldi."

We filled our water skins one last time from the falls and trekked north. After a few hours, the rock face dipped low, allowing us to pass with minimal climbing, just as Eldi had predicted. And just as Eldi had predicted, there was a small, lightly used goat path that we discovered before the end of the day.

Eldi's prediction of total travel time, however, was woefully ambitious. The goat path was, well, for goats. It was exceptionally narrow, which forced us to shuffle along sideways in a lot of places. It also got harder to breathe as we climbed, which resulted in more breaks than we would normally take.

Luckily, none of us were afraid of heights. In fact, Eldi seemed to love them. I frequently caught her leaning out over the edge of the path with a wild, gleeful grin on her face.

We ran out of food on day three, but there was enough water to keep us from dehydrating completely. Regardless, Serah and I were getting slower every day from the lack of proper supplies and the difficulty of the path.

Eldi, on the other hand, seemed to gain strength. She tried to hide it, but she had not eaten or drank anything since we left the waterfall. She didn't wrap up in blankets as often either, even though the altitude made it legitimately cold at times. Yet every day she stood taller, smiled more, walked faster, and kept talking!

After several more days on the trail, we came to the base of the mountain that Eldi called home. The ascent was steep here and the trail more narrow than usual.

Before long, my senses began picking up something vague yet ominous on the path as we climbed. I felt like I was being watched, but I couldn't tell what was watching me or where it was watching me from. An occasional, unnatural chill made me shiver from time to time but never in a consistent or obvious fashion. Maybe I was just getting delirious from exhaustion? By dusk I was tired of the feeling.

"Tinky, feel anything odd here?"

Her reply was timid and quiet. "Squeak."

She knew something was strange but not what.

"Serah, Eldi, do you feel what I'm feeling?"

Eldi shivered. "Damn straight I do! It's cold up here. I've been shivering my butt off!"

Serah shook her head at Eldi, rolled her eyes irritably, then looked at me with a much more serious expression. "I do. Most religions teach their clergy how to detect spirits, and the spirits here feel wild and restless. But there's nothing I can do for them right now. Let's get some sleep and finish the climb once we have daylight again."

I gulped, then nodded. The only "spirits" I had heard about were nasty things that the cave shaman summoned to keep orcs and hobs from smashing our camps into pieces. They were invisible, howling things that terrified even the largest orcs. I counted myself lucky, as I had never seen them personally. There were few goblins that had, and most of them were plagued by nightmares for the rest of their lives.

We made a small camp on a ledge, just wide enough for all of us to fit shoulder to shoulder. No fire tonight. Eldi, in another selfless act of naivety, slept on the outer edge. An inconveniently timed shove could easily knock her off the cliff.

Hmm. Just one push and no more talking. I grinned madly at the thought. So tempting, but she was helping us, and I doubt the Charred Maiden would forgive me if I killed one of her priestesses.

Sleep came quickly in my exhausted state, but my dreams drifted into horrid memories of things that I would rather forget. I tossed and turned in my sleep, though luckily didn't fall off the cliff. I was tired but happy when Serah woke me for my turn at watch.

Serah settled onto her blanket, and I stationed myself a little further up the path where I could keep a better eye out. A freezing chill had crept into the air, cold enough that my breath came out in a fog.

Maybe it was my previous dreams still lingering, but the uneasy feeling had gotten worse. Within the hour, my nerves were getting the best of me, making me jump at shadows and sounds that were probably just wildlife. I was on edge, highly alert, and judging from the beady eyes shining out from my shoulder bag, so was Tinky. That should have been a comfort, knowing it wasn't all in my head. Instead, it made me realize that the problem was real.

My neck hairs and ear tufts stood on end as I surveyed the area. A shiver crept up my spine. This was too much and getting worse. We should leave.

I took a deep breath and exhaled, preparing to wake up Serah and Eldi. My breath came out as a billowing cloud in the frigid mountain air. The white wisps of my breath wreathed around an invisible human face! I panicked, staggering back to the cliff wall and thumping my head against the stone. The face was gone the second my breath dissipated from the air, but it had been there. I was certain! It was so close that I could have spit on it!

A fog crept over my mind, diluting reality and forcing my thoughts inward. Visions appeared in my head, blurring and clashing with themselves, swirling over each other. Some of the images were of things I couldn't remember, things I had never seen or done.

Before long my mind was assaulted by sensations that accompanied the visions. Flashes of burning pain intertwined with the imagery of fire and smoke. An odd feeling of rage was building underneath, applying pressure to my skull. My hands gripped my head as the pressure turned into pain, quickly overwhelming me. It all grew in intensity; the burning sensations lingered, no longer a flash but a constant painful ache. Something was seriously wrong. I remembered the invisible face that appeared in my breath. Was this the work of a spirit?

A jagged whisper assaulted my thoughts in a hollow voice that I did not recognize. "Mine. It is mine. Give it to me!"

My body spasmed hard, then began trembling. My hands fell loosely from my head, then pushed at the ground, trying to force me upright.

What was this!? I didn't want to get up! I fought, resisting whatever this intrusion was. It pressed harder in response with a wave of rage and blazing agony.

I focused on my body instead of the intruder. "SIT DOWN, GLIK!" I shouted to myself. My voice did nothing, but my body dropped.

The barrage of rage and pain returned in full force. My hands moved on their own, dragging my body slowly toward Serah's sleeping form.

"Stop! Serah! Wake up!" My mind formed the words, but my mouth only responded in a quiet, wordless mumble. Why wasn't my body working? I could hear the pounding of my heart, see the panicked breaths I was taking, but my arms dragged me closer to Serah without any way to stop them.

Once I was close enough to touch her, my hand shakily edged its way down to the hilt of my dagger. Skraggafrakt!

A rapid series of pinpricks flew up my back, drawing my attention from the dagger. Tinky's furry body filled my vision, her tiny eyes narrowed at my own, less than a finger width away from my face. We stared at each other for a brief moment before the muscles in her face tensed. She opened her mouth wide, then clamped it shut as hard as she could on the fat part of my nose! She jerked her head hard, cutting deep into my skin, then spun around and gave my nose a hefty kick with her mechanical legs.

"OOOOOOOOOWWWWWWWW!!!"

My voice definitely worked that time! I dropped the dagger and my hands reflexively shot up to my now bruised and bleeding nostrils. My vision blurred as my eyes watered, and snot began to mingle with the blood on my assaulted face.

Serah's hand grabbed my shoulder and shook. I didn't respond for a while. It hurt too bad to care about anything else. I saw her lips move. I heard sounds coming out of her mouth. But my brain was preoccupied with assessing damage, shutting down the pain, and generally not giving a damn about anything else.

Finally, after what was probably the third or fourth time she had asked, I comprehended what she was saying.

"What happened, Glik?"

"Uuuuggg."

I responded with a groan, still holding my face. I heard Serah's voice speaking softly under her breath. "Aghti dak li matea ai." Another spell from the sound of it.

"SSSKKRRIIIIII!"

An otherworldly screech tore through the air as Serah's spell came to life. My eyes shot open in fear. The air around us sparkled with light, silvery dust. Serah stood over me, brandishing her amulet toward a translucent creature that floated at the edge of the shimmering barrier, unable or unwilling to enter.

The creature appeared as a ghostly person with charred skin and burning, hate-filled scarlet eyes. Remnants of seashell jewelry hung from its wrists and neck. Its face was the same one that I had seen in my breath earlier, but now that I saw it clearly, it looked oddly familiar. It was not Ixchel, nor Inyanga, but the similarities were striking.

The creature screamed at us with a ragged, almost disembodied voice that seemed to reverberate in my head. "Miiiiiinnnneee! MIII-INNNEEEE! Must have a body. Must have REVENGE!"

Its scalding eyes never left Serah. Whatever her spell was, it had pushed the spirit out, enraging it further in the process.

She answered the creature with emotionless neutrality. "A body for revenge? Let me help you. I cannot provide a body, but perhaps I can grant revenge. Revenge on whom?"

Help it? Sod that! What was she thinking!?

The spirit's eyes flared, illuminating the area with an eerie red glow. "Lies! More lies, snake! I will never believe lies from a forked tongue again! My family, my friends, my world, all ashes thanks to the lies of the outsiders! DIE!"

It rushed the barrier. Motes of silvery dust clung to the spirit as it entered, catching it in a net of dim light. It strained and pushed but could not come any closer. The dust held easily, absorbing the creature's momentum before pushing it back out. The spirit screamed at the barrier and began thrashing and clawing at it. Every swipe tore some of the silvery dust away from the barrier, but it stuck to the creature's hands, dimming them as though the shimmering dust repelled the creature's very existence.

Eldi sat cross-legged, studying the creature, somber and sullen. Her shoulders drooped as she realized something. Her eyes dropped to her hands, and she started fidgeting nervously. "Spirit? Does the name Naesbola mean anything to you?"

The creature flickered for a second, eyes cooling as it stared off into space, recalling some distant memory. "She was such a fun-loving, free-spirited child. My neighbor's daughter. My son's best friend. She used to cook with us and hunt with us when her parents were too busy to watch her. What do you know of her? Did she escape the outsiders?" The spirit looked at Eldi longingly, hopefully.

Eldi shook her head softly, not taking her eyes off of her hands. "No, but she will give you your revenge. Take your rage up the mountain, to the old temple of Agnit. She will meet you there."

"NO! No, no, no, no, no!" The spirit's rage collapsed, giving way to sorrow. Physical tears dripped from the spirit's eyes. It sobbed, holding its face in its hands for a few minutes as we stood in silence, afraid to reignite its furious rage with an interruption.

The spirit raised its head slowly from its hands as its sobbing eased. "How can she help? She was just a child."

Eldi smiled warmly and stood, finally raising her eyes to the spirit's gaze. She walked toward the limits of the barrier, stopping at the very edge of the cliff.

"Naesbola is much more than any of us could have ever imagined. Go, see for yourself. She will be happy to see someone she once knew. It has been millennia since she's seen a familiar face like yours. I know I would love to see an old friend after so many years alone."

The spirit straightened and leveled a finger at Eldi, regaining some of its hardened, threatening tone. "So be it. But if you are lying, I will return. No fork-tongued outsider will stop me if I do!" He gave Serah one last hate-filled glare before whirling around the barrier and disappearing through the face of the mountain.

I gave a massive sigh of relief and collapsed, torn between holding my throbbing head or my rat-bitten nose. Tinky had already made her way back to my shoulder bag, using it as a hiding place both from the spirit and from any potential retribution I might dish out. Little Okkikrumper bit me! She saved my life doing it too, so I couldn't get mad at her for it!

Serah kept her barrier up as a precaution, graciously waiting for me to regain my composure. "We should leave."

Eldi was still staring at the spot where the spirit had been. She whispered softly to herself, sad and sullen, but I could still hear her. "So much pain in that spirit. So much rage. The outsiders caused it all, but for what? Territory? Control? They would have had both if they had only asked. Oh Maiden, I understand why you want revenge, but without knowing why they do what they do, what hope do we have to prevent it from happening again?"

She shivered a little, then wiped her tear-filled eyes with a sniffle and turned to Serah and I. "Let's get on with it. If we push hard, we should be at the temple by dusk tomorrow."

CHAPTER 15
WHICH WITCH?

Several hours later, with dawn's glow breaching the horizon, we arrived at the summit. The air here was crisp and cool. I stretched my arms upward, then abruptly plopped to the ground, exhausted. A staggering view of the entire island graced my eyes as I caught my breath. I nudged my shoulder bag, signaling Tinky to come out and look.

Lush green jungle sprawled across the southern part of the isle, starkly contrasting the ziggurat at its center. A jagged mountain chain to the northwest dwarfed the walled goblin city at its base. Grasslands flowed like a sea of honey on the central plains. Foaming waves rushed undisturbed stretches of sand at the island's edges, giving way to the endless sapphire waters of the ocean. Blue skies with fluffy white clouds promised shade in small doses across the landscape.

Eldi broke the silence. "It never gets old. That view is one of a kind."

I glanced over at Serah. The look of awe on her face was a subtle expression, mostly in her eyebrows, but it was rare enough that it made me appreciate the weight of the moment. Eldi was right. This view would be something to remember for a lifetime.

We sat there, enjoying life for a few brief minutes. A goblin, a naga, a rat, and an irritating priestess, all in perfect harmony with the world. But all good things come to an end.

Gurrrgle.

My stomach protested the delay.

"Which way to the food, Eldi?"

She giggled and pointed to a crater off in the distance. A light-grey smoke wafted up from it, barely visible. "We follow the smoke to the crater. The temple is inside it."

I nodded. Serah was still staring off at the horizon, so I tapped her on the shoulder.

She jumped. "What? Oh. Yes, let's get going."

We had only been on the move for a few hours when my ears picked up a distant chant lingering in the wind. It was high-pitched, harsh, and chaotic. Goblin speech. I probably could have made out individual words, but Eldi was humming some catchy, annoying tune that would undoubtedly get stuck in my head for days. I sniffed the air a bit. We were downwind. Good for hiding, despite the nasty odor of never washed goblin. But there was something else in the air. A sick, rotten-sweet smell that was definitely not goblin or smoke.

"Tinky, what do you make of this?"

Her whiskered nose popped out of my shoulder bag and sniffed. She paused, then cocked her head and sniffed again.

"Squeak?"

So, it wasn't just me.

"What is it, Glik?" Serah had noticed my hesitation.

"Goblins most likely, but there's something else. Sickly-sweet smell, like rot."

Eldi stopped humming and started talking at her usual breakneck pace. "Well, there is a cult that comes up here every so often. They claim to be worshipping some fire god. I've never seen or felt any deity up here, other than the Maiden, and it's definitely not her.

Perhaps they are still worshipping the dead fire god, but I doubt it. Most likely they are just deluded fanatics praising some figment of their collective imagination. Then again, they might just be trying to make friends by forming a cult. I never understood goblin social practices."

We continued toward our destination quickly and quietly, while keeping an eye out for the source of the chanting. Before long I spotted six diminutive figures in robes. They danced around awkwardly at the edge of the smoking crater, singing as though they were performing some religious ceremony. The sick smell I noticed before became oppressively strong as we approached.

We hid behind a boulder once we were close enough to make out the individual words. I listened in to their conversation, hoping to gain some insight on how we should proceed.

Holy clubberfish on a stick! Serah and Eldi were lucky. They didn't understand Goblin. Listening to this gibberish was painful.

A robed figure balanced on one foot and screamed, "Oh, Fire God, feed me most deliciousest of all foods!"

Another waved a twig in the air. "Dearstest Goddess of Flame! Prove you endless power! Burn dis stick!"

A third dropped to the ground, prostrating itself before the crater. "Pretty Light Maker! Kill my enemies and this numpty beside me!"

The last "prayer" resulted in a minor scuffle, starting with a kick from the insulted goblin and ending with the two idiots wrestling around on the ground.

Serah grew impatient. "What are they saying, Glik?"

I was dumbfounded, at a loss for how to describe the bone-headed display. "You really don't want to know. It's nothing useful, just witless gibberish."

"Squeak."

I looked down at Tinky. Her head was poked out of my shoulder bag, and she wasn't looking at the cultists. She was focused on a large outcropping off to our left.

I trusted her nose. "Rotten-sweet smell, Tinky?"

She nodded.

"Eldi, Serah, we've got company. Outcropping to the left. I can't see them, but the odd smell is coming from there."

WHOOSH!

A tremendous blast of flame erupted near the cultists, engulfing the two morons wrestling around on the ground. They pulled themselves apart in a panic and tried to douse the flames.

The lead cultist threw his hands up in the air. "The God of Burning answers! We are blessed this day! We must sacrifice to honor our blessings!"

Behind the outcropping, a muffled cackle caught my ear. The image of a haggard old woman flickered, then became fully visible as she held her belly and her mouth, trying hard not to be heard but having trouble in her hysteria. She slid into a sitting position with her back to the rock.

Another old woman's voice emerged from behind the rock. "Shhhh! They'll hear you. You know how well goblins can hear."

The laughing old lady turned to face the empty space next to her and spoke with an eerily similar voice. "Pfft. We are downwind and they are too busy celebrating the power of their 'god' to notice us."

The goblins were indeed focused on their rituals. The two ignited cultists had fallen to the ground and stopped moving. The cult leader chanted some more gibberish and two of the others led the last of them by his arms toward the edge of the crater.

"... accept this sacrifice. We thank thee, oh Lord of the Flames! Bless us in our times of terror. Shine light upon the shadows of our minds!"

With a hefty nudge from its fellow cultists, the "sacrifice" jumped. It didn't scream at all. Quite an impressive display of faith for a goblin!

The three remaining cultists walked away shortly after, apparently done with today's festivities.

I nudged Serah and pointed toward the old lady. "Can you hear the two old ladies by the rock?"

Her eyes had already riveted onto the visible one. "No, but I see the one. We should be wary. Eldi, is there a way around?"

Too late. Eldi was hustling from rock to rock, covering the distance between us and the old woman in a flash. She was grinning mischievously from ear to ear.

Dagnabbit! If that numpty got herself killed, we'd have to find the temple on our own, and likely explain to her goddess why she died and why we were there. I hope Eldi knew something we didn't. Serah and I followed as quickly as we could without making noise, trying to keep the line of sight broken by the boulders between us.

As soon as the goblins were gone, the second old lady's image flickered into existence. What in the...? I looked back and forth between them rapidly, trying to decipher what my eyes were telling me. Every part of the two women was identical, from the facial features to their crooked posture. Even their clothing was similar, made of thin worn hides and scraggly mountain vegetation. Given their looks and voices, I suspect they were twins.

The first woman cackled some more. "Hahaha. It's too much. After five years, you'd think the goblin cult would run out of faithful zealots to throw in the crater. Yet here we are, still laughing at their gullibility!"

The second old lady responded, using sharp, jerking gestures to accent her words. "YOU are still laughing. YOU are easily amused. Can WE get back to collecting reagents now? I need that catalyst for the sleep potion. It's been weeks since I've had a good night's rest thanks to these damnable legs that wake me up every hour of the night."

The laughing old woman rolled her eyes at the chastisement. "Yes, yes. Same story as always, you need to sleep. That's obvious from your lack of a sense of humor."

Eldi was close enough that she could spit on them, hiding behind a boulder half her height. She leaned forward and crouched like a cat.

Her legs wound tight, preparing to pounce. I half expected her to shake her butt like she had an imaginary tail.

A second later she sprang into action, leaping over the bolder and sprinting toward them with reckless abandon. "GOTCHA!"

The old women shrieked, flinging their hands around wildly with what was some sort of defensive gesture or spell. Eldi dropped to the ground in a fit of laughter. Good thing too. One of the old ladies flung a nasty jet of flame right where Eldi's head had been. The other produced a puss green, semi-translucent barrier over the two of them.

Eldi sucked in air with a gasp, trying hard to stop laughing enough that she could speak again. "That works every time! You two are much more fun than the cultists!" She pointed at them and laughed some more, rolling on the ground and running out of breath.

The more serious of the two old ladies pointed a crooked finger and screeched. "DAMN YOU, ELDI! We should have roasted your hide on the spot!"

Eldi gestured to a charred black spot on the rock behind her, still laughing. "You tried!"

The two women sat down slowly, holding their chests and trying to calm themselves. Eldi had scared them heartily, but they apparently knew each other and treated this as some sort of game.

Eldi sat up with a bright smile plastered across her face and shouted for us to join her. I clenched my fists and hoped the goblins were already out of ear shot.

"Serah, Glik, come up here and meet Maya and Morgan! These two ladies have been hanging around the crater, tormenting the goblin cultists, and keeping me company every so often for the last few years. They are so fun to talk to and have lots of wild stories! Oh, oh! Maya, tell them about the mermaid girls! I always love hearing what mischief they caused you!"

Serah eyed me with concern. I shrugged and walked over. They hadn't killed Eldi yet, which told me they had exceptional amounts of patience and restraint. "Hello. Who is Maya and who is Morgan?"

The two women looked me over, eyebrows wrinkled in confusion as Eldi answered. "Maya is the fun one. Morgan is 'Miss Serious'."

Morgan gave a quick, sharp glare at Eldi, then smirked. "Traveling with a goblin now, Eldi? That's quite a surprise, deary. It speaks much better than the cultists. Is it another straggler from that stone-walled cesspool of orcs and hobs?"

Eldi waved off Morgan's assumption. "Nah, he was a prisoner in that jungle temple. He can't be too bad if those zealots hate him, right?"

I chimed in. "I was shipwrecked, actually. I'm trying to get off this island. Any help would be great."

Maya interjected. Her voice was so similar to Morgan's that I was glad I could see her lips moving. "Sorry, sonny. No way off but a boat, and that's been a problem from what we've heard. Otherwise, we'd have left already. There's not much here to keep us entertained." She scowled at Morgan with her last comment.

Serah joined us then, eyes wandering over the pair, reading their movements and judging any level of threat.

Morgan continued the conversation. "Well, Eldi, you've caught Maya and I unaware, yet again. Our previous 'agreement' is still in effect. You surprise us, you get one honest answer. What would you like to know this time?" She glared at Maya as though the "agreement" was a stupid game Maya had talked her into playing.

Eldi clapped her hands in excitement. "Birds! How do they fly? I know it's not magic."

Morgan shrugged, indifferent. "Maya, animals are your thing. I'll stick with my plants. They don't bite."

Maya smirked and mumbled under her breath, "My animals only bite who I want them to." She smiled and began explaining to Eldi in an almost condescending tone.

"Wings, my dear. Birds have hollow bones and feathers, which make them lighter than the wind. By flapping their wings and catching the breeze, the wind carries them off. Controlling their flight takes lots of practice, but they hatch with plenty of instinct."

Eldi put a finger up to her chin, childishly contemplating. "Hmmm. Makes sense. Thank you!"

I spoke up, wanting answers. "Ladies, if I may? I have told you why I am here. What brings you to this island?"

They looked at each other, barely hiding mischievous smirks, and answered together. Their tone and rhythm were slightly offset, creating an odd, eerie harmonic in their speech that raised the hair on the back of my neck.

"A little bit of tit for tat? Both of us agree to that. But for ev'ry answer that you seek, one from you, we shall reap."

I felt magic humming in the air. It was like Serah's prayers, but had an odd, sticky feel to it.

Serah whispered from behind me. "Be careful what you tell them, Glik, and even more careful of what you ask." She began a prayer of her own, mumbling the words quietly. "Lohe, vaata, känna till iqiniso. Aghti dak li matea ai."

A brief memory tugged at my brain. "... ata, känna... iquin..." Serah had said that same prayer when we first began our game of trade secrets, back on the *Dolphin's Tear*. My mind rapidly pieced the context together. No wonder she had trusted my answers so readily when we first met. She knew I was telling the truth!

Maya and Morgan watched Serah closely. Maya seemed curious, but Morgan stared meticulously, like she was memorizing Serah's words and movements.

I decided to play stupid and see where this went. "An answer for an answer. Seems fair. Why did the two of you come to this island?"

They nodded to each other with a slow, eerie synchronization. Morgan spoke first.

"We came here for a better life. Zealots hunted us on the mainland. Some people didn't like our magic. A mutual friend stumbled across this land in her research. It was supposed to be deserted."

Serah tapped me twice on the small of my back. I leaned back; my ear next to Serah's mouth. "Once for truth, twice for lies or deceit." She whispered as quietly as she could in Nomadic Orcish.

I watched the ladies' expressions as Serah spoke. A twitch of frustration in Maya's eyes gave her away. She heard but did not understand. Morgan was stoic and gave away nothing.

Maya spoke next. "Eldi said you were in the naga temple prisons. Did you meet an old lady there, similar to us? She was a friend of ours. More like a sister, really. We'd very much like to see her again, but she preferred the warm jungle to the cool mountain air. The weather was easier on her joints. We would have joined her in her humid jungle, but the plants are hell on my allergies." She gave another glare at Morgan, probably a jab at her botanical obsession.

Two taps on my lower back. Lies.

An odd, warm tickling sensation crawled up my throat, nudging words out of my mouth. "Yes. The naga might have sacrificed her at the dual moon festival. I did not see her when we made our escape." I raised my eyebrows in alarm reflexively. That was more information than I had intended to give, and all of it was true.

I hesitated, leery of the magical compulsion but still needing answers. "My next question is for both of you. I assume you cast a spell when we started this game. What does it do?"

They glanced at each other again, then answered in that eerie, harmonic unison. "It lets us know the truth of your words."

Double tap.

Eldi sat cross-legged beside us, eagerly learning and enjoying this game. She was completely oblivious to the magic, the undercurrents, and the lies. How had she survived this long? She may not be maliciously leading us into danger, but her ignorance was going to get me killed.

Morgan spoke next, her knowing eyes glinting with expectation. "Since Serah is not playing our little game, I will ask you. What does the spell that she cast do?"

The same warm tingling crawled up my throat. "It reveals lies." Why had I said that? They didn't need to know.

The pieces pulled together in my mind. That damn spell they cast! Skraggafrakt! It was probably the source of that tingling in my throat when I answered. Fine, if they were going to use magic to force me to tell the truth, then guile was not an option. I'd be as blunt as a cudgel and see how they liked the uncivil approach.

I cleared my throat and glared at them. "Answer this question in unison. You mentioned your sister was in the jungle. Where are the other ten members of your coven?"

Their lack of surprise gave them away fully. No raising of eyebrows, no narrowing of lips. They knew exactly what was going on. They knew I knew. The facade ended here. These were no magical old ladies. These were two witches, and for whatever reason, they were not with the rest of the coven.

They glanced at each other, then answered in unison. "We don't know." I didn't need to feel the double tap on my back to know they weren't telling the whole truth.

I called their bluff, cocking an eye and putting my hands on my hips. "Come on now, you can't expect me to believe that. At least tell me where they were last."

They waited until the silence got uncomfortable, then Maya spoke. "I shall give you this one for free, sonny. As a gesture of good faith. We did not lie. We don't know where they are at this moment. The last we heard; most of them were at the sea caves to the north. That was some years ago."

Single tap. Interesting.

Morgan put her hand on Maya's shoulder, locking eyes with her. They stayed that way for a few moments, sharing something unseen and unheard. Morgan gave an almost imperceptible nod, then began packing up her things.

Maya gave me a venomous smile. "What are you willing to do to leave this island?"

I shuddered involuntarily. The eager look in her eyes screamed "trap" even more than her wording. "What do you have in mind, considering you don't know how to leave?"

Maya's grin widened. "Our coven has a way off, but they won't let Morgan and I use it until the entire coven agrees to leave. You might convince them to help you; perhaps us as well."

These traps were getting old. "What's the catch?"

Maya opened her arms, feigning innocence. "We have a gift for them, something they probably want back. See, Morgan and I left in such a hurry and on sadly bad terms. We'd like you to show that we hold no grudges against them and deliver this gift."

She reached into one of her pockets and pulled out a small bracelet made of tiny bone charms. It looked like something a goblin shaman would have used to store magic.

I eyed it suspiciously. "Will it hurt me or my friends?"

Maya laughed. "So cautious, sonny. It won't hurt, not unless someone is allergic to leather or silver."

Single tap. I was beginning to hate truth even more than lies in this conversation.

I nodded and took the bracelet, worried that if I spoke the witches' spell would give me away. I had no intention of playing Maya and Morgan's little game.

Morgan chimed in as she finished packing their gear. "Time for us to go, deary. This was entertaining. Eldi, my dear, take care of your new friends."

Eldi, oblivious as always, bounced up to her feet with a radiant grin. "Thanks, you two! It's always a pleasure. Catch ya next time!" She winked at them, then waved childishly.

The sisters rolled their eyes, then set off. The sticky sensation of their truth extracting hex cleared almost immediately. I eyed Serah, expecting a follow up conversation. She calmly gestured me to follow Eldi, who was already heading toward the crater, skipping along like she had just visited her best friend.

Once Eldi was a good twenty paces ahead of us, Serah quietly gestured for the bracelet. I gave it up willingly. With her amulet in her other hand, she began another prayer.

"Pragata Fa'aalia. Aghti dak li matea ai."

The bracelet emitted a purplish glow for a moment, then oozed a nasty black ichor into Serah's hand. An acrid stench filled the air around it.

Serah crinkled her nose and held the bracelet out at arm's length. "This 'thing', is a tool of vengeance. Eldi's witch friends must have a problem with silver. It would have exploded, filling whatever room it was in with silver dust."

She sighed as she wrapped the bracelet in a rag. "Every statement those two made was riddled with subtle omissions. Half-truths are more dangerous than lies and much harder to detect with my spells. I'll hold on to this trinket until we can destroy it."

I nodded in agreement, happy to be rid of it. "If Maya and Morgan are this cruel and vengeful, what do you think their friends are like?"

She eyed me, probably debating on whether to ask me a question in return or if the danger merited just telling me. "Worse, if the histories are correct. There are benevolent covens, but they actively avoid the cruelty that Maya and Morgan are showing. Cruel covens yearn for power and rely on deceit. They charm and enslave anyone and anything that could strengthen them. They omit truth from their deals and hide secrets in their meanings so that no matter the outcome of the deal, they gain from it. Their lust for power at any cost corrupts everything around them. This bracelet is just a small token of that."

Serah paused for a second, furrowing her brow as she crouched to inspect a scraggly bush in our path. "Maya and Morgan should be corrupting everything here if they live nearby, but I don't see any signs. Maybe Eldi's temple protects it."

I shrugged. It looked like an ordinary, half-dead shrub to me, just like the rest of them on this mountain.

A few minutes later, we caught up to Eldi and looked over the edge of the crater. Its walls went straight down to a bubbling pool of molten rock at the bottom.

Eldi was giddy with joy. "This way, you two. We'll be home

soon!" She darted off to a small path that zigzagged down into the crater.

I shook my head in disbelief. I may not be afraid of heights, but the thought of burning alive in a pool of fire made me a lot more careful on this path than Eldi was!

CHAPTER 16

OUR MAIDEN OF FLAMES

T he descent to the temple only took a few hours. If Eldi had her way, it would have taken a few seconds. The woman was absolutely fearless when it came to heights. Ripples from the heat distorted the air around us as we moved down the pass. We had long ago stopped sweating, our bodies conserving what little hydration we had left. I had a nasty headache developing too and was getting a little dizzy. What did I expect? It was a volcano, after all.

The path ended about halfway down the crater at the entrance of a cave. Eldi led us into it and, after a few hundred paces, began lighting sconces along the rough, black stone walls. After a couple minutes of walking, we came to a massive stone entryway with gigantic double doors. They were at least ten times my height and wide enough that all three of us could have walked through them side by side with our arms stretched out.

Molten swirl marks scarred the stone door where it had partially melted, and the cave near the door appeared to have been mined away. I pieced together the clues. This wasn't a cave at all. It was the old entryway to an immense temple, but it had been filled in with lava from an eruption at some point. Someone had spent months chipping away the volcanic rock to regain entry.

I turned to Eldi, who was busy spitting on a torch.

"Hock, ptooey!"

WHOOOF! The torch ignited in a small burst of heat.

I stopped in my tracks, my mind trying to understand what I had just witnessed. "Eldi!? What the, how the, huh?"

She looked at me, eyebrows knotted in confusion. "Oh, the fire. We need to see better in here, and the maiden always loves the fire. I want to reroute the lava in here someday, but I'm not very good at building things."

I stared at her, open jawed. "Eldi! You lit the torch by spitting a mote of flame on it!"

She shrugged. "Of course. You mean you can't do that? Huh. Makes sense, I guess. I wondered why you two kept using rocks to light fires. Oh well. I've always been able to do that. Must be inherited."

I turned my wide-eyed gaze to Serah for answers. She was busy eyeballing Eldi with a stern look and her arms crossed. That's when it hit me. We'd been lighting fires with flint and tinder the entire journey all the way from the jungle to the mountaintop. Thanks, Eldi.

She ignored us and pushed one of the heavy stone doors hard, slowly creaking it open. Before we could follow, she held up her hand to stop us. She had her giddy "I've got a surprise" smile plastered all over her face.

"Wait here for thirty seconds, then come in. I want you to remember this!"

I hesitated reflexively, naturally suspicious of an ambush as a result of growing up with goblins. But Eldi had not tried to harm us yet, and it seemed unlikely she'd do so now. Thirty seconds went by quickly, and we slowly made our way through the door.

Eldi had lit the temple with spectacular, blazing light. Massive columns lined either side of the room, supporting a ceiling so tall it seemed to go on forever. The room was absolutely massive! Thousands of people could stand in this place and still have room to walk around. A ring of flame lined the entire outer wall of the temple and met at the far end of the room, creating a massive bonfire. Sconces in the columns provided extra light for the central area.

Every available surface of the walls and columns was covered with hundreds of murals and mosaics depicting all manner of stories and histories. It was hard to tell what they all meant, but my interest was piqued.

A worn red carpet as wide as the double doors led to an obsidian throne at the far end of the room. It was carved out of a single piece of volcanic glass, using odd-angled cuts and intricate sculpting work to form a polished, tall-backed shape. With the bonfire behind it, anyone sitting there would have an air of power and glory. Even the small, striped cat sleeping on the armrest seemed to have a feeling of authority and importance.

Eldi skipped happily down the red carpet once she saw us enter. She yelled at the cat as she got closer to it. "HI PAKI! I'M HOME!"

The cat flinched and flattened its ears, but it kept its eyes closed, trying to sleep.

Eldi turned to us once she got to the throne. "Welcome home! Do you like the place?"

Serah and I were overheated, dragging with fatigue and hunger, and otherwise ready to die. But we were amazed by the grandeur of the temple. As we approached the throne, I noted a dusty red cushion on the throne's seat and a sizeable pile of egg shells sitting on it. The pieces were thick and larger than any egg I'd ever heard of.

Serah nodded appreciatively as she approached. "It is an impressive temple, Eldi. Your Charred Maiden should be proud. But where are all the worshippers? Do you maintain this place yourself?"

Eldi cocked her head, confused. "Maintain? What do you mean maintain? There's not much to do. I take care of the occasional cleaning and such, if that's what you mean. As for worshippers, the Maiden has thousands, perhaps millions of worshippers. Anything that lives on, in, or around the island is usually a worshipper. They just don't come here. She prefers that they pray where they want, not in any specific place. She's quite practical in that matter, but it makes the place extremely lonely."

Gurrrgle

My stomach was done with the small talk. "Food, Eldi. Where's the food?"

"Ah, yes, let me get that."

She disappeared behind the throne and returned with two large skewers of dried meat and vegetables. She also produced two wineskins.

"I'll cook up some fresh meat later, but the dried stuff is really tasty. There are lots of little spices in them that grow here on the island. It's really dry, but it has to be. It will spoil otherwise. I usually take a sip of the wine first and let the meat soak it up in my mouth for a few seconds."

The skewer smelled peppery, and the wineskin reeked of cinnamon. I took a huge swig of the wine and instantly regretted it. My eyes watered as my body forced me to swallow instead of spitting it out. The flavor was a masterpiece, hidden under a guise of burning spiciness and the kick of almost pure alcohol.

I shoved the skewer in my mouth to tame my now burning tongue. The meat had a much better balance. It was salty and tough, but its taste was exceptional. I'll have to get this recipe. It might work well on fish.

Serah gnawed on her skewer absentmindedly. Her attention was on the throne and the large pieces of eggshell. She stepped up to it and turned her head every which way, trying to see the shell from as many angles as possible without daring to pick them up.

Tinky shifted her weight in my shoulder bag, reminding me that she hadn't been fed yet. I turned, keeping myself between Tinky and the cat, and gave her a few pieces of my skewer. Can't be too careful.

Eldi didn't bother waiting for us to finish eating before waving us back toward the entrance. "Okie dokie! Now that you've seen the place, let's not keep the Maiden waiting! Follow me back outside."

We took our skewers and headed back through the temple slowly, distracted by all there was to see. It would take days to look over all the murals and mosaics decorating the walls. Probably a ladder too. Serah's eyes roamed over them as we walked. She wanted to explore as much as I did.

Once outside, Eldi gave us a sly smile. "I've been waiting for this for a long time. Don't freak out."

She shuffled her feet backwards slowly, pausing once she was at the very edge of the path. She winked at me and spread her arms wide, then fell backwards off the cliff.

I rushed to the edge and looked down, Serah right behind me. Time seemed to slow around us as we watched something that we could not understand.

Eldi's body was stretching, fattening, changing. She was not falling so much as floating through the air, gracefully tracing circles around the inner walls of the crater as she descended toward the glowing lava beneath. Within seconds, Eldi's body had shifted into something new. It was a smooth, painless transition, not like the brutally feral shifting that Ixchel and Inyanga had gone through. Her skin scaled over, colored in the same mottled gold and crimson of the lava beneath her. She grew to over twenty times her original height, not including her long, writhing tail. Her head shifted, elongating into a set of bestial, reptilian jaws with glowing eyes that twinkled at us through vertically slit pupils. Long, blackened claws grew from her new, lizard-like hands and feet.

She was a dragon! Wingless, she soared up to us, head now twice as large as Serah, and winked again. With a high-pitched, childlike giggle, she did a backflip and dove, lightning quick, straight into the molten rock beneath.

I shielded my eyes from the heat as I watched her disappear. She began popping in and out of the lava, swimming gracefully; happy as a dragon could be. This was her home. No wonder she had been so cold on the way here!

Eldi pulled herself upright again, then dove hard and deep under the molten surface. A few minutes passed, then she burst up through the surface again, sending splatters of molten rock everywhere. She shifted magically back to a humanoid mid-air and landed gently beside us.

"The Mistress will join us shortly, but you don't want to be out here when she arrives. It gets really hot. Let's go back into the temple and meet her inside. And don't stand in her way, it's...uncomfortable."

I was overwhelmed. Eldi was a dragon! A sarding DRAGON! This was a greater adventure that I could have ever imagined! "How did you do that? Why didn't you tell us you were a dragon!?"

She looked up and away, avoiding eye contact and giving a mischievous shrug of feigned innocence. "You didn't know? I thought it was obvious. Besides, I didn't want to ruin the surprise! You should see your faces!"

We walked back to the temple, following Eldi's fast pace. She pushed both of the main doors wide open for greater effect. Serah and I stood just inside them and waited patiently. We could see straight through the rough rock cave all the way to the path and the crater outside.

BOOOOM!

The room shook violently, nearly knocking us off of our feet. A sudden blast of scalding air slammed into us from the crater outside. Within seconds, the lava had risen until it was level with the path outside. A human-sized figure arose from it, stepping steadily from the lava onto the rocky path outside the cave. The creature became clearer as it approached. Lava dripped off of it slowly, revealing more and more of the feminine shape before us.

The stench of burned hair and charred fat wafted into the temple and violated our nostrils as she came to us. She had no hair, no clothing, only a somewhat featureless form under cracked, blackened skin.

Small seashell jewelry was melted into the flesh around her wrists, ankles, and neckline.

Once she entered the cavern, her scarlet irises washed over us, flickering with pupils made of flame. Flakes of her skin blew off with each shift of the oppressively hot wind, leaving patches of ooze and cooked gelatinous fat exposed to the air. Despite this, her movements were normal. Not graceful, but not pained or corpse-like either.

The smell of ash and charred flesh grew worse as she approached. It likely would have made me hungry before, but something about it turned my stomach sour instead. I was so entranced by her, I almost forgot to get out of her way. I stumbled aside at the last second as the Charred Maiden entered her temple, not slowing in the least. But she didn't bother walking all the way to the throne. Instead, she turned around abruptly just after passing us.

Her image flickered every few seconds, revealing brief glimpses of an unremarkable tanned girl with sea-green streaked brown hair. She was young, perhaps in the ten to fifteen range, with brown, heavily flecked eyes, ears with soft, mostly round tips, and a somewhat crooked, button nose. Her clothes were strikingly similar to the ghost that we met on the mountainside, light enough to be worn on the humid island but practical overall. Her jewelry, which showed as melted sea shells in her burned form, was painted brightly with intricate designs and leather braid work. The fresh, cool scent of the sea filled my nostrils during these brief respites, but they never lasted. Each time, they reverted back to the stench of charred flesh, sulfur, and ash.

We stared at each other for a few seconds in silence, her gaze shifting back and forth between Serah and me. Those glowing eyes judged us, letting time stretch as she waited to see what we were made of.

Serah spoke. "We were tol—"

My vision blazed white as my entire body erupted with burning pain, dropping me to the floor. My hands clenched my head in agony. Every bit of my skin tingled and seared, sending wave after wave of misery ripping through my mind. Every second lasted an excruciating eternity.

After a while the sensation was the only thing that mattered to me. Pain, pain, and more burning pain defined my reality. But slowly, tediously, the pain twisted into hatred, anger, and rage.

My mind flared with the new emotions, hardening them into thoughts of action. Whoever had caused my pain would feel my wrath. I would return this torture to them, their families, every creature they had ever known or met! I would etch their ruin into the histories so that their very name became synonymous with revenge.

A few more everlasting seconds passed before an abrupt shift sent my senses into a spiral of abject terror. I was instantly drenched by a cold sweat as I shivered from fear's icy grasp. My vision returned, and I was hiding somewhere dark, scared of the inevitable end coming for me.

It was them, the snakelike outsiders. Naga, they called themselves. They took my friends, took my neighbors, took my family. They dragged us from our houses and ripped us apart like wild animals in the streets. They captured us, taking us to unknown torments, letting the imaginations of survivors run wild with fear. They strapped us to their alters and ripped out our hearts while we screamed, sacrifices to their cruel gods. We filled their prisons, were tortured and forced into a restless, nightmarish sleep, night after night.

They hurled us into the volcano, desecrating the holy place of Agnit with the bodies of his worshippers. I could see the last of our people, a young girl with green-streaked brown hair and seashell jewelry. They led her, blindfolded, bound, and gagged, to the edge of the crater. Boiling hate filled me as I watched, a strange, personal familiarity passing over me as I studied the girl. My vision raced towards her until my vision blackened, and I felt that I was in her body. I was her. The last sacrifice.

A hard shove sent me sprawling into the open air. I felt the wind blast through my hair, roaring by and drowning out my screams. The air burned my lungs, then my flesh, as I fell closer and closer to the molten rock beneath.

Time paused, holding me in perpetual agony. Something noticed me. Something gripped me, triggering a change, a pulsing of energy and a shift inside my soul. The volcano responded in kind. The lava rushed up to meet me as the volcano erupted, vaporizing my body and anything nearby, including the outsiders who had dared to sacrifice me.

All sensation ceased. I laid on the floor in my own body again, staring blankly at the ceiling of the temple. I was drenched with sweat, breathing deep, panicked breaths, and fighting the urge to yark up the meat I ate earlier. My mind was sore from the deluge of sensations that I had just experienced. It would need time to piece together what had just happened.

I let my head loll to the side. Serah was beside me on all fours with sweat dripping off of her face. Her face looked green, and she was breathing even harder than I was. Good to know I wasn't the only one having these wonderful visions.

Blinding rage and hate returned, wracking my brain and forcing me to clench my eyes closed. Images of the outsiders flooded my mind again, but this time it was the outsiders that were the victims. They were being dragged into the sea by animals or slaughtered and eaten. They succumbed to disease and famine. Even the plants were hostile to the outsiders, developing thorns and toxins to hinder them. Whatever means of pain and death were available, the island used them all to exterminate the outsiders in droves.

The anger slowly receded. Peace came to me as the outsiders vanished. I saw the island, years later, thriving without their presence. The jungle grew thick, food was plentiful, and wildlife was abundant. Sea creatures came and multiplied, both in quantity and in variety. Birds migrated to the island and frequently made it a permanent home. A few humanoid traders and smugglers visited briefly, enjoying the tropical beaches far away from civilization. The island had become a veritable paradise.

But the visions were not over. A stabbing pain invaded my skull followed by wave after wave of intense nausea. I saw blighted plants, diseased animals, and decaying land. Smells of sickening sweetness, rot, and filth accompanied the imagery. The island itself was weakening, succumbing slowly to some unknown corruption.

My mind's eye traveled out to the sea, where gargantuan tentacles grabbed ships, wrenching them to splinters and pulling them into the depths. Survivors were a rarity.

The view quickly pulled back, far into the sky, until the island was a small green mass below me. A shimmering wall of illusion and power formed a dome around the tiny island. I understood the magic's nature, it's intention. The dome stopped any magic that allowed the island's inhabitants to communicate or escape through it. Whatever this corruption was, it would stay here and die.

The sun rose and fell in a blur, showing the passage of years in a matter of seconds. The sickness grew larger and deeper, its poison seeping into the very rock of the island. Sea creatures abandoned the shores. Plants began dying or growing agitated and aggressive again.

There was a brief pause. BOOM! The island exploded violently, sending a shock wave through the air and flinging mountain-sized chunks of the island into the sea. Giant plumes of ash billowed into the sky from dozens of cracks in the land, raining pyroclastic hell down on anything left alive. Aftershocks and smaller explosions racked the island afterward, finalizing the decimation of the once lush paradise.

It was all over. I regained my own mind and spent the next few seconds laying on the floor of the temple, afraid to open my eyes again. Eventually, I got my bearings and sat up. Serah seemed more coherent than I was. She had gotten up to her knees and held her head in her hands. The Charred Maiden didn't seem to care. She turned toward the crater and started walking, not giving us another thought as she passed by us.

On instinct, I reached out to grab her leg as she went by. I wanted answers, clarification. My hand passed through her illusory leg, making no contact at all but blasting my mind with the same searing pain that the visions had started with. The pain was over as soon as my hand was all the way through the illusion.

Serah screamed at the Maiden, pleading. "Wait! I have questions!"

The Maiden's image flickered, but she made no sign of stopping.

Eldi giggled at us, leaning on the doorway and watching as her goddess walked by. "The Maiden doesn't like to focus like this for long. You should feel blessed! I haven't seen her do this for anyone in a very long time. It's hard for her to do detailed magic. Imagine trying to forge a needle with a maul or maybe cook a delicate dish with a burning building. If she's not careful, if she loses her focus, she burns everything she comes in contact with. There was also that time she accidentally blew someone up. You two are lucky AND blessed!"

Oh yes, I felt lucky and blessed all right. Sitting on the floor, drenched in sweat, and shaking all over from the mental assault of a full-blown deity. At least I shared my misery with Serah, who was now throwing up from the ordeal.

Eldi pushed off the doorway and opened a full wineskin, offering it to us as she walked over. "The Maiden told me to answer your questions, but telling stories is much more fun, so let me start! I've lived through most of the story that she just showed you."

She pointed to the shattered pieces of egg shell on the throne. "That egg up there was mine. I hatched on the same day that the Charred Maiden was reborn as a goddess. The volcano erupted when she inherited all the power of Agnit. Well, all that heat and power got me excited in my egg, and I clawed my way out."

Eldi sighed as she remembered more. "Poor Naesbola. She was the last of her people and the last of Agnit's worshippers. When the naga threw her in, they sealed Agnit's fate, and the god knew it. Without worshippers, he could never gain more power, so he gave Naesbola all the power he had left. It was his last, desperate act. I guess he wanted her to take his place and do better than he did."

She looked up as she thought about Agnit's sacrifice, moving her finger to her mouth. "Of course, her body burned into nothingness when Agnit set off the volcano, but Naesbola's soul was strong. All that anger and rage kept her here. And the power of a god? Well, it let her do amazing things.

"It took hundreds of years for her to control that power after the initial blast. But eventually she figured out how to feed the island with that power. Life returned and thrived wherever she focused her magic. In response, the new life feeds her back in a sort of symbiotic relationship. She doesn't talk much with the individual creatures, but they all feel her presence and she feels theirs. Now that I think about it, everything on this island feels her if they stay here long enough. I'd be surprised if those goblins in the city haven't noticed her by now."

Pfft. She was heftily overestimating goblins' affinity for magic. Most of us went our whole lives without noticing magic, even if the shaman showed it to us blatantly. Given, most of us die of sickness or battle before we reach the age of ten. I personally thought our shaman was just tricking us with some sort of clever deception and sleight of hand most of the time.

Eldi continued. "The Maiden and I have kept building up her power and the life on this island for about three thousand years now. We were best friends immediately since I was the only living thing that could talk with her, and we were both very lonely. She sort of incinerates everything that gets close, and you see how well I do with heat. She doesn't do it on purpose, mind you! Well, usually not on purpose. She just has far too much power and not nearly enough control. I think she's afraid to take physical form because of that, and she rarely does illusory forms like she did for you today. I'm so glad she did it for you!"

She gave me a sly wink. "I asked her to do that for you. Aren't you glad I did?"

I bit back a few choice responses, settling on giving her an annoyed glare.

She was too engaged in her storytelling to care what my response was. "I handle the little things, the in-person stuff that is too delicate for her to attempt. Anything that requires a physical form without charring the crap out of everything in the area. And, of course, answering questions! I'm sure you've noticed I like to talk, and there are far too few creatures on this island to talk with."

I interrupted. "What about the sickness, the Kraken, and the shimmering dome?"

Eldi nodded. "Ah, yes, our current predicament. In the last few decades, part of the island got infected by something. At first we thought it was some natural disease and didn't worry about it much, expecting nature to take its course. But about five, maybe ten years ago, it started spreading crazy fast! Something or someone is causing this corruption. Most likely someone.

"So the Maiden called in a favor with George to keep mundane means of transport under control. She also set up that dome and burned through a lot of power to do it. That thing prevents those stone steles from letting anyone off the island along with any other magical means of transportation or communication. Quite ingenious if you ask me, but I personally would have gone the opposite path and tried asking as many people as possible for help instead of isolating us.

"She tasked me with finding out who or what is causing the corruption, but I'm not very good at picking up on clues. I've searched for years and found nothing. That's why I wanted you to come up here with me. I'm hoping you can help. Something is slowly killing the island. Help us find it!"

I immediately thought of the naga and opened my mouth to state the obvious. Eldi cut me off before I uttered a single syllable. "It's not the naga. I confirmed that before they imprisoned me. The Maiden severely limited their goddess's influence centuries ago, right after the dwarf and elf coalition built that city-sized fortress and invaded the naga temple. The naga won that war, but they've never been able to grow or recover since."

My mind shifted to Maya and Morgan. That had to be it. From

everything that Serah had said, witches corrupt everything around them. If that coven was still on the island, thirteen witches would be making a big impact. But I couldn't tell that to Eldi. She'd never believe that the twins were hurting the Charred Maiden.

I looked to Serah. She had pulled out the bone charm bracelet from the twins and was eyeing it with contempt. She looked at me, then back at the bracelet, then back to me. She was thinking the same thing. Great. We were going on a witch hunt. There was no way that could end badly!

Serah put away the bracelet and got Eldi's attention. "What EXACTLY do the stone steles do?"

Eldi looked shocked. "You don't know? They've been here since, well, since before I hatched. Let me show you."

She led us to the back corner of the temple where a well-hidden stone door blended in perfectly with the murals on the wall. She opened it and led us to a small antechamber. Inside it was an obsidian stele with a spherical relief in the center. It was identical to the stele in the Stone'N, except this one was in pristine condition!

Eldi bounced her way up to the device and used her hands to elaborately "display" the intricate carvings. "THIS, is what I called a 'stone stele'. There are quite a few of them around. I think they only lead to specific destinations, but the destinations I've tried usually have another stele nearby that you can use to get back. It seems whoever lived here before wanted to get around quickly. I can't blame them. What better way to keep in touch!"

Serah and I exchanged a shared look of trepidation. That type of magic could be exceptionally useful. All of society would go to war for control of something that powerful.

Eldi continued, oblivious to us and the implications of what she was explaining. "I personally haven't used the steles in over a millennia. Flying is much more fun, and I never knew if someone would be there when I arrived at a destination.

"It took forever to figure out how they work too, so I scratched some instructions into the stone. The Maiden insisted I use that archaic language for my notes so that nobody would accidentally figure it out. Well, she said 'nobody', but I knew she just meant the naga. It took her years to teach me that language too. She's such a terrible instructor. So impatient!"

I kept the conversation going, hoping Eldi knew more. "So you know how they work, you can show us?"

Eldi nodded proudly. "Absolutely! But don't go trying out destinations on your own. Some of these will probably kill a non-dragon. I almost died myself a few times. Come over here and I'll show you."

She waved us over to the symbols on the stele and skimmed over the notes that she had scratched into the shiny obsidian. "Okay, I think I remember enough of it. First, it has to be activated. Hit it with any spell or just touch it with something magical. I don't know why that works, but without that magic touch, nothing happens. Once it's active, a reflective metal ball will float in the air along with magical versions of the rest of the symbols. If you catch the symbols in the right order, the symbols will stop moving, which means it's all ready to go. Touch the reflective ball and 'poof', you are at your destination!"

I was fascinated. I'd never heard of anything like this, not even in myth and fantasy. "Can we try it?"

She shook her head condescendingly. "Of course not, silly! Not until you've rested up and we've finished talking!"

She took a deep breath and tried to be a little more serious. "The goddess needs your help. If you want off this island, the fastest way will be to give her a hand. I'm sure she'll give you more than just a fond farewell if you do a good job. The Maiden may be an irritable, vengeful goddess, but she's also quite a stickler about fairness."

Serah narrowed her eyes at Eldi. "What specifically does she want, and what exactly is she offering?"

Eldi grimaced. "Well, she didn't exactly tell me what she's offering other than release from the island, but she wants you to find and destroy the source of the corruption. We are going to help you with the latter part of that. In the past we've done some 'controlled' use of the volcano to burn out natural sources of disaster. We'd like to try that again, but you'll have to prove yourself worthy first. She won't give control of that much power to just anyone."

Irritated at yet another trial, Serah clenched her jaw and spoke to me. "We don't have any better options. If the visions are correct, the stele won't take us off the island, and trying by ship is a lost cause with the kraken still around. I don't like looking for fights or destroying things. Those types of adventures usually end in death. But what choice do we really have? We can die while hiding in a goblin city or die trying to get off the island."

I knew there was a reason I liked Serah from the beginning. Survival is just in her nature. "Okay, Eldi. Serah has spoken. We're in. What's the test?"

Eldi hopped repeatedly and clapped her hands together, giddy with excitement. "YAY! I knew you two were the right ones to ask! That dumb gnome at the goblin city was too scared to try, except I don't think he really believed who I was. It's hard to show that you are the herald of an almighty goddess while trying to blend in with goblins."

"Anyway, to prove yourself, convince Paki over there that you are worthy." She pointed to the cat.

I scowled at her in disbelief. "The cat. A sarding cat holds the key to massive cataclysmic power! What do we have to do, eat it?"

That comment got Eldi to pause for a second. "Um, no? You have to talk to him; convince him you are worthy. His name is Paki. He's a bit snooty but nice enough once you get to know him. And don't try to pet him. He'll claw you."

Serah stopped me with her hand as I started walking toward the furry little monster, her eyes still focused on Eldi. "Eldi, why did we see a vision of the island exploding?"

Eldi perked up merrily as she remembered. "Oh, yeah! There's a time limit. If too much territory becomes corrupt, the Maiden won't be able to keep enough power to contain the naga. That's not acceptable. She'll blow the entire island out of existence before she lets the remaining naga get away.

"She would have done it already, but I convinced her that she needs to stay alive to prevent more naga from rising to power later. It's also possible that the naga here could attract the others from all over the world. She could survive such a blast, in theory, but she would be very weak until the life returned to the island. I'd hate to see her like that, and I personally think that it would kill her.

"Regardless, you probably have less than a month."

I rolled my eyes. "Splendid."

PAKI WAS sound asleep on the armrest of the throne. I scratched my chin, thinking. How do you wake up a cat without angering it? Tinky trembled in my shoulder bag. She had probably caught Paki's scent, which gave me an idea. I could wake up a cat the same way as I'd wake up a rat. Food!

I grabbed my skewer stick, which reeked of the spicy dried meat, and waved it in front of the cat's nose. The cat's nostrils flared, inhaling softly. Before long one eye lazily cracked open.

Sensing that he had company and a possibility of food, Paki opened the other eye. He stretched, yawned, and slowly rose to a sitting position. His tongue flicked out casually, licking the remaining oil and traces of meat off the stick. I put it on the armrest and waited. Minutes later Paki laid back down and tried to fall asleep, satisfied that the stick was spent. I wanted to smack him.

I cleared my throat. "Ahem."

The cat opened one eye and glared at me when I failed to leave.

I glared back. "You have something for us, Paki. Eldi said you would help us out with the whole 'destroy the source of the island's corruption' issue."

The cat managed to appear annoyed without removing the bored expression plastered across his face.

"Mrowr."

I buried my face in my hands. Surprise, surprise. What did I expect? Paki is a figglefroppin cat! Why would he speak anything but some sort of feline language?

Paki noticed my frustration and gave an amused snort. "Hmm. I can speak if I like, and I like speaking much more than reading the mind of a goblin. There are far too many nasty, un-catlike things in there."

I shrugged. He had me on that one. "What do we need to do?"

Paki rolled his eyes and yawned again. "To prove yourself worthy of having the destructive power of the Maiden? Why should I tell you? You'll never get it right."

I clenched my fists and prepared to tenderize some cat meat right as Serah stepped between us. She smiled at the cat warmly and offered him a full-sized chunk of meat that she had gotten from Eldi while I was distracted. In spite of Eldi's advice, she stood close to Paki and began lightly scratching him behind the ears.

He flinched at first but then rapidly melted into Serah's gentle touch.

Paki glanced up at her. "You, on the other hand. You might pass the test. The Charred Maiden wants to make sure that you can think clearly enough to find whatever is causing this blight. I'll ask you a riddle. Just one. If you get it right, the power is all yours. If you fail, it's your problem."

Serah kept rubbing Paki's neck and ears with a calm smirk. "Do we both get to answer or just one of us?"

The cat shrugged. "Both is fine. He'll never figure it out, and it is unlikely that you will either. But, if one of you does answer correctly, I'll give you the power."

I didn't see any other choice. "Fine, Paki. What's the riddle?"

"Ahem." Paki cleared his throat, then sat up in a regal pose. "I turn time on its side and spin the world round. Stone trembles in my wake. I am as gentle as the breeze, yet as loud as a thunderbolt. People strive to be me, yet never succeed. I turn bread brown and make blood red. Can you answer this riddle?"

That made no sense at all. Time on its side, perhaps an hourglass? Spin the world, maybe a compass? Maybe the two were iron. I suppose stone would tremble under an iron pickaxe. That didn't fit the gentle breeze line. It could be loud when striking something. People try to be hard as iron, except they always break in the end. I have no idea what the bread and blood could be.

I turned to Serah for help. "Any ideas?"

Paki cut me off. "AHEM! No helping! Each of you on your own."

Friklefrakt! Stupid cat.

"Fine then. Iron. The answer is iron."

Paki yawned at me; boredom painted all over his face. He spoke slowly, with just the right tone to call me an idiot without explicitly saying it.

"Incorrect."

Eager to get back to his nap, he cocked his head impatiently and looked at Serah. Her brow was furrowed, her mind deep in thought.

"Care to answer, Serah?"

She blurted out a response on reflex, waving her hand dismissively. "No." She realized her mistake as soon as the word crossed her lips. She closed her eyes, threw her head back, and clenched her fists.

Paki snapped his head back and folded his ears like Serah had just whacked him on the nose. "That's. That's. That's... Yes. You are correct, Serah. The answer is 'no'."

Serah's mouth fell open as she stared at Paki, dumbfounded by her luck.

Paki took a deep breath and settled back down into his regal pose. "So be it. Serah, you have correctly answered the riddle and have passed my personal test of trust. It was a bold move attempting to pet me, but your affection was genuine and your technique exquisite. Thereby you have my trust. You may pet me again at a later time, if you desire."

Serah gave me a wry smile as Paki continued.

"Take the seashell on my collar. Crush it when you are ready. It will send a signal to the Maiden, letting her know that you have found the source of the corruption and telling her its location."

Serah reached down and undid Paki's collar, removing a small, blackened seashell from it. Paki purred for just a moment, glancing up at Serah with approval as she reattached his collar.

"The Maiden might not be able to control the blast and may accidentally kill everything on the island while trying to destroy the corrupted area. As such, she's allowing you one day to get off the island. George will leave the sea alone for a while once the trinket is crushed, so you may leave by sea. But don't use the steles, as the dome will remain. I also warn you not to give the seashell to anyone else. Bad things may happen if you do."

Serah tied the shell to a leather strip and hung it around her neck with the amulet of her goddess. "Thank you, Paki." She smiled and gave the cat one last neck rub.

I glared at the cat and recalled a few recipes that involved small, furry varmints. Eldi looked at Paki with a warm grin. "Naesbola always loved cats when she was mortal. I see some of her mortal self survived the transition. She trusts cat lovers, what a surprise." She giggled at the memory.

I interjected, half because I needed information, half to stop Paki from gloating. "We're going to need a ship, Eldi. Any help would be appreciated."

She scratched her head. "I don't have one. But I could probably get you back to the goblin city. They have a few. Why don't you rest here first and share some stories with me?" She smiled hopefully, too clueless to realize how miserable the heat was making us.

"Eldi. It's sweltering hot in here. I couldn't rest if I wanted to. But some food and wine for the road would be great."

"Road? Why not use the stele?"

Trusting Eldi to properly operate a magic device seemed risky, but I was damn tired of walking through jungles and up mountains.

"If it involves food and no more trekking through the wilderness, let's do it!"

Serah nodded in agreement, reluctantly.

We stayed a few more hours despite the heat. There were many murals of ancient religious history depicted mostly through hieroglyphs and pictographs of various styles. Serah and I both made rapid notes of as many as we could before the heat became too unbearable, forcing us to leave.

Eldi was waiting by the stele when we were ready to go. "It's been a while, but I'm pretty sure the symbol for the city was this shining sun symbol here."

"Are you coming with us?" I asked.

Eldi laughed. "No. I'm still quite weak from my imprisonment. I also need to help the Maiden prepare for the upcoming destruction. It's going to take a lot of precision if you succeed or massive amounts of raw power if you don't."

She took a deep breath, then turned toward the symbols in the stele. Her hand clenched a few times as she concentrated, producing a faint glow on her fingertips. She gently brushed the image of interlinked circles, leaving a trace of the magic where she touched. The silver etched symbol echoed her touch, glowing a faint blue, then vanished.

Drops of liquid metal coalesced out of thin air, coming together to form a floating, mercurial sphere just in front of the stele. It was the size of the relief in the stone and showed our reflections as clearly as a mirror.

Faint, translucent symbols matching the silver runes on the stele appeared in the air surrounding the sphere. They floated lazily in rotating orbits around it, leaving a light blue haze in their wake.

Eldi watched the orbits carefully, then snapped both hands out to touch two symbols simultaneously. She almost missed, and her hands went completely through the wispy images of interlocking triangles. But both symbols responded, and the silver runes on the stele vanished as a result. She tapped the floating compass symbol next, which caused the silver rune on the stele to vanish, just like every symbol she had touched so far.

She glanced at me and smiled, then tapped the shining sun symbol. All of the blue symbols stopped in their orbits, then slowly dimmed. The few that Eldi had touched remained stationary and strong, but the rest faded into nothingness.

Eldi put her hands on her hips, proud of her achievement. "It's primed! Touch the metal sphere when you are ready to go."

I stared at the mercurial surface. It warped slightly here and there, adjusting out imperfections as the floating liquid fought against gravity. It scared me, yet I could not look away.

Serah sighed. "Let's get this over with." Her hand shot out toward the sphere.

Wait, what happened? I must have blinked or been dreaming or something. Eldi was still there, but Serah wasn't. There was no sphere, no wisp-like symbols floating in the air. The stele wasn't glowing either.

"Eldi! What happened?"

She giggled. "I guess you both had to touch it at the same time. I always wondered how it looked when someone else went through. Here, I'll reactivate it."

She followed the same process for me, producing the metallic sphere and floating glyphs once again. I stared at the mercurial sphere, my warped reflection staring right back at me. I took a deep breath and squeezed Tinky in my shoulder bag.

"Here we go, Tinky." I turned my head away and reached out a shaky hand to touch the sphere.

CHAPTER 17

TINKY BUTT 2.0

T he smell of well-seasoned tuna invaded my nostrils. I opened my eyes. The Stone'N! I was back at the Stone'N! That fish must be Chunx cooking! I turned my head and looked toward my outstretched hand...that was resting lightly on Chunx's chest.

SMACK!

Wow, she can hit hard with an open palm!

Spit sprayed from Chunx's mouth as she yelled at me. "First, snake lady knocks my fish in the fire! Next, her stupid friend appears out of thin air and touches me!"

She shivered with disgust and gagged slightly, then shoved me away and stabbed her finger in my direction. "Touch me again, I'll feed you your own hand!"

I stood there in shock, rubbing my cheek and trying to make sense of everything that had happened in the last two minutes. Serah was at the bar with a dozen jugs in front of her. She had soaked herself with water to cool off and had her hand over her mouth, laughing at my predicament.

I strode over to her, sat my bags to the side, grabbed a jug of water, and poured it over my head. I could be mad later. Right now I was too hot to care.

Serah stopped laughing long enough to dig out some coin for Chunx. "Sorry about the fish and the 'stupid friend'. I'll pay for the fish, take the room for another few days, and buy some more of that 'good stuff' you gave us last time." Serah looked at me and tried to avoid laughing again as I rubbed my cheek. "And for all the trouble we've caused you, Chunx, I'll pay you double."

Chunx glared at us, then sighed. "Fine. I owe you. Drink really is sake, not ale. I got more buyers after calling it that."

She eyeballed me suspiciously, then huffed and continued explaining as she got us some sake.

"Flugspur rarely showed up after you left. He came twice for 'his money'. Was scared of your friend studying the rock. Goblins and orcs stopping coming too. But others heard about sake and tried it. They came back for more." She gestured out to the room.

Sure enough, the room was over half full, impressive for this time of day. But it wasn't full of goblins, or hobs, or even orcs. It was everyone else! There were all sorts of people, from the two halflings to the elf in the corner. A handful of dwarves drank heavily at one table, and a few humans were gambling with Raylin. Of course, there was also the bouncer, Ruk, who had somehow come out of the Blood Pits alive and unscathed. I'd have to find out who gave him that magic he used!

Chunx chuckled at my confused expression as I looked back at her. "Kragga stopped by after you left. Tried my sake. He likes it. He says I make a better bar owner than Flugspur. Asked what I need to make LOTS of sake. Haven't seen Flugspur since. My partner now has everything she needs. Keeps the sake flowing, legit. No more hiding bottles under the bar."

A thousand thoughts ran through my head at this story. Maybe the non-goblins in town were just tired of the rotgut. That made sense. Maybe Flugspur was in debt with the hobs and this was a good time to take him out of the picture. Also made sense. Valas had a tendency to use magic a lot, so that might have scared off most of the previous customers, or maybe Chunx's ever-happy attitude towards people scared them off instead. But why would Kragga, the leader of the hobs, help Chunx instead of just taking over directly? It wasn't worth the trouble to learn the formula, or maybe it was better to have another person in debt to him?

A loud belch from the table of dwarves reverberated in my mind, shaking the thoughts loose. That was it. Had to be! They didn't want to deal directly with the non-goblins! Assuming Chunx didn't let any other tavern serve her sake, ALL the non-goblins that wanted a drink would come here too! She even served food they liked. This was also the closest tavern to the main gate. If Kragga wanted to make a move on the non-goblins, he had just set the perfect bait, and it was in a great location to use as a trap if needed. Besides, hobs providing services to non-goblins would have been terrible publicity, not to mention they simply wouldn't like it.

Chunx had nothing to lose (well, her life, but that was always at risk) and gained everything at minimal expense to her. Even if Kragga wiped out every non-goblin in town, Chunx's sake would still be a welcome alternative for the hobs, goblins, and orcs. They just didn't know it yet. Chunx didn't serve it to them because the few times she did, they didn't pay! I bet she'd shift her policy eventually, especially if Kragga made a move on the non-goblins at some point. She was in a dangerous spot, but she held a monopoly on a specific niche that no other tavern would touch. Even better, her monopoly was sanctioned by the city leader. Good for her!

It was then that I noticed the stele was cleaned but no longer being studied. Valas wasn't there, and all of his notes and scaffolds had been cleared. Maybe he was done, found another lead, or maybe he just had something else demand his attention. I hoped I could find out. I owed Valas a lot and enjoyed having him around.

I grabbed my gear and the bottle of sake that Chunx had left for me, tapped Serah on the shoulder, then headed over to Raylin. Today's game was some form of dice, and Raylin was losing. He never bet much, but he didn't win a single round the entire time I watched him. He seemed happy anyway, talking up a storm and enjoying a bottle, just like the others. I wondered if he was losing on purpose.

As soon as Raylin noticed me, he grinned and looked around the tavern. His gaze spotted Serah for a split second then snapped back to me. "Glik! You survived! I'm surprised I didn't hear that you were back."

"Just made it a few minutes ago. Serah too. Still gambling I see. Have any news?"

He pulled his money off the table and made his way toward me, soliciting disappointed groans from the table of humans that were enjoying a payday at Raylin's expense. "Not too much, but we should catch up anyway. I've still got that room. How about we grab some food and more sake?"

I could tell he was already a bit tipsy, but retreating to the room, outside of curious ears, was a good idea.

"Good enough idea for me, Raylin. I'll head to the room. You get Serah and the food." He nodded and handed me a shiny new key. Interesting.

I wanted to scope out the room before anyone had a chance to say much. It had been over two weeks since I was last there. Plenty of time to install peepholes, trap doors, you name it.

The first thing I noticed was that the door had been fully replaced. It was no longer an ill-fitting wooden scrap with crappy hinges that were installed from the outside. Instead, there was a well-fitted wooden door with iron reinforcements and a sliding peephole rigged up from the inside. A heavy lock was built into the door. I guess that explained the new key.

Inside, the room had changed quite a bit. There was still a way to bar the door, thankfully, but Raylin had created a need to have a solid door. The once barren room was filled with all manner of crap! He was using it as some sort of storehouse for all the stuff he'd accumulated while hustling the goblins and "selling" Gleeglum's excess goods. There were useless trinkets but also exceptional weapons, armor, jewelry, you name it. All scattered haphazardly everywhere. Raylin's habit of cleanliness apparently did not survive the loss of the *Dolphin's Tear*. But there was still enough room for the three of us to sleep once we consolidated some of the mess off of the furniture.

Raylin's voice interrupted my observations. "I've been busy. Go inside so we can close the door."

I shoved a pile of crap off of a chair and took a seat, grabbing a plate of partially charred fish from Serah. She cleared a bed, then sat and began eating with a fresh bottle of sake in hand. Raylin flopped his plate on his bed and began chugging what was probably his third or fourth sake of the day.

He took a breath, drank some more, then raised both arms, gesturing grandly to his modest hoard. "I've been busy!"

I glanced around, unimpressed. Yep, that'll get all kinds of unwanted attention. Serah didn't bother looking up from her plate.

Raylin dropped his hands in disappointment. "You two could at least fake being impressed. Some of this was damn hard to come by!"

Serah took a long draw of her sake, then kept her eyes on her food as she spoke. "How does any of this get us off the island?"

Raylin straightened up and put a smug grin on his face. "That all depends. Did you find a solution to the Kraken problem so we can sail out of here?"

I rattled off my response between bites. Charred or not, Chunx's fish was tasty. "Of course. 'George' is no problem at all! We just have to locate a hidden coven of elusive witches and make sure they don't kill us before we point them out to a vengeful fire goddess that plans to blow up the island as soon as we perform our task." Mmm. Tasty fish.

Serah piped in while chewing her food, her cheeks flushed red. "Don't forget. We've got less than a month to get it done, or the vengeful goddess will destroy the island anyway."

Raylin smiled skeptically and looked back and forth between us. "Ha. Real funny." Our semi-serious expressions didn't change. His smile disappeared. "You're serious? So you found a goddess in the jungle?"

I started picking at my teeth with one of the fish bones. "Nope. The goddess was on top of a volcano in the mountains. Eldi the dragon took us there. The jungle temple was a dead end. Probably even more dead now that two psychotic werewolves trashed the place after we all got imprisoned. Well, I guess we did meet a goddess there. Pixie bitch tried to eat our nightmares while her followers drugged us into unconsciousness every day."

Serah raised a finger with an uncharacteristically warm smile. "Don't forget, the jungle locals killed off my convoy. That was after the idiot Kiggles got us lost, and Raga abandoned the group with her hunters in tow." She furrowed her eyebrows, realizing how talkative she was, then held up her sake bottle and stared daggers at it. The bottle was set to the side as she switched over to a waterskin.

Raylin took a few seconds to process everything he had just heard. "That means... all we need is a ship?"

I threw a small fish bone at him. "That, and finding an entire coven of witches that doesn't want to be found! Minor detail, right? Assuming two vicious old twins and their ex-coven sister in the jungle prison can be trusted, the coven is at the sea caves that Gleeglum mentioned. I don't particularly want to blindly follow that backstabbing Maya and Morgan, so my next stop is Gleeglum. Hopefully he knows whether there's any truth to the sea cave lead and how we can investigate without ending up dead."

Serah squinted her eyes and cocked her chin up slightly, her gaze fixed on Raylin. "Out of that entire story, the ship is what you focused on? Not the goddesses, not the death and danger, not even the dragon. Just the ship. Why?"

Raylin grinned from ear to ear. "I know how we can get one."

～

I HEADED TO GLEEGLUM'S, mulling over the absolute idiocy involved with Raylin's plan. "Buy one from the hobs." "I can get a good discount since none of the citizens are allowed to sail." "Last captain died last week, so we might already have a crew."

Fat chance on the crew, genius. If they haven't sailed in years, the captain sure didn't pay them. No pay means no loyalty. Might be why the captain ended up dead. And buying from the hobs? At a DISCOUNT! No red flags there at all. They'll probably just wait until Raylin loads the ship full with whatever treasures he can, then board the thing, kill him, and steal everything he's accumulated. Not to mention, there's the issue with why he wants a ship to begin with. I'm sure all sorts of noses will be trying to sniff out that information. Imagine the hobs being able to lock down and control the only known way off the island. As if the hobs didn't already have enough power.

I growled and kicked a lot of rocks as we walked. Serah was walking with me to Gleeglum's tower. She had a few questions for Gleeglum, but mostly she didn't want me getting killed. She suspected that the three of us had been noticed by the city's leadership and were "of interest". Judging from the looks we got, she was right. Most of them were not fear and reverence anymore but curiosity.

Luckily, we made it to Gleeglum's unscathed, but I made a mental note to work by proxy for anything that involved travel from now on. Maybe Gleeglum would let me stay at his tower. No telling how many people knew about Raylin's stash of goodies at the Stone'N by now. He wasn't exactly discreet, and while Chunx's cooking was good, it was not worth dying for.

I knocked on the door using my unique knock from before. The door opened and Gleeglum practically ran down the stairs in excitement.

"Where'sTinky?   I'veBeenDoneWithHerUpgradesForOver-AWeek! WhereHaveYouAllBeen?"

I opened my mouth to respond to Gleeglum's verbal onslaught, but a loud "SQUEEEAAAK!" cut off any explanation. Tinky leapt out of my shoulder bag and hopped her way into Gleeglum's hands.

Serah smiled at me. "I'll be upstairs resupplying and checking out the books. Let me know when you three are done."

Gleeglum led us to his lab where we switched out Tinky's old prototype legs with a nice new set. It was as simple as removing a handful of screws and unplugging a couple of tubes. I couldn't believe what Gleeglum was capable of. The entire exchange took less than thirty minutes with Tinky awake and comfortable the whole time.

Gleeglum beamed with pride, making sure to take a deep breath and speak slow enough I could understand. "I tweaked the power output and regulation systems so you should be able to jump eleven percent higher on the same amount of energy. I also added a small gyroscopic balancer to help with any aptly ambitious acts of athleticism. Much better overall, don't you think, Tinky?"

"Squeeeeak!" Tinky raced around the room happily, testing out the new power and balance. She only fell over twice!

Gleeglum laughed whole heartedly with his hands on his hips and his chest puffed up with pride. "Her new prosthesis has several upgrades. An upgraded gem stores a little less raw power, but it has significantly improved regulation efficiency. In layman's terms, she can get more energy from less eating while also using less energy for her movements than before.

"The frame and casing have been replaced with a much more impressive material. It's strength to weight ratio is drastically superior to the original raw iron of the prototype. I also worked in a honeycomb structure at various points. This feature allows for added buoyancy due to trapped air bubbles and an additional reduction of weight. The cost is a reduction of the stress force limit by approximately eighteen percent, but because I upgraded the structural material, the overall resistance should be comparable to the prototype at these points, which aren't the critical failure points anyway.

"Then there are the utility sets!" Gleeglum held up Tinky's hind leg, displaying a set of shiny retractable claws and a small set of removable tools. "I surmised that Tinky would be climbing frequently or need additional forms of defense, but your bag would likely not survive weaponized claws. The retraction was somewhat difficult to perfect, but Tinky will have full control of them after some practice, of course. The tool set was also added per our original addendum to the specs, and lastly, I added in a self-lubrication system. No more field maintenance required."

He leaned back on his workbench and took a few deep drags off of his pipe, beaming at his accomplishments. Tinky had never been this happy. Even our escape from the goblin caves hadn't been as impressive to her. Honestly, I couldn't blame her. Those were some impressive legs.

Gleeglum led us up to his study afterwards, waving to Serah as we made our way up. He fired up the hookah, then set out some clean water and a few cheese wheels for us as we chatted. It was a much-needed relief from our previous weeks of rough travel and horrendous heat.

I led the conversation, hoping to get the obvious out of the way so we could make progress on leaving the island. "Alright, Gleeglum. What do you know about the witch coven in the sea caves?"

He glanced over to a small backpack with an elaborately decorated pickle etched into the leather. "Interesting that you should mention that. How about we start with why you need to know?"

"If we find them, the goddess who controls the kraken will call him off. All we have to do is track them down, mark the location while we are there, then sail off into the sunset."

Gleeglum narrowed his eyes. "You spoke with a goddess? I know of some mushrooms that cause those types of hallucinations, but I've never heard of any drug-induced prophecy that actually came true. At least, not of this magnitude."

I sighed. He had a point. Serah cleared her throat and glared at him. He fidgeted a bit, then continued.

"Ahem, but let's suppose you are correct. We'd still need a ship, and we'd need to know the location of the witches. How precise are we talking about?"

I snorted. "Not very. The Charred Maiden is planning to blow up the whole island if we fail, so I'm betting within a half-day's walk would be good enough. I can't imagine she'll do a precision blast smaller than that."

Gleeglum cocked an eyebrow, realizing our story had more credibility than he thought as he recognized the name. "The Charred Maiden? That's a name I've heard before, but only once. And it was here on this island."

I glanced at Serah. "So Eldi wasn't lying about Gleeglum not believing her story."

Gleeglum pointed at me. "How do you know that little scamp of a goblin? She asserted that she was the herald of the Charred Maiden, a fire goddess from the mountain. I've heard about those goblin fanatics up there and the imbecilic sacrifices they perform. You're telling me THAT goddess is legitimately real!"

I recalled the goblin cultists and their terrible, uninspired praying, then shook my head. "No. That cult of numptys is worshipping nothing. A pair of twin witches have a lot of fun tricking them. Eldi is a priestess that we met in the ziggurat's prison. She took us to a temple inside of the volcanic crater in the mountains, and she's able to change shape with her magic. She explained what the Maiden showed us through visions."

Gleeglum scratched his chin, glancing back and forth between us. "I don't like this, but it's the most promising lead I've had since I realized I was stranded here. Divine interference on a grandiose scale isn't unheard of, just highly improbable. Assuming we can locate the aforementioned witches, have you procured a ship?"

I side-eyed Serah and tried to avoid meeting Gleeglum's eyes. This was such a bad idea. "Raylin claims to have one he can buy. From the hobs. Original captain died last week."

Gleeglum stared at us for almost a minute, stone-faced. "Well then, I suppose we should find out about these witches."

Serah nodded. "I'll work with Raylin to get us a crew without letting the hobs know. If we stick to mostly non-goblins, we might have a chance of going unnoticed. Do you have a way to store provisions discretely?"

"We could accumulate the necessities in my tower. I'll pack up everything I need from the lab as well. I don't know how long our research will take, but at least everything we need will be ready."

"Be quick, Gleeglum. I think we've got about three days if I can keep the crew and Raylin quiet. After that the hobs will probably figure us out anyway. The ship may also sell to someone else if we don't act quickly."

Gleeglum took out some parchment and scribbled down a list of names. "Take this. These are my trusted suppliers and what goods they provide. They won't rat you out if you mention it's all for me. If any of them ask to join us, I think we should agree."

Serah scanned over the list as she got up. "Thank you. I'll come back when I have more information."

Gleeglum took a long drag from the hookah, then retrieved the leather backpack. "Pikle and I fought strenuously to do this expedition. The elders at the academy didn't see the merit, but Pikle was convinced that this island was important. She needed to get out of the library and back into the field. I was idiotic enough to follow her."

He sighed and handed me the backpack. "It's been almost a month since her things were returned to me, but I still haven't worked up the courage to look through them. Sentiment and emotions are unfamiliar territory for me, thoroughly illogical. But they are part of me anyway, regardless of my thoughts and wishes. Please, do me the honors. I will assist you as much as I am able."

Gleeglum's eyes were glossy, rimmed with tears. Strange. I wonder if Pikle was to him what Tinky was to me. Nothing I could do about it. I grabbed the backpack and flipped it open casually, pulling out a handful of vials, some clothes, an empty coin purse, and a thick notebook.

Gleeglum took one of the vials, shook it, then popped off the stopper and sniffed. "Water breathing concoction. I never understood her process for purifying the substances. She always insisted that calcination was the proper method, but it's so inefficient compared to distilling the material at higher temperatures."

More overtechnical explanation. Oi. I skimmed through the notebook. It was full of exquisite diagrams and detailing, but none of the text made any sense. It was in some language I had never seen. As I flipped through, one specific image caught my attention. The page depicted a large stone slab with a spherical recess in its center and thirteen symbols etched around its edge. She had found another stele in the sea caves!

"Gleeglum, take a look at this. What language is this written in?"

He took the notebook from me and traced his fingers over the text. He smirked at it. "I should have known. You always were secretive, Pikle. She never implied that she knew what was in the sea caves. She only said that the sunken temple was important. This proves it. She knew about the steles! If only she had gone drinking more, she would have found the one in the Stone'N first! She was so focused on the caves that she was blind to what was right in front of her."

His shoulders drooped. "If she were alive, she could have explained them to us. The text is an encryption. Only the members of our academy know how to translate it. I was hoping I wouldn't have to read her notes until I was ready, but you can help me. Peruse through them and indicate any drawings that might assist us. I'll work out translating the text on them as we go."

Gleeglum went over to a desk and retrieved some paper to work with. "Before we get started, why don't you give me a detailed account of the witches? And, Glik, make yourself comfortable. This is going to take a while."

CHAPTER 18

THE IMPORTANCE OF A PIKLE

P ikle's notebook was full of odd sketches and diagrams, mostly of ruins and specific inscriptions. I had to remind myself over and over again that I was searching for witches and that I could let my curiosity run wild later. If we succeeded, I'd have months at sea to dig through Pikle's notes in detail.

About two-thirds of the way through the notebook I stumbled across a sketch of something odd. It was an aquatic creature of some kind with the torso of an elf and a large fin instead of legs. Something about it reminded me of the myrrh that attacked us on the beach. "Gleeglum. What's this creature?"

He was at a small table making a quick-reference guide so I could assist him in decoding the text. He glanced up from his work as I held up the notebook.

"That is a merfolk. Interesting. I presumed they were extinct or a myth. There's not much text around the diagram. Mark it, and I'll translate it for you with the rest of the passages of interest."

I nodded and inserted a bookmark. Over the next few hours, I quickly scanned through every page of the book, marking over a dozen diagrams that looked out of place or overly interesting. Things such as a drawing of the inside of a quaint cottage, some sort of plant, and even a sketch of some old lady. When I was done, I handed Gleeglum the notebook and yawned.

He nodded. "It is getting late. I'll get a head start on the translations while you sleep. Tomorrow we can go through them together and see if anything is useful for finding witches. You can sleep here if you like so we don't waste any time."

I slept hard, but my dreams kept drifting back to the Maiden's visions. They had been so vivid and real. I felt every pain, every sorrow, even the blissful tranquility of the peaceful times on the island. My dreams relived it all, over and over again, until I awoke late the next morning.

Gleeglum had some fruit and cheese laid out for breakfast already. He was busy with the notebook on his lap, translating another page onto a nearby piece of paper. Dark rings appeared under his eyes, but he was far too excited to bother with sleep until his body failed him, or the task was done.

I grabbed some food and sat beside him.

"Glik, excellent. I wondered how long you would sleep. Take this. It's a translation guide that will convert Pikle's text into passable Imperial. With it, you should be able to convert any new entries you find without my help. It's a horribly rough translation, so if any passages catch your attention, give them to me and I'll decrypt the text again to ensure accuracy. It was no simple task converting directly to Imperial when the original text is written in encrypted Grass Gnomish."

I nodded and looked at the sheet. Whew! It might as well have been encrypted itself. This would take some getting used to.

Gleeglum handed me the handful of pages he had already translated. "I translated the introductions as well. They often hold the hypothesis and goals of an expedition, so may be of value directing our search."

I nodded. "Gleeglum. Where's Valas?"

If he were here, this would go a lot faster.

"Oh, he wrapped up his diagraming and note taking from the stele at the Stone'N and went to gather more information. Apparently, the hob's keep does have a small library, so Valas arranged to study there for a while in exchange for identifying some of the books for the hob leader. Kragga'k'tol is trying to learn the snake people's language, so he ordered the library to be protected. He's also collected as many books as he could locate within the city, except mine, of course.

"My theory is that Kragga is looking for more leverage over his poison supplier. Valas is simply taking advantage of the hobs ambition. He's always been resourceful, so I'm not surprised he found a way to access an otherwise restricted library. Luckily for me, he usually stops by every few days to borrow another of my books and restock on paper and ink. That gives us time to discuss his findings and any local gossip that may help keep us alive."

At least Valas was ok. Bolder than I would recommend, but ok. No help for now then. Time to get reading.

Day 1. Exp #6: Sunken Temple, Uncharted Isle 15X-22.7
Professor Pikle Kradulitz, Head of Field Research

Herein lies the notation of the 6th expedition of Professor Pikle Kradulitz, as funded by the Altrastian Order, and approved by said order's elders.

The purpose of this expedition is to explore the previously uncharted island located at 15X-22.7 of the standardized Dominion Navigational Charts. I hypothesize that this island holds elements of exceptional arcane and religious importance. My preparatory research indicates that the location of this island may correlate to the sunken temple of an unnamed sea god who took the form of a giant turtle. The temple was lost for millennia in the open ocean after an incident involving the other gods of the time.

According to legend, this temple once housed an obscure artifact said to empower the most powerful priests in such a way that they could traverse from the Dominion all the way to the Western Empire in minutes. Other records of similar devices are hard to come by, but the handful I identified noted that the artifacts were of such great importance that all of them were summarily destroyed at the end of the last golden age, some five thousand years ago. If the literature is correct, this temple was lost prior to the great purge of these artifacts, which leads me to believe that it may still be in the sunken temple.

Personal log: While I am thrilled to have funding, I suspect the elders are simply eager to be rid of me. I've given them no end to trouble through my cross-referencing and debunking of their theories. However, if I manage to find this artifact, even if it doesn't still work, a great number of texts will need to be rewritten, and an entire branch of magical science will begin!

Unfortunately, I had to drag Gleeglum into this. The poor creature is obviously under some chemical distress that has him smitten with me. He'd agree to almost anything I ask of him. I feel so guilty taking him along with us. He's no field researcher. He belongs in a lab. But oh, the things he can do in a lab! I couldn't match half of his formulas to save my life, and his improvisation techniques are unique, inspired, miraculous! I had to have those skills for this expedition.

That was definitely interesting. So there was evidence of steles outside of the island. It made sense logistically, but I was surprised that any history that old had survived. I glanced over at Gleeglum. I can only imagine what odd thoughts and feelings had clashed in his mind when he read her notes about him.

Still, this didn't help us at all regarding the witches. It explained why Gleeglum came all this way willingly and what Pikle hoped to discover. I wonder if the giant turtle god had any relevance.

I could figure that out later. For now, back to reading. I skimmed through another few pages, one diagram of a seabird, one diagram of some sort of fish, and another entry that turned out to be a copy of the captain's log (why Gleeglum bothered translating that is beyond me). Then I stumbled across this:

Day 44. Exp #6: Sunken Temple, Uncharted Isle 15X-22.7
Professor Pikle Kradulitz, Head of Field Research

We've arrived at the island as planned. It is much larger than originally indicated and sports a much larger variety of topographical features than we expected. Mountains line the eastern edge, presumably volcanic in nature, but there is also a major rainforest and a grassland on the interior.

Contrary to our preliminary research, the island also appears to be partially populated. There is a city, complete with walls, a keep, and docks that we shall visit shortly. Perhaps the inhabitants will be of assistance in locating the sunken temple.

Personal log: The crew of my expedition is overly eager to be off of this ship. While I share their enthusiasm for better food and freedom from such limited confines, I worry what we will find in this city. Any inhabitants of legitimate standing in the world would have likely stumbled across one of the shipping lanes and commenced with trade, resulting in the island being charted by the various major trade companies. But the island was still mostly unknown, and this city had over a dozen large ships in port. I hope I'm wrong, but we need to be careful. It may be that the inhabitants don't want to be found.

So Pikle wasn't just a book bound researcher after all. She had some instincts. I was surprised that she didn't attempt to land elsewhere and spy on the city first, but I suppose her crew could have overridden her decision. Probably cost them their lives, if not worse.

I scanned through another few pages, finding nothing of importance. Gleeglum's energy was finally waning. He handed me the notebook and blinked a few times.

"I left off at the quarter-way mark. Maybe you'll have better luck. I'm taking a nap."

I took a look at the guide and got to work. It was difficult at first, but started to make sense after I tried decrypting a few of the pages that Gleeglum had already translated and compared my notes to his. Confident that I could make a passable translation, I opened the notebook where Gleeglum left off.

By mid-afternoon I had found nothing and was getting frustrated. Pikle had done nothing but document her preparations and adjustments for the loss of her crew. Nothing at all about witches or the sea caves. They were stuck in the damn city.

Heck with it. I marked the page, then turned to the last few entries in the notebook.

Year 4, Day 163. Exp #6: Sunken Temple, Isle 15X-22.7
Professor Pikle Kradulitz, Head of Field Research

The three sisters met with me again today. I'm so fortunate that merfolk would talk to me! They promised to take me through the parts of the sunken temple that were not destroyed if I could find a way to breathe underwater. I would have to ask them more about their history and physiology as we spent time together. What an exceptional opportunity to share cultures!

It should be noted that the area near the temple seems to suffer from an unknown disease or corruption. The flora of the area appears less robust and tends toward toxicity when used in alchemical formulae. The fauna also appear to suffer from enhanced aggressiveness. Whether it is caused by irritation or affliction is yet to be determined.

Personal log: I hope I'm just being skeptical after my dealings with the goblins in the pirate city, but something feels off about these three sisters. Maybe they are just different. Being merfolk, that seems likely, but I can't figure out what they gain through our friendship. It could be a scholarly interest similar to my own, but their attitudes and questions don't reflect such an interest. I also find it strange that they are able to speak a fairly modern dialect of the Eastern Dominion language. Who had they met with already?

I translated the next few entries. Sure enough, these three merfolk sisters took her in and showed her the temple. For weeks their friendship grew and continued. I continued translating entry after entry, well into the evening, when Gleeglum woke up and joined me.

I waved him over. "Take a look at this section." I showed him my rough translations.

He chewed on some dried fruit as he read. "That is quite extraordinary indeed. This translation is also odd, specifically regarding the word 'sisters'. Didn't you say that there were two sister witches on the mountain? And didn't they refer to the other coven members as sisters?"

I nodded.

"By all means, keep reading then. I'll get started packing. It's unfortunate that I only have the one copy of Pikle's notes."

I read well into the night, focused like Gleeglum had been the night before. Page after page the three sisters kept Pikle company, learning some of her alchemy and teaching her some of the merfolk language so she could translate what few inscriptions remained in the ruins.

Year 5, Day 13. Exp #6: Sunken Temple, Isle 15X-22.7
Professor Pikle Kradulitz, Head of Field Research

Finally, real progress! After months of working with Tikara, Pricine, and Iratol, I have deciphered a passage in the temple that speaks of an antechamber I have not yet explored. This antechamber was loosely named "traveler's landing". The three sisters have avoided that part of the temple, but when I mentioned it, they agreed to take me there only if I could convince the other "guardians of the temple".

They admitted then that they were not simply living in the sunken temple but were part of a religious group dedicated to restoring it and preventing further decline. That was why they had helped me explore and why they had kept me away from specific areas.

The sisters informed me that they were the middle tier of the group, each with three acolytes underneath them that performed the more mundane tasks of the group such as gathering food. Above them is a high priestess named Jiris, who they reverently called "mother". She directs the efforts to restore and protect the temple.

The rest of the guardians were in a nearby cave network. When we met, I was surprised to find out that they were not merfolk, but a mix of land-dwelling races. Our meeting went well, and the group thanked me for my contributions to their understanding of alchemy, particularly the water breathing potions.

Now that my academic intentions have been confirmed,

Jiris has offered to escort me to the previously forbidden parts of the temple.

Personal log: I should be more worried about their deceit, but the sisters have saved me from more myrrh and aggressive sea animals than my orc bodyguard ever has. He doesn't even come with me on my underwater excursions anymore. If the sisters wanted me dead, they wouldn't have gone to this much trouble.

I took a deep breath at the end of that passage. If living with goblins and hobs had taught me anything, it was that there are much worse things than death. I kept translating more entries, fearing what was coming next.

Year 5, Day 19. Exp #6: Sunken Temple, Isle 15X-22.7
Professor Pikle Kradulitz, Head of Field Research

Jiris and the three sisters granted my request to see the "traveler's landing" antechamber today. It was in ruins, but I could tell from its design that it had been something special. Three badly damaged pieces of a stone stele lay on the floor in the center of the circular chamber. Time had worn off any adornment or decoration, but the spherical relief at the stone's center was apparent and the stele as a whole matched the descriptions of the artifact in the literature! This might be it! This might be what I've been searching for! I needed to run some tests and cross-check my research.

Personal log: I knew it! My gut was sending up red flags the second the sisters mentioned their "mother" and the religious purpose of their group. I drank one of my illusion-piercing concoctions before we left today. I was shocked, to say the least. The three sisters are indeed merfolk, but appear twisted, corrupted, and - for lack of a more academic term - evil.

Jiris is something else entirely. Whatever humanoid creature she might have been in the past, her decrepit magic had taken that form and contorted it beyond any recognition. Her true form was that of a hunched old woman with decaying flesh, a fanged maw, and distorted, monstrous limbs. I had not researched such a creature, but of all the creatures I had researched, only the truly malevolent shared similar features.

I can only imagine what the other nine guardians are in reality or what their true purpose may be. I fail to see how a sunken set of ruins could benefit them, unless of course, there is some active artifact to be found.

This discovery places me at an impasse. The very purpose of my last decade of research is here at my fingertips, but these thirteen creatures have some purpose for me or they would not have let me stay for all these months. I'm glad that the alchemy I have provided so far is mundane and beneficial in nature, though in the right hands, even the most trivial medicine could become a device of torture. I shall have to tread carefully and watch for signs that my welcome is nearing its end.

I got up quickly, heading downstairs in a rush. Gleeglum needed to see this. Dawn was approaching quickly, and in my sleep-deprived state I could have easily made critical errors. But if my translation was correct, we had found our witches.

I found him in his lab, packing. "Gleeglum, does this say what I think it does?"

He took the notebook and made his own translation, then read it twice with a surprised look on his face. "Well, she didn't specifically utilize the word 'witch' or 'coven', but the description seems accurate enough."

He looked at me and shook his head at my tired, disheveled state. He poured some water and powder into a mug and handed it to me. "Get some rest, Glik. This concoction will help. I'll translate the rest of the notebook and inform you of the details this afternoon. Thanks to your diligent efforts, I'm almost packed already. Serah's supply shipments started arriving an hour ago too. If all goes well, Valas should stop by today and Serah as well."

I eyeballed the water and shrugged. If Gleeglum wanted to sell me out to the hobs, he'd have done it long before now. I chugged it then headed upstairs for a long, hard, dreamless sleep.

CRASH!

The sound of shattering glass jolted me awake as Gleeglum kicked the hookah, smashing it against the wall. "DAMMIT!" He hurled Pikle's notebook at the wall, then flopped down to the floor and buried his face in his hands.

I cautiously stepped around him and picked up the page of translations he was working on. It was the last page of the journal.

Year 5, Day 27. Exp #6: Sunken Temple, Isle 15X-22.7
Professor Pikle Kradulitz, Head of Field Research

I have been studying the stele with the blessings of Jiris and the rest of the group. I informed her that I knew of her corrupted nature and assured her that my intentions were purely academic. As a result, she explained her predicament and her intention to let me continue my research.

She claims to be the last remnant of the original bloodline who built and kept the temple. Her family was cursed with long life and corruption for not defending the temple when it first fell, thousands of years ago.

She maintains that her coven is on a mission to restore the critical parts of the temple and carry on the original traditions, despite the hideous corruption that taints their bodies. They hope to cure Jiris's bloodline through redemption or perhaps through modern alchemy. That is why they were questioning my knowledge and also why they protected parts of the temple from my prior attempts at investigation.

With all deceit and secrets behind us, it is time to begin my study of the stele in earnest.

Personal log: I don't know why I didn't trust them before. I woke up with the strongest urge to come clean with them today, and it paid off exponentially.

Perhaps I should release my bodyguard. He's been sitting around camp bored every day instead of exploring with me since he hates swimming. He could return to the city and get paid if Gleeglum is still alive.

Come to think of it, I won't need any of my other gear either. I'm sure Jiris intends to provide all I need, and I could reside in the caves with them.

Maybe I'll stay after my study is complete and help them restore the temple to its former glory or at least restore it to a usable state. My skills would be exceptionally helpful. Can you imagine seeing a temple like this restored to its full glory?

That sounded far too good to be true. Gleeglum's ragged breathing and sobbing seemed to agree wholeheartedly with my assessment.

"Gleeglum?" I tapped him gently on the shoulder.

He raised his bloodshot eyes out from his hands and sneered at me. His voice took a vicious edge that I'd never expected from him. "Magical coercion sound 'witchy' enough for ya!?"

I backed off. He needed some time. I'd rather not imagine what sort of things the coven had in store for Pikle once she succumbed to magic like that. Yup, some things are definitely worse than death.

I headed downstairs and perused the library for an hour or so. Gleeglum had already packed up the volumes he wanted to keep, and I had looked over the shelves many times before so I didn't find much worth reading.

A knock at the door drew my attention. Gleeglum trudged down the stairs, still sniffling, and opened the door by hand instead of using his usual magical means.

Serah's voice carried up the stairs. "I see we need to talk. Let's go inside. Perhaps some hookah?"

Gleeglum responded irritably. "Yes, hookah. Ahem."

I joined them as they climbed the stairs, interjecting before the mood got any more tense. "Serah. We have confirmation that the witch coven was in the sea caves as recently as two months ago. No need to ask more about it. How are preparations going?" I gave her a stern look and stressed my question.

She glanced back and forth between me and Gleeglum but didn't question it. We'd been around each other for long enough now that it didn't take much for us to understand each other.

"We've got a crew, and only a few of them are orcs. The rest are non-goblins that want off the island as much as we do. I handpicked them quietly after Raylin gave me the rundown on what skills he was looking for. He was kind enough to point out a few of the more skilled sailors from his gambling and drinking too.

"We're all meeting outside Gleeglum's tower first thing in the morning. I've staggered the way the supplies are packed and procured extra. If we get attacked, we'll have enough provisions as long as we get the first half of it all loaded up before we leave. Gleeglum, I suggest we load your equipment first."

I smiled. Good news at last. Now hopefully the hobs hadn't figured out what was going on.

Serah eyed Gleeglum, who was sulking but no longer violent, then gave me the bad news. "Raylin is on his way to purchase the ship right now."

My hand made an audible "smack" as my palm met my face. If the hobs hadn't figured out what we were up to already, they definitely would know now! I had hoped Raylin would wait until the very last minute to buy the ship, when the only thing left to do was to load our gear and leave. Or even better, not pay at all and just take the kikklflaken thing! Hobs probably stole it to begin with anyway.

Serah continued, "He insisted that he needed to check and make sure it was seaworthy before we loaded it up. Unfortunately, he's correct. If we time our departure any tighter, and the ship needs repairs, we'll be caught in the open with the full crew and gear on display. At least this way he might mislead them into thinking that he won't be ready to use it for a few days."

My shoulders drooped. Patience was something hobs had plenty of when it came to traps and greed. They probably had one or two people watching the ship already. But once Raylin went in and bought it, there would be a full squad of cut throats waiting for their signal in the closest watering hole all day every day. That's if we were lucky. If we weren't, then there would be a lot more assailants, with a lot more skill. If they spotted Raylin and Serah together again, this would be a fast and rough escape. I'm sure the hobs remembered Serah's first day in the city quite clearly and would plan accordingly.

Our conversation was interrupted by another knock at the door. Gleeglum squeezed by us and went down the stairs. Valas entered the room shortly after with a serious expression, then noticed Tinky stuffing herself with another chunk of cheese.

He beamed at her. "Leave it to Tinky to brighten my day! And of course, Serah and Glik. So glad to see the two of you are still alive! You'll have to tell me all about it, but later. Right now..." His eyes veered over to Gleeglum.

The gnome crossed his arms and glared at us. "Enough! I've already had copious amounts of attention, and it does nothing to stop the deluge of regret and anger I feel regarding Pikle. I need work to focus and distract myself. Serah, what is the name of this ship Raylin is buying? I'm going to go examine it right now. Perhaps I can create some enhancements for it by morning."

"*The Red Tide*. It should be easily recognizable by the dead orc hanging from its bow."

Gleeglum nodded curtly. "Valas, care to join me? We have a departure to discuss, and perhaps a bit of vengeance."

He turned to Serah as he left the room. "Feel free to stay here, Serah. I won't be sleeping tonight."

I waved goodbye to Valas, then turned back to Serah. "Is this going to work? Did you really avoid detection while gathering a crew and supplies?"

Serah leveled her eyes with mine. "You tell me. You're the expert on hobs."

I sighed hopelessly, then gestured for Serah to follow me as I headed downstairs. "We're going to need more weapons and armor. Do you know how to make a bomb? How many times can you bite people in quick succession?"

CHAPTER 19
LOOK, TINKY! THEY'RE STILL READING!

G leeglum returned in the middle of the night and began banging out some sort of improvement for the ship, making lots of noise as he did. Judging from his loud and creative cursing, he was frustrated. It might have been because his good equipment was already packed, but realistically, he probably wasn't over the incident with Pikle. We both knew that any rescue attempt would be suicide, and even if she was alive, it was unlikely she would ever heal from what the witches were doing to her. One way or the other, Pikle was gone, and Gleeglum knew it.

I got a few more hours of sleep, then gathered my gear and prepared for a fight. I found some gnome-sized armor with metal rings in it, a short spear, and most importantly, a blank journal complete with a tight, wax-coated sleeve that made it almost water-proof. No more charred covers and soggy, ink-stained pages for this goblin!

Serah joined me after eating a moderate breakfast. She loaded up an entire bandolier of labeled concoctions from Gleeglum's stores and wore it around her waist like a belt. I hoped that more of them were acid bombs than healing potions. Then again, if she was really unlucky and an attacker broke a vial while it was still strapped to her waist...ouch.

A knock at the front door signaled the dawn, drawing a string of Gnomish curses from Gleeglum. A few seconds later, he poked his head into the room where Serah and I were finishing our preparations. His eyes were bloodshot, hair trussed all around, and he spoke faster than I had ever heard him speak.

"That'sYourCrewSoGetMoving. TheCratesLabeled'G'AreMine."

He cleared his throat and clenched his fists as he continued. "I failed to finish the intended ship upgrade, but I have a cluster of nasty surprises that will be complete in a few minutes. I'll leave with you once they are done. Raylin and Valas remained with the ship last night, so they will be ready to load as soon as you arrive."

He turned back toward his lab without waiting for a response. I caught a mischievous chuckle and a comment under his breath as he went downstairs. "Insufferable lack of focus. Can't wait to watch those witches burn..."

Serah and I headed to the door. Over two dozen people waited outside with carts, consisting of dwarves, elves, halflings, humans, a few orcs, and, of course, Ruk. Each of them had a small bag of personal effects and a big grin on their face. Not nearly enough of them had weapons.

I turned to Serah, my mind racing on how to get this done as quickly as possible. "Have the armed crew load up first. Send the fast ones up ahead to scout out our path. Send anyone who isn't armed upstairs to me. I'm sure Gleeglum won't care if I give away some of his mundane fighting gear since he didn't bother to pack it up."

She gave me a sarcastic "no shit" look and started barking orders. An hour later our convoy of carts was in full motion, and Gleeglum closed his doors one last time. There was a net full of vials on his back, each one containing a clear liquid.

He chanted a long, complicated phrase while waving his hands and splashing some yellow liquid on the door. With a last flick of his wrist, he turned to me and grinned maniacally. "Anyone opens that door, the whole city will be able to see the pyrotechnics from the docks all the way to the keep."

He paused and looked me square in the eye before turning to follow the convoy. "I left it unlocked."

Note to self: never, ever piss off an alchemist.

We traveled across town with little trouble. A few hobs and some children plied their usual pickpocketing schemes, which we summarily ignored. Let them have a handful of coins. We were getting out of here.

I brought up the rear of our caravan and spotted *The Red Tide* as soon as we reached the docks. It was hard to miss with the dead orc still hanging off the bow, though it would have been hard to miss anyway. It was decorated like an orcish war barge, which meant death, spikes, shields, and a thick coating of filth.

The hull was painted blood red, but it was chipped and weather-worn to wood in most places. Large iron spikes protruded from the railing, some still sporting skeletons and torn rags. They were intimidating, but judging from the rust on them, they were more likely to serve as extra weight and extra handholds for a boarding party. No real threat.

On the other hand, I would not want to be on another ship trying to take *The Red Tide* down. The bow had a heavy metal ram at its base, and the deck held a number of catapults and ballistae. A variety of extra rigging was in place, allowing crew members to quickly move around the ship or even board another. This ship was ready for a fight. I hoped the added weight wouldn't slow it down too much.

By the time I set foot on it, the crew had loaded up almost half of the cargo. They were moving exceptionally fast. I spotted Raylin at the top of the gangplank directing them. He was sober, alert, and brutally efficient. It reminded me of the first time we met, back when he was the ruler of his own little empire called the *Dolphin's Tear*. This island had brought out the worst in him. I hoped having a ship of his own would change that.

Serah and Gleeglum made their way to the captain's quarters to meet with Valas and unpack. I stood next to Raylin and started scouting the nearby crowds. There were more people around than I was comfortable with, and a lot of them were armed. I started to say something to Raylin, but he was far too busy for idle chat. I did a quick count of the crew and remaining cargo waiting to be loaded. About one-third to go and we'd be out of here.

A soft thud drew my attention down to my chest. A tiny dart stuck out of my armor, failing to pierce through.

"SQUEAK!!!"

Tinky's warning was late, but appreciated nonetheless. I kicked Raylin's legs out from under him, dropping him to the deck as I screamed, "ATTACK!"

Another dart embedded itself into the mast where Raylin had stood. Take out the leaders, then aim for the crew. My suspicion was confirmed less than a second later as two crew members collapsed onto the deck. Their bodies spasmed and jerked as foam spewed from the corners of their mouths. I briefly recalled the poor hob that Serah had bitten when we first arrived at the city. The hobs really did have access to naga venom!

Raylin scowled at me for tripping him, then noticed his poisoned crew members and sprang to action. "All crew on board! Abandon the remaining cargo! To arms! Riggers, weigh anchor and drop canvas! We're not sticking around for this fight if we don't have to!"

I was immediately glad it was daylight, despite my usual preference for darkness. The attackers stood out easily, despite several of them attempting to hide at the rails and blow darts at key targets. Gleeglum emerged from the captain's quarters with a wild grin on his face and his net full of vials in hand. He chose targets quickly and didn't bother aiming much as he flung vial after vial at the enemy. BOOM! BOOM! BOOM!

Each vial exploded where it made contact, creating a small divot in the deck, but also clearing the area of any attackers and leaving a smoke cloud that obscured their vision. One vial made a direct hit on a goblin attacker's foot, blasting his leg completely off and flinging him halfway across the ship.

I noticed at that point that all attackers were goblins. A handful of them on each side, surrounding us and creating confusion. They were poorly armed but well armored. Crap. Someone had spent money to make sure they took as long to kill as possible. This wave was a distraction. Hobs probably wanted to make sure we let down our guard once these few died, or they were buying time to get into a more strategic position.

I yelled a warning. "Don't let up, these goblins are just the first wave!"

A roar from below deck announced the second wave. They had probably hidden below deck before anyone else had gotten on board last night. Tricky hobs.

"RRRRAAAAAAAHHHH!!!"

Then again, that roar sounded familiar. Ruk stuck his head up from the stairs below with a feral smile and a wild look in his eyes. He held a dead goblin by its throat and scanned the deck for a target. His eyes locked onto an unsuspecting attacker and launched the corpse across the deck. The corpse met its target with a sick, meaty smack, knocking the attacker over the railing. Ruk's giant hand snapped out to another goblin's leg, flinging it off its feet as Ruk started using the goblin as a club. I was no longer worried about any enemies below deck. If there were any to start with, they would be more interested in escaping than attacking after watching Ruk's performance.

A spear flew by me, narrowly missing my head and reminding me to keep moving. I ducked, dove, and dodged my way over to the captain's quarters. Armor or not, I was no warrior. I was more likely to die than kill anyone with my martial prowess. Serah opened the door right before I got there. Her flail was out, and her eyes glowed a dark, eerie green. She noticed me and stepped to the side, opening the way so I could get inside.

As I nodded my thanks, I noticed a fast dark object in my peripheral vision. I turned my head to see it better, but it was too late. I watched in horror as an oversized hammer flew right at Serah. She had just enough time to follow my gaze and turn her body square to the attack, not realizing what it was.

WHUMP!

The weapon smashed into Serah's chest, slamming her into the wall behind her before it fell to the deck with a hefty thud. Serah abandoned her flail and slid down to a sitting position against the wall. The glow in her eyes died, replaced by a flood of tears as her hands reached the sunken spot in her torso.

I didn't need to trace the throw or hear the celebratory taunt to know what had happened. The hobs had sent in the muscle. The orcs were attacking us.

"RAAAAHAHAHAHA! Snake lady ain't too tuff now, is she!"

The distraction cost the cocky orc. A flying goblin slammed into the cocky assailant's face, screaming and clawing. The orc panicked at the attack and fell over the railing. Ruk bellowed with laughter, proud of his handiwork. It was greatly appreciated, but I had no time to celebrate, and there were more orcs coming over the rails.

Despite our best efforts, we were losing this fight. At least a third of the crew was already down, and the enemy was no longer waiting for us to tire. The hobs themselves started joining the orcs, pushing both numbers and combat strength into their favor.

Serah scrunched up in pain and coughed, spraying bloody spittle everywhere. I abandoned the battle, grabbed her by the shoulders, and dragged her back into the captain's quarters.

I pulled with all my meager might and screamed as loud as I could. "Gleeglum! Healing!"

It took a few rough seconds to haul her over, but it was enough for the gnome to catch up with us right as Serah's feet cleared the door. He shut it and threw the bolt. I snorted. Mighty lot of good that would do against a raging orc, but better than nothing, I guess.

Gleeglum took one look at Serah, then ran further into the room where he had already started unpacking his gear. The sound of clinking glass vials betrayed Gleeglum's haste in finding the right concoction. I kneeled over her to assess the damage myself.

The hammer had hit her hard, making a solid connection with the dead center of her chest. There was a visible depression where her chest caved inward. She took short, rasping breaths and sprayed blood out of her nose every time she tried to stifle her coughs. It was a kill shot. I was amazed she was still alive at all.

My vision flickered in and out suddenly, confusing me as I focused on Serah. Valas brushed my shoulder gently as he walked to the door, taking me completely by surprise. I had forgotten that he was inside with Serah and Gleeglum at the start of the battle.

One glance at him showed why he was the last into the fight and explained why my vision had flicked in and out when he was near. Deep streaks of darkness raged around his body, circling him in a brutal torrent of blackened winds. Whatever spell this was, it was serious, and judging from the look on Valas's face, it was difficult to control.

He casually opened the door, stepped onto the deck, and ended the battle in less than a second. Weapons clattered and bodies thumped to the deck followed by a handful of splashes in the water below. The air thickened with a heavy, tense silence that was only permeated by muffled choking, gagging, and the low-pitched whipping noises of Valas's dark wind.

The silence beckoned me to peek out the door. Every living thing in sight, crew and assailant alike, was writhing in agony on the deck. Black tendrils of magical darkness restrained each person individually, ripping at their faces and throats. Any attempt to get up was met with dark, violent winds that slammed the creature hard into the deck.

Valas, eyes solid black, spoke to us calmly, not looking away for a second. "Dispatch them quickly. I don't know who is crew and who is enemy."

Eyes wide, Raylin hesitated at first. He then grabbed his spear and stabbed each helpless enemy, one by one. I didn't wait for him to finish. The immediate threat was gone, and Serah was dying on the floor behind me.

Gleeglum had upended two vials into her mouth, but she choked them up, unable to swallow. The contents oozed down her cheeks, mixing with fresh blood.

"This isn't working, Glik. Help me get this tunic off. I need to see the wound."

We cut away her tunic as fast as we could with a dagger. There was a weeping hole that barely broke the skin, but the sunken structure underneath stopped my breath. Her ribcage had caved in, her entire sternum shattered. The impact likely punctured her lungs, causing her rough breath and bleeding. It was a miracle her heart still worked with that much nearby damage. Her skin was perforated with several tiny cuts where small, black shards of something stuck out. Her symbol of the Gatekeeper, goddess of secrets, was bent out of shape from the impact.

Gleeglum shook his head. I knew what that meant. Something inside snapped, filling my eyes with tears. I had lost people before, but this was different. She had been there with me through all of this insanity. I wouldn't lose her now. She trusted me, a goblin, when she trusted so few others unless she had no other choice. It may get me killed, but she was my friend, just like Tinky. No, I wouldn't accept this. I wouldn't let go.

My memory kicked in, scanning and searching for anything that might help. I watched Serah's lips quiver as her hand slowly reached for her disfigured holy symbol. That was it.

I took a deep breath and pulled Serah's hands up to her amulet, grasping it with my hands clasped over hers. I closed my eyes and focused on the symbol. I recalled memories of our time together, the oddly calm feeling of sleep with someone watching my back, the joy of Serah's random bouts of sarcasm, and my will to see her live.

The words left my mouth softly. "Dear goddess of secrets, I hope these are the right words. Aghti dak li matea ai!"

My hands warmed, and my toe blistered with pain. I held my breath and timidly cracked open an eyelid, chancing a glance at what was happening. A blinding glow poured from the amulet in our hands just above Serah's chest. Her flesh shifted under the light, knitting itself together as her body laid there. She shook and spasmed, unable to control herself under the torrent of healing magic reshaping her. It lasted a few seconds, then the light dwindled and faded to nothing as her body settled and relaxed.

I sucked in a hard breath and collapsed on the deck beside her. My head throbbed and my toe screamed for attention. I stared at the ceiling of the captain's quarters, not wanting to move. Slowly, three familiar faces came in to view, looking down at me in awe.

"What? Never see a goblin do magic?"

Valas chuckled and shook his head as Gleeglum answered dumbfounded. "That's beyond any restorative magic I've ever seen. She was as good as dead."

Raylin smiled with relief, then cocked his head to the side and bent down to pick a small piece of blackened seashell out of Serah's skin. "What's this?"

Small... blackened... seashell. Fuck.

"Um, Raylin. Let's not go to the sea caves for a witch hunt. Let's get out of the blast area before this island explodes instead."

By the next morning, I was puking at least once every hour. We had lost almost half the crew in the fight, which left enough hands to manage the ship but not comfortably. Raylin had them double up on some of the easier duties to ensure everything was covered. True to his prior meticulousness at sea, he ran a tight ship and didn't let up on anything, including cleaning duties.

Gleeglum provided all of us, including the crew, with some sort of anti-fatigue concoctions that helped a lot. He brought extra ingredients on board in case we needed more or something similar. Turns out Gleeglum was an excellent cook too, and many of his alchemical ingredients served well in the food as spices. Having an alchemist on board was amazing!

Serah slept the rest of that first day and most of the night. According to Gleeglum and Valas, her recovery was going to take a long time, even with the help of a few Gleeglum's concoctions. She may always have soreness in her chest after this, particularly when breathing hard or when the weather changed.

I went to the rail of the ship and took a long look back at the island. Sunrise loomed just over the horizon, creating a stunningly beautiful scene. Such a wild adventure. I really hoped it was all over. I could use a long stay at some tavern, feeding stories to the locals, enjoying a daily bed, and stuffing myself with juicy tuna.

A ripple tore through air around the island, followed by a chaotic rumbling. The entire ship jerked as the shockwave hit, knocking me off balance as the world itself seemed to spasm.

BOOOOOM!

The explosion blasted away my hearing, giving me a massive headache and overwhelming my ears with a piercing, ringing sound. I put my hands on my head and laid down on the deck, trying to recover.

Once the pain subsided to manageable levels, I got up and looked back at the island. A large plume of dust and ash erupted from two places on the horizon. I went to the wheel and grabbed Raylin's spyglass for a better look. A towering column of pyroclastic ash and smoke roared from the crater at the Charred Maiden's temple in the mountains, blasting impossible amounts of burning death into the air.

The second plume of ash came from the mountain near the

pirate city, but the city itself was no longer there. The mountain had exploded outward toward the city and buried it with dirt and stone. Where once was civilization, there was naught but rubble and ash.

More thundering explosions cracked the air in the distance. Large fissures split the grasslands all the way from the goblin city to the sea caves. The mountains were cracking open, spewing lava in some places, ash clouds in others. Half the island was belching out smoke and flame.

Serah's calm, neutral voice brought my focus back to the ship. "What do you think that means?"

I glanced at her. Her hair was a mess, partially stuck to her face with sweat, and her eyes reminded me of the dead. Sunken in and blackened with fatigue. "You shouldn't be up."

She put a finger in her ear and made a face, trying to stop the ringing. "Could you sleep through all that noise?"

She started to sigh, but grimaced instead. "Everything hurts, especially breathing, but I'll survive."

I huffed, then handed her the spyglass. "I think this means we screwed up."

She held it up and inspected the island. "If the Maiden thought we triggered the shell in the wrong place, she wouldn't have blown up anything. I think she lost control, and the power went wild. Blowing up an island probably has a lot of uncertainties. Go ask Gleeglum, I'm sure he could give you a full, mind-numbing analysis."

"Huh. Good point."

She scanned the horizon quietly for a few minutes, letting her thoughts slowly collect and come to the surface. "What do I owe you for saving my life?"

I smiled and clenched my toes. The ring had gotten so hot that it blistered all three toes that touched it and left a small black mark on my boot. It was so bad that I had to wear the ring on my other foot while it healed. "How about a secret?"

She sighed, put down the spyglass, and hung her head. "What secret do you consider an equal trade for my life?"

"Aghti dak li matea ai. Every spell I've heard you cast ends with that phrase. Aghti dak li matea ai. The same words saved your life. What do they mean, and why do you say it?"

She side-eyed me. "That's two secrets, Glik."

I clenched my jaw, tired of waiting for the answer. "Then ask me a question after you tell me what the words mean!"

She turned around and leaned against the rail with her back to the island. "Aghti dak li matea ai. 'Give me what I need.' A long time ago, I learned that getting what I want rarely got me out of trouble. I learned that sometimes what I thought would solve my problems, didn't. I learned to trust. So every prayer, every spell, I end with that phrase. It opens up the magic so the goddess will give me what I need, not just what I want." A warm smile overtook her face as she reflected on her past. "It does make for some interesting moments when I get something I don't expect."

I eyed her suspiciously. "You. Trust? When you can't cast a spell to make sure the other person is telling the truth?"

She chuckled. "I am capable of trust, even when I'm lying on the floor coughing up blood. It may take a long time or an extreme situation to earn my trust, but once it's there, it's damn strong. Now for my question, Glik. Why do you think the goddess of secrets granted a spell to you, a non-worshipper?"

I shrugged. "Selfish deity probably just wanted to save one of her clergy."

"Pfft. You obviously haven't studied my goddess enough."

I narrowed my eyes. "Ok, Miss 'I know my own goddess but ask you about her so you look like a numpty'. Why do you think she granted me a miracle?"

Serah smiled warmly, pushed herself off the rail, and slowly walked toward the captain's quarters. She looked over her shoulder for just a second to give me my answer. "Maybe we both needed a trustworthy friend."

I grinned and looked back at the sunrise. So this was it. This was adventure. No heroic deeds. No epic armies clashing in glory. Just a bunch of luck swaying back and forth. Lots of trying to not get dead. Tons of miserable, boring travel. A few friends and a lot more enemies. But in the end, I was still alive to tell the tale, where so many others were not.

I pulled out my fresh new journal and sat it beside the old one with its charred cover and water damaged pages. The tale had survived, the story would spread. That was what mattered most. Now, time to embellish a bit and make it fun!

LIKE WHAT YOU READ? THEN GO FEED TINKY!

Help the author create more stories:

- Donate to the Feed Tinky fund. Seriously, this rat eats a ton. Go to www.gliksfables.com and select the "Feed Tinky" tab to make a donation directly to the author (who of course, feeds Tinky, and pays for all the other expenses life incurs while trying to write interesting novels!)
- Spread the word! Tell your friends and family about the book. Talk about it on social media. Read a physical copy in public. Anything to get the word out!
- Post a review (Goodreads, Amazon, social media groups, wherever you like!)
- Buy more books. There are multiple formats for each book, and books make a great gift for those reader friends.
- Consider asking your local library about adding this book to their collection.

About the Author

Glik is an adventurous goblin storyteller, out to make his name known and spread the wealth of stories that he is collecting on his adventures. When not out adventuring, he spends his time at whatever tavern he happens to be staying at, regaling the regulars with embellished stories and adding to his repertoire of recipes, per Tinky's request. There's simply too much good food and drink to not try as much as possible.

amazon.com/author/hdscott

facebook.com/hdscottcreations

goodreads.com/hdscott

instagram.com/hdscottcreations

twitter.com/hdscottcreation

7ed7e316-a776-4ac9-8397-91194863d731R01